AN

Affair

OF

Poisons

No one looks kindly on
the killer of a king

AN

Affair

OF

Poisons

ADDIE THORLEY

PAGE STREET
PUBLISHING CO.

PAGE STREET
PUBLISHING CO.

Copyright © 2020 Addie Thorley

First published in 2020 by
Page Street Publishing Co.
27 Congress Street, Suite 105
Salem, MA 01970
www.pagestreetpublishing.com

Distributed by Macmillan, sales in Canada by The Canadian Manda Group.

24   23   22   21   20   1   2   3   4   5

ISBN-13: 978-1-64567-015-5
ISBN-10: 1-64567-015-5
Library of Congress Control Number: 2018963767

Cover and book design by Kylie Alexander for Page Street Publishing Co.

Printed and bound in the United States

Page Street Publishing protects our planet by donating to nonprofits like The Trustees, which focuses on local land conservation.

TO SAM,

for believing in me before I believed in myself.

AND TO KATO,

who sat with me through every word.

1

Paris, 1679

MIRABELLE

My laboratory reeks of death. Not of blood and flesh and decay, but the garlicky bite of arsenic, the musty essence of hemlock, and the sweet smell of oleander—like rose water and citrus. The lethal perfume tickles my nose as I rush about the hearth, stoking the fire and whisking the steaming concoction in my cast-iron kettle.

Today I will kill a man.

Not directly, as I won't be the one to tip the poudre de succession into his wine, but my hands made the poison, so I suppose I am responsible in part. This should probably strike fear into my bones or make me tremble with remorse or, if nothing else, have me worried for my soul, but a smile bends my lips as I add a pinch of sulfur to the draught and watch the garish yellow particles flutter down like snowflakes. Sinking and swirling and vanishing.

While the mixture bubbles, I return to the sideboard and thumb through my notes. *Is it belladonna or lead I need next?* The poison is a new one, called Aqua Tofana. Mother acquired the formula from an associate in Italy. It's a devilish little brew, rumored to be most effective at disposing of bothersome husbands and rivals at court—one of Mother's many services.

Some claim she's a witch. Others a saint. I see no difference; the people of Paris worship her either way.

Behind me, the potion hisses, hungry for the next ingredient. I pick through a bowl of dried belladonna, grind the darkest, most potent berries, and tip the powder into the pot, adding an extra scoop for good measure. I'll spare no mercy for a lecherous toad like the Duc de Barra. Not when I've seen the purple bruises marring the duchesse's arms and that ghastly cut across her cheek. Not when I've heard her wailing from Mother's salon, recounting how the duc beat their son near to death for attempting to shield her.

Gritting my teeth, I raise my spoon like a dagger and plunge it into the cauldron. Beads of sweat trickle down my face, and my woolen dress clings to my chest, but I stir with ruthless vigor until the concoction reduces into a shimmering crystalline powder. Careful not to touch a speck of it, I spoon the poison into a phial and bury the cork with the heel of my hand.

De Barra's death will not be quick or painless. I made certain of that. His reckoning will burn like fire down his throat and eat like maggots through his flesh. He will see red, breathe red, *bleed* red until not a drop of life lingers in his veins. Until he's cold and stiff, lying facedown on his parlor rug.

Ordinarily, I take no such pleasure in death—I can count on one hand the number of times I have provided poison to Mother's clients—but if ever I were to relish the role of reaper, this is one such occasion.

Au revoir, Monsieur le Duc.

I situate the phial on a tray and return to the hearth, where my more innocent elixirs are boiling. The largest cauldron holds an elderberry infusion to counteract headaches; the one beside it contains a watercress and fennel seed hunger tonic, which we distribute to the beggars on the rue du Temple when the rutting Sun King fails to issue rations; and the hanging copper teapot brims with a valerian root extract that smooths even the deepest wrinkles.

A little something for everyone. That's the Shadow Society's promise. And Mother will have my head if her order isn't ready by sunup, when her consultations begin. Which will be any moment now, judging by the pale gray light streaming through the shutters, casting ladder-like shadows across the floor. My heart leaps into my throat and my hands flutter like frantic birds as I dash from pot to pot. I was so absorbed with the Aqua Tofana I paid little heed to everything else.

I dip a finger into the plum-colored elderberry infusion and wince—still cold and clotted—and when I peek inside the copper teapot, a sticky, sour-smelling syrup spatters my face.

Merde. I can already hear Mother hissing her customary diatribe. *Don't you care for the cause, Mirabelle? For the people of this city? Who will succor them if we do not? Surely not the glorious Sun King. If it were left to him, the better half of the kingdom would die of pox and he'd be glad of it. Then he could reallocate the funds he uses to put moldy bread in our bellies to build more gilded palaces like that monstrosity at Versailles.*

Mother's intensity may be overwhelming, but her goals are admirable. We are the saviors of Paris. And if I want her to respect me and trust me and welcome me into her inner circle, I must prove I am more responsible than Father.

"Gris, I need the watercress now!" I bellow over my shoulder. He's hunched over the ancient claw-foot table in the center of the room, furiously chopping herbs. The laboratory isn't large— it's a one-room garden house with crooked shelves built into the stone walls—but it's more chaotic than a battlefield. Curtains of steam hover about our heads, thick as cannon smoke, and the rumble of the bubbling cauldrons sound like a hundred marching feet. I can hardly hear myself think.

I cup my hands around my mouth to call out again, but Gris leans over me and sweeps the herbs into the appropriate pots. Then we stand there, watching, as the bubbles devour the tiny particles. "I added a pinch of butterbur to the elderberry infusion," he says. "It should come into effect twice as quickly. And three sprigs of rosemary to the wrinkle salve. Now it doesn't smell like feet."

"Good, good." I reach for my stirring spoon and expect Gris to do the same, but he thumbs the cutting board and continues to peer into the cauldrons.

"Do you think she'll notice?"

No. Mother never notices the improvements we make to her draughts. But I can't bring myself to say this. Not with Gris standing there looking so hopeful and earnest, with his cinnamon eyes peeking out from beneath his sandy mop of hair. He's the most imposing person I know—a good head taller than me and built like an ox—but where Mother is concerned, he will always be a skinny, orphaned eight-year-old desperate to prove she did right by taking him in.

I seize Gris's goggles from the hook beside the hearth and fling them at his chest. He yelps and scrabbles to catch the strap. "What was that for?"

"A watched pot never boils. You know that. And if we fail to finish these draughts before Marguerite arrives, Mother will *definitely* notice that." I tighten my own goggles for emphasis.

Gris glances once more at the pots, then quickly out the window at the house before finally donning his eyewear.

Like two parts of a well-oiled machine, we fall into the easy rhythm of our work: he whisks the curls away from my face when I lean forward to grind herbs, and I dab the sweat from his brow while he stirs the cauldrons. After more than a decade of toiling side by side, his arms feel like an extension of my own; we know what the other needs without having to utter a word. We're so consumed with our alchemy, I scream and Gris bangs his head against the hanging pots when the laboratory door flies open.

"Must you barge in here like a brigand?" I whip around, ready to scowl at my sister. But it isn't Marguerite who has come to collect Mother's order.

It is Mother herself.

The stirring spoon drops from my fingers and rolls into the coals, making the fire crackle. Gris straightens and furiously brushes the yellow flecks of camphor from his hair and tunic. Which seems a wasted effort, since Mother herself looks so uncivilized. I gape at her filthy, loose-fitting shift. Stare at her dirt-smeared cheeks and the threadbare cap atop her tangled hair. She looks like a fishwife. And, worse, she smells like one. I cover my nose, but the vile odor seeps through my fingers, strangling me.

"Lady Mother!" I stammer. Ordinarily, she is immaculate—clad in the finest satins and silks. Rumor has it that it's more fashionable to be received at our shabby house on the rue Beauregard than the palace at Versailles, but she looks nothing like the most powerful devineresse in Paris or "Queen of the People" at present.

She pins me in place with her inky stare and clears her throat.

I hurriedly draw out the sides of my soot-stained petticoat and lower into my most practiced curtsy. Gris follows suit and sketches a bow. "To what do we owe this honor?" I ask.

She waves a hand and ventures into the room, sidestepping a stack of dusty grimoires and an overturned sack of milk thistle. "Can't I visit my beloved daughter and favorite son without cause?"

Gris looks like he might die of happiness, and for half a second, I allow myself to hope. But then Mother flashes her most honeyed grin—the one she reserves for noble clients—and dread coils in my belly like a sickness. She does nothing without reason. And she hasn't stepped foot inside the laboratory in years. The garden house reminds her too much of Father. *I* remind her too much of Father.

I quickly scan the laboratory for the true purpose of her visit, and my pulse pounds at my temples. She has a dozen reasons to eviscerate me. The mess, for one. When Father was chief alchemist of the Shadow Society, these floors were as pristine as glossed parquet and the cauldrons gleamed like fresh shoe polish. But my mind works better when I am mired in mixtures. When I'm surrounded by my phials and bottles and barrels—a part of my alchemy, both body and spirit. Besides, Father's methods proved ineffective. What use are alphabetized cupboards when your experiments are so explosive that they quite literally blow you to bits? Mother should be glad that I strive so hard to be his opposite.

So it must be the late order. I rush to her side, already babbling excuses, but instead of stalking to the hearth and clucking her tongue at the disastrous array of half-finished tinctures, she moves to the board instead. "Is this my *special* concoction for the Duc de Barra?" she asks, holding the Aqua Tofana toward the firelight.

I nod.

"And you altered it according to my instructions? So it kills upon contact with the skin?"

"Of course." Aqua Tofana is usually dispensed in liquid form, but Mother asked me to reduce it to a powder. So it's twice as potent. "He'll be dead from the barest brush of his fingertips."

Mother's grin curls all the way up to her eyes, and she looks truly pleased. Proud, even. Then she does something that has happened only in my most outlandish of dreams. A favor usually reserved for my older sister. She places a hand on my back and leans in close. Her dark hair dances around my shoulders and her almond-scented breath puffs against my cheek. "Well done," she whispers.

I do not move or breathe or blink for the space of five heartbeats as a tiny seedling of pride sprouts inside my chest. I know better than to let it take root. She will change her mind. Or her praise will transform into a barb, as it always has before. But when neither happens, the shoots curl around my heart and grow. Mother is like the sun. Vibrant and flashing. It's impossible not to bask in the warmth of her esteem—no matter that I'll likely be burned.

Though, perhaps not. This could be a sign—a beacon of change. Perhaps she's finally beginning to trust and appreciate me.

I look again to Gris, and we exchange a bewildered smile.

"Don't stand there gawking like a dullard," Mother says with a laugh, linking her arm through mine. "We've much to do."

That jerks me from my stupor and I spring toward the hearth. "Of course. The rest of your order is nearly ready. We'll bring it along—"

"Gris can finish the order." Mother tightens her grip on my elbow. "You shall come with me."

My eyes widen and I try not to stutter. "Surely I'm not invited?" She has never welcomed my presence at her consultations; she and Marguerite handle that side of the business. I am hardly better than a servant. A lowly lab rat. Unless that is changing too . . . A thread of excitement hums through my core, but I bite down hard on my lip. Best to keep my delight hidden, or Mother will sniff out my desperation. She despises weakness above all else.

"Don't be daft." Mother shakes the phial at me. "You are the genius behind the poison, so you must witness my triumph."

My brow furrows. I fail to see anything particularly triumphant about watching a man suffer—even one so wanton and despicable as the Duc de Barra—but I know better than to argue. If Mother considers his death a victory, it must be. And she wants *me* to take part in it.

Gris beams and raises a celebratory fist as Mother tugs me into the garden. The morning air is deliciously cold and it slams down my throat like a hammer, enlivening my mind and making my skin tingle. Every window of our cottage is ablaze with candlelight and movement. Shadows dash behind the velveteen curtains as Marguerite and La Trianon arrange their gilded Marseille decks and fill the scrying bowls with water. In lieu of morning birds, the chatter of anxious customers queuing up and down the rue Beauregard welcomes the sun. Like a windup clock, the Shadow Society is grinding into motion, and *I* am to be a part of it.

Matching Mother's stride, I hold my head high as we slip through the kitchen door. *Command respect. Prove you belong.* But my feet stutter to a halt the moment we enter her salon, and for once it has nothing to do with the oppressive black curtains and damask papering. The room writhes like a hornet's nest, packed wall to wall with visitors. And these are not the poor serving girls or the cotton-headed duchesses they often entertain. These are the leaders of the Shadow Society.

La Trianon, Mother's second, quits pacing and fastens her watery eyes on me. Ordinarily the old woman's eyes glint with fire and spark with mischief, but today they are drooping and exhausted—the same dirty gray as the snow in the gutters. Mother's infuriating lover, the royal sorcerer, Lesage, winks at me from where he lounges on a divan, and Marguerite whispers with her fiancé, Fernand, in the corner. On the other side of the room, Abbé Guibourg, the priest who oversees the Society's spiritual affairs, pulls his rosary beads through his knotted fingers. And beside him, Mother's most prominent client, the Marquise de Montespan, former maîtresse-en-titre to His Majesty, Louis XIV, whips her lace fan back and forth with agitated strokes.

Warning bells blare in my mind. Why are they assembled at such an hour? They can't all have a vested interest in the Duc de Barra. He is one man, of little consequence, especially to someone as elevated as Madame de Montespan.

"What's all this?" I ask, trying to keep my face blank and serene. Like Mother's.

"We are waiting for you. *Clearly.*" Madame de Montespan rolls her eyes as if I am the simplest creature alive. I cringe without meaning to, and she titters behind her fan. *I wouldn't be laughing had the king dismissed* me *in favor of a younger mistress,* I long to snap at her, but I bite my tongue and turn to Marguerite. She will enlighten me. But she looks pointedly at Mother's arm, linked through mine, and her lips flatten.

My sister and I are either best friends or mortal enemies depending on one important variable—Mother's favor.

"Up. All of you. It's time to be off." Mother claps and waves down the hall. Abbé Guibourg rises with a grunt and shuffles to assist Madame de Montespan, but La Trianon wrings her gnarled hands through her skirt and looks pleadingly at Mother.

"Please reconsider, Catherine. This is madness. We'll burn at the Place de Grève."

Mother's dark eyes flash, and she advances on the old woman. Not yelling. Mother never yells. She whispers, which is far more terrifying. "Do you mistrust my judgment?"

"Of course not." La Trianon retreats behind the divan like a mouse cornered by a cat. "I wouldn't dream of it."

Mother points down the hall. "Then go."

Lesage extends his arm to La Trianon in vicious mockery, and with Mother watching, she can't refuse. Marguerite sends another glare in my direction, then stomps down the hall with Fernand. But her hostility wicks away like water off a duck, for Mother continues walking arm in arm with *me*. She clutches the crook of my elbow tightly in one hand and the poudre de succession in the other. I try not to look overly pleased as I climb into the six-horse carriage waiting on the street.

We ride in silence over the Pont Neuf and out of Paris, onto the dusty, rutted country roads. I glance around the carriage, at

Mother beside me and Marguerite across from me, certain they'll tell me where we're headed and what they've planned now that we're en route. But they purposely avoid my gaze.

I swallow back a knot of disappointment and shift in my seat. I suppose this is to be expected. It's my first foray into the Shadow Society. In order to be trusted with greater knowledge, I must first prove myself in small things. And if this is some sort of initiation or a test of loyalty, I intend to pass. Better than pass—I intend to excel. I paint a smile on my lips that I hope mimics Mother's— oozing lethal confidence—and fold my hands in my lap.

After some time, Mother peeks out the curtained window and I catch a glimpse of the enormous red and white palace at the end of the road, the golden crenellations and blue roof shimmering like pearls in the sun. The palace at Versailles. A tiny thrill courses through me and I lean forward to get a better look. The king's new residence is said to outshine the Louvre the way the sun outshines the moon. It is swiftly becoming the beating heart of his royal court.

Which shouldn't interest you, I remind myself before Mother has to scold me. I sit back and stare straight ahead. The palace is nothing but a lavish den of iniquity. A mockery to the people.

The footman drops us in front of the sprawling château, where a massive crowd of petitioners writhe before the gilded gates. On the last Friday of each month, King Louis comes to the courtyard fronting the palace to receive petitions from his people, but I cannot fathom why we would come now. It will be far more difficult to slip inside and poison the Duc de Barra during such a disturbance.

We gather in a tight circle at the back of the crowd. "Is everyone in place?" Mother says softly, though no one could hear us over the cries of the petitioners.

Marguerite and Fernand nod.

"What do you mean, 'everyone'?" I ask, looking at our small group.

"Quiet, Mira," Marguerite snaps.

"Excellent. Wish me luck," Mother says, "though I shan't be needing it." She dons a pair of gloves, uncorks the phial of poison, and sprinkles it into a roll of parchment that the Abbé Guibourg procures from his robes. Then she disappears into the rabble, pushing toward the gate.

"What is she doing?" I demand. "I thought . . ."

"Watch and see." Madame de Montespan points to the palace.

A queer feeling rises in my gut, as if I've eaten spoiled meat. I fan my face furiously, but I'm sweating like a smith at the forge. There are so many petitioners making so much noise. I try to fall back, but Marguerite and Fernand grip my wrists and drag me forward.

"We need a better view," Lesage mutters, bludgeoning people out of our way.

The Abbé squints his tiny eyes. "Where *is* she? Do you see her?"

"There, there!" Madame de Montespan points to the left, where the crowd is thickest around the gate, and I catch a glimpse of Mother's blue cap. Hundreds of people thrust their arms through the gilt swirls and flourishes, waving their petitions wildly, and Mother joins them.

She's naught but a single stalk of wheat amid a vast and rolling field, but I see the exact moment the Sun King notices her parcel. It's as if he's bewitched. His eyes contract and he strides purposefully down the fence line, his cape billowing like a banner behind him. The dauphin, in sky blue velvet, tugs his father's arm and whispers in his ear, but the king shrugs him off and continues on his course. Straight to Mother.

"She isn't. We wouldn't . . ." I babble, looking for someone to confirm I am mistaken, that this isn't what it seems. "We came to poison the Duc de Barra!"

"Did we?" Marguerite says with a laugh.

Time slows as Louis XIV reaches for the scroll. His gold and silver rings flash in the sunlight. The ruffles at his wrist dance in the chilly breeze. A scream builds in my throat as his fingertips brush the tainted parchment. *Stop!* I want to shout, but my clenched teeth are a prison, trapping the word.

The poison is deadly quick—just as Mother ordered. As soon as he unfurls the missive, a high-pitched wail spills from the Sun King's lips. He staggers to his knees, and my own lungs burn as I watch him rip open his doublet and claw at his lace collar. His face turns purple then blue, and for a terrible moment, everything is frozen. Silent. Then the dauphin bellows—the low, guttural keen of a dying animal—and the stillness shatters like a broken pane of glass.

Mon Dieu.

The petitioners rear back, dashing about the courtyard like a flock of chickens with a fox in the coop, and I watch in horror

14

as the dauphin yells his father's name, shouting for help, crying for a healer.

All too late.

The king collapses face-first to the cobbles. His immaculate wig topples from his head and his crimson cape pools around him like blood.

An invisible fist slams into my stomach, and I vomit all over my shoes.

"Better steel your nerves, girl," Lesage says. Then he flings his arms into the air and emerald fire bolts crackle from his fingertips. A deadly living fire called désintégrer.

The fire smashes against the palace gates, and amid the screech of rending metal, figures in jewel-toned cloaks and velvet masks race past, appearing from nowhere and spreading throughout the crowd—like a swarm of flies, a descending plague.

The whole of the Shadow Society.

Marguerite and Fernand don velvet masks of their own and shout as they rush into the fray. They probably expect me to join them, but my shaking legs refuse to cooperate. Another wave of nausea drops me to my knees. This is madness and all my fault.

I haven't rid the world of one abhorrent duc.

I have murdered the King of France.

2

JOSSE

There are a good many chores I should be doing. Rixenda's list is endless: peel the turnips, scour the pots, sweep the scullery, harvest the leeks. On and on and on. Sneaking over to the royal château and hiding in the hedge beneath the second-floor window, third from the left, is decidedly not on that list. But I can't be blamed. Not really. I was headed to the garden to dig up the leeks when the morning sunlight struck the path in such a way I couldn't *help* but notice how round and smooth the pebbles were, shining like precious drops of silver.

The perfect size for tossing at windows.

A thrill shivers through me as I lob the first stone, picturing Madame Lemaire up there, coiled like a dragon inside the keep. The old governess is far uglier than a serpent, and her tongue is sharp enough to spit flames, which is precisely why I must rescue my sisters.

Plink, plink, plink.

The rocks bounce off the gilded shutters like bullets. A few more go unanswered, but I am nothing if not persistent.

Come on, you old crone.

Three more and the shutters fly open.

Without waiting to hear her bray like a donkey or watch her wrinkles flap like a turkey's wattle, I grip the trellis and scamper up. I've had loads of practice climbing. Mostly trees in the garden to avoid tumbles with the courtiers' brats when I was young, and now the curtain wall surrounding the maids' quarters for a different sort of tumble.

Madame Lemaire spots me immediately, but before she can call me a flea-bitten bastard hog and slam the shutters, I dive through the window and nearly knock her on her backside. She screams and crashes into the cream and pink papered wall, and her curled wig plummets to the floor. It looks so much like one of Madame de Montespan's miniature poodles, I half expect it to bark. Or bite me.

Anne and Françoise shriek with laughter—the best greeting I could have hoped for—and I rush across the room and snatch them from their chairs. Their teacups clatter to the floor and I stomp through the steaming brown liquid, making an even bigger mess. Madame Lemaire is right: I'm quite like a pig, sullying the rich mulberry rugs with my muddy boots, shaking leaves and twigs from my hair. I do it on purpose. First, because it's amusing to watch Madame Lemaire clutch her chest and sputter. And second, because it's easier to blow around like a tornado and make a wreckage of everything rather than stare at the mahogany bed frames and silk-threaded coverlets and try not to compare them to my thin straw mat in the servants' quarters.

"How are my girls?" I ask, balancing one on each hip. At five and seven, they're almost too big to carry, especially with their full satin skirts, but I grit my teeth and boost them higher so we can rub our noses back and forth. Our special greeting.

"Better now that you're here," Françoise, the elder of my half sisters, says. She pats my cheek and my heart melts like a warm pot de crème. "These lessons are awfully dull."

"We hoped you would come for us," Anne says behind her hand. Only she hasn't quite mastered how to whisper, so Madame Lemaire hears every word.

The old woman smashes her wig onto her head and advances on us, arms outstretched to the girls. "Come along, sweetings. Lessons may be dull, but they are necessary. Children who ignore their studies end up like *him*."

I gasp and crumple my face so it looks like a crab apple and, coincidentally, a good deal like Madame Lemaire's. "We wouldn't want that now, would we?"

My sisters giggle and shake their heads. Their silky auburn curls brush my cheeks and tickle my nose. They smell of honeysuckle and rose water. Like happiness and home. I squeeze them tighter because despite incessant conditioning from their maîtresse-en-titre mother and their snub-nosed tutors, they *do* want to be like me. They *want* to see me, and not just to laugh at my expense. They're the only ones who give a piss about me— besides Rixenda, I suppose.

"You cannot take them." Madame Lemaire folds her arms and positions herself before the door. "We are in the middle of an important etiquette lesson. You would do well to sit in on a few such lessons yourself, Josse."

"Ah, but then I might be expected to act princely, and we can't have that. I am, after all, just a kitchen boy."

I see no point in trying to win the king's affection when my fate will be the same as my mother's: cast aside like rubbish as soon as the novelty fades. As soon as he tires of watching his ministers drop their forks to stare at me—his spitting image— pouring wine and serving mutton in the great hall. I am a trifling form of entertainment, like a dancing monkey.

"Release the girls this instant," Madame Lemaire demands.

Smirking, I dodge the sweep of her arm and hold my sisters tighter. "One hour," I beg. "Look at their faces—so wan and melancholy. They need sunlight, exercise. It's unhealthy for young girls to have so many lessons."

"I've had a terrible headache all morning," Françoise adds with a dramatic sniff.

"What they need is to be kept away from scoundrels like you. Their mother has forbidden it." Madame Lemaire puffs out her chest, making herself as large as possible. I will have to tackle her to get through the door, and she likely outweighs me.

"It seems we're out of luck, ladies," I say.

Anne whimpers and blinks tears to her eyes, but Françoise squares her shoulders and levels a steady finger at their governess.

"You will stand aside, Madame Lemaire, unless you wish to be dismissed. I am a daughter of France and you are nothing but a lowly retainer who has been sent to serve *me*. Father will be most displeased to hear of my unhappiness."

Madame Lemaire's cheeks pale. Her perpetually frowning mouth drops open but not a sound escapes. I almost feel sorry for her as she bobs a shaky curtsy and removes herself from the door, tripping across the room like a brittle, wind-tossed leaf.

Françoise tips her head and laughs. "That's how it's done, brother. Proceed."

I steal a glance back at Madame Lemaire—even though I know she doesn't want my apologetic shrug—and carry the girls into the hall. They're chattering away as if nothing is amiss, but the bravado I felt before, the laughter and excitement and warm sense of belonging, curdle in my belly like sour milk. I'm all for riling the old bat, but *that* was cruel and demeaning. I like to think my girls are different from the other nobles, but Françoise sounded so like Louis or Father or their mother, Madame de Montespan.

A current of ice trickles through my bones. *How long until she says those things to you? Until they realize you are the son of a scullery maid? Even lower than Madame Lemaire?*

Technically, the girls are bastards like me, but the daughters of the royal mistress are a far cry from the son of a servant.

I don't realize I've stopped walking until Anne pokes her finger into the side of my face. "Josse? Are you ill?"

I blink and force a smile. "There was a stitch in my side, but it's better now."

"Then let's *go*," Françoise says. "I'm desperate to visit Rixenda. She promised to let us pluck chickens."

I raise a brow. "You *want* to pluck chickens?"

"Oh, yes," Françoise says, and both she and Anne bob their heads energetically. "We've been dying to try it for ages. Madame and Mother never let us have any fun."

Fun. Not the word I would choose to describe my chores, but I swallow my annoyance.

"Then to the kitchens we go," I say, raining kisses on their cheeks. They clutch my neck and giggle in my ears and I feel both better and worse. I hate myself for ever thinking poorly of them. They are nothing like the others. Will *never* be, if I have any say in it.

We race down the spiral staircase and out of doors, past the guardhouses where the ceaseless petitioners batter against the golden gates, and burst into the smoky galley. A dozen maids in plain gray dresses flit about, stirring pots and tending the ovens, but none of them acknowledge me. They never do. No matter that I've been slaving beside them all my life. To them, I'm half prince. To the courtiers, I'm half commoner. Which makes me one hundred percent invisible to everyone besides Rixenda.

"It's about time you showed up, you worthless bag of bones!" she crows, slapping her floured hands on her apron. "You'd best have harvested the entire crop of leeks for how long you were gone."

"I brought you something even better." The girls peek out from behind me, and Rixenda's smile broadens until her wrinkles cover the better part of her eyes. How I love that ugly, crinkled grin. My antics usually make her frown and fret—she says I'm the reason her hair's gone so white—so it's good to do something right every now and again.

She leads us into the courtyard and the girls attack the waiting barrow of chickens like starving weasels. I thump to the ground beside them and shiver. The spring breeze still has the frosty chill of winter on its breath, and it slices through my tunic like a knife. Anne and Françoise don't seem to notice—they're too busy blowing smelly feathers at each other. And it clearly hasn't deterred the petitioners. There are twice as many as usual, and their fervent cries carry back to where we work.

"What do you think it is this time?" I ask Rixenda, nodding at the commotion. "Are they as greedy and ungrateful as Father claims? Or is he as callous and condescending as the broadsides report?"

"The riot at the gate has naught to do with us, Josse, and thank the Lord for it. And you shouldn't be reading those treasonous pamphlets." Rixenda tweaks my nose.

I squint at Father and Louis pacing the fence line, their heads tilted together in official business. Sometimes I wonder what it would be like to be included in their diplomacies. How it would feel to wear Louis's pearl-embroidered doublet or Father's silken cape. But most of the time I want to march over there in my feather-specked tunic, knock the massive wigs off their heads, and force them to see, to really look, at the peasants dressed in rags.

Rixenda's withered hand pats my knee. "His Majesty thinks it best you work with me for now."

Of course he thinks it best to banish me to the kitchen, where he doesn't have to lay eyes on me unless he needs a laugh. I am an embarrassment. An unsightly stain on his otherwise pristine line.

With a touch more vigor than necessary, I slam the plucked chicken into the barrow and am reaching for another when a blood-curdling cry erupts from the gate. A second later, a wave of ungodly heat hurls me to the ground. My head collides with the cobbles, bits of plaster and brick pelting my back like hailstones. Vibrant green sparks rain from the cloudless sky, and the gate clatters and clangs like shattering dishes. I press my palms against my ears, but it does little to block out the noise; the entire world is screaming.

My sisters loudest of all. Their high-pitched voices rake across my skin like claws. A surge of panic lifts me to my knees, and I crawl to where they're huddled safely beneath Rixenda—thank God. Beyond them, it's utter chaos. The palace gate collapses with a crash so violent that the ground shudders beneath me, and a cloud of dust plumes into the air, thick enough to devour the sun. The petitioners stream onto the grounds and run for cover, pointing at cloaked figures flying toward the palace like bats in the night.

Where's my father? The musketeers? His porters? *Anybody?*

"What's happening?" Françoise shouts.

I haven't a clue, but we need to move. *Now.* I swing Anne onto my back and yank Françoise up by her hand. "This way," I yell, but Rixenda hobbles in the opposite direction. I catch her elbow and spin her around. "What are you doing?"

"Go on! I'll only slow you down."

I shake my head and tighten my hold.

"Go! Get the girls out. I'll meet you outside the palace." She presses the knife she brought to debone the chickens into my hand and shoves me off with far more strength than a woman her age should possess. "Be strong, Josse," she calls as she skitters around the curtain wall.

I stare after her, my eyes watering, my heart screaming. Another flash of emerald lightning smashes into the palace, and Anne shrieks in my ear, "Run, Josse!"

I tuck the knife in my boot and spin toward the outer wall, but the gatehouses are overrun with figures in purple and green cloaks. Arrows assail the courtiers attempting to flee, putting them down like deer on the hunt. I look back to the grand château, but hordes of intruders are charging up the steps. Inside the palace, eerie green light streaks through the hallways, setting the draperies aflame.

There's no way out. Nowhere safe.

Think, Josse.

I close my eyes and imagine each hall, each level of the palace, until my attention snags on the hidden passage beneath the stairs outside the Venus Salon. My best friend, Luc Desgrez, and I discovered it years ago, when I was desperate to evade my chores and he wanted nothing to do with the Latin lessons his scholar father taught Louis. It used to be a discreet entrance for carpenters and masons during construction—my father couldn't have commoners traipsing across the cour d'Honneur—and it leads from the main château to the stables and into the woods beyond. Brilliant.

With a grunt, I boost Anne higher up my back and tug Françoise toward the nearest window. I've never stepped foot inside this wing of the palace—the dauphin has expressly forbidden *bastard scum* from entering his apartments—but it's the fastest way to the hidden passage, so I smash my boot through a window and duck past the shards of glass.

For all I've heard of its beauty, Louis's bedchamber is a scorching, incendiary hell at present. The gold damask walls are spattered with sickening green scars that drip onto the parquet floor, and two gentlemen of the bedchamber lie in the center of the room, their skin greener than leaves and their faces frozen in agony.

I look away and charge ahead, willing myself not to scream.

The stairs. Get to the stairs.

I careen through the door and into a wood-paneled antechamber, where I slam into an intruder. The man is my height but twice as broad, and his face is covered with an intricate black mask. "What luck," he says with a husky chuckle. "Just the girls I was looking for." He leans forward in a mock bow and reaches into his scarlet cloak.

Anne and Françoise scream, and I don't wait to see what he's grabbing for. Rage flash-boils the blood in my veins. I have never killed a man, never trained with a sword like Louis, but my time in the kitchen serves me well. Faster than I've ever moved, I set Anne down, pull the knife from my boot, and plunge it into the man's belly. Up and in. Gutting him like a pig. He coughs and sags against me, his blood rushing warm and thick over my hands. I wait for my arms to tremble with horror, for nausea to squeeze my throat, but I only feel fury. A ferocious desire to stab him again for even *thinking* of harming my sisters.

I dump him on the ground, return the knife to my boot, and take Françoise and Anne by the hand, cringing at the blood that smears their skin. The smoke thickens as we run through the next antechamber. Servants pour from the dauphin's library and grand cabinet, screeching and crying as ghostly green flames blaze down the hall. "Everything's going to be fine," I call, as much for myself as the girls.

We burst into the forecourt and the marble staircase comes into view. So close. But a cry pricks my ears as we pass the Diane Salon, and my stomach bottoms out.

I think I recognize it.

Clenching my teeth, I take another step. If our roles were reversed, they wouldn't stop for me. Anne and Françoise are my only responsibility, the only ones I care for in this rutting palace. But the cry comes again, even louder. Wrenching me between the two halves of my life.

Be strong, Josse, Rixenda's voice echoes.

I whirl around and pound on the door. "Marie? Are you in there?"

The door flies open and my half sister, Madame Royale—the king's eldest daughter—pokes her face into the hall. Her porcelain complexion is blotchy enough to be poxed, and her eyes are swollen into slits. She's coughing so hard she's unable to speak, but silence from her isn't unusual. In my eighteen years, we've only exchanged a handful of words.

"What are you still doing here?" I demand.

"There's nowhere to go. Louis says we simply cannot rush into the fray."

"Louis?" I choke on his name. "He's here? But I saw him at the gates. . . ."

"When Father was struck—" she begins, but she collapses in the doorway, weeping. Anne and Françoise burst into tears again, and I scoop them up and step past Marie.

The Diane Salon is the most decadent of all the sitting rooms, with rich violet hangings and ebony furniture, but like the dauphin's apartments, it has been transformed into a picture of gory contradiction. Three intruders lie strewn across the glittering tiles, swimming in pools of blood, and the Grand Condé, the most celebrated general in the French army, sags against a divan and clutches his side, a deep red stain spreading through his ivory justaucorps. Beyond him, Louis leans over a table laden with snuffboxes, quills, and decanters arranged in the shape of the palace. He points to a wall on the far end of the table, and the Condé shakes his head. His Royal Highness roars a black oath.

I'm tempted to turn on my heel, grab the girls, and leave the court to sort out their own escape. They will never listen to me, and every moment could be the difference between making it to the passageway. But Marie moans into her palms, and my insides wring like a washrag. Deserving or not, I cannot leave them to die.

I situate my sisters against the wall and stride toward the men, clearing my throat since neither of them have bothered to acknowledge me. "I know a way out," I announce.

They jerk at the sound of my voice, and even though he's halfway to death, Condé manages to frown down his bulbous nose at me. "Thank the saints! The royal bastard has come to save us."

"This is hardly the time for politics," I bark. "Come."

The old general waves a hand. "They've posted guards at every gate. They'll kill us on sight."

"Thankfully my way doesn't require a gate. Follow me. And *make haste.*"

Louis's blue eyes flick up from the table and flay me open like a butcher's knife. "If myself and the Grand Condé cannot find a way out, *you* certainly cannot."

"Fine. If you have a death wish, I'll happily leave you to rot."

"I would be careful, *brother,* how you address the King of France," Louis quips.

Louis is king? That means our father, the Sun King, is dead.

I hardly knew the man, but I still feel the loss deep in my gut. Like the heel of a boot. "The queen?" I whisper.

The Condé glances at Marie, who bursts into another fit of tears, then he quietly says, "Her Majesty is dead on the veranda. I was defending the dauphin and didn't reach her in time."

I toe the masked corpses strewn across the carpet. "Who are they?"

"Hell if I know," the Condé says, "but the court magician, Lesage, is leading them. Turncoat rat. He'll burn us all to cinders with his devil magic."

A shiver races through me from crown to toe. "Please come."

Louis slams his fist against the table and bellows, "Be gone!" At the same moment, the window nearest the door shatters. Bolts of fiery green light shoot into the room and strike the wall a hair's breadth from where Anne and Françoise stand. Hissing green ashes nip their arms, and they yowl like mice caught in the traps beneath the kitchen cupboards.

No, no, no.

I fly across the room, scoop them up, and brush the burning soot from their skin. Then I leap over Marie, who stares at me with a pained expression before rising to her feet and clinging to my tunic. To my surprise, the heavy thump of the Condé's step and Louis's grumbling about how *he* should be leading our exodus trail us down the hall.

Fancy that. Following a bastard is preferable to burning alive after all.

"This is your brilliant plan?" Louis says when I press the notch on the stair rail and the panel slides. I'll admit, it looks a bit ominous. The walls are splintered and bowed and the sharp tang of rot makes me cough. Louis hesitates, but thankfully he's a good deal shorter than me and slender as a bean pole, so I shove him inside, hard enough that he falls to his knees. Without an apology, I push the others in behind him. Then I crowd in and bar the door.

Blackness swallows us. The air is heavy and sour, and the damp walls soak the sleeves of my tunic as we inch forward. Marie sniffles, the Condé groans and lists against the wall, Louis curses as he tries to keep the old general on his feet, and the girls cry silently onto my shoulder. That's when I notice the specks dotting their skin like freckles. They're round with raised centers that glow a faint, otherworldly green. My ribs squeeze around my heart, and I hold my breath as I wipe my thumb across a spot on Françoise's finger. It doesn't smear.

Damn.

No one utters a word as we blunder through the dark. My arms ache from the weight of my sisters. It feels as if we've been walking for hours. Days. I take a deep breath and readjust for the hundredth time. Whatever it takes to keep them safe.

Except you've failed already, I think, looking at the sores and feeling sick.

When we reach the hidden door behind the stables, Louis lets out a whoop, but it's quickly followed by a horrified scream from

Marie. As soon as I emerge from the tunnel, I bite back a scream of my own. The south woods are drenched in molten-orange flames. Heat lashes my face, and smoke pours down my throat like gravy. I have led us straight to the gates of Hell.

The Condé's scowl bores into the side of my face. "Don't stand there staring while we burn alive, boy! You brought us here."

I cast around for the safest route while praying for Rixenda to hobble from the barn or beckon from the forest's edge. Guilt drags at my feet until they're heavy as boulders. It was foolish to think an old woman could make it through the chaos.

"It seems *I* must lead us to safety." Louis shoots me a disgusted look as he charges into the north woods. I raise my eyebrows but decide not to mention that the Petit Parc is the nearest thing he's seen to wilderness—and he gets lost on those manicured paths.

With one more glance at the barn, I follow the others.

We tromp through the underbrush, slower and more painfully than a royal procession. Flames crackle through the canopy and fiery leaves rain down atop our heads. They fall faster and hotter as we aimlessly twist and turn, wandering farther from civilization and help. I need to say something, need to *do* something—I've picked mushrooms in these woods hundreds of times; I could have us to the road in minutes.

Be strong, Josse. Rixenda's admonition plays in my head so loudly that I whip around, hope banging in my chest. But it's only the blaze, spitting and snapping at our backs.

I shake the sweaty strands of hair from my eyes, heft the girls higher, and make my way to the front of the group. "We need to head north along the road and find a carriage out of Versailles, perhaps out of France entirely."

Louis glares at me as he mops his forehead with a silver-stitched handkerchief. "The king cannot flee his own country."

"You won't be king if you perish in these woods," I retort.

"Watch yourself, boy." The Condé moves a trembling hand to his sword—as if he could cut me down in his condition. But by some miracle, when I stomp off, he and the others follow.

We pick our way through the burning trees, the fire dying out as we near the road. Gruff voices shout orders, and a chorus of whimpers follow. My heart thuds in my throat as I squint through the branches. Two masked intruders are herding a cluster of bloodied servants and courtiers down the road at sword-point. And there, second from the front, is Rixenda. Her petticoats are charred and her white hair billows around her like a storm cloud.

Relief crashes through me, and my eyes fill with a blurry wash of tears. She's alive. But for how long? Desperation blows me forward like a violent gust of wind, and I dodge through the underbrush.

Momentarily forgetting that I'm carrying my sisters, a twig rakes across Anne's cheek and she yelps.

The voices on the road go silent. The line of prisoners grinds to a halt.

"Show yourself!" one of the masked intruders calls.

The girls tense in my arms, and Louis mutters an oath.

Rixenda peers over at the trees, her face pinched with a brazen expression I know all too well. Fingertips of worry trace up and down my spine. I hold every muscle still. The sky is dark and thick with smoke and we're a good ways back from the road. *Look away,* I plead. But her pale eyes lock on mine through the bramble.

One of the men starts toward us.

Rixenda wipes her palms down the front of her apron and stands taller. Sparks from the fire dance in her eyes, and I know what she's going to do.

No, I want to shout, but it's too late. She hefts her petticoats to her knees, steps out of line, and runs in the opposite direction. Drawing the attention away from us.

The intruder wheels around to give chase. The man at the head of the group glances at the trees, then back at his line of prisoners. Torn.

"Go!" Louis whispers as he runs deeper into the forest.

The others follow, but my feet are rooted to the spot. My throat burns as if I'm screaming, but I'm not making a sound.

The man overtakes Rixenda in less than ten steps. His sword slashes through the flesh between her shoulder blades, and her shriek raises every hair on my body. Pain shudders through me like an earthquake as I watch her hit the ground. A raw, warbling sound sputters from my lips as her blood seeps across the road.

Marie clamps a hand over my mouth. "Don't waste her sacrifice," she says softly. Then *she* is dragging *me.*

I want to curl into a ball and weep. I want to lie down in the leaves and let the fire devour me. But as Rixenda's screams fade away, her final words to me linger in my mind.

Be strong, Josse.

So I force myself to inhale. Force myself to boost my sisters higher and run. Tears streak my soot-caked cheeks and numbness settles over me—as murky as the charcoal sky. By the time we finally stop to catch our breaths, my bones have turned to jelly.

Louis leans against a tree and mumbles something about scampering about like godforsaken rats. His words slowly permeate my grief-stricken haze and spark something inside me.

"Rats . . ." I repeat.

"What about them?"

"If these rebels want to treat us like rats, we might as well oblige."

Louis eyes me like I'm out of my mind. And maybe I am.

With a wave to the Condé at the rear, I forge ahead, marking a straight course toward the last place anyone would think to look for royalty.

3

MIRABELLE

Our carriage rumbles away from the smoldering remains of Versailles, trailing a wake of corpses. I sit straight as a lance and stare at the frayed window curtain flapping in the breeze. Each time it billows, an icy gust whips through the compartment, but I am too numb to feel it. My tongue is too raw to form words. I squeeze my eyes shut, but the Sun King's face fills the blackness: foam dripping from his mouth, fingers clawing at his standing ruff. I see the green glow of Lesage's désintégrer and the courtiers' bodies strewn across the manicured lawns, their satin gowns and jewel-encrusted doublets riddled with arrows and seeping scarlet.

What have we done?

I grip the edge of the bench, tighter and tighter until my forearms quake. No matter how deeply I inhale, I cannot catch my breath—as if invisible hands are cinching my stays. I know better than to utter a word of objection, but I must look like a cauldron threatening to boil over, for Mother takes my chin in a firm grip and forces me to look at her.

"Trust me, Mirabelle."

I wet my lips and swallow hard. *How can I trust you? You deceived me, used me. We poisoned the king.*

Mother makes her voice as smooth as honey and brushes a wayward curl from my face. "This was necessary. For the greater good. We will care for the people of Paris far better than the Sun King ever did. There will be no hungry, no infirm."

Everything inside me goes quiet. So still, I can hear the blood pounding in my ears. What does she mean, *we* will care for the people?

"As someone with intimate knowledge of our former ruler, I can assure you he deserved this fate," Lesage adds in a breathy voice. He leans against the carriage wall, so weak from expending his magic that he can hardly keep his eyes open. I glare at the ghoulish green light still radiating from his fingertips, fear and fury scorching through my veins like wildfire. *I* gave Lesage that power—or, my alchemy enhanced it. He was nothing but a performer, a conjurer, creating illusions that vanished like smoke before *I* invented a tonic that made his magic tactile. Until I turned him into a sorcerer at Mother's behest.

Another bout of nausea surges up my throat, and I lean out the window, retching my sickness down the side of the carriage.

"Really, Mirabelle. Show some fortitude," Mother barks, though I notice her own face is as waxen as a tallow candle.

Marguerite straightens and inclines her chin so she's looking down at me. "Do you suppose the great Charlemagne united an empire without some bloodshed?" She sounds as if she's reciting from historical texts to impress a tutor. It works. Mother's countenance lightens considerably at the comparison. "It is better that a few might perish in order to help the majority."

"And think of all we will accomplish with the royal coffers at our disposal," Lesage puts in. I cut my eyes at the auburn-haired jackal. Of course the coffers are his primary concern.

My fingers begin to tingle. My vision shimmers gray and black. *Breathe, Mira.* The king was a gluttonous, slothful man. An abhorrent leader. Perhaps Mother is right. The people will fare better without him.

The remainder of the ride passes in silence, though it's not the somber quiet of a torn battlefield or the reverent stillness of a graveyard. It is a raucous silence. A giddy, rasping hum that grates on my ears and makes my skin crawl with weevils. Fernand and Marguerite continue whispering, as always, and the Abbé Guibourg strokes his crucifix, a satisfied smile on his withered lips. Even La Trianon looks pleased, shaking her head and fanning her flushed cheeks.

Madame de Montespan is the only person other than myself who doesn't join the silent celebration. I had thought she was in on Mother's scheme, the instigator even, but when Fernand and Marguerite donned their masks and rushed toward the palace, she collapsed beside me in the dirt and wailed at the top of her voice.

Now she's ashen and listless, knocking into the carriage wall whenever we round a bend or rumble over a pothole. She fingers her limp corn-colored curls, and her azure eyes stare through me. She mouths the same two words over and over again: "My girls, my girls."

For once, Mother and Lesage do not rush to console her. They purse their lips and shoot her wary glances.

I was not the only one deceived this day.

As we pass through the Faubourg Saint-Germain and approach the left bank, the sprawling yellow fields give way to crooked half-timbered houses that teeter and lean like tired old men. The familiar stink of bilge water and the haze of chimney soot coats our throats. Marguerite breaks the silence with a long sigh. "We shouldn't have burned the palace at Versailles," she laments, peeling back the curtain to stare longingly at the distant pillar of smoke staining the skyline. "It was so much grander than the reeking city center."

"That is precisely why we burned it." Mother flings the curtain shut. "We are nothing like the former king, tucked away in a lavish country château where it's impossible to see to the needs of our people. *We* shall live in the heart of the city. We will open the gates of the Louvre and welcome all to court. The worst has passed," she says emphatically.

I nod along with the others. Forcing myself to believe it. Willing her declaration to be true.

Despite Mother's promise, the nightmare continues.

We sequester ourselves in the belly of the Louvre while battles rage in the outer baileys. Cannon fire shakes the great stone walls. I take a small measure of comfort knowing we aren't attacking unsuspecting citizens this time. The ministers and courtiers residing at the Louvre surrendered as soon as they saw the host of Shadow Society rebels scaling the battlements, and the servants happily switched allegiance when Mother offered to double their pay. And the citizens of Paris voiced no objection. On the contrary. They cheered in the streets and stitched banners of emerald, cerise, and plum-colored rags in support of Mother, their champion.

Our only opposition is the Paris Police. The officers are as relentless as roaches and just as impossible to kill: more skilled with the sword, more organized in their battalions, and more prepared with reserve armories scattered about the city. They have every advantage. Save for magic.

"I need another draught," Lesage says, bursting into my new laboratory. It is a cold subterranean chamber that used to be a dungeon. Menacing hooks and chains still dangle from the walls, and soiled rushes litter the floor. I could have chosen any of the gilded salons with velvet divans and marble mantelpieces abovestairs, but then I would have been forced to hear the clashing swords and ear-splitting screams. My windows would have overlooked the carnage. Down here, it is muffled. Apart. If I close my eyes, I can pretend I'm back in the garden house—*if* I can ignore the stink.

Lesage clips across the chamber and deposits himself on a stool. He has always been thin and sallow, but now he looks like a corpse brought to life. His tunic is spattered with gore, and dark bruises sag beneath his bloodshot eyes. I doubt he's slept since Versailles. His fingers quiver as he rolls up his sleeve and lays his arm across the table. When I don't spring for my lancet, he glares at me.

I fold my arms and stand my ground. "I thought we agreed to fight by natural means? Mother said seizing the Louvre would be simple compared to—"

"Does that sound simple to you?" He gestures wildly overhead. Even deep beneath the palace, the blasts shudder through the walls, rattling the phials. Grout crumbles from between the stones. Not for the first time, I gaze up at the ceiling and wonder how heavy it will be when it buckles and buries us.

Gris gives me a gentle nudge. "Perhaps Lesage is right." He shuffles across the room and offers me a porcelain bowl and lancet. "We are a society of alchemists and fortune-tellers. It's foolish to think we can battle officers hand-to-hand."

I glare at Gris. Groveling to Mother is one thing, but to Lesage is another. I've done more than enough for the sorcerer, and I intend to remind Lesage of this, but another explosion groans through the ceiling. Shaking the cabinets. Rocking my stomach until it threatens to expel the few gulps of tea I choked down this morning.

"Fine." I take the equipment, Lesage makes a fist, and I nick the blue vein below his elbow. Rivulets of blood snake down his arm and drip into the porcelain bowl. I have to turn away, knowing the violence it will bring.

Gris lays a hand on my shoulder. "The sooner we quell these dissenters, the sooner we can return to making curatives."

I nod and cast him a weak smile. I want to believe him, but trapped in this unfamiliar laboratory with the king's death on my conscience, brewing naught but Lesage's blood magic, it's hard to believe I'm capable of anything beyond destruction.

Gris prepares the cauldron while I grind stinging nettle, monkshood, and horehound and add them to the pot. Then I return to Lesage to collect the basin of blood. He coughs and collapses against the table, his face gray and his hair slick with sweat. His shallow breath rasps like stones.

"You're going to kill yourself if you keep this up," I say over my shoulder as I incorporate his blood into the mixture.

Lesage lifts his head just enough to look at me. "Shouldn't you be glad of that?"

"*I* would be exceedingly glad. But *Mother* would not." I place a tin cup before him and fill it with the crimson draught. "Pace yourself, magician."

Chuckling, he downs the potion like ale and wipes the bloody dregs on his wrist. "Would that I could, La Petite Voisin." He pats the top of my head, specifically because he knows I despise it, and flashes a peevish grin. The same weaselly smile he wore two years ago when he first appeared in my laboratory, asking prying questions about my abilities, about Father's death. I didn't trust him from the first. He reminded me of a slippery, squirming leech, attaching to the plumpest vein. I told Mother as much, but she ignored me, as always. And she didn't resist when he began courting her the very next week. She saw only a powerful man who looked on her as if she were a rare jewel, who bowed to her every whim, who kissed her knuckles and whispered pretty words. All the things Father never did.

I watch Lesage totter away, so weak he can hardly make it abovestairs without aid, let alone vanquish the Paris Police. But the following morning, the palace is deathly quiet. The walls have stilled and the bellowing in the courtyards has ceased.

Thankfully, I did not witness the massacre, but Marguerite flits down to relay every gory detail. How Lesage conjured beasts made of smoke that tore the officers limb from limb, sparing only the lieutenant general, whose head is now spiked on the Louvre's curtain wall. A warning to anyone else who might challenge our rule.

"You see? The worst has passed," Gris says, echoing Mother.

I am so desperate to believe him, for my life to return to some sense of normalcy, I agree to attend Mother's victory banquet the following night.

I glide down the Grand Galerie, my navy skirts whispering against the gleaming parquet, my hair parted down the center and curled on either side of my head. I'm tempted to peek at my reflection in the leaded window panes—I doubt I'd recognize myself, bedecked in all this finery like a proper courtier—but I do not look. I am an alchemist, first and always, and once Gris and I resume making curatives, everything will be as it was before. Only better, as our reach will extend a thousandfold with the Shadow Society controlling the city.

The banquet hall is so bright with golden filigree, I squint as I step through the doors. Gilt roses and curling vines snake up the walls and pilasters, crisscrossing in a glittering canopy overhead. Intricate chandeliers spit flares of bronze candlelight, and sumptuous tapestries adorn the walls. The impossibly long table is littered with buttery yellow goblets and platters heaped high with sugar plums and pomegranate seeds, with roe deer and spiced sturgeon.

"Isn't this a dream?" Marguerite slides into the seat beside me. "Even the utensils are bejeweled." She lifts a ruby encrusted fork like a scepter and uses it to point to the chair on my other side, at the head of the table where Mother will sit. I stand and trade her seats without complaint. I would rather not sit too close to Mother and Lesage anyway.

The banquet begins, and I glut myself on strawberries with cream and duck confit, hoping the rich food will fill the wound festering inside my stomach. But everything tastes of ashes, and my appetite sours entirely when Fernand reenacts the king's final moments, complete with wine frothing from his lips. There are irreverent toasts and boisterous laughter, but to my surprise, Mother and Lesage do not participate. They're too consumed by their whispered conversation, looking up only to cast furtive glances down the table.

When dessert arrives—pear tartlets and steaming bowls of persimmon pudding—the reason for their distraction becomes clear. As soon as Madame de Montespan finishes her pudding, she lurches in her seat. Her enormous blue eyes double in size and beads of sweat pour down her cheeks, cutting runnels through her powder. She bursts into a fit of coughs and grips the table so hard that my goblet rattles.

The hairs prickle down my neck. If I didn't know better, I'd say she'd been . . .

I push my plate away, wishing I hadn't eaten so much. I expect the rest of the table to do the same, but none of the Society members shy away from the feast. Nor do they rise to assist the marquise.

"Are you unwell?" Mother asks. Her voice is soft with concern, but her dark eyes are slitted like a serpent's.

Madame de Montespan doubles over, hands clutched to her stomach, and when she tries to speak, droplets of blood spatter her golden plate. I scream as she collapses into her bowl. Poison. Undoubtedly. But why would Mother poison her ally? And where did she get it? I think of the Aqua Tofana intended for the Duc de Barra, and my insides go cold. Who knows if any of my draughts are ever delivered into the proper hands?

Mother stands and raises her goblet. "To loyalty," she bellows. The other members of the Shadow Society echo her and drink. "If anyone else feels compelled to pen letters to the royal army or encourage the Duc de Vendôme to organize the former nobility to rise against us, this will be your fate." She waves a hand at Madame de Montespan, then looks meaningfully from the Duc de Luxembourg to the Duchesse de Bouillon to the Marquis de Cessac, continuing down the line of her highest-ranking clients. Her features are painted with disgust, but I notice the slightest tremble of her arm, how she cannot bring herself to look at Madame de Montespan's face.

"Fortunately, we've no cause to worry," she says, forging on. "Thanks to the magical wards Lesage wove around the city, no one can come or go without my express consent. Which means the royal army never received word their king is dead. And if the Duc de Vendôme rises against us from within the city, we will quell his attack long before he breaches the Louvre—through *poisonous* means, if necessary."

The others shout their approval and bang their goblets against the table, but I shove backwards. Out of my seat. The ground sways, and I barely manage to steady my balance on the table.

"Is there a problem?" Mother demands.

Yes. You promised the worst had passed. You promised this was for the greater good, yet we continue poisoning people.

I attempt to speak, but my thoughts are thicker than an overboiled draught. I'm trying to trust Mother, but she must see this has gone too far.

Irritation flickers in her eyes. When I remain standing, she glares as if she will wring my neck. "Excuse us for a moment," she says to the table, finding a radiant smile for her guests. Then she grips my forearm and drags me to the corner. "What the devil is wrong with you?"

"Why must we poison Vendôme and his men? Surely our numbers are great enough—"

"Our numbers may be greater, but we're trained in tarot cards and tea leaves. And our followers are farmers and tinkerers, not soldiers. You know what happened when we battled the officers, and Lesage is still too weak to use his magic. The task falls to you, Mirabelle. If the duc and his men refuse to stand down, we will poison them."

"*No.*" The word slips out before I can stop it. Not loud, by any means, but loud enough. Several heads turn to peer at us. Whispers tangle down the table.

Mother grips my wrist, her nails slicing half-moon cuts into my skin. "Do you think I enjoy this? Do you think I am any less horrified? My dearest friend lies dead on the table." Her voice warbles and she draws a deep breath. "But in order to serve the people how we ought, we must squash these rebellions and establish a government that prioritizes the common men and women. So you will do as I say and make my poison, or I will find you *other* duties. Away from Gris and your precious laboratory. Do you understand?"

I curtsy on wobbly legs and sprint for the doors, falling to my knees as soon as I reach the hall.

I do not understand.

And I won't do this.

All night I stew. Pacing my chamber, crying into my pillow, and screaming until my throat tastes of blood. By the time the sun rises, I am delirious and more than a little unhinged, but I have a plan. Mother requested poison, but she never specified what *type* of poison, so I brew a simple sleep poison made from mushroom spores and blue vitriol. It slows the heart and causes paralysis, but the effect is painless. Vendôme and his men will simply drift off to sleep and never awaken. It's the best death I can give them.

Unfortunately, Mother anticipates my scheme. As soon as I deliver the poison to her salon, she administers a few droplets to a pair of doves she keeps in a gilded cage. Her lips flatten and her fingers tap with increased speed and agitation against her dressing table as the birds drop from their perch without a sound.

"Do it again," she snaps, overturning the tray so the remaining phials of poison shatter across the floor. "And this time, make Viper's Venom."

"But—" Viper's Venom is horrendous. The most violent of poisons. Victims suffer brutal trembling fits, their backs arching and twisting until the bones break, and then the hallucinations and vomiting set in. The torment lasts for hours.

Mother presses her fingers against her temples. "Do you know what the Duc de Vendôme is claiming? That the dauphin and princesses live, since we have yet to produce their bodies. He wants them returned to the throne."

"You said the royal children perished in the fire."

"They did," Mother says forcefully. "Which is why we must send a message. All of France must know the consequences of rising against the Shadow Society, and drifting off to sleep is hardly fear-inducing."

I close my eyes and try to take a breath, but the lump in my throat feels like a cannonball. "What happened to caring for the people?" I say in a small voice. "I know you would never do anything that wasn't in their best interest," I add quickly when Mother stiffens, "but doesn't this seem extreme?"

Mother takes my hand. Her cold fingers coil around my knuckles like snakes. "We *shall* care for the people. We would be already, were it not for these rebellious nobles. Now stop acting like your father and distill my order. This is the only way."

Stop acting like your father. She means it as a slight. A cutting remark to cow me into submission. But a seedling of an idea takes root in my mind. Perhaps Father is exactly who I *should* be channeling.

Late that night, while the rest of the household sleeps, I scurry down to the laboratory like a clever kitchen mouse and pry open every crate brought over from the garden house. I comb through decaying ledgers and scrolls, digging for something I swore I destroyed two years prior.

In the bottom of the third dusty trunk, I find it: Father's grimoire. The red leather flashes in the torchlight and my hands hesitate on the binding, years of Mother's warnings ringing in my ears.

He loved alchemy more than he ever loved us. He was reckless and obsessed, and it killed him in the end.

She isn't wrong. Father was so consumed by his experiments, we fell into financial ruin and would have starved to death had Mother not resorted to palm reading and selling love potions—the beginnings of the Shadow Society. And he perished in an explosion that could have been avoided had he heeded Mother's plea to brew only the safe, familiar recipes she required for her customers. But Father brewed what pleased him. The potions he deemed most important. I still remember how Mother cried at night after Marguerite and I were tucked in bed, begging him to be more careful. Begging him to come in for supper and be a father to us. Begging him to love her.

But Father loved only his alchemy, and unlike Mother, I didn't mind that he treated me more like a laboratory assistant than a daughter. I was glad to have even a measure of his attention. And I had learned to love alchemy nearly as much as he did.

I run a tentative finger along the spine of Father's grimoire. What if his convictions weren't as preposterous as Mother claimed? Perhaps he was onto something—trusting his own instincts over her commands.

You will be a great alchemist one day, he used to tell me. *Greater even than I.*

I pry the grimoire from its hiding place and clutch it to my chest, inhaling the sweet scent of sage that wafts from the paper—the same scent that always clung to Father's doublet. "What would you do?" I whisper, but I already know the answer.

Experiment. Innovate.

My mind immediately goes to the Viper's Venom, and I spend the next three hours poring over Father's notes, determined to distill a compound that will nullify the poison's horrendous effects. But the curative is extremely temperamental. Too much stirring, and the ingredients separate. And it boils over with even the smallest amount of heat. After five failed attempts, dawn is beginning to seep through the curtains and I want something to show for a whole night's work. So I close Father's grimoire and focus on counteracting one of my own recipes instead—one in particular that I wish I'd never invented: Lesage's désintégrer.

After scribbling four pages of notes and checking my calculations twice, I tip two parts ambergris and one part periwinkle into a pot. The petals wilt into the foul-smelling paste, and I stir continuously until bubbles swell and pop across the surface. When it turns a deep pearl gray, I siphon it into a large phial and hold it up to the light, watching the liquid churn and eddy. The next time Lesage shoots his fire bolts, I will attempt to reverse the effects.

Smiling, I skitter across the chamber to hide the curative, but the door swings open.

Merde.

My heart slams to a halt and my feet follow suit. I quickly slip the phial into my apron pocket. Then I whirl around, fanning my face to draw attention away from the telltale bulge. "Prop that door open. It's hotter than hell in here," I say dramatically.

Gris nods as he lumbers through the door. I'm so relieved to see him instead of my sister or Fernand or Lesage that I let out a loud, breathy laugh. "Thank goodness you're here. I'm anxious to begin."

He scratches his sleep-tousled hair and studies the cluttered board. "It looks to me like you're well under way. Since when do you rise before dawn?"

"I couldn't sleep, so I thought I'd get started."

He frowns at the messy table, fingering the periwinkle petals and sniffing the mortar bowl where I ground the ambergris. "Get started making what, exactly? Obviously not Viper's Venom. And what's this?" He reaches for Father's small red book, but I snatch it off the table and stuff it down my bodice.

"Nothing."

"Mira?" Gris narrows his eyes.

I lunge across the table, extract a sprig of witch's thimble from a jar, and bat the purple flowers against his nose. "Do you remember the first time my father taught us to use witch's thimble?"

Suspicion and hurt flicker across his features and he pushes the sprig aside. "I know the unrest has lasted longer than expected, but please tell me you don't pity Vendôme and his army of noblemen. That you're not secretly helping them."

"How would I help them? There's no antidote for Viper's Venom."

He eyes my bodice—more specifically the grimoire hidden within it. "They deserve this. You know what they did to me."

I look down at the board and fiddle with a bit of twine. I'll never forget the day Mother brought Gris home—he was two years older than me, but so skinny and frightened, he looked a good deal younger than my six years. You could see every rib protruding through his thin, filthy skin, and bruises peppered his arms and legs. He didn't speak to any of us for months, but Mother told me what happened. He'd been beaten and left in the gutter to die by his master, the Chevalier de Lorraine, after his father, a footman, was hanged for stealing a golden button from a waistcoat. A button that was later found in the rushes of the chevalier's bedchamber.

Mother was Gris's savior. The Shadow Society became his new family.

Gris viciously tugs an apron over his head and mutters about *merciless, cold-blooded courtiers* as he ties the strings.

"I'm not helping them. I swear it," I say, glad I can tell the truth. But guilt still squirms through my chest like a worm through a rotten apple, because part of me *wants* to help them. Despite how the nobles mistreated Gris, despite how they look down on us rabble, I'd pity anyone who meets their end by Viper's Venom.

Gris studies my face, and after a long, prickling silence, he cups my cheeks in his kettle-sized palms and plants a kiss on my forehead. "If you say you're not helping them, I believe you. But I do wonder what you're doing. . . ."

"Just experimenting," I reply, busying my hands with the herbs.

His big eyes fall. *You can trust me,* they say. *Haven't I earned it?* And he has—a thousand times over. When Marguerite was busy clawing through the ranks of the Society and hoarding Mother's favor, Gris offered to apprentice with Father alongside me, claiming he shared my love of alchemy. I suspect he wanted to protect me from Father's volatile moods. When we got older, he taught me to play quinze and let me tag along with him and the other boys. And he laughed and talked with me long into the night, the way my sister used to before she abandoned me in favor of Fernand.

There's no one I love or trust more than Gris. Which is why I keep my lips pressed tight.

It's the only way to protect him—in case I'm found out.

The only way to keep him from hating me.

"Sometimes you're just like your father," he grumbles as his knife cuts across the herbs.

Oh, Gris. If only you knew.

Over the next three days, Mother sends delegations to negotiate with the Duc de Vendôme, but he and his horde of incensed noblemen refuse to swear fealty to the Shadow Society. They continue their march, turning Champ de Mars into an army encampment, so Mother sends Fernand, Marguerite, and a contingent of Society members to poison their horses and food.

"It was horrific," Marguerite whispers when they return later that night. We haven't slept in the same chamber for several years now—at *her* insistence—but she tucks herself beneath the counterpane and nestles in beside me. I stiffen, annoyed at her tears wetting my dressing gown and her hands quivering like leaves beneath the blankets.

"Go cry to Fernand," I protest.

"Please. I can't let him see me like this. Or Mother. I've nowhere else to go."

I'm glad we can be sisters when it's convenient for you, I imagine saying as I shove her to the cold floor. But I'm curious to hear what happened, so I let her take my hands. She responds with a faint squeeze of gratitude, and despite myself, I'm transported back to our childhood. To the nights we held each other like this, singing quietly to drown out our parents' quarreling.

"There were so many of them," Marguerite says in a choked voice. "Writhing like slugs across the ground—foaming and bloody and shrieking. I know they deserved to die—they were coming to attack us—but I keep thinking of the wives and children they'll never return to."

I gape at her through the darkness. My heart batters against my rib cage, and I tighten my grip on her clammy hands. I never dreamed my sister might be plagued by the same sliver of guilt. "Margot, do you think it's wrong, what we're doing?"

She stiffens, and when she speaks, her voice is careful and cold. "Of course not. Mother would never lead us astray. The massacre may have been difficult to witness, but that doesn't mean it was wrong. Those men needed to die for the greater good of the people. Now that our hold is secure, all will be well. Mother plans to open the palace gates and welcome all to court. And there's to be a victory procession." She stitches a smile across her lips. Brittle and steely. Eerily similar to Mother's.

I let out a breath and stare up at the lacy bed curtains, wondering how she can lie to herself. And whom I'm supposed to believe. And how I can possibly march in Mother's procession when the last thing I feel is victorious.

4

JOSSE

I always imagined Hell would be hot—a lake of fire and brimstone and all that. But Hell, it turns out, is being trapped in these dank, freezing sewer tunnels, helpless to stop the eerie green specks from spreading like ink beneath my sisters' skin. It's hearing them cry my name and being unable to ease their suffering. It's the feel of their brittle arms and legs withering beneath their dresses, smaller and smaller until I could snap them like twigs.

Every waking moment feels like a nightmare, and during the fleeting snatches when I accidentally nod off, I am bombarded by actual nightmares. Sometimes I'm carrying the girls through a blazing, endless forest, only to discover they've been dead all along, corpses clad in dresses. Other times I'm standing at the edge of the road, watching the blade sink into Rixenda's back over and over again. But always, no matter the dream, Father's voice taunts me, hissing and popping like the crackling flames: *You wished for this. My death is on your head—as will be your sisters'.*

I wake up sweating, shaking, and sometimes even sobbing. Yes, I wished for change, for acknowledgment, but never like this. Everything is twisted and wrong. I finally have access to my sisters only to watch them die. My siblings and I share the same status and accommodations, but they're squalid and putrescent, even worse than the servants' quarters.

The Devil must be having a good laugh.

"When can we go home?" Anne asks, as she has every morning for the past two weeks. Only today she coughs so violently between words, droplets of blood dapple her lips. Frowning, I offer her a sip of water we collected in a shoe and tug my waistcoat tighter around her shoulders, wishing, for the millionth time, we had a proper bed and blankets. A torn burlap sack in the corner of the chamber where the ceiling drips the least is the best we can manage.

The entire room is less than twenty paces across and barely tall enough for me to stand. The floor is jagged and misshapen and sudden gusts of reeking wind threaten to strangle us—made worse by the Condé's decaying body. The wound in his side wouldn't stop bleeding, and he died not long after we reached the tunnels that first night. I dragged him as far away as I could, but it isn't nearly far enough.

I smooth Anne's hair away from her clammy cheeks and adjust her dress to cover the ghastly green bruises creeping across her shoulders. "We'll go home soon, love," I lie. "Now close your eyes and rest."

Marie dabs a soaked bit of satin she ripped from her petticoats across Françoise's forehead, but her fever's burning so hot, the cloth dries the moment it touches her skin.

"What do we do, Josse?" Marie whispers.

I don't know, I want to cry. I don't know how to be the steady one, the strong one. No one's ever noticed me, let alone depended on me. The ghost of Rixenda's wooden spoon thwacks the back of my knuckles. Her gravelly voice is close, as if she's sitting in the puddle beside me. *Quit simpering and crying. You know what to do. I taught you.*

"Tear more compresses," I say, motioning to Marie's petticoats. "Keep them cool against the rocks and rotate them every few minutes." It probably won't help. Nothing has. But it's worth a try. In two weeks, the girls have gone from round-cheeked cherubs to wasted shells. I'm afraid to imagine what will become of them if we're trapped down here for another two weeks.

The sewer was never meant to be a permanent solution, but finding alternate lodging and arranging transportation when you're supposed to be dead—and cannot be seen, or else you truly *will* be dead—is next to impossible.

But I haven't given up.

Once the girls finally drift off into a fitful, whimpering sleep, I pull on a tricorne hat that I nicked from a market stall and creep across the chamber. Louis scowls as I pass. He badgered me relentlessly those first few days, arguing that he should accompany me up above. But I flashed a pointed look at his opulent clothes, flaxen hair, and his altogether recognizable face— with that long, straight de Bourbon nose—and he muttered an oath and stayed put.

This is the first and only time being the nameless, nobody bastard has benefited me.

It's too dangerous to venture out the grate we entered through—smack in the middle of the bustling rue Montmartre—so night after night, I scour the stinking tunnels until I find the hatch leading up into Madame Bissette's pâtisserie. She's a shrewd woman of business and agreed not to hand us over to the masked intruders in exchange for a few seed pearls and sapphires, which I took great pleasure in ripping from Louis's extravagant frock coat.

For the past week, I've been creeping around Les Halles marketplace, stealing carrots and tomatoes and cabbages and listening in on conversations, which is how I know the attack on Versailles was orchestrated by the devineresse, La Voisin, and her Shadow Society. A witch masquerading as a fortune-teller, aided by poisoners and alchemists and magicians, like Lesage. They've taken the Louvre and are murdering courtiers and police officers to secure their hold on Paris.

I haven't a clue how to stop them, but thankfully that isn't my responsibility. Louis can figure out how to retake his throne. My only concern is getting Anne and Françoise to safety and a physician.

With fingertips trailing either side of the tunnel, I race through the passageways. Two rights, four lefts, and another right. The blackness is so thick, it's tangible—dense and scratchy like a wool blanket soaked in rat piss. I hold my breath until I reach the iron steps beneath the pâtisserie, where the smell of baking bread combats the stench a fraction. After rapping on the overhead hatch four times, I bounce with impatience while I wait for Madame Bissette's ruddy face to appear. She has at least three chins and smells of yeast, but when she opens the trapdoor each night, she looks more beautiful than God's heavenly angels, doughy cheeks all radiant and glowing in the moonlight.

"Josse, my boy, come up, come up." She clucks and pecks around the hatch like a mother hen while I bound into the sweet shop. "Let's have a look at you." She brushes off my tunic and breeches. A waste of time. I haven't anyone to impress down there, and no one gives me a passing glance up here. I look like any other street urchin.

Skirting around her, I make for the door, but she catches the tail of my tunic and pulls me back to fuss over a smudge on my cheek. I grit my teeth and count the seconds till she's satisfied. *For the girls. Think of the girls.*

Madame Bissette licks her fingers and slicks back a dark strand of my hair that's fallen from its queue. "There now, that's better." She straightens my collar. "If only you weren't illegitimate. Such a handsome face and all for nothing."

"Yes, such a pity," I agree, straining for the doorknob.

Madame Bissette sidles her large body between me and my goal. "Can I get you something to eat? Before you go?"

I can't steal enough cast-off vegetables from Les Halles to keep us from starving, so Madame Bissette has been selling me her day-old baked goods for the small price of another jewel.

There's also the unspoken promise that when we rise again to power, overthrow the Shadow Society, and reclaim the throne, she'll be appointed royal pastry chef.

I grab a hunk of rye off the counter, stuff it in my mouth, and toss her a pearl as I head for the door.

"And the others?" She waddles after me. "Surely they're hungry too?"

"I'll purchase more when I return. To surprise Louis for breakfast." I screw on my most dazzling smile, as if I care for frivolous things like fresh bread—or pleasing my brother—but his name is like a magic word, so I use it as often as possible.

"Oh," she exclaims, fanning herself at the mere mention of him. "How *is* his Royal Highness?"

He's trapped in the sewer. How do you think *he is?* I ratchet my smile a notch higher and pat her shoulder. "He's been better, obviously, but staying optimistic. Mostly thanks to your hospitality." I give her a wink and tip my hat. "It's been a pleasure as always, Madame Bissette."

"Be careful out there, Josse. This is no time to be gallivanting about. *They've* taken to the streets, readying for the procession tomorrow."

I sweep out the door. "Thanks for the warning, ma chérie."

Despite the late hour and pouring rain, the rue Saint-Honoré teems as if it's midday. Everywhere I turn there are black masks and velvet capes. Shadow Society miscreants crowd the taverns and spill into the streets, and the common folk are out en masse.

I had expected at least a little resistance or fear from them—the Shadow Society is murdering the courtiers and police officers, after all. But they seem delighted to see one of their own risen so high. La Voisin is something of a hero. Apparently there's hardly a man or woman in Paris who hasn't consulted her for some sort of remedy or tincture, upper and lower classes alike. And they're all lining up to secure the best view of the victory procession, which will parade through the streets tomorrow afternoon.

With all eyes on the Shadow Society, it's the perfect time to flee with my siblings. But in order to do that, I'm going to need help.

I skirt through the Place de Grève, past the pillory and old docks where grubby children try to pick my pockets. The sandy soil is so flooded, my toes damn near freeze inside my boots. It hasn't stopped raining for weeks now. *As if God is mourning the king,* Louis likes to say.

He's the only *one mourning the king,* I think. But my palms are sticky and my mouth feels dry, and I know I'm not being entirely honest with myself. I am mourning him too. Not a lot. Not how a child should grieve for a parent. But more than expected. And I don't like it. I tell myself it's only residual guilt from reading those broadsides, from his voice haunting my dreams. Or maybe a tiny part of me resents him for not teaching me how to shoulder this responsibility better.

The point is, I don't miss *him.* He didn't want to be my father, so he has no right to my pain. Rixenda is the voice inside my head. *She* is my true parent. Every time I close my eyes, I see her there on the road. Her gaze burning with determination and love. Giving me that final gift. Father never would have sacrificed himself for me, and the swell of crushing gratitude and guilt I feel for Rixenda relegates the king to his rightful place in my heart. I stomp his memory beneath my boots.

When I reach the Méchant Meriée, I pull my hat brim low and shoulder through the swinging doors. It smells of sour ale, soggy wool, and sweat. The gaming tables are crowded with exhausted laborers and dirty, unkempt thieves. A pair of sailors shoot to their feet, arguing, and when one of them overturns a table, I have to press myself against the wall to avoid the flying tankards. I like a rowdy hand of cards as much as the next lowborn, but this gambling den is too dodgy, even for my taste.

But it's precisely the sort of place my best friend, Luc Desgrez, would come—if he's alive. It's a dangerous thing to be a member of the Paris Police these days.

But I have cause to hope.

For the past two days, the stationers in Les Halles have been grousing about a black-haired brigand who's cleaning out the pockets of everyone at the lansquenet tables—boasting as he does so—which pretty much sums up mine and Desgrez's routine for the past three years. Each night after I finished in the kitchens, we'd make our rounds of the gambling dens, leaving with stacks of silver livres that were inevitably accompanied by black eyes and busted lips—thanks to Desgrez's big mouth.

I squint at each table, not knowing what to look for exactly.

He won't be wearing his officer's coat with the golden epaulets, I know that much.

An enormous bearded man sporting a ruby-encrusted baldric knocks my shoulder. Another rams me from behind. I'm about to abandon my plan and slink back to the sewer when I hear a familiar whoop of laughter from the back corner table.

I spin and elbow through the crowd, a prayer on my lips. I know better than to call his name, so I cup my hands around my mouth and make the hooting noise we used as boys to signal that the palace halls were free of guards.

A man at the table stiffens and turns, and I practically sob for joy at the sight of his familiar face. Desgrez is wearing a tattered gray tunic topped with an overlarge vest, his black hair hangs in greasy strands across his eyes, and his feathered cap has been replaced by a dark, shapeless hood.

"You look like hell," I say in way of greeting. It's supposed to be a jibe, but my voice is so thick with emotion that it comes out small and choked.

He drops his cards, shoves out of his chair, and buries me in an embrace. "You're alive. I didn't dare to hope."

"*You're* alive. How?"

"Thanks to my proclivity for disguise, obviously." He grins and tugs his disgusting vest. The other men at the table shout and pound the boards, but Desgrez abandons his hand, loops his arm around my shoulders, and drags me toward the door. "I think it best if we take our reunion elsewhere."

We duck into the midnight rain and wind around several corners until we find a quiet storefront with an overhanging roof. He releases me and scrunches his nose. "You smell awful. Have you been rolling in a midden heap?"

"Close to it," I say. "How did you survive the battle against Lesage's beasts? I heard it was horrific. Not even the lieutenant general made it out alive. His head is currently spiked on the castle's curtain wall."

Desgrez shudders. "I know, and I would have perished with them, but since I was the lowest ranking officer, Le Reynie sent me to fetch ammunition from the reserve armory behind the Port Saint-Antoine. By the time I returned, the battle was over. I saw the bodies of my comrades strewn across the courtyard, shed my long coat, and ran in the opposite direction." He's silent for a beat. "Does that make me a coward?"

"No. It makes you smart. What good is rushing to the aid of dead men?"

Desgrez shrugs, but his lips are drawn and he refuses to look up from his boots. "They were my brothers in arms," he says softly. "We took an oath to defend the city—and each other— and I left them, broken and bleeding on the cobbles. I know there's nothing more I could have done, but I still feel I failed them somehow. . . ."

I nudge his shoulder. "Redeem yourself by helping me get the girls to safety."

That makes him look up quickly. "The girls live as well? But

Versailles burned to the ground. The Shadow Society claimed the entire royal line was eradicated."

"We nearly were, but I snuck us out through that builders' passage we discovered beneath the stairs—me and Anne and Françoise. As well as my *royal* siblings."

The whites of Desgrez's eyes grow as round as the moon and he lets out a low whistle. "That must be *interesting*. Where are they now?"

"Follow me," I say, filling him in on Anne and Françoise's condition as well as my plan to flee the city as I lead him back to Madame Bissette's.

"Smart," he says. "But I think we can do even better. I still have the keys to the armory. Let's move a cannon into one of the buildings along the procession route—maybe that church near Voisin's residence, Notre-Dame de Bonne Nouvelle—and blow it to smithereens when the poisoners march past. God willing, the blast will kill La Voisin and Lesage. In the chaos, they'll be forced to call reinforcements from the road blockades, and we'll ride out of Paris free and clear."

I blink up at Desgrez. "That's ingenious."

"I know." He preens as we enter the pâtisserie.

Madame Bissette looks up from behind the counter and shrieks when she sees someone come in on my heels. She brandishes a knife, and I hold up my hands. "It's okay," I say, "this is Des—"

"Captain Desgrez." Desgrez rushes forward and kisses the back of her wrist as if she's a bedamned courtier. "Of the Paris

Police. At your service, madame."

She makes a high-pitched cooing noise and brings her other hand to her chest. I roll my eyes and open the floor hatch. The first night we met, Madame Bissette threw four plates at my head and nearly took off my fingers in the trapdoor. Then I spent the next three nights groveling and bribing and begging her not to turn us in. But one look at Desgrez's slate gray eyes and charming grin—no matter that he looks every bit as haggard as me—and she's falling all over herself to accommodate him. She even gives him a baguette, free of charge, after which she greedily collects two seed pearls from me in exchange for a sad-looking barley loaf that will barely feed my siblings.

"Well, she's rather charming," Desgrez says, stepping off the moldering ladder and into the sludge. He takes a large bite of bread as he turns to inspect the tunnel. "This place . . . not so much."

"*Captain* Desgrez?" I snatch a piece of his bread and shove it into my mouth. "Really? You're the newest member of the Paris Police, only a year on watch."

"True, but since I'm now the *only* member of the watch, I'm captain by default."

I scoff and set off into the suffocating blackness. "Keep up, Captain."

"Mock me all you'd like, but who's the dauphin more likely to listen to: Officer Desgrez or Captain Desgrez? Just let me do the talking."

When we enter the chamber, Anne and Françoise push up to

their elbows and smile at Desgrez. Before he joined the police, he was a permanent fixture in our escapades, preferring to wreak havoc round the palace with me and the girls instead of assisting his father with Louis's lessons.

"This is a secure hideaway!" Louis bellows at me. "You cannot bring your rabble-rousing friends—"

"Forgive the intrusion, Your Royal Highness." Desgrez sketches a perfect bow. "Captain Desgrez of the Paris Police."

"Captain? How did you of all people rise through the ranks so quickly?"

"My exceptional skills, of course. Skills I wish to lend to you. I've come to escort you from this hellhole to safety."

Louis looks him up and down with a dubious frown.

"I obviously can't wear my uniform, given the circumstances, but I served directly under the lieutenant general." Desgrez spouts off a litany of names and titles and eventually Louis nods.

"Very well, go on."

"We've devised a plan to remove you and your sisters from Paris, but it will require your cooperation and assistance."

Louis crosses his arms. "What do you mean, *we've* devised a plan? Surely you don't mean him?" He juts his chin at me.

Desgrez shoots me a warning glare and turns back to Louis. "The circumstances are dire. We need every capable man on our side."

Louis grunts as if to say, *Precisely.*

I toss my hands into the air. "I saved your life! If it weren't for me, you'd have burnt to cinders with the palace. You're the one who's completely incompetent. I'm beginning to see why Father had to hold your hand so tightly."

"Silence!" Louis punches the dripping stone wall and then immediately yelps and cradles his fist. It's abundantly clear he's never punched anyone or anything, and I can't help but laugh. Desgrez looks like he wants to strangle me. Marie gapes as if I'm a monster. I'm generally not *quite* so brazen, but Louis needs to know I won't be intimidated.

Desgrez grabs me by the shoulder and hauls me behind him, then he fawns and grovels until Louis finally calms down and listens to our plan. "We obviously don't want you to be anywhere near the explosion—we can't risk you being injured or seen—so you will collect a cart, which I'll hide for you near the pâtisserie. Situate the girls in the back beneath blankets, and then meet Josse and me at the intersection of the rues de Richelieu and Saint-Honoré."

The chamber is silent as Louis digests the plan. "I don't like it," he says at last. "If I leave the city, I may lose it entirely."

Look around! It's already lost! I want to shout, but Desgrez glares at me out of the corners of his eyes.

"This is your best option, Your Highness," Desgrez says. "You're not gaining any ground hiding in the sewer. You must get out of the city and rouse your allies in Anjou and Brittany and Savoy. Plus your sisters cannot wait much longer." He glances over at Françoise and Anne, tossing and turning in the corner.

The silence stretches and I brace myself for Louis to say something awful, like, *We cannot put little girls above the well-being of a nation.* They are technically bastards, after all. Not to mention girls. But he grinds his teeth and mutters, "Fine. But if this ends poorly, you are to blame." He jabs a finger at me. "Father, God rest his soul, would have never supported such a preposterous, dangerous plan."

Louis's words wheedle beneath my skin, and I have to shut him up before the guilt seeps in, before Father's taunting voice crushes me with doubt. I *do not care* what he would think. I refuse to care. I am going to save my sisters and prove them all wrong.

"Caution got our father killed," I yell. "He disregarded the majority of his people and they assassinated him. Pardon me for not wanting to follow in his footsteps."

I turn on my heel, fist the back of Desgrez's vest, and drag him across the chamber. I need to be free of these stinking tunnels and Louis's condescending scowl.

"Thought we agreed I'd do the talking," Desgrez says once we're out of earshot.

"You were too busy kissing Louis's feet to say what needed to be said."

"You're both impossible. Would it kill you to show him a little respect?"

"Yes," I say as I charge up the iron steps and burst through the hatch into the pâtisserie.

Desgrez rolls his eyes and dons his hood, and we slip into the heaving crowd on the rue Saint-Honoré.

5

MIRABELLE

Mother has requested curatives. Hundreds of remedies she wishes to dispense to the crowd during our victory procession: Cadmia for ulcers, Arcanum Corallinum for gout and dropsy, Oil of Brick for palsy and tumors, as well as dozens of salves and syrups for headaches and fevers and coughs. As many tinctures as Gris and I can manage in a week's time.

I stare dubiously at the note Mother's attendant delivered to the laboratory.

"You see." Gris stands behind me, reading over my shoulder. "It's just as La Voisin promised. We've silenced the dissenters and can resume the true business of the Shadow Society."

I fold the note into my apron pocket and try to muster a hopeful smile, but the voices of the dead still call to me from the dust. Condemning me.

Gris watches me with a frown. "Did I miss something? Isn't this a good development?"

"Yes. Yes, of course."

"So why do you look like you're going to be sick?"

I fidget with a pile of fennel seeds on the counter. "I'm pleased we're returning to healing, but all of the curatives in the world will never bring back the dead."

Gris places his hands on my shoulders. "Sometimes succession is ugly. But we can rest easy in the knowledge that those who perished deserved their fate." I start to protest but he speaks over me. "We tried to be reasonable, but the nobles kept rising and fighting and forcing your mother's hand. She would never *choose* poison or Lesage's magic. She was backed into a corner and did what was best for the majority."

I nod grudgingly. "I suppose you're right."

"This order is proof I am. We have to trust her, Mira. She's done nothing to make us doubt."

I can't argue with that. Since Vendôme's slaughter, there have been no more uprisings. Mother hasn't ordered additional poison. Even Lesage has been strangely absent from my laboratory— requesting only one more blood draught.

A warm ember of hope flickers inside my chest.

"Very well." I tie back my curls and flash Gris a genuine smile. "Let's get to work."

Gris and I throw ourselves into distilling curatives, waking with the sun and burning candles long into the night. The healing scents of basil and cinnamon and lavender slowly overpower the pungent remnants of Viper's Venom and the rusty tang of Lesage's blood draught. We amass trays and trays of curatives until they crowd every corner of the board and cabinet. Even the crates and boxes and floors are cluttered with colorful packets and bottles. It's the most beautiful sight I've ever seen—proof that all has been set to right—yet the trickle of unease in my veins refuses to run dry.

Sleep continues to evade me. My hands tremble on my pestle and mortar. And I am haunted by images of withered, bleeding bodies.

The only time my mind is truly quiet is when I'm alone in the laboratory, distilling my treachery. I know I should stop. It's dangerous, treasonous, and above all, useless now that we've returned to brewing curatives. But the need to experiment lingers like an itch. A terrible twitching sensation that makes me sweat. Father's little red grimoire feels like a living, breathing entity tucked inside my bodice. It calls to me like a siren song, wrapping its wicked tendrils around my legs and guiding them back to the laboratory.

In the dead of night, when even Gris has gone to bed and only ghosts haunt these chambers, I tiptoe down the spiral staircase, bar the laboratory door, and slip into my secret world of alchemy. Under Father's imaginary direction, I modify the cure for désintégrer until I'm certain I have it right. Then I tuck a pouch filled with the ingredients beneath my stays so I'm ready at a moment's notice. Once formulated, the potion only keeps for an hour or two, and I want to be prepared to test its effectiveness should Lesage unleash his magic without warning. While I may trust Mother, I will never trust him.

On the morning of the procession, I climb the stairs to Mother's chamber feeling calm and hopeful and almost entirely like my old self. I'm eager to leave the palace and distribute our medications, to interact with the people and chase away the final vestiges of my guilt. I even smile at Marguerite and Fernand when they fall in stride with me on the second-floor landing—which may be a bit overzealous.

"How nice of you to clean up for the occasion." Fernand plucks a bit of straw from my hair. "Have you taken to sleeping in your laboratory too? Or maybe not sleeping at all?" he adds, pulling at the bottoms of his eyes. "You look terrible."

"Still better than you," I retort. It's a mystery to me what my sister sees in him. Fernand's thin black hair is even stringier than usual, and his velvet mask, which he *never* removes, clings to his cheeks like a second skin. I don't know if I hate him because he's a weaselly, scheming mercenary or if it's because Marguerite used to whisper with me before he came along and widened the gap between us.

Marguerite turns around and cuffs Fernand on the head. "No one asked you."

It seems that only *she* is allowed to harry me. A development that suits me quite well, if I'm honest. We've been oddly amiable since that night in my bed. Marguerite saved me the last religieuse after dinner two nights later, and when she and Fernand and his cohorts downed an entire cask of ale and sang bawdy drinking songs until dawn, I did not shout complaints. Marguerite and I even sat by the fire in my chamber and worked on our samplers together Thursday last.

"Are you still afraid?" she'd asked in a hushed voice, even though we were alone in the room.

Something about the way her dark eyes burned like the coals in the hearth made me nod. "A bit, I suppose. But not nearly as much as before. Are you?"

She shrugged, which was more confirmation than I expected. After a long pause, she whispered almost too soft to hear, "Sometimes I can't sleep. Their cries still haunt my thoughts." She became very intent on picking at a loose thread in her stitching, looking so small and timid, so unlike my older sister, I wanted to say something to comfort her. Something genuine to return her honesty.

"I think we're all haunted by ghosts. Sometimes I think I hear Father. I talk to him."

Marguerite's hands stilled and her eyebrows arched. "What do you say?"

"I ask what he makes of all this."

Marguerite was never close with Father. She craved bedtime stories and kisses and rides on his shoulders, but she had no predilection for alchemy. "Does he answer?"

"In his way," I said, thinking of his grimoire hidden beneath my bodice. "But I don't think we have any cause to worry. The worst has passed."

"The worst has passed," she agreed, repeating Mother's words with reverence.

There's a certain air of camaraderie between us as we stroll through the doors of Mother's chamber and leave Fernand grousing in the hall.

"Ah, my girls, at last," Mother croons from the vanity, where her ladies are powdering her face and arranging her chestnut curls. They are swept up into a high pompadour that somehow makes her look regal and dangerous all at once—like a lioness. Only at her temples can you notice the threads of gray running through her hair, and her shadowed eyes are as large as a doe's— black, depthless marbles set against the porcelain whiteness of her face. She hardly looks old enough to be my mother, but then, she's been slathering her face with youth restoratives and drinking alchemical mixtures since she was my age.

She waves her maids away and rises with a flourish. Hundreds of golden two-headed eagles shimmer through the folds of her ceremonial cape, and the sumptuous velvet billows around her ankles, creating the illusion that she's walking on wine-colored clouds. She is beautiful. Resplendent. A proper hero of the people.

Mother approaches me first and kisses my cheeks. Marguerite bristles, even though I was simply standing nearer. I try to catch her eye, but she purposely looks away, the easy energy between us doused as quickly as a candle.

"Mes petites Voisins." Mother takes both our hands and guides us across the chamber. "Come, I have a surprise for you."

Marguerite balks. "For us both?"

Ignoring her, Mother leads us through the dark-paneled sitting room and into her robing chamber, which is larger than our entire house on the rue Beauregard. "For the procession," she announces, gesturing to the identical gowns draped across the cedar trunks.

"They are. . . ." *Scandalous. An abomination. The most hideous things I've ever seen.* The black and crimson silk is so delicate, it's all but translucent, and the square neckline is so low, my hands fly to cover my breasts.

"We are to match?" Marguerite's voice is flat. I lift my gown by the sleeve and hold it at an arm's length—like it's more poisonous than the vats of distilled mandragora in my lab.

"It's so chilly outside." I lace my voice with concern. "And raining constantly. Don't you think a bit more fabric . . ."

Mother's carefully penciled eyebrows lower. "Are you belittling my selection?"

Catching the venom in Mother's voice, Marguerite takes up her gown and holds it to her shoulders with an excited squeal. "*I* think the gowns are exquisite. Mira knows nothing." She elbows past me and kisses Mother's cheek.

"Don't stand there like a dolt, Mirabelle," Mother says with a clap. "Dress. Or we shall be late for our own procession."

Reluctantly, I bring the gown to my chest, and my fingers brush against something hard beneath my bodice.

Father's grimoire.

Merde. I've grown so accustomed to its presence, it's like a second heart beating outside of my chest. I didn't even think to remove it. The herbs to counteract Lesage's emerald fire are in a pouch beneath my stays, but if the maids succeed in removing my dress, there will be no hiding the grimoire.

All the air leaks out of me, and the monstrous gown slips from my fingers and plummets to the parquet floor.

Mother scowls and points at the rumpled heap. "The work of the finest seamstress in Paris and you toss it to the floor like rags."

"F-forgive me," I stammer as I pick it up. "It's exceedingly beautiful, but I fear I won't be able to maneuver through the crowd to dispense curatives wearing such a *delicate* design. The dress I'm wearing is far better suited—"

Mother sighs loudly. "The dress won't be an obstacle because you won't be distributing curatives."

"*What?*" I feel like I've been hit in the head with a cudgel. My breath comes in bursts. "But you requested medicines. I've been preparing all week."

"Gris and other servants will distribute the syrups and salves, and you will ride beside me—in *that* dress. You're a member of my inner circle now, Mirabelle. It's time you took on duties beyond the laboratory."

My chest wrenches painfully. I've been waiting a lifetime for her to say those words. Gris's voice bellows in my head: *Be grateful. Cooperate.* And I would if I could. As desperate as I am to tend to the people personally, I could get over the disappointment. But I cannot remove my dress.

She cannot see my treachery.

"Don't the people need to see us distributing the medication?" I say quickly.

Mother waves a hand. "The people know the medication is from us. What they need to see is a united leadership after the perils they've been through. Now dress." She orders the maids who aren't busy lacing Marguerite to assist me.

I scramble back, dodging their eager hands.

"Keep still," Mother insists, but I kick and flail and jerk. Marguerite giggles as two maids dive to unlace my boots, while another three take me by the shoulders and tug the laces of my brown work petticoats.

Father's little red book slips down the front of my stays in the jumble, and I let out a strangled cry. "I need no help." I swing the hideous gown like a shield. "I am perfectly capable of dressing myself." But there's a rattling quality to my voice now, and Marguerite's ears prick.

"Enough of this nonsense. *I* shall dress her." She elbows past the maids and tugs on the front of my dress.

No. I lock my arms across my chest and dart back, begging with my eyes. *Please, Margot. We are friends, allies.*

But we're not. Not really. Her desire for Mother's favor will always outweigh her loyalty to me.

Her lips curl as she reaches for my bodice, and she pitches her voice low. "Surely you aren't too modest to accept the help of your loving sister?" With a heave, she yanks the brown wool from my shoulders and the grimoire tumbles to the floor.

Marguerite's black eyes—eyes that are a mirror of my own, a mirror of Mother's—quadruple in size. "*Mother!* Come see," she shrieks.

My feet tingle, itching to flee, but I keep them firmly planted. It would be pointless to run with masked sentries guarding every window and passage, so I cross my arms over my chest and stand as still as the statues in the Tuileries, naked and exposed for all to see in my chemise and stockings.

"Leave us," Mother whispers, and like a sudden draft of wind, her maids blow out of the chamber. I look longingly after them, wishing I could escape so easily.

The folds of her cape shush across the polished floor, and the bones of her corset creak with each step. Her expression is stony, but her hands tremble ever so slightly as she smooths the invisible wrinkles in her gown. Her eyes glimmer with flashes of raw pain—even after all these years.

"Antoine," Mother whispers—love, anguish, and animosity distilled into one word. She adored Father. I think a part of her always will, no matter how desperately she tries to hate him now. They met when Grandmére fell sick and Mother ventured into Father's experimental apothecary shop, looking for a cure. He was young and smart and charismatic, a genius with spagyrics, even then, and Mother loved him from the first day he winked at her from behind the counter. Back then, he wasn't too consumed with his work to notice a pretty face.

He doted on Mother in the beginning, making her delicious caramel syrups and false love potions he threatened to slip into her supper. They tended the herb garden together and even ran a small jewelry shop side by side when they were first married—the trade given to Father by his father, which he enhanced by transmuting his own metals. But over time, such things fell by the wayside as Father's experiments devoured him.

Mother stares at the book, her face flushing until it's redder than the rouge staining her cheeks, redder than the grimoire. She bends over, catches the book between her fingers, and waves it in my face. I press my back against the papered wall, and droplets of icy sweat race down my neck. "You swore you burned his deplorable grimoires and notebooks."

"I kept only one to remember him by," I squeak. "A memento."

"Lies!" Marguerite sidles around Mother, her face so close, I want to scream. "Mira told me the other day that she *talks* to him."

This betrayal hurts more than I expected. For a moment, I can do nothing but gape. "I told you that in confidence!" I shout at her. Then I turn back to Mother. "It's not what you think. . . ."

"Silence!" Mother frowns down at the grimoire, and after what feels like an eternity, storms across the room to destroy the book in the hearth. The flame is long dead, however, so she settles for hurling the book into her strongbox instead. Then she returns to her dressing table and trails her fingers across the silver combs and pots of rouge. My sweaty palms stick to my chemise.

When at last she speaks, Mother's voice floats across the

room as if on the wind. "I gave you so much freedom, so many responsibilities. Now I see it was a mistake. If you insist on acting like *him*, I cannot trust you. And if I cannot trust you, you cannot manage the laboratory. From now on, Gris will oversee production, and you will be assigned different duties. Away from such temptations."

"No!" I choke. It feels as if all the air has been siphoned from the room. My pleas pour out in an endless stream. "I'm sorry. It will never happen again, I swear it. Gris won't be able to keep up with your orders. What about Lesage's draught?"

"Gris is more than competent—he'll figure out the formula for the blood draught. And I'll hire him help, if need be. There are dozens of alchemists in this city who would jump at the chance to work for the Society."

"None as skilled as I."

"Perhaps not, but I won't risk losing you to your father's obsession. You may hate me now, but eventually you will thank me for protecting you."

A tiny sob bursts past my lips. I stumble forward and throw myself at Mother's feet. She cannot do this. She cannot bar me from the laboratory. I don't know who I am without my work. "Please, Mother."

She looks past me, pretending I haven't spoken. With lethal grace, she collects a whalebone hairpin off her vanity and rolls it between her fingers like a knife. "Groveling will do no good. My decision is made."

She slams her fist to the table with such force, the hairpin stabs deep into the mahogany.

I pull on the hideous dress without another word.

The streets of Paris are a riot of color and noise and fanfare. The former king's blue and white fleur-de-lis standards have been rent from their poles and replaced with banners emblazoned with the Shadow Society's double-headed eagle. Our gleaming black warhorses are fitted with armor and emerald plumes, and the multitude of carriages are draped with raucous red and purple silks. Revelers herald us with trumpets and lutes while jesters and acrobats dance and sing in the streets. Hordes of commoners clad in velvet masks—the newest trend in fashion—whistle and clap as we pass. It's so vibrant, so bright and dizzying.

The maids somehow twisted my mouse-brown curls into an intricate waterfall that tumbles down the front of one shoulder. Marguerite matches me exactly, but while she basks in the men hooting and hollering at our scandalous necklines, I sink lower and lower, desperate to become one with my saddle. My breasts nearly spill out every time my horse steps, and when I try to cover my chest with my hands, Mother shoots me a death glare.

Lesage leads the procession, using his harmless magic to conjure flocks of exotic birds—indigo peacocks and marigold swans, pearl-gray doves that wing and flit above the crowd before dissipating like candle smoke. Mother smiles and waves from the back of Louis XIV's white stallion. She throws alms to the people and directs Gris and the other servants as they distribute curatives. A select few peasants are even ushered forward by her guards to receive her "blessing."

"Hail La Voisin!" the multitude chants. "Hail Lesage!"

Gris catches my eye as he hurries back and forth, loaded like a cart mule with bags and trays and bottles. *See? All has been set to right.*

I manage a smile for him, but it doesn't reach my eyes. Of course I'm glad to see the work of the Shadow Society resuming, to see the people so overjoyed, but I feel apart from it. Never again will I experience the euphoria of watching two substances combine. Never will I feel the thrill of discovering a new remedy, the elation of knowing it will help someone who was otherwise without hope. How many people might I have saved if I hadn't been so foolish? So careless? The ache in my chest feels like forceps squeezing my heart.

You will be a great alchemist one day.

"Quit looking so miserable," Mother says through her teeth. "Smile. And wave."

But I can do neither. I squirm in my saddle and wring my fingers through my horse's mane. I look over at my sister, searching for what, I don't know. But she's too preoccupied with batting her eyelashes and blowing kisses to notice my plea. Abbé Guibourg ripples like a massive slug on my other side, and La Trianon trots behind me. I'll find no comfort in any of them.

I let out a long breath. Gaiety reigns all around, but I feel listless and limp. Where do I fit in this world if not in the laboratory? Flaxen cords of panic wind around my throat like bonnet strings until I am coughing and choking. I teeter precariously over my horse's neck.

Gris jogs up beside me and places a steadying hand on my leg. "You look like you're going to fall. Are you unwell?"

I am far past unwell. I need to get down. Back to the laboratory. Away from all of *this*. I kick out of my stirrups, but Gris catches me around the waist and holds me in place.

"I know it's crowded and chaotic, but I'm right here with you, Mira. Try to enjoy—"

Cannon fire rattles the sky like thunder.

Flames explode from the building to our right, and a blistering orange wave rolls toward us. Pain washes over my skin like scalding water and I know I'm screaming, but I only hear silence—as thick as clotted cream in my ears. Followed by ringing. A maddening, high-pitched keening.

My horse rears, and this time Gris isn't there to catch me. I fall through the smoky air and dash my head against the cobbles. Blood wets my hair and dribbles down my neck. Hooves strike like lightning all around me. Balls of fire and shards of glass continue to erupt from where a church stood mere seconds before.

I grip my forehead to steady my vision, trying to comprehend what's happened. It must be one of Lesage's illusions. But then I spot him through the haze, cursing and clinging to his rearing horse.

If he isn't behind this...

We've been attacked.

The Sun King's bloated face fills my vision, followed by Madame de Montespan crashing into her pudding and Vendôme and his men, twisted and broken and retching in the grass.

I stare into the chaos, heart thudding, head throbbing. Thousands of Parisians flee in every direction. A mob the likes of which I've never seen. It would be so easy to get lost.

To disappear ...

Before I realize what I'm doing, I steal a purple cloak off a motionless guard, throw the hood over my bleeding head, and vanish into the pandemonium.

6

JOSSE

Desgrez and I burst from the fiery skeleton of Notre-Dame de Bonne Nouvelle a breath before the roof collapses. White-hot ash and burning rocks pelt the rue de Richelieu like flaming arrows, but we charge through the cinders like knights of old, marching to battle. I toss my head back and whoop at the mayhem.

Such a pity Louis can't see how brilliantly my *preposterous* plan is coming along. Smoke chokes the street and people dart everywhere, screaming and shoving and fleeing for their lives. It looks like the world's largest tavern brawl, which should provide ample time to race back to Madame Bissette's, collect my siblings, and drive like the Devil through the blockade around the city.

As we barrel through the haze, I scan the masked Shadow Society members strewn across the cobbles, praying I'll see La Voisin or her sorcerer.

"Save yourself the trouble." Desgrez nods up ahead, where La Voisin and the leaders of the Shadow Society slowly appear through the smoke. They're trapped in the center of the teeming street, their horses rearing and churning like a dark, deadly whirlpool. We lit the cannon just seconds too early. My stomach drops and disappointment drags at my legs. Killing them would have made everything so much simpler.

"Don't look so defeated. They could still be trampled to death," Desgrez says as a rider pitches through the burning sky.

"We can only hope."

The crowd grows thicker and thicker as we shove down the street. I slam into the back of a man's sweaty doublet. When I try to step around him, I meet more shoulders and backs and fists. We're like sheep trapped in a too small pen. It takes an eternity to elbow our way down half a block. We'll never even make it to my sisters, let alone through the blockade, at this rate.

I lower my head and heave forward like a battering ram, trying not to see the children with tears streaming down their cheeks. Trying to block out the deafening cries of the injured. But they are everywhere, pressing all around me, hot and sticky and screaming. Fingers of guilt strum my heartstrings because I didn't even consider them when I made this plan—didn't think how the explosion would affect the innocent. And now that I'm in the thick of it, it feels eerily reminiscent of the attack on Versailles. Except I am the one leading the destruction.

No. This is nothing like that. This had to be done.

Would the people agree? Is it okay to sacrifice the whole to save a few?

Yes. The girls are worth everything.

Behind us, La Voisin's voice rises over the tumult, calling her

Society to arms. Her scream is like nothing I've heard before—like banshees and ghouls, the wail of the damned. Chills race down my arms, leaving me suddenly cold.

Desgrez glances back and shouts a stream of colorful curses. I ball my fists and peek over my shoulder, expecting to see Shadow Society members charging down the street, but instead of people, we are beset by beasts.

A brigade of Lesage's smoke creatures take to the air, and a scream tears up my throat like a blade. These are not birds and butterflies like before, but winged dragons and three-headed serpents that are so much more threatening, so much more *tangible*. They roar and gnash their teeth as they slither through the clouds. From half a block away, I can see each glittering scale of crimson, green, and gold. I can feel the heat from their breath, and there's no mistaking the tang of rotten eggs in the air—the distinctive scent of sulfur and brimstone.

After the beasts, Lesage sends a bolt of cerulean lightning streaking across the sky. It slams into a row of half-timbered townhouses, and emerald flames engulf the thatched roofs in seconds.

"What the hell is that?" Desgrez demands.

"*That* is what's killing Anne and Françoise," I say, lurching forward as needles race down my spine. I cringe at every scream, at every blast of stone behind me. *I'm sorry*, I want to shout to the people trapped in the streets. But it will never be enough. The Shadow Society doesn't know who lit the cannons. I thought that would be a good thing—as they can't hunt us specifically. But I never dreamed they'd hunt *everybody*. Striking out at random.

Why didn't it occur to me that they would retaliate?

Reckless. Careless. Your fault. Father's voice chases me down the block, and I have no doubt these gory scenes will be added to my nightmares.

We reach an intersection and Desgrez and I cut through an alleyway, making good time once we're away from the main thrust of the crowd. "Faster!" he keeps yelling, even though I've never run so fast in my life. We fly down five more blocks and reach the pâtisserie at last.

But there's no cart.

No sign of Louis or the girls anywhere. Just bodies and mayhem and the impossible distance between us and the road out of Paris.

Every molecule of air drains from my lungs. I'm going to murder Louis. I should have known he'd pull something like this. Should have planned for it. We shouldn't have included him at all. *Stupid, stupid, stupid.* Tears sting my eyes, and vomit burns my throat. It was all for nothing. All of this carnage. I turn a frantic circle and trip over my feet. Desgrez steadies me, spitting even blacker profanities. Precious seconds tick away. The Shadow Society's boots sing across the cobbles. The heat from the smoke beasts grows closer and warmer. A strike of lightning levels a laundress shop across the street.

"Still think I should show *His Royal Highness* a little respect?" I growl. Then I take off in the opposite direction, as fast as my exhausted body will allow. If escape is out of the question, we must keep the Shadow Society away from the hidden sewer entrance. Far away.

We run. Down one alleyway after another. My legs turn to feathers and everything is on fire: my muscles, my watering eyes, my burning lungs. The broken cobbles jut from the ground like pikes, biting my ankles and threatening to bring me to my knees. A few steps more and we'll reach the Pont Neuf. We can cross the stone bridge and take cover in the overcrowded Île de la Cité, with its countless houses and chapels and narrow, twisting streets.

We are steps away from safety, and I'm so grateful I'm practically weeping, when a shadow moves beneath the bridge. An enormous shadow. Desgrez and I barely have time to stop before a dragon made of smoke rears up from the Seine and slithers across our path. It's taller than a two-story building, with orange and yellow scales that flare like sparks. Its colossal head and long, pointed snout remind me of a crocodile, and the heat of its breath is so intense, my skin bubbles like candle wax.

"Move!" Desgrez shouts as fire pours from the serpent's teeth. He grabs my tunic and yanks me back, saving me from the worst of the blaze. I gape at the cobbles—charred black where I stood just seconds before.

While I stand there reeling, Desgrez springs to action like the captain he pretends to be. "You go right and sneak across the bridge. I'll draw it left." He sprints away before I can stop him and slashes his blade across the dragon's hind leg.

Inky blood oozes from the cut; the creature growls and turns fully on Desgrez. He waves for me to run, but my feet are cemented to the cobbles. Only a rutting coward would leave him to face this monster alone. I can't bear to lose him, too. I crouch to extract the dagger from my boot, and in that split second a flash of green crackles overhead, so close it would have slammed into my chest had I been standing.

I whip around and shout at Desgrez, "Get down!"

The smoke beast rolls sideways and contorts its long neck, but Desgrez is not so quick. The green fire hits him square in the gut. His eyes go wide and his breath wheezes out in a grunt. Ropes of electricity snake up and down his torso, and he strikes the ground like a felled tree.

Blood rushes in my ears. My feet tingle as I stumble to where he lies. His skin is cold and chalky, and his face is frozen in a scream. "Don't be dead, you bastard," I whisper, holding my fingers to his neck. I heave a sigh when I feel a faint, fluttering heartbeat.

But my relief is short-lived. Orange sparks flash in my periphery.

The smoke beast rears above us.

A vicious calm settles over me, same as when I gutted the intruder in the dauphin's apartments. I don't think; I just move, prying Desgrez's rapier from his fist and swinging to face the creature. If I must die, let it be defending my friend—in the name of my sisters.

The dragon rears up on its hind legs. I bellow and charge forward. Seconds before we collide, another bolt of lightning whizzes past my head. I flatten against the ground. Once again, the creature dodges too, twisting to avoid the flame.

The beast quickly regains its feet and turns on me with a hiss. Instead of hefting Desgrez's sword, I glance up at the bolts of aqua lightning smashing into the ground like hailstones. Then down at the rubble from the obliterated shops. The smoke beast lowers its head and opens its jaw. I roll and grab a ragged slab of tin roofing. But instead of using it as a shield, I dive to the left—directly into the path of a green lightning bolt.

The force slams me into the muddy ground and pain jolts up my spine, but I manage to keep the scrap raised. The lightning rebounds off the metal and smashes into the smoke beast's belly. It's yellow, feline eyes widen, and a second later it explodes into millions of tiny ashes that glow as they flutter through the sky.

I sit there, stunned and gasping. I killed the creature. But the pit in my stomach still feels deep enough to drown in. If the lightning is powerful enough to kill Lesage's monsters, Desgrez and my sisters are doomed.

Don't think like that. They're still alive, which means there's still a chance.

I stagger back to where Desgrez lies, grip him beneath the arms, and drag him onto the Pont Neuf. The man is heavier than an ox. I barely manage a hand's breadth with each tug. Ribbons of aqua lightning continue to fly back and forth beneath the clouds, striking all around us. Chunks of rock and mortar whir through the air like throwing knives.

There's no way I can carry him. Not fast enough to outrun Lesage's magic.

"I'm sorry," I choke out, thinking of all the fights he picked on my behalf, of all the nights he went without sleep, teaching me how to toss a dagger and throw a punch. He's the brother I never had, and even though he's barely three years older, he's far braver and more capable than I'll ever be.

If our roles were reversed, Desgrez would find a way—get us to safety. The least I can do is continue trying until the smoke beasts devour us or Lesage buries us in a coffin of verdant flame. I steady my grip and brace my arms to tug again, but something rustles behind us.

I spin and draw the rapier, ready to slaughter whoever—or whatever—stands between us and freedom, but my hand falters.

It's a girl.

A lone girl, wearing an oversized purple Shadow Society cloak. If she's supposed to be guarding the bridge, she's doing a piss-poor job of it—leaning against the wall and wheezing. Her face is haunted, and she looks from Desgrez's stiff, glowing body to the colorful streaks of light exploding overhead.

"Move!" I yell. Another smoke creature with a blunt snout and massive curling horns has drifted dangerously close; the gray water of the Seine boils and pops beneath the bridge. Scalding steam ripples through the chilly spring air.

"You'll never outrun them," she whispers.

"I'm sure as hell going to try." Green ash flutters down, kissing our cloaks with a hiss. The beast's growls shake the struts of the bridge.

She bites down on her lower lip and looks back across the bubbling river—at the ghostly Louvre, at the fire and lightning and chaos. "He'll die without treatment."

"Where do you think I'm going?"

"Not the kind of treatment you can give. Not against Lesage's magic."

Lightning strikes less than a length behind me. Fragments of stone explode into the air, strafing my arms and hat. Her eyes widen and she retreats. *At last.* But when I move to go around her, she grits her teeth, tucks her frizzy hair behind her ear, and rushes toward me.

I fumble with my weapon, but she brushes past me and lifts Desgrez's legs. The rapier falls to my side. "What are you *doing?*"

"Getting us across the bridge and into the nearest alleyway."

"What?"

"*Move* unless you want to be scorched!"

It feels like a trap, but her voice is so fierce and her gaze so intense, I sheath the blade and lift Desgrez by the armpits. Then we scramble across the bridge into the muddy, cramped passages of the Île de la Cité.

We slink along, unnoticed—with so many injured, it isn't even strange to be carrying a body—until we reach a tiny chapel, half hidden by larger edifices. The girl nods to enter. I've never been the religious type, and Desgrez would sooner die than have a member of the Shadow Society pray for his soul, but we haven't a better option. The larger churches are sure to be occupied by priests.

I squint at the sudden dark as we fumble into the nave and trip on a wayward hymnal. The girl gestures to one of the benches, and we carefully lay Desgrez out. His body glows unnaturally beneath the gothic archways and unlit niches.

The girl reaches into her bodice and extracts a small leather pouch from between her breasts.

"What are you doing?" I ask.

"We need to work quickly," she says, readjusting her bodice, though it doesn't help. She's a breath away from spilling out. She rips the sack open with her teeth and dumps the contents onto the bench. "I need fire, a bowl, and your blade."

A hysterical laugh bubbles up my throat. "You can't expect me to hand over my weapon."

"I am trying to *help* you."

"Why?"

Her small frame flinches and her voice is tight when she speaks. "That out there, it isn't what we do. Or, it wasn't."

All the comebacks I'd been planning stick to my throat. "I don't understand...."

"You don't need to understand." She motions to Desgrez, whose skin has turned a sickly shade of green. Twice as green as the blotches marring Anne and Françoise. "Do you wish to save him or not? He hasn't much time."

I look at Desgrez's wan face, his shriveled, sunken chest.

"What *is* it?"

"A form of alchemical magic called désintégrer. The fire bolts liquefy victims from the inside out. So every second you waste doubting me, your friend's liver decays, his heart withers, and his bones dissolve into ash."

Vomit rises up my throat. *His bones will dissolve into ash?* Swallowing hard, I dash behind the wall of icons surrounding the sanctuary. With a complete lack of reverence, I rummage around until I find a collection plate and a sermon to use as kindling. Then I nick the sanctuary lamp and a piece of flint, hoping God won't strike me down, and rush back to Desgrez.

I arrange the papers in a cluster and light them with the torch. The girl situates the collection plate over the heat and squeezes a foul-smelling paste and a pinch of herbs into the bowl. As she stirs the mixture with one hand, she returns the pouch to her dress with the other.

When she clears her throat, I realize I'm staring directly at her breasts. *Again.* Heat singes my cheeks, and I tug at my collar as I kneel beside Desgrez. The girl tears open his shirt and slathers the ointment across his concave chest. The paste is light gray and smells worse than the sewers, which I didn't think was possible. I cover my nose. "What *is* that?"

"Periwinkle and ambergris," she says, watching Desgrez's chest rise and fall. She stands, blows the curls away from her face, and kneads the mixture more forcefully into his skin.

"And you conveniently happened to have it on hand?"

"Yes. It's my fault Lesage can conjure désintégrer, so I developed an antidote."

"Antidote," I jeer. "What do you know of healing?"

The girl's hands still and she glares at me with so much loathing, I swallow my laughter and lean away. "You'd best hope I know a lot, monsieur, if you want your friend to live. Now your blade, if you'd be so kind." She holds out her hand.

I unsheathe the rapier but cannot bring myself to surrender it.

"If I wanted to kill you, you'd be dead. And if you want him to live, you'll give me what I need." She seizes the sword with a grunt, then after adding a bit more ointment to Desgrez's chest, she places the tip of the blade directly beneath his breastbone. I grip the bench and try not to say anything, but a choked squeal rushes from my lips when she applies pressure. Blood seeps around the blade, running deeper and darker.

"Are you sure this will work?" I ask when the pool below his chest is nearly black.

The girl nods, but her expression wilts with every passing second. "It—it should. I checked my calculations dozens of times. . . ."

"You mean you've never done this before?" I'm about to shove her aside when Desgrez's face breaks from its frozen mold. He vomits over the side of the bench, and the girl releases the rapier. It clatters to the stone floor, the sound echoing around the chapel.

Desgrez twitches and howls with pain, but the green tinge is already fading and the pits and hollows in his chest slowly rise and reform. The blood from the knife wound clots as it mixes with the foul-smelling paste.

It worked. The girl's antidote worked!

Relief douses me like a bucket of ice-cold water, and I laugh as I reach for Desgrez's hand. He squeezes back, and hope takes flight in my chest, soaring up to the carved stone angels keeping watch from the rafters. If she healed Desgrez, perhaps she can heal Anne and Françoise. I turn, ready to toss the girl over my shoulder and make for the sewer, when Desgrez moans and coughs up another mouthful of dreck.

First things first.

He attempts to sit, but his arms quiver and his eyes roll back. "I feel like death."

"You look like it too." I laugh, gently easing his shoulders back down to the bench.

Desgrez waves away the slight and mumbles that he's still better-looking than I am. We sit for several minutes in silence while he regains his breath. Slowly, his glassy eyes rove from the niches in the north aisle, across the garish yellow and crimson nave, and slam to a halt on the girl. He squints at her for a long moment, then his eyes bulge. He grips me by the collar and pulls me close. "What is *she* doing here?"

"You need to stay calm. She only just healed you."

"*Healed* me?" Desgrez's hands fly to inspect his face and torso. He winces at the knife wound. "It doesn't *feel* like she healed me."

"Well, she did. When you were hit on the Pont Neuf, she

helped me carry you here and brought you back to life."

"You expect me to believe that?" He glares at the girl, and the girl glares back. It's like watching the cocks circle each other before a fight, and I position myself strategically between them.

"It's the truth. I saw it myself."

"Fine." He waves a hand at her. "She saved me. But I cannot comprehend what she's still doing here."

I stare at my friend, my frustration rising like the smoke from the collection plate. *She can help the girls,* I want to say. But I know better than to mention them in front of a member of the Shadow Society—no matter how helpful she's been. "I couldn't turn her out," I say stiffly. "The streets are still a riot."

"You could have and you should have. Do you know who she is?"

"I know she's one of *them,* but—"

"She isn't just one of them. That is La Voisin's daughter. I fought against her in the battle at the Louvre."

I wheel around and stare at the girl. In the lengthening shadows, she looks far more sinister than she did on the bridge, with those slashing brows and dark eyes. Black as tar. Black as Hell itself. Nausea grips my belly, and I have to steady myself on a bench.

"That was my sister," the girl says. "I didn't fight."

"Yes, I'm sure you're entirely innocent," Desgrez snaps. "I know the true nature of your black heart. Be gone! Run back to your mother."

The girl glowers at Desgrez. "Are you really so thankless?"

"Yes," he says without hesitation.

"Fine." She skulks to the door and throws it wide. A breeze rips through the chapel, scattering the singed papers, and a chorus of screams reverberates off the archways and frescos. La Voisin's daughter hesitates, sucking in a shaky breath and gathering the purple cloak around her. An unexpected twinge of sympathy shudders through me. A rush of gratitude.

"You don't have to go out there," I tell her, glaring at Desgrez. I jog to the door and close it with a decisive thud. "We can all sit civilly until the danger passes."

Desgrez groans and clutches his head. "If she so much as looks in my direction . . ."

"I should have let you die," the girl snips. She turns on her heel, marches to the front of the church, and sits down hard behind the pulpit, completely out of view.

Desgrez eyes the space. When she doesn't reemerge, he waves me over to his bench and yanks me down so we're face to face. "We have to kill her."

"But she can help the girls."

"We can't take her anywhere near the sewer. She's recognized us. That's the only reason she would heal me—to win our trust so she can lead the Shadow Society to your sisters and Louis."

I roll my eyes. "You're the son of a tutor and I'm a servant. No one would recognize us."

"Are you certain? Lesage certainly performed often enough to recognize *all* of the king's children. And who knows how many spies they had within the palace."

I try to tamp down my fear, but it bubbles and swells, coursing through me like frothy, crashing waves. I want to slap myself for being so daft, for not seeing their plot sooner. I'm always making the wrong choice: reading those illegal broadsides, failing to protect my sisters, putting thousands of people in danger today. And now this.

"So what do we do?" I ask.

Desgrez parts his lips, but the girl rises from behind the pulpit and I leap back. Which only makes us look more suspicious. She frowns and perches on a bench at the front of the nave, hugging her knees to her chest, helpless and shivering like a kitten in the gutter. She may look small and innocent, but Desgrez is undoubtedly right. She cannot be trusted. Her family is responsible for murdering half of the nobility. My father and the queen included.

But she's my sisters' best chance at survival.

Their only chance.

Desgrez shoots me a look and nods toward his rapier. I make the mistake of peering at the girl again—so peaceful, with her eyes closed and her lips parted—and my muscles seize.

With a vexed look, Desgrez staggers to his feet and retrieves his blade from the floor.

"What do you think you're doing?" I demand.

"Simply apologizing for my boorish behavior." He makes a show of sheathing the rapier, then hobbles closer to the girl. She bolts upright.

"My sincerest apologies, mademoiselle," Desgrez says with a bow. "Thank you for healing me." He offers his hand and the girl considers it, chewing her lip before cautiously placing her small hand in his. Desgrez kisses the back of her wrist, and at the same moment, drives his other fist into the side of her face. Leveling the girl who just saved him. She collapses like a rag doll, slides off the bench, and sinks into her black and red petticoats.

I can't stop the cry that surges up my throat.

Desgrez rubs his knuckles and gives me a hard look. *"What?"*

Shame and indignation burn my cheeks. "Are you going to kill her?" I ask, trying and failing to keep my voice from cracking.

A sly grin crawls across Desgrez's face, and he shakes his head. "Not yet. You're right. I think we can use her . . . in more ways than one."

7

MIRABELLE

Merde.

I writhe against the ropes but the knots hold fast, and the more I struggle, the soggier I become. Shivering and choking, I turn on my side to avoid the freezing puddles that reek of urine. Mother would be appalled if she could see me—tied up like a hog, rolling around in the muck. The longer I squirm and cry, the more I'm certain she's here. Watching. I catch glimpses of her dark eyes in the undulating blackness. I hear snatches of her voice in the biting drafts of wind.

Serves you right for running away. For brewing forbidden tinctures and healing our enemies.

Perhaps she's right. I saved a boy's life, protected him and his friend from Lesage's magic, and this is how they repay me: by binding me and leaving me to rot in a moldering dungeon. A chamber pot!

"Help me! *Please!*" I scream through the gag in my teeth. The muffled cries reverberate off the cramped walls, growing softer and softer until they fall away completely. No one comes, and the hours pass. The darkness is so complete, I am unable to make out my own feet, let alone an exit, nor can I determine how long I've been trapped here. It was sundown when that ungrateful lout put his fist to my face. *After* I healed him.

I should have let him perish on the Pont Neuf. His friend, too.

A ribbon of guilt slithers beneath my ribs. That's what Mother would have done. But we are supposed to be protecting and caring for the people. We are supposed to be better than Louis XIV. And I promised myself I would test my antidote if Lesage unleashed his magic. Which he did. And it worked!

I bark out a laugh, my breath puffing like a cloud above my face. A flood of pride, as warm and sweet as the lemon verbena tea Father used to drink, seeps through my core, combating the cold a fraction. It is the sole spark of light, of hope, in this dismal situation—in this dank, dripping cavern or dungeon or wherever it is they're keeping me.

I try to cling to that monumental victory, but with every passing hour the ground grows colder and my skin grows wetter. The puddles soak through the flimsy silk of my gown, chilling me to the bone. The men relieved me of my cape, and this deplorable dress offers no protection. The rocky floor digs into my hips and bites at my shoulders, and it isn't long before shivers overtake me. My teeth clink together, making my head pound and my thoughts jumble. Will I freeze to death before Mother finds me? Do I *want* her to find me?

A tear streaks down my cheek and drips off my chin. And then another. They come faster and faster until great, gasping sobs hammer my sides like fists. I tell myself I'll only carry on for a moment. Then I'll pull myself together and devise a plan. But waves of fear and regret continue to pummel me, so fast I can scarce catch my breath between swells.

I cry for Gris, whom I left in the chaos of the procession to be trampled beneath the horses' hooves.

I cry for the innocent people who were caught in the crossfire of Lesage's lightning or scorched by his smoke beasts.

And I cry for myself because I am a fool, deceived on too many counts to fathom.

It feels as if I've been lying here for days, months even, when something rustles far off in the blackness. I cock my head and strain to hear. Slowly, like an eerie, disjointed melody, the sounds form into footsteps and voices. Pounding and arguing. Drawing nearer.

My captors have returned to kill me. Or torture me.

I flail against my bonds with renewed determination, twisting and straining and stretching. But nothing has changed in the hours or days since they left me. The ropes dig bloody rivets into my wrists and ankles. My shoulders howl in agony—bent at awkward angles like an injured bird. Crying with pain, I press myself against the dripping wall and pray for deliverance, though my pleas are surely in vain. I doubt God looks kindly on the killer of a king.

A flare of light pricks the darkness. It's so bright against the suffocating gloom, it scorches my pupils. I yelp and shut my eyes, but the imprint of the flame continues to dance behind my eyelids. Footsteps splash through puddles of filth, and the voices slowly become discernible.

"It's been *one* day. You cannot feed her yet," someone complains.

"I most certainly can," another voice answers. This one, I recognize. Bit by bit, the boys from the bridge emerge through the shadows, ducking down a long, low-ceilinged passageway. The single torch they carry between them highlights their faces from below, making them look devilish and menacing. My heart beats so erratically it pulses in my throat. I dig my heels into the floor and thrust deeper into the corner.

"She isn't going to die after one day without food," the boy I healed says. "If anything, it will make her more cooperative."

"She saved your life. She eats," the other one says firmly.

They're close now, maybe twenty paces from where I lie. I'm in some sort of cavern, it seems, because they're no longer stooped but standing at their full height, looking like giants from where I squirm on the floor. I'm determined not to look like a sniveling worm, so I raise my chin.

The boy I saved shakes his head and clenches his fist on the hilt of his sword. "Were it up to me, she wouldn't eat until she's healed the girls and we've heard from her mother."

So that's it. They plan to ransom me back to the Shadow Society?

"Well, it isn't up to you, is it?" the other boy says through gritted teeth.

The first boy throws his hands into the air and storms back

down the tunnel. The other glares after him for a moment before yanking his tricorne hat lower and striding toward me. He's even more haggard and filthy than the last time I saw him; not even the beggars in the streets look so ravaged. His brown hair is a tangle of knots, his doublet is torn, and a thick layer of grime covers his breeches. His cheeks are gaunt, and his chin is scruffy with stubble. If I didn't know better, I would say he was a prisoner himself.

My eyes break away from him and scan the cavern, taking in the few details I can distinguish in the torchlight—the dripping walls, the rusted grate in the far corner, the tunnels branching off in numerous directions. I should have gathered where I was from the dampness and smell alone. This isn't a dungeon or a cave—it's the sewer. Not even vagabonds would inhabit such a place. Which means my captors are more desperate still.

The boy lumbers closer, and I scrutinize him with greater care, looking for a crest on his doublet or some feature that might identify him. He's taller than average with a strong chin, green eyes, and a thin scar through the corner of his lip. And his friend mentioned healing "the girls." What girls?

"What are you looking at?" The boy glowers down at me.

I avert my eyes but refuse to cower, channeling Mother's cold, imperious demeanor. She would never grovel to these ruffians. Then again, she would never be in this situation because she would have left them to die on the bridge.

The boy squats down beside me, and I squeal. My head knocks

against the cavern wall and bursts of light explode like stars in the darkness. He waits for me to steady my balance before speaking. "I thought you might be hungry." He reaches into his coat and procures a butt of bread.

I stare at the offering and choke on a fresh wave of tears. My stomach is so knotted with hunger it feels as if a sword is sawing through my middle, but I cannot accept a morsel of food. It's undoubtedly poisoned. They probably think themselves clever—poisoning the girl who poisoned the king—but I won't eat.

"Don't you want food?" he says more forcefully.

I shake my head and press myself against the moldy wall. Naturally, my stomach chooses that moment to gurgle, making noises more befitting a cow than a girl.

The boy's sigh sounds as weak and exhausted as I feel. He scoots closer, and the heat of his body sends shivers through my frostbitten skin. When his fingers slide through my hair and untie my gag, I quiver at the wrongness of his touch. It paralyzes me from head to toe, as if I've ingested monkshood. Long, painful seconds tick away, and when at last I regain control, I peer through my wet, clinging eyelashes and find the butt of bread hovering before my lips. It's old and stale, the crust flaking off in brittle pieces, but it smells like garlic and rosemary, and my empty stomach roars with longing.

I shouldn't eat it. I *will not* eat it.

The boy tears off a corner and holds it out, and, curse my lacking discipline, I bite it from his fingers as if I am a mangy, starving mongrel. He doesn't say a word as he breaks off bite-sized chunks and holds them to my lips, nor does he look at me. Whenever I lift my gaze, he is examining the floor, the puddles, the walls. Anything else.

Too soon, the bread is gone, and the boy brushes the crumbs from his fingers and stands. My insides still throb with emptiness, and I'm tempted to slither forward like a snake and lick up every speck. But I tighten my fists and keep to the corner. He cannot see my desperation.

"You saved my friend's life. It's only right I return the favor," he says brusquely. "If you cooperate, I think we can continue to help each other. There are others in need of healing. Save them, and perhaps we can negotiate your freedom."

I had resolved not to speak, but his suggestion is so ridiculous, I can't help but laugh. "Negotiate my freedom? How dim-witted do you think me? I healed your dreadful friend and look where it got me. I'll heal no one else."

The boy grinds his teeth, and his voice rumbles low. "Consider your actions carefully. If you fail to oblige, we will have no reason to spare you."

I shrug as if my own life is of little consequence, but in truth, I'm so terrified, my hands twitch and tremble behind my back. I don't want to die, but it's not that simple because I don't want to return to my former life either—back to Mother and the Society to dole out poison and death. So where does that leave me?

I squeeze my eyes shut, wishing I had developed a draught

to render myself invisible. How blissful it would be to vanish, to slip away to some other city and live some other life. To shed the skin of Mirabelle Monvoisin and become someone new, someone who doesn't have to live in fear of her mother and compete with her sister and flounder every second, wondering if she's crossed a line. Or if she was standing on the correct side of the line to begin with. At what point does gray bleed into black?

I wave the boy off. He can offer nothing I want. I don't know the answer myself.

The boy's face hardens. "You *will* help us, La Petite Voisin."

That cursed moniker makes me flinch. I am not Mother's perfect miniature—not anymore—and that anyone thinks so, even this boy, makes me want to scream. He marches into the curling shadows down the tunnel, and my fury escalates with every step he puts between us. "I am *not* La Petite Voisin," I shout.

To my surprise, he halts, shoulders tense, as if he's forgotten to breathe. "What do you mean, you're not her? Of course you're her."

Maybe the food in my belly is making me bold. Or maybe I know, deep down, it doesn't matter what I say or do: I'm dead regardless. But I glare up at him and shake my head.

"Then who are you?"

"Mirabelle."

The boy grips his forehead. "I don't give a damn what your given name is. It makes no difference to me."

But it makes a difference to me, and I shout my real name, *Mirabelle,* again and again as he vanishes into the blackness.

The boy returns with bread the next day. And the day after that. At least, I assume another day has come and gone. In the dark, there's no telling how much time has passed, but I've noticed a pattern in the routine. Each time after I eat, the faint sounds of coughing and crying reach me from somewhere down the tunnel. It lasts for what feels like an eternity—through the day?—then it's quiet as death until the boy comes again.

He hasn't bothered retying my gag. I stopped screaming days ago because I lost my voice, and it's pointless besides. No one can hear me in this dank, dripping place. After a week of imprisonment, my hips and back are covered in raw, oozing sores and my fingers and toes are so cold, I'm afraid they'll need to be amputated.

But I haven't given up.

Each time the boy comes to feed me and beg me to heal *the girls*—I still haven't figured out *which* girls—I pepper him with questions of my own, hoping he'll slip and say something I can use against him.

"Who are you?" I ask through mouthfuls of bread. "I know you're someone of consequence."

Nothing.

"My mother will never let you get away with this. She will hunt you and kill you. Lesage will torture you with désintégrer."

Still nothing.

After several days, I blurt, "Are your *girls* dead yet? They must be getting close. Supposing they weren't hit directly by Lesage's fire, they haven't much time. The longest I've seen anyone survive is a month."

His eyes flick down the tunnel—the only reaction I've been able to provoke. Which means I'm on the right path. "They'll die a horrible, painful death. A death *I* could prevent, if only I could trust you. . . ."

But the boy doesn't spare another glance for the tunnel. He is made of stone: cold and hard as granite.

It near kills me, but I refuse his bread and water the following morning. He grunts and scowls and even tries to wedge the bread between my lips, but I eat nothing and drink only from the puddle beneath me. The water tastes of silt and iron and all manner of dreck. With every swallow, I feel it tainting my innards and poisoning my humours. Sickness gathers in my chest. Fever heats my cheeks. My limbs grow steadily heavier until they become boulders, too dense to budge. My head is an anchor, an anvil, a cannonball. I don't even have to remind myself to close my eyes and take only rasping breaths in the boy's presence.

After I have refused food for four days, the boy doesn't even attempt to feed me. He sighs and drags his feet to where I lie, nudging me with the toe of his boot. "Damn you," he mutters. "Do you *want* to die?"

When I don't respond, he limps back across the chamber,

but he doesn't make it more than three steps before he halts, his breath quickening. I hear it too—the heavy tread of boots and garbled stream of cursing. I slit my eyes just enough to see his hateful friend burst into the cavern. His black hair is tangled across his face and he's heaving for breath, waving a torch in one hand and an opened missive in the other. A bit of parchment stamped with a crimson double-headed eagle seal.

Mother's seal.

Hope surges through my frostbitten body. Little as I wish to return to the Louvre and the Shadow Society, anything would be better than perishing of jail fever at the hands of my captors. A hint of a smile bends my lips at the thought of dry clothes and a full belly.

But then the boy I healed begins shouting. "She refuses to negotiate!" He thrusts the letter in the other boy's face and points at me. "La Voisin doesn't want her."

What?

The smile melts off my lips. My heart ceases to beat. I'm tempted to launch up from the floor and demand to see the missive, but I bite my tongue at the last second and keep still, swallowing the bitter panic gathering in my throat.

"Impossible," the boy who feeds me cries.

He's lying, I assure myself. *Of course Mother wants you. She needs you in the laboratory.* Only that's no longer true. I've been stripped of my title, barred from my concoctions. She caught me with Father's grimoire.

"Give me that." The boy snatches the letter from his friend and paces as he reads, silently mouthing the words. I wish he'd read aloud, and at the same time, I'm grateful he doesn't.

Mother has always led the Society with an intensity bordering on ruthlessness, but she has always been my *mother* first: teaching Marguerite and me the arts of chiromancy and face reading, supporting our family with her fortune-telling when Father shirked the task, and even after he died, when her eyes brimmed with tears every time she looked at me, she protected me by enforcing stricter laboratory rules. I will never be her favorite, but she would never disown me like this. She wouldn't.

Unless it was for the "greater good."

The boy stops abruptly, crumples the terrible note in his fist, and hurls it across the chamber. When that doesn't satisfy him, he snatches the tricorne hat off his head and slams it to the ground with a curse. His eyes are wild and manic in the torchlight, laced with strands of molten lead. His voice rumbles low and hoarse. "What do we do now?"

The boy I saved stares at the battered, soggy hat. "What can we do? We have no leverage to negotiate our way out of Paris and no allies within."

"We have to do something," the other boy shouts. "Anne and Françoise—" he cuts himself off and glances at me. I hold my breath, hold every muscle still.

"Is she dead?" the boy I healed asks.

"Probably," the other says.

But I am not dead. And finally, *finally*, he has said something useful. Anne and Françoise are the names of Madame de Montespan's daughters. *The girls* he's been speaking of are the bastard daughters of the king. And without his hat, I can better see the prominent cheekbones and gooseberry green eyes of the boy who feeds me.

Devil's claws, I could slap myself for being so blind!

For weeks, the Sun King's face has haunted me, and the boy is his exact likeness. Not the dauphin, as he's fair as a fawn, but undoubtedly a bastard son. And if three siblings survived, I'd wager the dauphin and Madame Royale are nearby as well.

All of the king's children, here in the sewer.

And I helped them.

I bite the inside of my cheek, harder and harder until warm, rusty blood slides down my throat. I'd scream if I could. Even if I wanted to return to the Louvre, it's impossible now. Mother knows I've been with the royals. The only way she will welcome me back is if I lead her to this hideout. Or if I kill them myself and return to the Louvre bearing their heads on a platter. It would be my ticket, my sanctuary. With that one act, I would secure her throne, become her favorite daughter and a hero to the Shadow Society.

"We're out of options. Out of time," the boy I healed says. "I say we abandon this hellhole and seek refuge and allies in Savoy. Between the two of us, perhaps we can best the rebels at the blockades."

"You honestly think we can battle a dozen guards?"

The boy flashes a cocky grin. "I *am* captain of the watch now."

Of course he's a police captain. Only an officer would be so cruel and calculating. The screams of his comrades near drove me to tears during the siege of the Louvre, but now I happily imagine Lesage's smoke beasts tearing this deplorable boy into a million bits. Guilt slowly creeps in and I scold myself for entertaining such wicked thoughts.

The bastard princeling casts a sidelong glance down the tunnel. "Do you think the girls can make it that far? They can hardly sit upright."

"What other choice do we have?"

"She could help them, how she helped you. . . ."

The officer rubs the back of his neck. "She made it perfectly clear she won't help. I say we finish her off, dump her in the Seine, and leave at first light."

"First light?" the princeling sputters. "We haven't any supplies or transportation. And we can't simply dump her in the river. She helped us; I won't have her blood on my hands."

"Better hers than ours." The officer turns on his heel and knocks the princeling's shoulder as he saunters down the tunnel. "Like you said, she's half dead already. It will only be *half* our fault."

I close my eyes and press against the jagged floor until pain blossoms across my forehead. If I do nothing, the royals will kill me at first light. If I return to the Louvre without their bodies in tow, Mother will do the same.

This is hopeless. Impossible.

Nothing is impossible. Father's defiant voice pricks my memory. *Think!*

My heartbeat quickens. My thoughts whir. In an abstract way, my situation is similar to developing new compounds in the laboratory. All I have to do is run the calculations, find the proper ingredients, and make the circumstances combine to my benefit.

Alchemy in its purest form.

Here's what I know: The bastard can't afford to kill me. Not while his sisters need my antidote.

Letting out a breath, I drag myself up from the ground like a corpse rising from the dead. "Your plan will never work," I say. "Not without my help."

8

JOSSE

La Voisin's daughter arrests me with those fathomless black eyes. Crimson blood trails from a scrape on her forehead and drips off her chin. It makes the hairs on my arms stand on end. "Y-you're alive," I stutter like a fool. "I thought—"

"Now that the horrid police captain is gone, perhaps we can speak reasonably, princeling." She accentuates the title.

I cough and reel back. "How do you know—"

Her grin spreads wider. "You bound my hands, not my ears. Such a pity Anne and Françoise are unwell. Are the dauphin and Madame Royale ailing as well? These foul accommodations can't be helping matters."

Indignation burns my cheeks, and I drag a hand through my hair. What I really want to do is shout. Or punch something. Why did I slip and say their names? Another costly mistake. The more I fidget and mutter, the more the girl smiles. I draw a deep breath and blow it out through my nose. *Be calm.*

"I've learned better than to negotiate with your kind." I wave at the crumpled missive from her mother. "La Voisin doesn't want you, which means you are useless."

I turn on my heel, retrieve my hat from the floor, and slam it over my head. Rivulets of dirty water stream down my face and drench my coat. Fantastic. On top of everything, I'll have a soggy, sleepless night.

"I'm not useless." The girl's ragged voice chases me down the tunnel. "*They* need me. Your sisters."

"We need nothing from you," I retort.

We both know it's a lie.

"We'll find treatment elsewhere," I say.

"No. You won't."

"*Yes*. We will," I bark at the girl. *Mirabelle*. But I'm not about to call her by name. Not if Desgrez is going to kill her in the morning. It'd be like naming the hen you plan to slaughter for supper. "The girls are strong. They can make it to Savoy."

She shakes her head slowly. "An ordinary physician cannot help them, and they'll never make it that far. None of you will."

"How could you know that?"

"The blockades around Paris are warded by magic. No one enters or leaves the city without my mother's consent."

"*Magic?*" I yell, stomping back to where she lies.

She nods. "Lesage is behind it, so you can bet it is ironclad. And vicious."

"You're lying," I say in a rush. "You'll say anything to save your skin."

"Why do you think the royal army has yet to storm the city

and retake it?"

I groan and clench my fists, wanting to strangle someone—mostly myself.

"You're the son of the king," she continues, her voice silky and hypnotic. "You can do as you see fit. Release me, and I will help your sisters."

"I am the *bastard* son of the king. I'm nobody."

She rolls her eyes. "You have plenty of influence. And you're a fool if you allow that pigheaded police captain to tell you what to do."

"That *pigheaded police captain* is my best friend."

"I pity you if he's the best friend you can find. Your sisters deserve to live, and so do I. You owe me that, at least. Put your horrible friend out of your mind and find a way."

There is no way. Can't she see that? We're all doomed.

I turn and trudge through the murky puddles, shouting an oath that chases me down the tunnel.

"The bread is stale," Louis grumbles as soon as I enter our chamber. He picks at the crust and flings it into a puddle, where it's instantly devoured by gray sludge.

Normally I can ignore his grousing, but not tonight. Not on top of everything else. I stomp to where he sits, propped against the wall with his ankles crossed, and pry the remaining bread from his fingers. It *is* stale—hard enough to chip a tooth—but even if it wasn't, Louis would complain.

"My apologies," I mutter. "I'll remove this from your sight and tell Madame Bissette to prepare sugar comfits tomorrow." Then under my breath I add, "We wouldn't be stuck down here, eating this stale bread, if you had done your part during the procession."

"How many times must I tell you? I tried to maneuver the cart to the pâtisserie, but the streets were impassable. I would have been crushed. The fault is not on me, but on your inadequate plan."

I start to bite back at him, but the poisoner's confession about the wards around the city stops my tongue. Louis may be right. The thought makes my stomach churn.

Shooting him a glare, I clip across the chamber, break the bread in two, and hand half to Marie. Usually she whispers in thanks and nibbles quietly, but now she bursts into tears. Of course.

"Where the devil is Desgrez?" I yell. I want to wring his neck for leaving me to deal with my siblings alone.

"He went above," Marie stammers. "He said he needed a drink."

"Don't we all," I grumble.

"How much longer must we eat these castoffs?" she continues. "When can we leave this place?" She looks at me with her wet blue eyes, and I haven't patience for crying either. I take the bread back—she doesn't even protest—and continue to Françoise and Anne, who are mercifully silent. They're too weak to sit up, but they smile when I ease down beside them.

They take the bread eagerly, and Anne stuffs the entire piece into her mouth. Before she can swallow, her body heaves and crumbs spray across my lap. She deflates next to Françoise and disappears beneath their damp, colorless blanket.

"This is an outrage," Louis cries. "You can't expect me and Marie to eat nothing."

"Too late," I say with a cruel grin. "Stale bread is too far beneath you anyway. Think of it as a fast. You've always been so pious. What could be nobler, more Christlike, nay, more *kinglike*, than feeding homeless bastards? Father would be proud."

Louis's thin lips press into a line and he leans against the wall with a begrudging huff. Unlike me, he's always been devout, attending daily mass with Father since the time he could walk. And, also unlike me, he cares what our dearly departed father would think.

He laces his fingers, closes his eyes, and begins praying. Aloud. His voice makes my skin crawl, but at least his complaints aren't directed at me. Though I should probably apologize to God—I doubt even *His* patience is infinite enough to endure my half brother's moaning.

When I glance back down at my two smallest sisters, my breath hitches. They're almost unrecognizable, with hollow, sunken cheeks and skin so transparent that I can see each blue vein tracing up their arms. How has it come to this?

I run my fingers through their hair. Not long ago, it was thick and glossy, tied with ribbons and bows. Now it's brittle and comes away in tangled clumps.

"Josse?" Françoise murmurs. Her fingers wrap around mine, so light you'd think she was a ghost. It kills me to think those same hands used to pick beans in the garden, and help Rixenda carry the wash, and yank my hair when she rode on my shoulders. A ferocious cough folds her in half, and her hand slips away.

"Why must you always leave us?" she asks in a wispy breath. "It's so cold without you. . . ."

Briars wheedle beneath my skin and plunge into my heart. I would give anything to take their place, to take their pain. My eyes prickle, but I blink the tears away. The girls need me to be strong. "Hush, I'm here now." I take off my doublet and drape it around her shoulders. "I never want to leave you, but I must find us passage out of Paris and get you to a doctor."

She droops against me. "Louis says it's hopeless. We're all going to die here. Me and Anne first."

"He said *what?*" Rage flashes through me, and I glare across the chamber at Louis, who's still mumbling supplications in the corner. "You're not going to die," I promise. She looks at me with glazed blue eyes. Her lungs rattle with each shallow breath. "I won't let you die."

I think of La Voisin's daughter down the tunnel. She can help them—I watched her save Desgrez's life—but she'll never agree.

"Tell us a story." Françoise tugs on my shirt.

"All right. Which would you like? The one about the enchanted locket? Or the fairy queen's horse?" I reach across Françoise to poke Anne. "I know that's your favorite."

Anne doesn't respond. Frowning, I nudge her again. Harder. Her skin feels cold beneath her dress and she's unnaturally still. Not coughing. Barely breathing.

Suddenly I can't breathe either.

I surge to my feet. Françoise topples from my lap with a cry, but there's no time to comfort her. I crouch beside my smallest sister. "Annie, wake up," I say, prodding her gently. Her face lolls to the side like the limp, broken head of a flower. "Wake up!" I shake her harder. My voice sounds foreign in my ears, too high-pitched.

Louis stops praying. Marie screams and slaps a hand over her mouth.

"Don't let her be dead," Françoise wails, reaching for Anne's hand. "Josse, don't let her be dead! You promised."

My gaze flies desperately around the chamber and lands on the pouch of supplies we took from La Voisin's daughter. I've tried to recreate the curative several times now—it didn't look so difficult when she healed Desgrez. But the paste always separates and smells wrong and I'm not about to cut my sisters open to test my work. I grit my teeth to keep from sobbing. My sisters' salvation is within reach, but the ingredients are useless in my hands.

But not *hers*.

I scoop Anne up, retrieve the sack of alchemy supplies, and rush for the tunnel. Let Desgrez punish me. Let La Voisin find us and torture us in the end. Let me rot in Hell for lying to the girl and using her. I cannot sit back and watch Anne die.

"What are you doing?" Marie cries. "Desgrez said. . . ."

"I don't give a piss what Desgrez said!"

Marie covers her face with her hands. Françoise continues shrieking. The color drains from Louis's cheeks, and his eyes grow round with terror. "I won't allow this! If you untie the poisoner, she'll kill us all."

Ignoring them, I brace Anne's tiny body against my chest and sprint into the dark.

9

MIRABELLE

I've nearly drifted off to sleep when shouting erupts down the tunnel, followed by the *slap, slap, slap* of boots on stone. I bolt upright. Cool tendrils of fear trickle down my neck, and I shiver as I stare into the blackness. The bastard prince is coming to kill me— or the officer, more like. Why wait until morning? The only thing my reckless negotiating bought me was a few less hours of life.

The steps grow louder. Nearer.

Move, Mira.

I thrash against my bonds, but the ropes cut deeper into my wrists. Thankless, rutting royals! Healing the police captain should've convinced them that the Shadow Society isn't wholly wicked—that some of us are still reasonable and capable of incredible, lifesaving innovation.

Serves you right for betraying us, Mother hisses.

A frustrated scream burbles up my throat, but I'm not sure who I'm screaming at: Mother for being right, the royals for being heartless, or myself for being so stupid.

"You! Girl!" The bastard's voice echoes around the corner,

gruff and strained and manic. A second later, he materializes through the shadows and barrels toward me like a bull. I'm sure the loathsome officer isn't far behind. Wild with panic, I press myself against the dripping wall and will the rocks to swallow me. I tense every muscle, waiting for a blow to the head or a sword through the ribs, but I feel a whoosh of air instead. The boy drops to his knees beside me, carrying a limp sack of something.

No.

Someone.

"Heal her," he begs.

I blink at him. Mold must've sprouted in my ears. Or perhaps they've frozen shut.

"Please." He chokes. In the low light, I can just make out the tears coursing down his face and the shape in his arms—a small girl. Sallow and thin. So very, very still.

"You didn't come to kill me?" I whisper.

"You said you can save her." He fights to keep his voice steady, but his shoulders lurch and he buries his face in the scraps of the little girl's dress. "Do it. I'll give you whatever you want."

I purse my lips and wait until he meets my gaze. "You know what I want."

The bastard swallows hard but nods. "I'll let you go, I swear it. Just help her. Quickly."

He's lying. Mother's voice cracks like a whip. *You know he cannot set you free. Don't let one pitiful girl cloud your judgment and threaten all we have accomplished.*

And what exactly have we accomplished? I want to shout back at her. How is executing our opposition and reigning with an iron fist any better than the Sun King forsaking the peasants?

I look down at the girl and finger the satin hem of her dress. She wasn't a willing party to any of this—she was caught in the cross-hairs. Like myself. We are all cannon fodder in our parents' war.

Mother's voice grows louder and more frantic: *If they live, the nobles will continue to rise against us.* But I clench my teeth and banish her from my mind. I'm through dancing like a puppet at the end of the Society's strings. They refused to negotiate for my life. And barred me from the laboratory. I owe them nothing. I would rather cling to the original goal of the Shadow Society and rely upon my healing concoctions—hold fast to my convictions like Father—than be poisoned by power and ambition like Mother.

"Cut the ropes," I say. "We haven't much time."

With a strangled gasp of thanks, the princeling lays the girl on the floor and severs my bonds. At first, my arms refuse to move. After being bound for so many days, they're creaky and stiff, and my shoulders are on fire. I grit my teeth and wrench them forward, shouting a stream of curses that would put even Fernand to shame. Then I crawl through a puddle to where the little girl lies. She's breathing, only just.

"Right, then—I can work here, but I'd prefer better lighting and drier floors."

The bastard looks from his sister to me and then down the tunnel, biting his lip into a pulp.

I huff out an exasperated breath. "The longer you waste mistrusting me, the worse she gets. I am not your enemy. I knew nothing about the attack on Versailles, I helped you escape Lesage's beasts, and I healed the police captain when I should have killed him."

He looks at me, actually looks me in the eye for the first time in days, then lifts the girl and motions with his head for me to follow. Neither of us speaks as we wind through the pitch dark. It takes all of my concentration to navigate the slime-covered floor thanks to my bleary eyes and weak, aching muscles. Sweat dribbles down my cheeks, but I welcome the wetness. It means my fever has broken.

We round several corners and ascend into a chamber lit with flickering torches. As soon as I duck through the grate, the quiet clip of conversation ceases and three pairs of blue eyes lock on my frame. I nod at each of them, but the royals don't return my greeting. Madame Royale, who looks to be my age, regards me like the walking plague, scrunching her nose and narrowing her eyes. The girl beside her, a slightly older replica of the one in Josse's arms, dives behind her older sister's skirts, while the dauphin sits in the farthest corner, his blond wiglet dangling in his piqued face, his arms crossed over his blue and gold doublet.

He shoots to his feet. "This is an outrage! She'll poison us. Or attack us with her wicked magic."

Marie squeals and shields her face.

"Enough!" the bastard princeling shouts. "She isn't going to harm anyone." He glares at me, daring me to contradict him. "She's here to help Anne and Franny."

"Be reasonable, Josse! You can't honestly believe that," Louis says.

"I have to." The bastard—named Josse, apparently—turns his back on the dauphin and sets the little girl down. He straightens her dress and tucks her mahogany hair behind her ear, his fingers surprisingly gentle as they skim across her cheek.

"This is another one of your doomed and reckless plans," Louis says in a dangerous voice. "And I won't allow it."

Josse rounds on him. "Do you have a better suggestion? Shall we let the little ones die? Or perhaps you don't care because we're bastards."

When Louis fails to respond, Marie steps forward, wringing her hands through her grime-coated skirts. "Of course we don't want the girls to die. It's just . . ." She looks at me again and winces.

I lift my chin and clench my fists. Can't they see I'm trying to *help?*

You haven't always helped.

The realization makes me retreat a step, and I'm suddenly unable to meet their eyes. Louis XIV wasn't just a king. He was their father.

And I killed him.

Not intentionally. I couldn't have known. I stab my nails into my palms to fend off the image of his bloated, foaming face. Then I blow out a breath and nod at the unconscious princess. "We should hurry. . . ."

Marie closes her eyes and presses her fingers against her lids—the perfect, poised aristocrat—but as soon as I move toward the little girl, she darts around me and flings her slender body over her younger sister. "Please don't hurt her."

My brows lift in shock. A full-blood sacrificing herself for a bastard. Marguerite wouldn't do the same for me, and our blood is identical drop for drop. "Stop being ridiculous," I bark to conceal my astonishment—and the thread of niggling guilt. "If you don't let me work, the girl *will* die. I am not the risk here."

Not anymore.

Marie blinks at me, and her tear-filled eyes scrutinize my every movement. It makes my skin prickle. "Fetch me a torch and a bowl," I say, so she'll stop staring like I'm inhuman. Something *other*. "Now!"

Covering her shriek with the back of her hand, she scurries across the chamber and brings me a torch. Josse procures the bowl, and I make quick work of mixing the paste. They've clearly been meddling with my supplies. I had enough herbs for half a dozen doses, but now there's only enough for the girls and maybe one more.

"Your dagger," I say to Josse in my most commanding voice.

"Don't!" Louis shouts. "She can't be trusted with a weapon." But Josse flips his blade around and offers me the handle. He keeps hold of the hilt a touch longer than necessary, his eyes glinting with warning.

I yank the knife away, annoyed by his lack of confidence, and more so by how his worry leeches into me. My fingers tremble as I slather the ointment across the girl's stomach. The blade slips when I press the tip to her flesh. I have done this only once before.

What if it was luck? These girls have been deteriorating for weeks rather than minutes. What if it's too late? What if I kill her?

You will be a great alchemist one day—greater even than I.

At the first sight of blood, Marie whimpers and clutches the small girl's shoulders in a vise grip. Josse's boots nudge up against my back. Even Louis falls silent and leans forward to watch.

I swallow hard and hold my breath as the blood swirls with the thick gray ointment. When the girl's color finally returns, I let out a sigh of relief. I want to leap and dance and shout for joy, but I keep my head. "Press her dress tightly over the wound and apply constant pressure." I show Marie how to go about it. "And bring me the other girl."

My voice is stronger now. My hands steady.

This is who I am, what I was born to do.

I imagine Father sweeping me up in his arms and swinging me around the laboratory, as he did once long ago—the first time I correctly brewed a sleeping draught. The faint echo of his laughter rumbles in my ears as I repeat the process with the older girl, Françoise. But her treatment proves far more difficult. She squirms and kicks so violently, Josse has to pin her shoulders to the floor. I work as quickly as possible, and once both girls are bled and bandaged, I melt to the freezing ground. Despite the puddles and stench, I want to press my blazing face against the cold stone and sleep for days.

Marie leans against a wall and fans her flushed cheeks, watching me with alternating expressions of awe and mistrust.

Josse stalks across the chamber like a lion guarding its cubs. And Louis continues glaring at Josse, cursing and muttering under his breath. I am all too familiar with the hard set of his jaw and unabashed sneer; it's the same bitter expression I've seen a hundred times on my own sister. Though I doubt these two share the morsels of friendship that make the intolerable stretches bearable. My sister and I may quarrel more than we get on, but it's underscored by love—I think.

What are you doing now, Margot? Is she worried for me? Did she beg Mother to negotiate with the royals on my behalf? Or is she relieved to be the only daughter of La Voisin?

Eventually, Josse tires of pacing and eases down beside the girls. His devotion is mesmerizing: the way he adjusts his coat over their shivering bodies and smooths their ratted curls; how the tenderness on his face softens his sharp cheekbones and pursed lips. I study the thin layer of stubble on his chin, the way his dark hair flops into his eyes. He's younger than I thought—perhaps a year or two older than I am—and handsome, I suppose, now that he isn't threatening to kill me.

"Do you like what you see, *poisoner?*" Louis's nasally voice drones from across the chamber.

I jolt and avert my gaze. "I haven't a clue what you mean."

Louis's laugh is harsh and tinny. "You're practically devouring my bastard brother with your eyes. If you'd like, you can take him off our hands. He would be quite useful in your line of work, with all of his kitchen experience."

Josse grinds his teeth so hard the muscles near his temple jump. Marie glares at Louis. "Enough," she snaps.

"What?" Louis says. "Can I not speak the truth? He's no prince. He's a kitchen boy. Our father never approved of him, so I see no reason why I should."

Josse's eyes flick up, full of fire. "I didn't *want* the king's approval. Though there's no denying who he'd find more competent now. At least I'm trying! You just sit there and complain while the Shadow Society takes your city. Even the poisoner is more useful." He flings a hand in my direction. I know he's trying to cut Louis, but still I flinch, hating that word. Hating what I've done. Hating that no matter how many times I prove myself, I will never step out of Mother's shadow.

"You will regret those words, *brother*," the dauphin spits out.

Josse's laugh is scornful and vicious. "What do you plan to do? Bind me with your silk ribbons? Batter me with your red-heeled slippers? Or, I know, smother me with your ratted wiglet?"

Louis's cheeks blaze and his mouth bobs open and closed. "I demand silence," he stammers at last.

"Gladly." Josse stretches out on his back and slams his tricorne hat over his face. Marie curls into a ball on her side. I long to follow suit. My arms tremble like leaves and my eyelids flutter. *Do not fall asleep,* I command myself. *There's no telling what the royals will do to you.* But Marie doesn't seem so bad, merely overprotective. Louis would never risk touching unwashed vermin. And Josse fed me. He trusted me to heal his sisters. He promised to release me. . . .

Gray blotches cloud the edges of my vision. How long has it been since I've slept well? Days? Weeks? Darkness wraps around me, and I'm sinking, drowning. So unbearably heavy. I sag against the wall and give in to the exhaustion. The royals may well kill me, but at least I tried to redeem myself. I proved who I am and where I stand with my final act. Satisfied, I drift out of consciousness with a tiny grin on my lips.

I wake to a sound I haven't heard in ages: Laughter. High and trilling and merry. I bolt upright, and my body screams in protest. A kink in my neck makes it near impossible to turn my head. I blink through the darkness, momentarily blinded as I wipe the sleep from my eyes.

The little girls are sitting up. They have to clutch the wall for support, and the smaller one, Anne, is still frightfully pale—but they're alive. And no longer speckled with awful green bumps. Josse kneels before them, telling them a story. He waves his hands above his head and tweaks Françoise's nose. Her delighted squeal tugs at the corner of my lips.

I'm so engrossed with watching them, I fail to hear Marie approach until she collapses beside me and takes my hands in hers. "Thank you," she gushes. "A thousand times, thank you."

Josse turns at the sound of her voice. His smile is more radiant than the sun at midday, his eyes greener than the hills in summer. My chest constricts, and a funny tingling seeps through my core. After everything I've done, I never thought anyone would look on me with such hope and gratitude. Nor did I think they would hold my hands to their chest, wetting my fingers with tears the way Marie does now. I even catch Louis grinning in the corner, and a surge of emotion swells within me.

"It worked," Josse crows. He rushes over and smothers me in an embrace. I yelp with surprise, and the girls giggle. The sound fills my bones with warmth and strength and *rightness*. "You're brilliant," Josse continues. But his praise lands like a slap across my cheek, and my body goes rigid.

I'm not the hero they think. I may have saved the little girls, but I still killed their father.

Josse leans closer before releasing me, his lips at my ear. "I'll see you safely home. I swear it."

I shuffle back a few steps. I have no desire to return to Mother and the Shadow Society. And it's impossible, at any rate, thanks to their misbegotten ransom note. Even if I claimed I escaped, Mother knows I've been with the royals, which means she will expect me to lead the Shadow Society back to this hideout. She will slaughter these innocent *children*. Guilt twines tighter around my neck, and a foul taste fills my mouth.

"No," I whisper.

Josse stares at me as if I just refused all the gold in the Sun King's coffers. "But you said—"

"I said I wanted *freedom.*"

His green eyes blaze into mine. "I'll find a way to keep my promise. Trust me." Then he takes my arm and ushers me toward the girls. "What do you say to Mirabelle?"

Mirabelle. Not poisoner. Not La Petite Voisin. *Mirabelle.*

Françoise looks down shyly. "Thank you for healing me. I'm sorry I caused such a fuss."

"No need to apologize." I offer her a hand to shake in truce, but little Anne pounces. She drags me to the floor and climbs onto my lap, nestling against my chest. I feel as if I've been kicked in the gut, only it doesn't hurt, exactly. It's more of a blooming, burning sensation. A rush of heat that dislodges my heart and presses it up into my throat. Slowly, and with extreme caution, I wrap one arm around Anne's shoulders.

"I'm glad you feel better," I say, but my voice comes out hoarse. She squeezes tighter and I close my eyes, desperate to store this feeling, this wholeness, until the sharp clang of metal makes my eyelids fly open.

I jerk away from Anne, Marie curses, and Josse leaps to his feet.

"Unbelievable!" The police captain towers at the entrance of the sewer chamber, his sword vibrating at his feet.

My stomach drops.

Josse hasn't time to keep his promise.

It's morning.

And the officer has returned to kill me.

10

JOSSE

"Would you care to explain why your sisters are *embracing* our prisoner?" Desgrez seethes.

"It's about time you arrived," Louis interjects. "It's an outrage. The bastard has—"

"She healed the girls," I cut in, patting Françoise's head and flashing Desgrez a timid smile. Hoping it's all the explanation he'll need. Praying it will somehow change his mind.

His face crumples—with rage, yes, but other, more unexpected emotions simmer beneath the surface. Hurt glistens in his eyes. Betrayal drips from his downturned lips.

Which is so much worse.

I loosen my collar, but I can't catch my breath. My heart pounds so loudly, Madame Bissette can probably hear it from her pâtisserie. Slowly, Desgrez bends and retrieves his blade. When he straightens, his features are ironed into a steely expression. He adjusts his grip on the rapier and clenches his jaw. I have less than ten seconds to make a decision before Desgrez makes it for me.

I accidentally look at Mirabelle and she stares back, her eyes as round as saucers. *You promised,* she screams without saying a word.

Behind her, Françoise's lip begins to tremble. Anne grasps for Mirabelle's hand. I know what my father or his ministers would do: rip the promised freedom from her hands like the morsels of bread they pledged to the peasants. But that's not who I want to be. I am a different sort of royal, and if I want the girls to follow suit, I must lead the way. Stand for something.

Be strong, Josse.

I blow out a breath, wipe my clammy palms down my breeches, and stride across the chamber to Desgrez. "Can we speak in private?"

He scowls but allows me to hook my arm around his shoulders and lead him into the tunnel. It would be cleanest and easiest if I let him dispose of Mirabelle. Her people did murder my father—even though she claims innocence—and if I set her free, she could easily betray us to her mother. I must think of my sisters' safety above all else.

But my sisters wouldn't be alive if it weren't for her.

"Well?" Desgrez shoves me off as soon as we round the bend. "What could you possibly have to say?"

"I'm sorry." Then I kick out and slam my boot into his wrist. As his blade clatters to the ground, I smash my fist against his temple. A low whine leaks from his lips and he crumples to the wet stone floor. I cushion his fall as best I can. "I really am sorry," I whisper before sprinting back the way we came. He'll come around in minutes if we're lucky. Seconds if we're not.

"We have to go *now,*" I shout as I burst back into the chamber.

Louis clambers to his feet, his eyes wild. "Where is Captain Desgrez? What have you done now?"

He tries to block my path, but I plow through him. "It doesn't concern you." I offer Mirabelle my hand and pull her up. "I hope you can run."

"Traitor!" Louis bellows. He retrieves his rapier from his small pile of belongings and levels it at me. His shoulders heave and sweat stipples his brow. The steel blade glints in the torchlight, the edges sharp and flashing. "You cannot set her free."

"Stand aside. I don't have time to fight you," I say, but we both know I couldn't best him with a sword if I had all the time in the world.

"Get back." Louis flicks his wrist, and his blade whizzes past my cheek, pausing just below my chin. Anne and Françoise gasp, and Mirabelle shrinks behind me.

I roar with frustration and reach for the dagger in my boot. It won't do much good against his rapier, but Mirabelle and I can't be in these tunnels when Desgrez wakes. He won't hesitate to kill her, and he'll make me wish I were dead. I'm about to lunge when something white streaks through my periphery. Marie dives into Louis with a bloodcurdling cry and they careen sideways, crashing into the stone wall. Louis groans and his rapier spins off into a puddle.

"Go!" Marie gasps. "Get her out!"

I gape at Madame Royale for half a second, then tighten my fingers around Mirabelle's wrist and dash into the tunnels. We sprint blindly through the dark, chased by the echo of our boots. *What have you done?* The words pound in my ears. *You betrayed your best friend. Endangered your sisters.*

Yet still I keep running, the rightness of my choice spurring me on. A life for a life. *Three lives*, if we're truly keeping count.

I emerge through the floor hatch into the pâtisserie, pull Mirabelle up behind me, and nod to Madame Bissette as we bolt for the door. But the old woman takes one look at Mirabelle's sparse dress and lurches after us.

"Oh no you don't, you wicked, sneaking codpiece!" She drops the trapdoor and flour billows into the air. While I cough and stumble, she charges through the haze like a wolf through the snow. "What did I say about bringing whores to my shop?" She catches a strand of Mirabelle's hair between her gnarled fingers and sniffs. "Filthy, stinking whore. If she brings lice or vermin . . ."

I dig my elbow into Madame Bissette's ample side and race out onto the rue Saint-Honoré. Her shrieks chase us down street after street until we reach the Place de Victoires and duck behind a chandler shop. It's so early, the stores are dark and barred—not even the vendors are out with their carts. I release Mirabelle and hunch forward, hands on my knees. She leans against the wall, making noises halfway between sobs and laughter.

The air up here smells of rain instead of pottage, and the cobbles are slick and glittery in the early-morning light. I breathe deeply through my nose until the tension in my shoulders slackens. "I can't believe we made it," I say.

"I can't believe you freed me." Mirabelle's dark eyes are wide with disbelief.

"I promised I would."

"Yes, but . . ." She looks back the way we came, then at me, and eventually shrugs. "I suppose we're even, princeling."

She pushes away from the wall, straightens her tattered red skirts, and starts down the street without looking back. Without so much as a thank-you. Rather rude, considering I've risked everything to help her. But that's only half the reason my stomach tightens: If she leaves, she could go anywhere. Do anything. *That's the point of freedom,* I remind myself. But up here, with the city sprawling out in a thousand different directions, freedom seems a little *too* free. Desgrez's warnings seem very real. And very possible. She could have lied about not returning to her mother. She could have saved the girls just to gain my trust. She could be plotting to lead the Shadow Society back to the sewer chamber.

No. I saw the look on her face when she healed the girls. I saw how she flinched and shrank when Desgrez condemned her for being a poisoner. She won't betray us.

Are you willing to stake Anne and Françoise's lives on it?

Cursing, I wipe my sweaty face on the inside of my tunic and jog after her. "Where are you going?"

Mirabelle quickens her step. "I don't see how that's any of your business."

"I suppose it's not, but I'd feel better if—"

She holds up a hand and whirls around. "You kidnapped and

threatened to kill me. I'm not concerned with *your* feelings."

"Yes, but I also saved you. . . ."

She shoots me an exasperated look. "Like I said, we're even." She rounds another corner and starts up the inclined streets toward Montemartre—the hillside neighborhood overlooking the city center. I watch her go, my toes itching inside my boots.

You will not follow. There's nothing more you can do.

Pebbles crunch behind me, and I check over my shoulder. The hairs bristle on my neck as I stare into the sinister swaths of shadow and darkened corners. Desgrez could be anywhere. Or her mother, La Voisin. Even if Mirabelle doesn't return to the Louvre, the Shadow Society could capture her and force her to divulge my siblings' location.

My sisters aren't safe unless she's safely hidden.

I flip my collar high, tug my hat brim low, and trail her at a distance. Up we climb, past sordid gambling dens and rows of maisons de tolerance, with their red-painted doors. "I know you're still there," Mirabelle says with an aggravated sigh. She pivots and folds her arms across her chest. "Why?"

I raise my hands and step out of the shadows. "I'm only trying to help. Desgrez will be hunting us. And the city is overrun with your mother's lackeys. . . ."

"I know. I'll avoid them."

"How?"

"Again, I don't see—"

Footsteps ring out on the cobbles. Before we can even think

to dive for cover, a group of avocats round the corner in a flurry of polished leather cases and powdered wigs. Mirabelle sags with relief, but I remain as rigid as stone, glaring at the side of her face until the lawmen are out of sight and she finally looks at me.

"What?" she hisses.

"If that was Desgrez, you'd be dead!"

"What do you expect me to do?"

"Hide. Like a reasonable person." I look up and down the road, and my gaze snags on an abandoned millinery sandwiched between two gambling dens. It's dark and unassuming, the windows boarded up and the steps crumbling. "How about there?"

Mirabelle's brows lower and she starts to shake her head.

"Just until tonight—to ensure Desgrez isn't trailing us. Wait until the streets are empty, when you can blend in to the midnight shadows."

"The sun is barely up!"

"Fine. Don't. But I'll be forced to keep following you. For your protection."

"Don't you have anything better to do?"

"As much as I'd love to get my sisters out of this treacherous city, we won't get far if the Shadow Society captures you and forces you to compromise our location. So, no. I don't have anything better to do."

Mirabelle tilts her head back and groans as she crosses the road to the millinery.

I wait a moment, check up and down the street, and jog after her.

"I cooperate, yet still you follow," she snips as I catch up with her on the stairs.

"Where else do you expect me to go? I'm not exactly welcome in the sewer anymore."

"There's got to be another abandoned shop in this city. Preferably on the opposite side."

I shut the millinery door, and a thick coating of dust drifts down from the moth-eaten hats and ribbons dangling overhead. We stumble through the fog, coughing and tripping over each other. I bang my knee on the long, low counter in the center of the room and then crash into the shelves lining the back wall. They're littered with buttons and thread and bent needles—one of which bites my finger. Even the shelves are unwilling to support me.

I'm so tired of fighting—with Mirabelle, with Desgrez, with Louis and even Madame Bissette. I am weary to my bones. More exhausted than after a long day of scrubbing in the scullery.

I slump to the floor beside one window and let my legs sprawl out in front of me. Mirabelle stalks to the other window and peers through the slats.

The minutes tick by slowly. I watch the pink and orange rays of sunrise crest the hillock, setting the thatched rooftops ablaze. Slowly, the streets fill with carts and carriages and people buying bread and cheese. At one point I think I see a man in a long black overcoat marching toward the shop and I scramble to my feet. But then I remember Desgrez no longer wears his uniform, and I slide back to the ground.

Mirabelle ignores me with stalwart determination, and I try to do the same, but my rebellious eyes keep darting back to her, wandering along her clenched jaw and trailing down her long, slender neck. Even in that stained scrap of a dress with her hair in wild tangles, she's one of the most stunning girls I've ever seen.

And the last person on earth you should think of that way.

Yet she claims she had naught to do with the attack. . . .

Of course she would say that.

She glances up from beneath her fan of dark eyelashes. "What?"

My cheeks burn. I'm not about to tell her I was admiring the smattering of freckles across her nose, so I skip straight to the second bit: "How could you not have known about the attack on Versailles?"

"I wasn't a member of my mother's inner circle. I hadn't a clue she planned to poison the Sun King or storm the palace or take Paris. None of it. I was just as horrified as you."

"I highly doubt that." I shudder at the memory of the blood dripping from my hands, the wall of ravenous flame, Rixenda crumpling to the dirt. Nightmares that haunt me still.

"I was horrified enough to defy her," she says to her hands. "To turn my back on my family and the Society and everything I've spent my life working for."

Oh, wow, what a sacrifice. How awful it must be, turning your back on a throne-stealing witch. . . . That's the response that immediately springs to mind, but she looks so miserable, sitting there with her scrawny arms clutched around her knees, so instead I say,

"You don't have to feel that way."

Scornful laughter pops from her lips, and she faces me with one eyebrow raised. "How could you possibly know what I'm feeling, princeling?"

"Well, your mother left you to die at the hands of her enemies, and now you're on the run without a plan or protection. So I'd imagine you're feeling abandoned, betrayed, alone, inadequate, hurt. Shall I go on?" She stiffens, but before she snaps I quickly add, "I have a bit of experience with those feelings, being the king's unwanted bastard."

She bites down hard on her lower lip and is silent for so long, I figure the conversation is dead. But then she says softly, "I tried so hard. I did everything she asked—*anything* to win her approval. Devil's claws, I was a fool. Like a dog begging for scraps."

I nod sagely. "The trick is not to care. If you don't want their acknowledgment, they have no power over you. They can't hurt you."

Mirabelle turns to face me, the light from the window slanting across her skeptical expression. "You had no desire for the king's approval?"

"None."

"I don't believe you."

I bristle. Even *she* thinks me a groveling pissant. "I haven't wanted it for years. You can ask anyone at court. I was the bane of His Majesty's existence."

Mirabelle purses her lips and studies me. "What about your sisters?"

"What about them?"

"It's obvious you care for them."

"What does that have to do with my father?"

She rolls her eyes. "*Why* do you think you're so doting and protective? Why do you think you're trying so desperately to be the hero now? To prove you're better than Louis?"

"First, I *am* better than Louis—that doesn't require much effort. And second, I love Anne and Françoise because they're the only ones who have ever loved me. Protecting them has nothing to do with pleasing *His Royal Majesty*."

"If you say so." Mirabelle's expression is pitying—as if I'm as sad and confused as she is, which I most definitely am not. That sniveling little boy who needed his father's approval died a lifetime ago. I buried him myself.

"I don't know why I bothered," I mutter. "It was foolish to think a poisoner could understand."

Mirabelle flinches, but I don't apologize. Her dark eyes bore into the side of my face from across the shop, but I refuse to look at her.

Finally, she huffs and looks away. "*You're* the one who initiated the conversation."

"Well, I shouldn't have."

"Fine."

"Fine."

We sit in silence as the hours pass.

A prince and a poisoner.

Trapped in the same room, but on opposite ends of the world.

11

MIRABELLE

I ball my fists in my skirt—mostly so I don't fly across the millinery and throttle the bastard princeling—and watch the sun make its languid arc across the sky. Morning shifts to midday then evening. As eager as I am to leave this place, he's right—it will be safer under the cover of night. So I drum my fingers against the floor and count the seconds until it's dark and I can be free of him.

Never in my life have I known anyone so bullheaded. So willfully obstinate! Sitting over there with his devil-may-care attitude. *I see you!* I want to shout. *You are just as desperate for approval as I am. Maybe even more so, since you're too blind to recognize it.*

I glance over and hope to catch him staring again—so *I* can make a barbed remark. But he's drifted off to sleep. His long legs are stretched out in front of him and his hands are tucked behind his head, his hat propped partially over his eyes. He looks younger in sleep—the hard set of his jaw finally slack, his brows released from their perpetual scowl. A strand of dark hair has slipped from the queue at the nape of his neck and dangles down the side of his face. My fingers twitch, inexplicably wanting to tuck it behind his ear.

He's impossible. And infuriating. But also desperate and lonely and aching.

Like me.

You don't have to feel that way.

I want to say his words back to him. Not to rub salt in his wounds, but because they're true. We're more alike than either of us would care to admit. In another life, we might have been friends.

But not in this one.

He may be a bastard, but he's still royal. He grew up at court, oblivious to the hunger and sickness and poverty I've spent my life fighting. There's also the undeniable fact that I killed his father. I don't know why I omitted that rather large detail when he asked about Versailles. Maybe I don't want to accept my part in it; I may be less culpable than Mother and Marguerite, but I'm hardly blameless. Or maybe it's more self-serving than that. He would never grant my freedom if he knew the truth.

Josse insists he wanted nothing to do with Louis XIV, but it's a lie. Deep down, he loved the man. Desperately.

Which is why we'll go our separate ways. I have an agenda to keep, and it doesn't include hiding away like a coward while the Shadow Society ravages the city. Not if I can help the people and quiet the nagging finger of guilt that's prodding me in the belly. I push up to my knees and peer between the boards nailed across the window, waiting until the night is half gone and the gambling dens on either side are silent. Then I gather up my skirts and tiptoe across the millinery. At the door, I steal one more glance at Josse—the moonlight dancing across the sharp planes of his handsome, but entirely irksome, face—and slip into the chilly night.

After a quick scan of the street, I head south toward the river. More specifically, toward the Louvre.

I may not be able to change what I've done, but I can attempt to redeem myself.

I creep toward the city center, past the Palais Royal, which is no doubt overrun with Shadow Society loyalists, and I'm about to turn on to the rue Saint-Honoré—the street bordering the northern wall of the Louvre—when a hand snakes out of a shadowed alcove and catches me by the throat. A moment later, fingers slap across my lips, muffling my scream.

"You filthy little liar!"

I had expected to find Fernand or Marguerite or another high-ranking member of the Shadow Society. But Josse's gray-green eyes blaze down at me. His fingertips press bruises into the skin above my collar bone.

"Unbelievable," he seethes.

"Y-you!" I stammer when his hand slides away from my lips. "You were asleep."

"No. I was testing you. And you failed. Running straight back to your mother, despite your pretty promises. I should have let Desgrez kill you."

I wrench my arm back, but his hold tightens. "I'm *not* running back to my mother."

Josse narrows his eyes. "You just happened to fancy a stroll past her stronghold?"

"I *happen* to have a plan of my own." I rear back again, and this time I stumble free.

"And what plan is that?"

I wrap my arms around my chest, rubbing his angry red fingerprints from my skin. "I don't see how it's any of your business, but I plan to continue the work of the Shadow Society— our *true* work," I add when he scoffs. "Murdering the king and seizing the city was never our aim. Our concern has always been for the common people: brewing curatives and hunger tonics and love potions."

"I still fail to see how that requires returning to the Louvre. You can't honestly hope to recruit La Voisin's followers to your cause."

"No, but I can steal back my alchemy supplies."

He's silent for a moment. His heavy breath billows between us in the cold. "While your intentions are noble . . . *if* you're telling the truth," he adds with a deliberate pause, "I can't allow you to put yourself in such a precarious position."

"Why not?" I cut him off. "The common folk aren't worth the risk?"

His eyes flare. "I am a commoner."

"Are you? Truly?"

He tugs at his collar in frustration. "That's beside the point. I must focus on getting my sisters safely out of Paris before your mother finds us, which is why I can't allow you to flit about raising a ruckus and getting yourself caught. It's madness to think one person could make a difference, anyway."

"Is it, princeling?" I take a bold step closer, the toes of my boots knocking his. He's a good head taller than me, but my indignation raises me up to his height. "Did I not make a difference when I brought your sisters and Desgrez back from the dead?"

"Yes, but—"

"Don't others deserve such a mercy?" His lips part, but I don't let him speak. "I'm not asking for your permission. I'm free to do as I please. You're free to go on your way, help me, or kill me. And since we both know you can't stomach the third option . . ."

He rips off his tricorne hat and rakes his fingers through his messy hair. "I haven't time to help the whole bedamned city!"

"So don't. Scurry back to the sewer." I charge from the alcove and continue down the rue Saint-Honoré toward the gatehouse in the palace wall, though I'm not entirely sure how I'll get inside. Perhaps when the guards change. . . .

I stop beneath the awning of a butchery across the road and study the gate, with its sharp iron teeth digging trenches into the ground. I tilt my head back and frown up at the ramparts that soar higher than the roofs of the half-timbered houses.

"Do you have a death wish?" Josse materializes beside me,

grabs my elbow, and pulls me down the street. "You'll be caught within the hour if you try to get through there. Follow me. I lived here half my life. I'll get you inside."

"I thought you didn't have time to help?"

"I don't. But I'll have even less time if you're captured."

He leads me past the palace, down the muddy, sloping embankment of the Seine, and plunks me down in the reeds. The cold mud seeps through my skirt, and I shudder as the midnight breeze skiffs across the river. "This doesn't look like the inside of the palace," I say.

Josse glowers and removes a dagger from his boot.

I eye it warily but refuse to flinch. "Ah, I see. You've decided to kill me after all."

"We both know I'm not going to kill you," he murmurs, turning the blade to offer me the handle. "Cut off your hair."

My hands instinctively reach for my curls. "Why?"

"Why do you think?" He makes large swirling gestures all around his head that are offensive and altogether exaggerated.

"It isn't that unruly."

"You'll be recognized in an instant. Hair is a small price to pay to be the *savior of the people*. Cut it off."

Grudgingly, I take the dagger and do as he says, sawing off my curls just above my ears. By the time I finish, I'm surrounded by piles of light brown hair—it looks like I sheered a lamb—and I silently mourn the long, curling strands as they blow away across the river. My ears have never been so cold. "Now what?"

"Now we wait."

We sit, shivering and soaking, for what feels like an eternity, until the outline of the Louvre glows gray and pink. As the sun rises over the water, a group of palace maids file down the embankment, strip off their dresses, and splash into the Seine.

I shoot the bastard prince a wicked grin. "Dare I ask how you know when the maids come to the river to bathe?"

"Be quiet and take a dress."

"Will they recognize you?"

"Only if you keep talking and draw their attention."

We slink forward on our bellies to where the girls left their clothes, and I pull on a scratchy slab of wool with a grunt. It's still warm with body heat and the underarms are slightly damp. My eyes flick to the river. Some poor girl's going to come out of the freezing water to find nothing but pebbles and reeds, but I haven't time to feel overly guilty because when I look to my left, I see that Josse has somehow squeezed himself into a gray maid's dress as well. I laugh and slap my hand over my mouth.

"Not a word," he says as he viciously ties the bonnet strings beneath his chin.

The pathway from the river to the palace is short, and we reach the postern gatehouse in a blink. Thankfully, the masked sentries are too busy playing cards to notice a pair of maids in ill-fitted uniforms, so we hunch our shoulders and shuffle inside without trouble.

At once, we are enveloped in a flurry of activity. Masked

Society members swarm the outer courtyard. Some march in single file while others spar with rapiers and daggers. Colonels in plum-colored livery pace atop the curtain wall, barking orders. The sight makes my breath catch. I knew the Society was large, but it's staggering to see them all in one place. And even more unsettling to see them drilling like a proper army.

Josse gapes around the courtyard, then looks at me askance. As if I singlehandedly recruited every one of them. Or conveniently forgot to tell him that Mother had legions of soldiers. But I'm every bit as shocked. *This isn't who we are.*

"Let's keep moving." Josse says, his voice low. "The servants' outbuildings are located behind the castle proper." He leads us along the curtain wall and around the nearest watchtower, but the moment he enters the courtyard, he slams to a halt. I crash into his back and start to curse him for smashing my nose, but he's already cursing enough for us both.

"Damn, damn, damn."

A massive steel cage has been erected in the center of the square. The crude bars are as thick as my middle and rise higher than the castle walls. Inside, Lesage's smoke beasts snort and snarl. There looks to be around ten of them—half created during the battle with the Paris Police and the other half from the procession. Their semi-translucent bodies slither and glide over one another like a tangle of shimmering yarn. The grass and cobbles around the pen are scorched, and a pillar of smoke billows skyward. I choke on the foul stench of brimstone.

I created those monsters. Without my alchemy, they would have dissipated like smoke. But I gave Lesage the power to make them tactile. I was so desperate to prove myself to Mother, I didn't consider the consequences. Just as I didn't consider the consequences of making the poison she used to kill the king. Maybe Josse is right. If I weren't so hungry for acknowledgment, I would have been more prudent. At the very least, I should have rendered the blood draught so I could control the beasts as well. They are half mine.

Which means the fault will be half yours when Lesage releases them again.

Shame and regret nip at my heels as we run down the narrow paths that snake around the cage. The beasts blow fire at our backs, attempting to incinerate anything that moves, and we narrowly dodge the flames. My feet burn like they've been branded by a hot poker. Josse's boots hiss as he splashes into a puddle, but it seems we've gotten off easy. There's a long line of servants with blistered arms and singed petticoats hobbling into the castle through a creaky wooden door near the midden heap.

We fall in line, and I glance nervously at the other servants, laden heavy with linens and barrows and missives. We'll stand out like a violet in a patch of belladonna if we don't appear to have a duty.

"Relax," Josse whispers. He grabs a water bucket waiting behind the door and hefts it to his hip. Then he leads us down the hall and past the kitchens, which smell of rye and roasted duck, to a corner stairwell.

I take the lead from there, guiding us down into the depths of the palace. The air grows colder as we descend, prickling across my skin and sitting damp and heavy in my lungs. It smells of rot and urine, and I pull my sleeve over my nose and quicken my step. While I miss my work and Gris, I haven't missed this miserable place.

Doors blur past, branching off into holding cells and torture chambers, and a cacophony of discordant music follows us down the twisting halls: the clink of iron manacles, the shouting of guards, and the painful wails of prisoners. Shivers overtake me, and I practically run the last few steps to the familiar gray door.

I crouch and check the gap to make certain it's empty—not even Gris should be working at such an early hour—then I burst into the laboratory. My feet carry me straight to the board, and I trace my fingers over the wood, touching every bottle and phial and spoon. Expecting them to welcome me like old friends. But everything feels cold and unfamiliar. The warm, pungent air assaults me like a bouquet of awful memories: Louis XIV's foaming lips, brewing Viper's Venom for Mother, Lesage's scarecrow arm dripping blood across the board.

This place is a cruel mockery of my garden laboratory. An insult to the Shadow Society.

I hate it.

"Fascinating," Josse says, perusing the shelves. He leans over to inspect the athanor and swings the furnace door open and closed.

I slap the back of his hand. "Don't touch anything. Stand over there and keep watch."

He grumbles but moves to the door. I retrieve several empty satchels from the cabinet and get to work, eager to be free of this place. I stuff fistfuls of fresh herbs and entire jars of the dried variety into the sacks followed by mortars and pestles and phials. Everything I'll need to resume healing. It will be obvious the laboratory has been pillaged, but I must collect as much as possible.

Gris's goggles call to me from their nail beside the hearth, and I run my finger along the leather strap, wishing more than anything for his help. But I leave the goggles be. Better that he's not involved in this madness. It would be selfish to ask him to take such a risk. And I'm not certain he'd side with me. I may be his best friend, but Mother is his savior. Not to mention I'm working with a royal—albeit it a bastard royal, but I helped the others as well.

In a matter of minutes, I have three bursting satchels waiting by the door and I'm teetering on a stool, reaching for one more sprig of juniper berries, when Josse mutters a black oath and dives behind a cluster of cauldrons in the corner.

That's all the warning I get.

A second later the door swings open and Gris strides into the laboratory, as if my longing summoned him. He immediately spots me on the stool, and the sack of eye bright in his hands hits the floor. "Do you know what happens to maids who steal from the Shadow Society?"

His voice rattles the shelves like the boom of a cannon, and I stand there paralyzed, seeing him for the first time how others must. Not as my clever and kind-hearted best friend but someone to be feared; he's as tall as a house and thick as a bull, with sinewy arms and a broad, heaving chest. His hands close around my wrist, but before he can hurl me from the stool, I throw my cap back and shout, "Gris! It's me!"

His eyes widen, and he releases me, reeling back against the table. "Mira?"

Up close, I see that his usually tanned face is deathly pale, and his tunic is so rumpled and stained, I doubt he's changed in weeks. The bags beneath his eyes are the color of a new bruise: purple and red, bleeding into blue. Mother's working him to death.

"You're alive," he chokes out. "How? Where have you been? Why are you dressed as a maid?"

"Thought I'd try my hand at cleaning." I flash a small grin, but Gris continues blinking as if I might vanish. Tentatively, he reaches out to touch my cheek. I lean in, the gentle brush of his fingertips sending shock waves through my body. I place my hand over his and a cry bursts from my throat—relief and comfort and something I can't put into words. Like waking from a horrifying nightmare to a world of brilliant, golden sunlight.

"You're alive," he says again, pulling me into his arms. "Everyone will be so relieved. La Voisin said the royals refused to negotiate for your life and slaughtered you to send us a message. The Society's been in a frenzy ever since, planning our retaliation."

Lies. Like always. "Mother is the one who refused to negotiate for my life."

161

Gris lifts a heavy brow as he guides me to a stool. "What do you mean?"

"When the royals sent word they'd captured me, she gave them leave to slaughter me."

He sucks in a breath and shakes his head, his honey-colored curls flying. "No. She wouldn't—"

"Are you certain?"

After a long pause, he collapses onto the stool next to mine like an empty bellows. "I'm sure she thought it was the only option. Or that rescuing you would put the Society at too great a risk. Or maybe it was a show of faith—she knew you could escape. Speaking of, how did you manage it? The royals would never let you go unless . . ." His voice takes on a note of wonder. "Did you kill them?"

"I took care of them," I say tightly, clutching my stays to push down the discomfort thumping in my belly. Technically, it's the truth, but Gris would never guess that I *literally* took care of our enemies.

"So why come to the lab? Why not go straight to La Voisin and tell her the good news? It was wrong of her to abandon you, but now that the royals are disposed of . . ." Gris shoots to his feet. "This will change everything."

"I'm not returning to the Shadow Society," I interject.

"Why not? Why are you here then?" His gaze wanders around the ravaged laboratory, stopping on the overflowing satchels.

"Mother's so obsessed with securing the city, she's forgotten our most important duty is to the people. While she's busy doling out poison and vengeance, I plan to resume making tinctures and curatives, and I need supplies to do it."

"But the unrest is only temporary. Until we quiet the dissenters."

"And when will that happen?"

Gris buries his fingers in his hair. "What would you have your mother do? The nobles swear fealty then betray her right and left. She asked them to contribute funds to rebuild the merchants' shops and homes that were burned during the procession. Not only did they refuse, but they organized against her! They've left her no choice. The only thing we can think to do is threaten them with Viper's Venom."

A small intake of breath comes from behind the cauldrons. Gris's eyes narrow and he turns.

"You see!" I clench Gris's shoulder and spin him back around. He nearly topples from his stool. "It will never cease! And what happens to the common folk in the meantime? They're forgotten, as they always have been. I have no wish to be a part of Mother's killings and carnage. I want to give life." *Make amends,* I think, but I know better than to admit this aloud. Gris would argue that we have nothing to be sorry for. "I won't force you to help me against your will. Just don't tell Mother where I am. Or what I'm doing. At least not yet."

Gris purses his lips and stares at me like he did the first time I suggested we alter some of Mother's recipes.

"I'm not doing anything contrary to the Society," I assure him.

"Only what we've always done. Think of the people."

Eventually, he nods. "What do you need me to do? And please tell me you weren't going to stroll past the porters with all that?" He points to the bursting satchels.

"It isn't so much. . . ."

"Devil's horns, it's a good thing I caught you, or you really would be dead." He pinches the bridge of his nose, then casts me a withering look. "I'll deliver your supplies, as well as some kettles and cauldrons so you're not limited to small quantities of medication. Just tell me where to find you."

"Thank you!" I throw my arms around him and kiss his cheek. "You can have my portion of meat for a month."

That makes him laugh; it's the same silly promise I made when I wanted him to scrub my share of the cauldrons when we were children. I look adoringly up at his face. With that broad smile crinkling his eyes, he almost looks like his old self—if I can ignore the purple bags.

Gris ruffles the remnants of my hair. "We're family. There's nothing I wouldn't do for you, Mira. You know that."

His tender words slide between my ribs like a dagger and the grin melts off my lips. *How can you betray him like this?*

But it isn't a betrayal so much as a small omission about my involvement with the royals—and it's for the greater good, like Mother always claims.

"I'm working in an abandoned millinery on the rue de Navarine in Montmartre. Right between two gambling dens."

He leans over the board to make a note. "Finish collecting everything you need, and I'll bring it later tonight. I'm supposed to meet La Voisin in her solar now to discuss this week's order." He crosses the room but pauses in the doorway. "Take the servants' stairs when you go; they're less crowded. And, Mira?" His eyes lock with mine. "Be careful. I couldn't bear to lose you a second time."

12

JOSSE

As soon as La Voisin's lackey lumbers down the hall, I spring to my feet and get all tangled up in my bedamned skirts. "Did you hear what he said?" I demand as I emerge from behind the cauldrons.

"He's going to help me procure supplies," Mirabelle says with a clap. "That went far better than I could've hoped."

"That went horribly! Your mother is planning to execute the remaining nobility. I may not know much about alchemy, but I'm going to assume something called Viper's Venom isn't pleasant."

Mirabelle looks away, suddenly very interested in a double-barreled contraption on the counter. "It's not."

"We have to stop her. Or help the nobility. *Something*." I wait for Mirabelle to agree, to erupt with righteous indignation and suggest—no, *insist*—we rush to their aid as she did for the common people. But she simply watches me stalk back and forth. "Well? You dragged me into this palace full of poisoners *in the name of the people*. Shouldn't that include poor and rich alike?"

Mirabelle folds her arms across her chest. "Of course I'd help them if I could, but there's no antidote to Viper's Venom."

I gape around the laboratory, at the hundreds of colorful bottles lining the walls, refusing to believe that none of them contain the necessary elixir. "Nothing?"

"Nothing."

"Well, then *make* something. You are an alchemist, aren't you? How hard could it be?"

"Viper's Venom is the most sophisticated poison known to man. My father, who was a far better alchemist than I, developed the compound, and his grimoire full of notes is locked in my mother's strongbox. In her bedchamber. *If* she hasn't destroyed it."

The way she tacks on the last excuse suggests this isn't likely. La Voisin has the book. We just have to steal it. My eyes flick up to the ceiling. "How hard could it be to pop abovestairs and take a book?"

"Out of the question. It's too dangerous."

"Too dangerous? We're already inside the palace! What's a little more risk?"

"A *lot* more risk," she fires back. "I have what I need to resume making curatives. That's enough. I see no reason to—"

"You don't care what becomes of the nobility." I bang my fist on the board, rattling the phials.

Mirabelle slams her own fist down with equal force. "Why do you suddenly care so much? I thought you despised the nobility. You're always so adamant you're not one of them."

"I'm not . . . Not wholly, anyway." I groan and drag a hand down my face. "I don't know what I am, but I do know—no matter how much I loathe the aristocracy—if we allow La Voisin to exterminate them, we will never have enough strength to overthrow her, which will seal her hold on the city and make it impossible for my sisters and I to flee."

"Ahhh, there it is. The real reason." Mirabelle gives me a condescending pat on the cheek. "This may be difficult for you to believe, princeling, but there are others to consider beyond you and your sisters. Hundreds of thousands of them."

"Exactly! Your mother is desperate and grasping and dangerous. Things are no better for the people under the Shadow Society than they were during my father's reign. He may have ignored the rabble in favor of the rich, but how is that different from exterminating the nobles? Half the city is still forsaken. More than half! You're stealing alchemy supplies because the poor are being neglected."

She opens her mouth to argue, so I quickly add, "How much can you honestly hope to accomplish—a single alchemist, working alone, in hiding?"

Mirabelle tilts her head back and lets out a loud breath. "What do you suggest we do? There's no solution."

Oh, there's a solution. But it's so preposterous, I'm afraid she'll laugh me out of the Louvre. I suppose people have been doing that all my life. "We do what neither my father nor your mother could accomplish. We *unite* the nobility and the common people."

She barks out a laugh.

"It could work! The noble families still have enough power and influence to overthrow La Voisin, but only with the strength of the commoners behind them. Then, once the Shadow Society is removed from power, we reestablish the monarchy."

Mirabelle scoffs. "Only the aristocracy will be in favor of that. If you want the people's support, they need a voice, a vote. Representatives from among them who will bring their concerns to the king, along with a guarantee that he will address them promptly and to their satisfaction."

"I'm certain Louis could be open to that . . ." I say, even though I'm not certain at all. If we get to that point, I'll *make* him open to it.

Mirabelle chews her lip and studies me. "I thought you weren't interested in helping *the whole bedamned city*."

"I didn't say I wasn't interested—I said I didn't have time. But if uniting the people and retaking the city means my sisters will be safe in Paris, I'll gladly choose the plan that benefits the majority. If you're as passionate about serving the people as you claim to be, it's what you'll choose too. Unless you're pleased with current events . . ."

Something flashes in her eyes, and I know I've hit a nerve. I place my hands firmly on her shoulders. "If we fail, you can still make your curatives in secret, but why not try? You have nothing to lose."

"Except my head if Mother discovers us." She glances nervously at the door, as if La Voisin can hear our treachery from across the palace.

"This will be far more effective than doling out curatives one by one and ignoring the larger problem. You wouldn't treat a man's cough if he was dying of White Death."

"Fine," she says. "But I'm in charge. And if someone discovers us traipsing through the palace, I'm telling them I escaped and brought you back as my prisoner."

I chuckle, but Mirabelle doesn't join me. Which is when I realize she's serious. "I snuck you into the palace. You wouldn't forsake me so easily!"

"I suggest you ensure we don't get caught." She shoots me a pointed look and sweeps out of the laboratory.

We retrace our steps to the end of the hallway and sneak up the winding staircase, past the intoxicating smell of freshly baked bread wafting from the kitchens, to the gilded ballroom above. Then higher still, to the royal residences in the uppermost levels of the palace. I was never permitted to enter these rooms when Father held court at the Louvre, but I delivered enough tea trays to recognize the receiving chambers—the white door carved with peonies and swallows leading to the queen's solar. And on the floor above that, the long corridor with soaring ceilings and buttery damask papering outside the queen's chambers.

Mirabelle streaks down the hall and ducks into a windowed alcove near the towering double doors. She pulls me in behind her and yanks the velvet draperies around us. "What are we doing in here?" I ask, but the horrid smell of must coagulates in my throat and my words are consumed by coughs.

"Quiet," Mirabelle hisses. As if I'm choking and sputtering on purpose. "Most mornings, Mother takes breakfast with Lesage and Marguerite and Fernand in the great hall, which means we shouldn't have to wait long to sneak into her chamber."

I nod and we watch the doors in silence, my fingers tap-tap-tapping against my sides. The minutes pass with excruciating slowness. There isn't enough space in here; the entire length of Mirabelle's body is smashed against mine, which under different circumstances might not be unpleasant, but she's quivering and fidgeting and her elbow keeps jabbing me in the ribs. Not to mention she's sucking up all the air with her quick, anxious breaths.

Just when I think I might suffocate, far-off bells chime the hour and the doors swing open. La Voisin parades from her chamber looking like the rising sun itself in an impressive golden gown with slashed sleeves and tiny cream-colored pearls sewn at the neck. Her crimson cloak completes the ensemble, and a gaggle of maidservants trail her down the hall to ensure the train doesn't catch on the furniture or drag through dirty rushes.

I suck in a breath as she passes our alcove. I've seen her previously but only from a distance, and I don't know what I expected up close, but she looks old. And tired. Her steps are slow and heavy, her eyes swollen and shadowed despite a thick coating of powder. Before she rounds the corner, she adjusts her cloak, sending the double-headed eagles flashing, and raises herself up as if she's a puppet whose strings have been pulled taut. Then she lets out a breath, her face takes on a mask of perfect calm, and she glides away, the peerless leader of the Shadow Society once more.

But now I've seen the fissures underneath.

I reach for the edge of the drapery, but Mirabelle smacks my wrist and holds up a hand. She must count well past fifty before finally moving.

Carefully, we draw the curtain aside and scurry to the ornate double doors. They're made of gilded ebony and groan as they swing inward. The room is gargantuan, with a floor-to-ceiling mirror along the back wall that makes the space look even larger. A tall bed with sumptuous green curtains occupies the center of the chamber, and rose settees line the walls. An unexpected pang wallops me in the stomach and stops my feet.

My servant mother never occupied the queen's rooms, of course. But that didn't keep her from dreaming. Rixenda told me how my mother would bargain with the other maids, taking on extra scrubbing and chopping so she could deliver the queen's breakfast each morning and steal a second in these rooms. Imagining how it would be if the king acknowledged their relationship.

"Come on." Mirabelle nudges me forward and makes straight for the vanity atop which sits a medium-sized box made of black lacquered wood. She tries the lid, but it's locked, so she rummages around the miniature bowls of powder and parfum.

"The key isn't here. Like I knew it wouldn't be." She slams her fist against the box and glares at me. "This was a waste of time."

"Thankfully, getting into things I shouldn't happens to be one of my specialties." I take the box from her, find an ivory hairpin on the vanity, and insert it into the lock. After a few twists and jiggles, it clicks, and I throw back the lid with a triumphant grin. A pocket-sized book made of worn red leather shines up at me. A strangled sob bursts from Mirabelle's lips and she snatches it with a speed that rivals the pickpockets in Les Halles. Then she holds it to her chest and inhales deeply.

She looks so vulnerable, gripping that book as if it's the most precious treasure in this palace. I fidget. It's undeniably intimate seeing someone love something so much—like cracking a window to the innermost part of their soul—and it makes me so uncomfortable, I blurt something peevish so she'll stop. "Do you still think this was a waste of time?"

She smacks my shoulder with the book, stuffs it down her bodice, and finally moves toward the doors.

A chambermaid emerges from the adjacent garderobe when we're halfway across the room and crashes into Mirabelle. Who in turn crashes into me. The maid drops the ewer of water she was carrying, and it shatters with a crack so loud it sounds like every windowpane in the palace is breaking. Louis and my sisters probably heard it from the sewer. Which is bad enough, but then the girl starts screaming.

I lunge forward to silence her, but Mirabelle beats me to it. She hefts a water pitcher off the bedside table, closes her eyes, and whirls. The jug makes a wet thunking noise against the girl's head, and she collapses into the spilled water and broken bits of porcelain, lying perfectly still, arms and legs splayed at awkward angles.

We both stare down at her, stunned.

Mirabelle drops to her knees. "Please don't be dead," she mutters as she places her ear near the girl's lips. After several excruciating seconds, she sags with relief. "She's breathing. A bit of butterbur for her head wound and . . ."

Mirabelle keeps talking, but I'm no longer listening. I check the chamber door, then look back at the unconscious girl. I don't mean to be insensitive, but La Voisin will have the portcullises lowered and every corner of the palace overturned if she finds a body in her bedchamber. And we cannot return to the lab for butterbur—whatever that is.

I bend over, lift the girl gently over my shoulder, and carry her from the room.

"What are you doing?" Mirabelle demands.

"What needs to be done." I stuff the maid into the alcove in the hallway and pull the curtain strategically around her body.

"We can't just leave her."

"We can and we will." I hook Mirabelle by the elbow and drag her back toward the servants' stairs. "It's just a knock on the head. She'll be fine."

Mirabelle glowers at me.

"Well, she may have a skull-splitting headache for a few days, but it won't kill her. I, on the other hand, will be executed the moment I'm discovered, and since you made it my duty to ensure we don't get caught, that's what I'm doing."

Mirabelle looks back at the alcove once more but eventually sighs and follows.

"You can make up for nearly killing her by healing another," I say as we wind down the stairs.

Mirabelle kicks the back of my ankle, and I trip, nearly smashing my nose on the stone steps. I suppose I deserved that.

As we hurry past the kitchens, a woman in a black dress with a severe gray bun spots us and insists we follow her, but I break into a run. I'm not about to be caught now, when we're so close to pulling this off. We batter through the servants entering the castle, then slow to a walk, our heads bowed as we make our way across the crowded courtyards and past the porters at the gatehouse.

Even after I've shed my disguise and we've blended into the bustle of the busy streets, we continue to plow past vegetable carts and shopkeepers waving baguettes and children selling flowers until the decrepit millinery comes into view. It feels oddly reminiscent of running through the streets the day before, when I freed her from the sewer. That same breathless, buzzing energy. That same *rightness*, dancing across my skin, warmer than the midday sun. Our boots pound the cobbles in perfect cadence. The air between us feels charged and electric. I'm as raucous and jittery as if I spent the night playing winning hands of lansquenet.

"We seem to have a knack for narrow escapes," I say.

Mirabelle allows a tiny smile and her fingers brush the front of her dress, where her father's grimoire hides. "I suppose we do."

13

MIRABELLE

I cannot stop staring at Father's grimoire. Cannot stop running my fingers over the crumbling leather binding. It's truly in my possession—his thoughts, his handwriting, that sweet, sweet scent of sage. I bury my nose in the brittle pages and pull a deep breath into my lungs. Holding it. Imagining Father's wily, wicked grin. How he would have loved this intrigue!

That's my girl, risking all in the name of alchemy!

I lie down on a pile of scraps in the corner of the millinery and will myself to sleep. I need to be well rested and ready to begin making curatives the moment Gris delivers my supplies.

But Josse has other plans.

"I don't know how you can sleep!" he says, tromping around the shop all wide-eyed and red-cheeked, like a child on May Day. "There's so much to do, so much to plan."

"It's simple. You shut your mouth and close your eyes and lie very still—which I'm beginning to realize may not be simple for you . . ."

He laughs as if I'm joking. "Are you always so calm and practical, poisoner?"

"Are you always so loud and overzealous, princeling?"

He scrunches his brows and strokes his chin. "Why, yes. I do believe I am. And you should thank me for it. You wouldn't have accomplished half as much without me."

"*I* convinced *you* to sneak into the Louvre! You demanded I stay hidden in this dusty hovel."

"Did I?" He waves a hand. "I didn't mean forever, obviously."

"Obviously," I bite back at him. But a hint of a smile creeps across my lips. He's a bit like a puppy: exuberant and excitable and thoroughly agitating, but so jaunty and eager you can't help but want to pat his head. The thought makes my smile widen, and I turn toward the wall to hide it as I drift off to sleep.

Just after midnight, a faint tap finally sounds at the millinery door and I scrabble to my feet. Josse jumps to follow but I wave him back, silently motioning for him to hide behind the counter. Gris may not recognize him right away, but Josse and his big mouth would undoubtedly blabber something revealing, and Gris cannot know the royals live. And he definitely cannot know that I'm working with them. He may be willing to overlook me brewing curatives in secret, but he would never overlook me aligning with the king's children. Bastard or not.

I crack the door open and peer out into the dark. "Gris?"

"Who else would deliver supplies at this hour?" A towering cloaked figure removes his hood, and the alabaster moonlight transmutes Gris's sandy hair to gold. He holds the satchels aloft.

"Come in, come in," I say.

"Not the fanciest of establishments, is it?" He frowns at the cobwebbed corners and moth-eaten curtains. I follow his gaze across the room, horrified to see Josse's tricorne hat hanging from the edge of the counter. My throat constricts and I scramble to invent an excuse, but Gris's gaze passes over the hat as if it isn't out of the ordinary.

I suppose it isn't, in a millinery.

A nervous burst of laughter sputters from my lips.

"What's so funny?" he asks.

"Nothing. It's nothing."

Gris arches a brow.

"It's just . . . this millinery is certainly preferable to that soul-sucking dungeon laboratory at the palace."

"I can't argue with that." Gris hefts the other two sacks onto the counter and starts to unload the phials.

"Don't trouble yourself. It's late. I'll do it."

"I don't mind. Like you said, it would be nice to make curatives again for a change."

He edges around the counter close to where Josse is hidden, and I shout, "*Don't!*"

Gris stumbles, knocks his hip against the corner of the table, then turns to gape at me.

"I-I'm so exhausted from sneaking in to the palace earlier," I explain. "I'm in no state to brew anything. And it would be unwise to keep you from the Louvre any longer. What if someone notices your absence?"

"It's the middle of the night."

"When has that ever stopped Mother? You know how she is." I take his arm and tug him gently toward the door. "I can't have her asking questions."

Gris works his jaw. "I still don't understand why—"

"It's all too much. You of all people know what I suffered at the hands of the royals. I need time to recuperate." I draw a shaky breath and make a blubbering sound when I exhale.

Gris's face immediately softens—like I knew it would. He pulls me in to his broad chest and tucks my head beneath his chin, whispering soothing words while petting my ragged wisps of hair. Then I really do want to cry because I'm the most deplorable liar in all of France. And the most deplorable friend in the entire world. Using him. Manipulating him. But what choice do I have? I would tell him if I could, if I thought there was a sliver of a chance he'd understand. But he only sees his father's bruised and battered face swinging from the gallows when he looks at any member of the nobility. They are all the Chevalier de Lorraine. And Mother saved him. He will always defend her, and I can't blame him for it.

"Get some rest," he says softly. "I'll keep your secret, and keep you safe, until you're ready to return."

I offer him a teary smile and follow him to the door, not bothering to remind him that I'm never returning.

As soon as he disappears around the corner, I race to the board and tear open the satchels, eager to get my hands on the supplies. Distilling tinctures and tonics will quiet my grumbling conscience. It will allow me to help the people. It's the answer to everything. It always has been.

Josse pops up from behind the counter, shaking his head. "This is why you can't be trusted: One moment you're crying, and the next you're cackling with glee. Poor bugger." He looks to the door and tuts.

"I should have let Gris find you," I grumble as I untie a bundle of blackberry leaves and begin chopping them into perfect squares. "Yet for some reason I'm deceiving my dearest friend for *you*."

"Not for me. For 'the cause.' Which is bigger than us all. Now where do we begin?" Josse leans across the counter and flips open Father's grimoire, sullying it with his grubby fingers, thumbing through the pages as if they contain common kitchen recipes.

My ears ring, and a tidal wave of rage rises up within me. I crash into him and wrestle the book from his hands. "Don't touch that!"

"You could have just said so." He brushes off his breeches and stares as if I attempted to bite him. "I'll just—" He reaches for one of the satchels, and this time I restrain myself. Slightly.

"Don't!"

He tosses his hands into the air and blows out a frustrated breath. "How am I supposed to assist you if I'm not allowed to touch anything?"

"You're not."

"But I thought—"

"You thought wrong."

He drags his fingers through his hair. "How are we supposed to unite the people if we cannot even unite ourselves?"

"Simple. You manage your side of the bargain and I'll manage mine. Once you've convinced Louis to give the common folk the same consideration as the nobility, I'll start working on your antidote to Viper's Venom. In the meantime, I'll be making curatives. As planned."

"If you recall, I betrayed my brother and my best friend in order to free you from the sewer, which means I'm not exactly welcome to return anytime soon."

I heft a gallipot to the hearth and arrange the sad remnants of half-charred logs into a pile. Then I strike a bit of flint to start a fire. "You're going to have to face them eventually if our plan is going to work."

"I know that. But I think they'll be more inclined to listen if we've laid the groundwork first—if we can show them the commoners are open to the idea of reinstating the royal family. I don't know why you're being so difficult. I thought we were past all this."

"You thought we were *past all this?*" I turn to face him, my arms crossed and my voice low. "Just days ago, I was tied up in the sewer and you were prepared to kill me."

"But I didn't. And we've been—"

"Then once I was supposedly 'free,' you followed me because you still didn't trust me—even though I had proven myself, *twice*, by healing your sisters and Desgrez. Forgive me if I'm not ready to hand over my most prized possession and the secrets of my trade. Trust goes both ways."

Josse opens his mouth, and then promptly closes it. Speechless for the first time in his life, I'd wager. "If I can't assist you and I can't return to the sewer, what do you expect me to do, exactly?"

I remove a kettle from one of the satchels and hold it out. "I need water. I saw a trough behind one of the gambling halls. And once you've done that, you can collect firewood."

"Anything else?" His voice has taken on a cold edge and he yanks the kettle from my hand.

A fingertip of guilt needles my side as he storms out of the millinery. It was low of me to relegate him to the role of a servant, but it's not as if he's treated me as an equal. Why should I be the first to bend?

I begin chopping watercress and fennel leaves for hunger tonic, expecting the familiar work to blot out the world and lull me under its spell as it always does, but my gaze keeps returning to the door. That invisible finger keeps jabbing my ribs.

Eventually Josse returns, banging the full kettle down on the table and tossing an armful of wood beside the small fireplace.

Then he skulks to the far wall and plunks down with a thump. "Is this far enough? Or am I still too close?"

"That's fine," I say. Then I add, softer, "I don't mind if you watch."

"How magnanimous of you."

I set my pestle down and look at him. "I'm not trying to be cruel. It's difficult for me to trust anyone. Surely you understand?"

He laughs. "I'm afraid you're sniveling stories and quivering lip won't work on me."

"I was trying to apologize."

"Were you? An apology usually includes the words *I'm sorry.*"

"Perhaps you should heed your own advice—you have just as much to be sorry for." I take up the pestle and resume dashing it against the mortar bowl. Pretending it's the princeling's head.

Neither of us speaks for well over an hour. I finish the hunger tonic, portion it into phials, and begin a vermifuge of agrimony and garlic.

"What are you making now?" Josse asks. "It reeks to high heavens."

"I thought you weren't interested."

"Well, I've nothing else to do—you've made certain of that."

I stifle another twinge of guilt. He was brimming with excitement when we first returned from the Louvre, and now he's slumped in the corner like a whipped mule. I sigh and offer him a sliver of information.

"It's a vermifuge."

"And that is?"

"It expels worms from the gut."

He grimaces as he gains his feet and slowly makes his way to the counter. "That explains the smell. And that other remedy you made?"

"A hunger tonic. We distribute it to the poor to ease the emptiness in their bellies and provide enough sustenance to keep them from starving." Josse is silent for a long moment, watching me stir the viscous mixture. My arms ache and sweat pours down my cheeks. I wipe my face on my sleeve and readjust my hands, but it's too late. Angry blisters are bubbling across my palms.

"Alchemy looks like backbreaking work."

"I am more than capable," I assure him.

He holds up his hands. "I never said you weren't. I didn't realize the Shadow Society provided actual remedies. I thought it was all love potions and inheritance powders."

"Of course you did. It's easier for all you rutting royals to assume we're witches."

"Just as you assume all us *rutting royals* are pompous, self-centered puttocks." I scowl but he holds my gaze, daring me to look away first. When it becomes apparent that neither of us is going to back down, he says, "Did La Voisin teach you all this?"

"No, my father taught me."

"Lesage? The sorcerer? He doesn't seem like the healing type."

"Lesage is *not* my father." I stir the vermifuge so violently that droplets spatter across the counter. "Just one of Mother's many lovers. My real father, Antoine Monvoisin, was a jeweler by trade, though he didn't acquire his gold and silver through traditional channels—if you take my meaning."

"He transmuted it. He was an alchemist, like you."

"The best in all of France," I say proudly. "Far more than your average false coiner or immortality chaser. His true talent was in spagyrics—plant alchemy. This was his life's work; he developed hundreds of substances. . . ." I place my palm reverently over the grimoire, as if Father's heart still beats within its pages.

"He took me as his apprentice when I was only seven. Mother said I was too young, but Father insisted I was ready. He snuck me a rope and instructed me to climb down from my chamber window that night and join him in the laboratory. I did so every night thereafter, and by the time Mother discovered our deception, I had learned to make simple salves and fever tonics, so it was easier to persuade her to let me continue; I was already a benefit to the Society. Father was always encouraging me—and sometimes shoving me—into action. He still is."

The memory makes me smile and ache all at once. After Father's death, Mother tried to warp my perception of him with her resentment and pain—and I was so desperate for her approval, I nearly gave in. But now that I feel Father's determination rising up within me, he is everywhere. His spirit permeates everything. And I know he is proud of me.

"My mother was something of a troublemaker too," Josse says with a wistful smile. "Well, technically she wasn't my mother, but she took me in when my true mother—a scullery maid whom

I never met—was dismissed shortly after my birth. Rixenda treated me like her own. When I was ten, I began listening to Louis's lessons through the window because the noble children mocked my inability to read. One day I sneezed and the tutor discovered me. He lashed my palms thirty times, and when Rixenda saw the bleeding welts, she made straight for the palace, shouting words so filthy even the stable hands blushed.

"'He won't be touching you again, my boy. I promise you that,' she said when she returned, wiping her hands on her apron like she did after skinning a rabbit. The next morning at breakfast, the man's eye was a deep shade of plum and he was telling everyone he'd fallen off his horse!"

I laugh. "She sounds fearsome."

"She was. But delightful, too. My father was the Sun King, but it was Rixenda who shone brightest at the palace. She lit up even the servants' quarters with her charm and wit."

"You have that in common." The words slip out, gliding along the easy ebb and flow of our conversation. I tighten my grip on my spoon and pray he didn't hear. But when I glance up, the princeling is grinning like a fox.

"You think me charming?"

"As charming as a snake," I mumble at the vermifuge to hide my burning cheeks. Curse the princeling for wheedling beneath my defenses like that. And curse myself for allowing it.

I turn to the hearth, but Josse follows, leaning languidly against the wall. "Where's your father now?"

"Dead," I say flatly.

After a beat he replies, "Rixenda's dead too. She was stabbed during the attack on Versailles and left to bleed on the roadside. She distracted the rebels so we could flee."

The ground seems to roll beneath my feet and my stomach flips. I sag against the wall.

"Are you all right?" Josse searches my face, his eyes full of concern. The knot of remorse swelling in my throat makes it impossible to answer. He lost everything that day—both mother and father.

Because of me.

I poisoned the king. I made it possible for the Shadow Society to seize his home and stab Rixenda.

Tell him.

He will see how impossible our partnership truly is. It will be the swiftest and simplest way to be rid of him. I'll no longer have to worry about him constantly peering over my shoulder and suspiciously watching my back—following me like he doesn't trust me.

He shouldn't trust you.

I wet my lips and turn, but he's looking at me with the oddest expression. Thoughtful and faraway. "In a strange way, you remind me of Rixenda. Obsessed with your pots and recipes—she was mistress of the kitchens—and always ordering everyone about. Pretending to be prickly to hide the softness underneath."

"I'm sure we're nothing alike," I say vehemently. But a warm, melty feeling is unspooling in my chest, and I jab the handle of my stirring spoon into my stomach to stop it. *Tell him before he makes any more ridiculous comparisons.*

But when I glance around the millinery and try to imagine the space without him in it, I can't. The quiet is suffocating.

"I'm going out," I announce.

"But it's so late—"

"I need to think."

"About what?"

About the fact I killed your father and feel guilty about it—and feel even guiltier for growing used to your company . . . "Viper's Venom!" I practically shout. He won't argue with that. I grab Father's grimoire and head for the door. "Alone," I add when I hear his footsteps follow. "I prefer to work out troubling compounds on my own."

"I wouldn't be much help anyway. I'll just stay here and . . . not touch anything." Josse's voice is playful and altogether too familiar, and it sets a hoard of pesky butterflies to flapping in my belly.

I do the only sensible thing I can think to stop them. I slam the door and bury myself in my work.

14

JOSSE

I try not to be bothersome, really I do, but after five days of watching Mirabelle slave over her curatives from dawn until dusk and experiment through the night, working out the antidote to Viper's Venom, I'm feeling rather bored and useless. Like the universe is having a good laugh at my expense. I had suggested she hide out and do nothing, which is precisely what *I'm* doing now.

I'm also desperate to see my sisters. It's been nearly a week. They haven't a clue if I'm alive, or if I'm ever coming back. And I haven't a clue how they're healing. Mirabelle keeps assuring me they should be back to full strength, but I won't relax until I see it for myself. And I cannot return to the sewer until we've good news to report to Louis and Desgrez. Which means we need to leave this miserable shop and begin distributing tinctures and tonics.

"I know you're *sensitive* about other people touching your supplies, but perhaps if I help, the work will go twice as fast," I suggest yet again, only now I've resorted to begging. "I'll do exactly as you say. You can even measure the herbs and hand me the appropriate phials so I don't foul up your organization." *Even though there doesn't seem to be any method of organization.* Herbs are scattered across the table and half the phials are tipped on their sides.

Mirabelle pauses in the middle of stirring some fever draught or another and wipes her sleeve across her forehead. It sends her close-cropped curls into disarray. "What about either of those things sounds quicker than simply doing it myself?"

"If you'd just allow me to—"

"What are the four humours? What is the difference between fusion and fixation? How do you operate an alembic?"

"Oh, hell, not the questions again! You know I don't know the answers."

"Then you're not prepared to work as an alchemist. It's a precise science that requires a lifetime of study. It isn't something you can—"

I let my forehead plunk against the wall. "Are you almost finished, then? Not that I'm trying to rush you," I add when she shoots me a withering look.

"I will never be *finished.* There will always be more curatives to brew."

"Yes, yes, of course. What I meant to say is, have you brewed enough to begin the actual healing portion of our plan?"

"Are you growing weary of my company, princeling?"

At moments like this, I want to shout a resounding *YES!* But I bite my tongue because from the way she accentuates *princeling,* it's clearly no longer a slight. It isn't a compliment, by any means, but I'm fairly positive she's growing less weary of my company.

And aside from feeling utterly worthless, I've almost come to enjoy watching her work. It's fascinating to see how seemingly common ingredients combine into powerful elixirs. Nearly as fascinating as watching Mirabelle herself. Her eyes take on this glassy, dreamlike quality, and she becomes a part of the laboratory—her arms are the spoons, her hands the phials, and with every pinch of herbs, she adds a bit of herself into the elixirs.

After three more days of brewing and stockpiling, the cupboards are filled with an array of healing tinctures and tonics, and Mirabelle has finally managed to distill an antidote for Viper's Venom.

"We won't know how effective it is until it's administered," she says, holding the phial to the light and inspecting the blue-black liquid as you would a diamond.

"So what do we do? Wait around until we hear rumors of nobles dying?"

"Do you have a better suggestion?"

I grumble but shake my head.

"I'll sew a phial of the antidote into the hem of my skirt, so we're prepared at a moment's notice."

"What about the rest of it?" I nod to the vast collection of bottles.

Mirabelle's lips lift into a grin and she finally says the two glorious words I've been waiting for: "We're ready."

I jump from the floor, where I was becoming too well acquainted with dust bunnies, and shout, "Thank the saints! I was beginning to think I'd die of old age before we actually accomplished anything."

"Poor, neglected princeling." She pretends to wipe a tear for me. "*You* may have accomplished nothing, but *I* accomplished more in a week than many alchemists could accomplish in months. Now, have you seen the milk cart beside the cottage at the end of the street?"

"Of course." I've spent so many hours staring out these windows, I could account for every pebble in the road.

"Good. Go borrow it."

"You mean steal it!"

"It isn't stealing if we plan to return it."

"And what if I'm caught?"

Mirabelle shoots me an exasperated look. "You've been begging to help for a week, and when I finally give you a duty, you complain. It's the dead of night and the cart's sitting out there for the taking. If you bungle that, you deserve to be caught."

I suppose she has a point. I slink out the door, creep down the moonlit street, and return a few minutes later with the creaking cart in tow. Mirabelle describes the contents of each bottle as she adds them to the cart. "Does this mean I'll actually be permitted to touch them in order to distribute the medications?"

"If you're lucky." She flashes me a goading smile. "Now keep quiet and stay close." She clips down the street, clinging to the shadows as we scurry from building to building.

I heave the rattling cart forward and try to keep up. The sky is beginning to gray at the edges—so late that the revelers have finally retired, but early enough that the fishermen have yet to set their traps. The cool spring air ruffles my hair and whispers across my neck, sending chills dancing down my limbs. Or perhaps they are chills of excitement.

"How much farther?" I whisper.

Mirabelle peeks around a corner, then waves me forward. "The encampment is just up ahead, on the rue du Temple. It's where we originally began healing the poor and sick and establishing the Shadow Society's reputation. We've been helping them for years."

"Then won't their loyalty be to La Voisin?"

"You've never been hungry, have you?" She looks at me as if I'm sporting Louis's jewel-encrusted doublet and powdered wig. "Their loyalty belongs to whoever has aided them most recently. And, lucky for us, Mother's been too busy putting down rebellions to distribute any kind of relief."

We dash down two more blocks. The lights of dozens of tiny fires prick the darkness, but just before we cross the final intersection, a group of Society soldiers round the corner.

I leave the cart and dive into an impossibly small gap between townhouses. Mirabelle smashes in behind me. The space is too narrow to be considered an alley, and her wild heartbeat pounds against my chest. Her hot breath races across my neck. My hands are pressed into the bricks on either side of her face, and she squeezes her eyes shut, digging her fingernails into the grout.

"That house there," one of the soldiers says, and the others rumble a reply. Every muscle in my body tightens and I draw my fingers into a fist. They won't take us without a fight. I watch the entrance to the alleyway for their crimson cloaks and masked faces, but a door bangs open several houses away and a woman screams.

"Where are the royals?" they shout at her. "Your neighbor reported hooded figures coming and going at odd hours of the night. And a fleur-de-lis pendant flies from your back window."

"Lies!" she wails. "I haven't heard or seen anything of the sort!"

The soldiers continue shouting and the woman continues crying until, finally, their footsteps *thump, thump, thump* down the street.

When I peek around the wall, the woman is sprawled across the threshold of her door, sobbing and clutching the frame.

A cold sweat beads across my face, and my legs twitch. I want to go to her, pick her up, and tell her how sorry I am. I knew the Shadow Society would be hunting for Louis and my sisters, but I didn't know it would involve banging down doors and accosting innocent people. How many are suffering in our stead?

Mirabelle touches my shoulder gently. Her dark eyes lock on mine and she tugs my cloak. Woodenly, I take up the cart and follow her the final block to the rue du Temple. But then another wave of horror knocks me upside the head the moment we enter the encampment. The reek of excrement and unwashed bodies is so intense, I have to clench my teeth so as not to gag, and the few ramshackle shelters are naught but piles of rotted wood and crumbling stone. Most people lie sprawled out in the gutters, their tattered clothes revealing gaunt ribs and bone-thin limbs.

The conditions are too squalid for rats, let alone people.

How could Father have been so heartless and unseeing? How

could he allow people to live in such squalor? But then a more sobering thought comes: I am hardly better. I was content to hide away in the palace, raising hell and feeling sorry for myself, instead of considering what might be happening beyond the gates. I may be a bastard, but I am infinitely more privileged than some.

"I-I didn't know." I turn a slow circle, sickness rising in my throat.

"It's a lot to take in at first." Mirabelle casts me an encouraging smile and urges me down the street. We veer toward a pile of pallets burning in the center of the road—it seems to be the center of activity. Old men warm their hands over the flames while middle-aged women dry their sodden petticoats. A group of teenage girls cook unidentifiable scraps of meat on sticks.

I can feel their eyes on us—on the cart specifically.

"We've come to help," Mirabelle says, removing a jar and holding it aloft. "We've brought hunger tonic and other curatives." Without a trace of hesitation, she turns to the nearest man, uncorks the bottle of watery green hunger tonic, and offers him a spoonful.

He leans forward and sniffs. Then he slowly, slowly brings his lips to the spoon. The people shift as he swallows, their muscles coiling and bunching as if they are cats readying to pounce.

The man smacks his lips and sighs. Tears run down his face, cutting channels through the filth. "'Tis hunger tonic indeed."

That's all it takes. The decrepit hovels groan, and scores of people scurry toward us like termites out of the woodwork.

"Ready yourself." Mirabelle shoves a phial of coughing syrup into my right hand and hunger tonic into the left.

"I don't know how—"

"It's easy. Just help them."

In the next instant, we're swarmed. People rush around us like a raging river, and I struggle to keep my head above the current. A thousand different hands grasp at me; a hundred voices plead. The night is freezing but I am suddenly drenched in sweat.

Where do I even begin?

Wide-eyed, I look over at Mirabelle, and the sight makes me pause. The crowd is shoving and shouting and waving all around her as well, but her face is serene. Her hands are sure and steady as she leans forward to offer a mud-caked child a spoonful of hunger tonic. She turns to them one by one, caressing their cheeks and taking their outstretched hands. She's so slight that she should be lost in the clamor of the teeming street, but she burns brighter than them all. A candle flaring in the dark.

She looks over, as if she can feel me watching, and flashes a smile filled with such overwhelming joy, it knocks something loose inside of me. She gives me a quick nod of encouragement and turns back to the people. I swallow and do the same.

I'm tentative at first, but I cast around until I find a face that looks almost familiar—an old, toothless woman with white snowstorm hair. It isn't Rixenda, of course, but the similarity makes it easier to be bold. She's clutching her chest and hacking into a sodden handkerchief, so I pull her close and administer the coughing syrup with a timid smile.

She smiles back and plants a sloppy kiss on my cheek. I still for the briefest moment, then burst out laughing and return the kiss. The crowd roars their approval, and I turn to the woman directly to her right—a mother holding two squalling babies. And then to a bearded man easily twice my size. On and on and on, until my bottles are empty and I wish, more than anything, I could somehow conjure more.

Mirabelle was right when she said her work would never be finished. There are so many who need help. So many I hadn't considered until now.

The shame of it drags at my shoulders.

When I first suggested we use Mirabelle's curatives to unite the peasants and nobility, I was thinking solely of my sisters, determined to keep them safe. I didn't care about the poor and downtrodden. I was no better than my father.

"We'll brew more remedies and return straight away," I call to the scores of people still waiting. "You have my word."

My promise is met with a chorus of cheers. "Our thanks to La Voisin," a voice shouts. Others take up the cry, and I have to climb atop the milk cart to get them to quiet down.

"This goodwill is not from La Voisin," I declare. "She and her Shadow Society have proven no better than the former king, forgetting their duty to the people as soon as they gained control."

The people whisper back and forth for a moment, then "Ayes" of agreement ripple through the throng.

"These curatives are from the royal family."

Someone barks a derisive laugh. "Sure they are. Do they also wish to dress us in silks and put us up in their palaces?"

A dozen other shouts and scoffs join in.

"It's true!" I yell. "Louis, the dauphin, is alive and wishes to make amends."

"That will take a fair bit more than coughing syrup!"

"Which he is prepared to give. In exchange for your support, he will continue to provide treatment and aid, but he also wishes to give you a voice—representatives who will bring the concerns of the common people before him, and together you will devise acceptable solutions. A union of the common man and noble man!"

"Lies!" A handful of voices cry immediately. "Who are you to make such high promises?"

I blow out a breath and stand taller. "I give you my word, as Josse de Bourbon, bastard son of the late king. I was spit upon and downtrodden, like you. Hated and cast aside. I'm not the same breed of royal who left you to freeze on this street, and if you'll lend me your trust, I promise you'll be given the respect you deserve. My mother was a scullery maid. I am one of you. I'll fight for you—if you'll let me."

No one cheers, but they don't boo me either, which feels rather miraculous, given it's my first speech. The people huddle into groups to whisper, and after what feels like a lifetime, a woman

steps forward and asks, "If he's the bastard prince, who are *you?*"
She points a crooked finger at Mirabelle.

"I am . . ." Mirabelle's voice trails off. She cannot use her given
name, as it will undoubtedly get back to her mother. She sputters
and looks to me, panic flashing in her eyes.

"La Vie!" I bellow the first thing that comes to mind. "This is
Mademoiselle La Vie." I offer Mirabelle a hand and pull her up on
the cart beside me. "It was she who created your salves and tinctures.
She who brought your plight to my attention. She is your true savior
and the leader of this revolution. Tell everyone who will listen."

Mirabelle blinks up at me, repeating the name as if I said
something miraculous. The men and women take up a chant, and
the name swells louder and louder as we hop down from the milk
cart and make our way back up the rue du Temple.

"La Vie! La Vie! La Vie!"

Life, life, life.

"That name—" Mirabelle says reverently. "I don't deserve it."

"Of course you do. You're brilliant." The words tumble out before
I can help them, and Mirabelle inhales sharply. I failed to use a
mocking tone or don a teasing smirk. I have never complimented
her in earnest, and my mouth bobs open and closed like a codfish's.

She nudges my side. "You're not so bad yourself, princeling.
Healing suits you. And the people adore you." She gestures to the
men and women clustered all around, and their grateful smiles
turn my bones to slush. Their cheers fill my belly like warm soup
on a frigid night.

It's wondrous.

And terrifying.

I am not a hero.

I duck my head and tighten my grip on the milk cart. "They're not cheering for *me*. They're cheering for the curatives *you* made. I'm just the delivery boy."

"Delivery boys don't generally make such impassioned speeches. It's okay to care, you know. You don't have to put on your act for me. Or them."

What act? I want to retort. *There's only me—Josse. Bastard. Rake. Hellion.*

Healer, a new voice whispers. *Brother. Leader.*

I try to shoo the thoughts away, but they buzz back like horseflies. Biting me. Insisting they have always been there— hidden. It's easier to be vexing than vulnerable. Safer to push people away rather than be turned away. Less painful to live up to low expectations than attempt to rise above them and be found wanting. I was so convinced I would never earn Father's approval, I pretended not to want it.

And now I will never have it.

You shouldn't want it, I scold myself. *Look around. Look what he permitted.*

And I do look—at the people clapping my back and calling my name. For the first time in my life, I am a success rather than a disappointment.

I feel like cheering and retching, both.

What if I prove them wrong?

What if you prove them right?

Echoes of Rixenda's final plea hum in my ears, and shivers flash down my arms. Is this the reason she always thwacked me with her spoon and ignored my complaints? Was she trying to tell me I could use my position for good—if I was willing to try? I may not be able to earn the king's approval, but I already had Rixenda's. And I could honor that by caring for *her* people.

My people.

When we reach the end of the rue du Temple, Mirabelle and I give a final wave and slip into the shadows. Overhead, the velvet sky has lightened to heather gray, and soft pink brushstrokes paint the underbellies of the clouds. Shopkeepers draw back their curtains and open their doors. I inhale the sweet scent of rising dough, marveling at how the city feels fresh. New. Reborn with possibility. As if I'm standing atop the towers of Notre-Dame, watching our next steps unfold like points on a map.

If we immediately distill more remedies, perhaps we can return to the rue du Temple as soon as tomorrow night. Once we've helped all of the poor, then we can turn our focus to the nobility.

My plan will work. I'm sure of it now.

I bend a glance at Mirabelle, and she's quick to meet my gaze. As if expecting it. Hoping for it, even. Neither of us speaks, but I can tell by the hopeful smile spreading across her face that she feels it too—how the air between us hums like a bowstring, vibrating with energy and possibility as we make our way back to the millinery.

Once we're safely inside, Mirabelle returns to the counter and I drop into my corner, no longer perturbed in the least to watch her work. But she bangs her fist on the table. "Well, don't just sit there, princeling. There's work to be done."

My eyebrows arch. "I thought I wasn't permitted to assist you."

"You can't be trusted with the recipes, of course. But I suppose you might be allowed to do some chopping. We might as well put your kitchen skills to use." She flashes a teasing smile and slides a knife to the edge of the counter.

The rest of the day passes in a blur of frenzied activity. I mince mountains of lemon balm and yarrow while Mirabelle distills more hunger tonic and coughing syrup and a tincture to counteract White Death. One remedy after the next until the air is thick with steam and my limbs feel like overcooked cabbage. Even then, we press on, propelled by the fire that burned in the eyes of the poor. The fire that sparks and crackles and lashes between Mirabelle and me. Hope and exhilaration and something *more*. A camaraderie and enticement that makes our gaze snag from across the room.

Two nights later, we return to the rue du Temple and distribute more curatives to the homeless. And three nights after that, we make our way to the Hôtel-Dieu, the old, moldering hospital on the Île de la Cité, which my father allowed to fall to ruin since it was "overrun" by the rabble.

It's a sorry sight; the stones are cracked and pitted and black mold dangles from the slatted windows. The air within is musty and damp, like the inside of a cave, and it reeks of rotting leaves and sickness. My gut clenches with what is becoming an all too familiar indignation, and I charge into the nearest ward.

The tiny room is crammed with dozens of rusted beds, each filled with two, sometimes three people. I remove my hat to greet them, but before I can say a word, a woman pushes up to her elbows and cries, "Mademoiselle La Vie! Thank the saints! We've been praying you would come."

Mirabelle lets out a loud breathy laugh and looks up at me. Her eyes well with tears as the name pings around the room, and she's still breathless and misty-eyed when we leave the Hôtel-Dieu hours later.

"They knew. They'd heard. And so quickly!" she gushes. "Can you believe it?"

I'd believe her capable of anything when she's grinning like that. Her smile is so dazzling, it could set the world ablaze. I have to keep a sharp eye on the cobbles to keep from drifting into her. And Mirabelle is definitely walking closer to me than she ever has before. I'm acutely aware of the flutter of her purple cape against my leg. Transfixed by her arm swinging so close to mine. The warmth of her fingers makes mine tingle in response. It would be so easy to reach out and take them.

The Josse of a week ago wouldn't have dared.

The Josse of today doesn't hesitate.

15

MIRABELLE

The bastard princeling is holding my hand.

And I don't hate it.

A part of me may actually *like* it.

I gape down at our intertwined hands, screaming at myself to pull away, but my rebellious fingers tighten. His hands aren't soft like a royal's should be, and I like the way his calluses slide against my palm, the way they fit so perfectly with mine.

"*La Vie*," he whispers. My heart pulses faster, beating in time to that glorious name.

It's the most beautiful sound in the world—to be life instead of death. To be loved instead of feared. I feel as giddy and as weightless as I did when Father used to hoist me onto his shoulders and we'd spin around the laboratory in a whirlwind of gold dust and sage leaves.

Josse stops and turns to me, bringing his other hand to my face. His feather-light fingertips trace across my cheekbone and tuck a wayward curl behind my ear. I implore myself not to look up, but like my fingers, my eyes refuse to obey. They explore his hopeful face; his strong square jaw and full lips; the dark strands of hair escaping from his tricorne hat; the way his eyes reflect the sunlight on the wet slate rooftops—gray and green and gold. Brash and brazen and beautiful.

And so eerily similar to the Sun King's, I suddenly can't breathe.

Can't move.

Can't do this.

I lurch back so swiftly, I topple into the gutter and soak my skirts.

Josse's hand hangs in the air for a moment before falling slack at his side. His face falls with it. "What's wrong? I thought—"

"There's nothing to think." This is absurd. Impossible. Josse would agree if he knew I'm the one who poisoned his father. He would be horrified for ever thinking there could be anything between us. So I clamp my lips together, wave my hand as if swatting a fly, and stomp up the road.

"I know you felt something," he calls after me.

"I'm not having this conversation here." I'm not having this conversation *anywhere,* but I know better than to say so or we'll be out here arguing all day. "We must return to the millinery *at once.*" I point down the street, at the candles flickering to life in several windows. "Not to mention a Society patrol could round the corner any moment."

Josse heaves the empty cart forward with a jerk. "Only if you tell me what changed your mind."

"Can't you just enjoy our accomplishment and not ruin it with all this?" I gesture between us.

"No."

"Fine. You want a reason?" I rack my brain for an excuse, since admitting that I'm scared of these feelings, and that I killed his father, are both out of the question. "Because you're royal," I blurt. "This is all a means to an end for you. Once Louis is restored to the throne, you'll return to your lavish palaces with your sisters and never spare a second thought for the thousands of people who still need aid. Or me."

The words feel like poison spitting from my lips. Horrible, disgusting lies. But it would be worse to admit the truth and see the hurt and revulsion on his face. There would be no more hiding. No more pretending or forgetting. I would be forced to face the horror of what I've done. Forced to accept that I'm just as guilty as the rest of the Society.

Josse's jaw tightens and he charges ahead, but two steps later, he drops the cart and pivots. "Is that what you honestly think of me? Was everything you said about 'healing suiting me' and 'the people adoring me' a lie?"

I bury my fingers in my hair and tilt my head back. I'm going to scream. Or blurt the truth just to be done with it—done with *him*. But halfway down the block, the creak of a door rends the quiet and we both dive behind a cluster of empty wine casks stacked outside a townhouse. The casks are on the small side, and we have to huddle low and close to stay hidden. The jagged cobbles bite my knees, and when I adjust my position, Josse makes a production of ensuring we don't touch. It takes all of my restraint not to push him into the road.

Shooting him an annoyed glance, I shift to squint through the casks. A lone man steps into the road. He's wearing a fine emerald frock coat and kidskin breeches with a cane clutched tight to his chest. His eyes flick up and down the street like a rabbit's, and he sets off at nearly a run, the ribbons on his coat trailing behind him.

Seconds after he rounds the corner, a tavern door on the opposite side of the road bangs open and another man stumbles out. He's mostly hidden beneath a black cloak, but I can see the high shine of his boots from here. All these lecherous noblemen, staggering back to their wives and children after a night of debauchery. This man heads in the same direction as the first, and I almost don't give him a second glance, but there's something about his painfully thin stature and off-kilter gait— the way he slinks more than walks—that sets the hairs prickling down my neck.

I know that walk.

I crawl to the edge of the wine casks to watch him pass. Through the sumptuous folds of his hood, I spy an intricate black mask framed by strings of long, greasy hair.

Fernand.

My body stiffens and the cobbles beneath me feel suddenly colder. Harder.

When he reaches the intersection, he quickly checks over his shoulder, then continues down the adjacent street walking much faster than he had been moments before—all vestiges of drunkenness gone.

"Hurry!" I nudge Josse. "Follow him."

"Why would we follow a drunkard home from the tavern?"

"Because that drunkard is my sister's fiancé, and I suspect he isn't drunk at all. He's up to something." I scurry out from behind the casks and Josse follows without complaint. Miracle of miracles!

The streets are winding and narrow, and by the time we reach the intersection, Fernand is vanishing down another. I clench my fists and break into a jog. We turn and turn again, leaving the crowded city center behind and entering the bourgeois neighborhoods. Lemon yellow and sage green villas line the road, each with a walled garden, dainty cast-iron balcony, and hanging plants.

Josse shoots me a meaningful look and we quicken our pace.

A dark, streaking shadow vaults over the wall surrounding the largest château at the end of the road. Fernand's so light-footed, I would have thought him a stray cat or a cloud passing in front of the moon if I didn't know to look for a man.

Josse and I hurry to the château and flatten ourselves against the wall. "Give me a leg up," I whisper. Josse cups his hands and hefts me up so I can peer into the garden and the house beyond. It's a towering stone behemoth with turrets on either end and a sharp, spired roof. The iron gate is festooned with flourishes in the shape of a family crest—a red cross surrounded by blue eagles.

I recognize it at once. Those banners flew from many a carriage in front of our house on the rue Beauregard: the esteemed Duc de Luxembourg—maréchal of France and perhaps Mother's most notable client, besides Madame de Montespan. Though their high status did them little good in the end.

The sound of crashing glass comes from somewhere within, and a moment later a bloodcurdling cry that's swiftly muffled.

I grip the top of the wall and hoist myself over, landing with a thump in the swampy ground. "Hurry!" I hiss to Josse. While he heaves himself over the wall with considerably more difficulty than Fernand, I fumble with my skirts and rip free the phial of antipoison I sewed into the hem of my maid's dress. If Fernand used Viper's Venom, we haven't long to administer the antidote.

We creep along the outside of the château and wait beside the servants' entrance. The tiny phial trembles in my fist. My pulse roars in my ears, so loud I lose track of the minutes. We cannot venture in before Fernand leaves. Neither of us could best the mercenary in a fight.

I never see Fernand, but I hear the slightest disturbance of pebbles in the road and nod at Josse. He throws his shoulder against the door and we race inside. My boots slide across the polished parquet as if it's ice.

"Monsier le Duc!" The hall is wide and soaring, and my voice rebounds off the wood paneling, shouting back at me. I pause to listen for an answer. When it doesn't come, I charge up the nearest staircase.

Abovestairs, the walls are adorned with heavy silk tapestries that billow and flap as we barrel into the great hall. It too is empty. Or has the appearance of being empty. I can feel dozens of eyes watching us from behind pillars and spying around corners. The house is crawling with servants but not a single one answers our call. Not a single one comes to their master's aid. I don't blame them. They've no way of knowing if the danger has passed.

I call out again, and this time, there comes the tiniest croak, hardly more than a wheeze.

"There!" Josse points to what looks to be a pile of soiled rushes in the corner, but now I see the man. The duc lies prostrate on his back. His hands jerk and flap at his sides, but his gimlet eyes are fixed and opened, so wide that they look to be protruding from his head.

I drop to my knees beside him and bite the cork from my phial of antipoison. "Drink." I tip the phial to his lips. He looks up at me and a low, guttural scream rattles from his lips. He thrashes violently, and Josse crouches down to hold his shoulders—as he did when I healed Françoise. "I am not my mother," I roar. "Drink if you want to live."

The fight goes out of him, and he stills long enough to allow the antipoison to dribble across his lips.

The hammering of my pulse counts the seconds.

I haven't a clue how long it will take.

When I reach six, the duc's jaw falls open and a virulent mixture of blood and phlegm spills over his chin. I try to turn him on his side, but he wails and arches back, his spine twisting at a sickening angle.

"Why isn't it working?" Josse stammers. His face is as pallid as the swath of moonlight pooling beneath the window. He looks like he's going to be sick.

"It will." I fumble again for the phial. According to my calculations, the man should have needed only half, but I pull him onto my lap, jam the bottle between his lips, and tip every last drop into his mouth.

You will not die.

I don't know if I think it, or whisper it, or scream it. But it booms like thunder in my mind. I barely knew the duc, and what I did know I didn't particularly like, but now I need him to live as surely as I need to breathe. I need my antipoison to be effective.

I grip the standing ruff of his collar so tightly, it rips away from his shirt when another tremor overtakes him, this one even more forceful than the first. He twists and moans, his bones snapping like the crack of a whip. His hand tightens around my forearm and his fingernails pierce my skin like five tiny blades. They cut deeper and deeper, until suddenly the pressure is gone. His legs give a final jerk, then he's still. Sprawled across my lap.

I shake him, even though I know it's useless. I shake him and shake him and shake him, as other grotesque, bleeding faces flash through my mind: the Sun King, Madame de Montespan, the Duc de Vendôme and his men.

How many more?

I whimper into the back of my hand, and the duc slides from my lap. His flaccid cheek presses into the floor.

"It was supposed to work. Why didn't it work?" I'm unsure if I'm talking to the duc, or Josse, or myself, but the words pour from me like the blood that poured from the duc's mouth. Drenching me until I'm shivering and shaking, rocking forward and back with my palms pressed to my eyes.

Spirits of hartshorn, camphor, and a strong brine of salt. Simmered for five hours and pushed through a sieve. I mentally review the recipe again and again.

I did everything right.

"Mira?" Josse touches my arm but I don't respond. "We need to go. There's nothing more we can do here."

I hunch over the duc's body like a vulture. There *is* more. I should be able to do more. If I could only just . . .

What? I may be an alchemist, but I've no Elixir of Life or panacea. I can't even brew a proper antipoison. I am a failure. A disgrace.

Josse begs and pleads, prods and pushes, but I sit on the floor, my skirts soaking up the Duc de Luxembourg's blood, until Josse loses patience. Muttering oaths, he crouches beside me and slides an arm around my back and beneath my arms. "I'm not being indecent. I'm just helping you up."

I'm too numb to fight him. He hefts me off the floor and I sag against his side, boneless and tripping as he guides me down the hall. Some far-off, distant part of me is mortified, but the part of me that failed to save the duc is too empty to care.

16

JOSSE

Mirabelle feels like a corpse in my arms—as if she is the one who perished from Viper's Venom. Her glassy eyes stare out at nothing. Her arms hang, leaden and swinging, as I retrace our steps down the stairs and into the garden.

I boost her over the wall and tug her down the street. The entire time she looks as if she's sleepwalking. I clear my throat and glance down every few minutes, imploring her to look at me. I haven't a clue what I'll say, but some sign of life would be comforting. She looks as brittle as a wasp's nest. Hollowed out with grief.

A light rain begins to fall, and I tug my hat lower to shield my face. Mirabelle does the opposite, tipping her head back, so streams of water trickle down her cheeks. They almost look like tears.

"You shouldn't be so hard on yourself," I blurt out when I can't stand the silence any longer. "You've saved scores of people. Think of the poor on the rue du Temple and the sick in the Hôtel-Dieu. This is just a minor setback."

"A minor setback?" she shouts, wheeling around. We both

flinch and scan the road. She steps closer and continues in a furious whisper. "How can you say that when you've seen what my mother is capable of? The good we've done won't matter. It isn't enough."

"So we'll do more . . ."

"I *can't* do more." Her voice cracks on the word *can't*. "My father believed I would be a great alchemist, but I can't even brew a simple antipoison."

"The Viper's Venom antipoison is hardly simple! You said so yourself."

"Forget everything I said. I haven't a clue what I'm talking about." She charges ahead, her fists clenched at her sides, and my breath comes a bit easier as I jog to catch up. I may not have consoled her, but anger is better than the blank nothingness of before.

Anger means she hasn't given up.

At long last, the millinery comes into view. I drag myself the final excruciating blocks, practically salivating at the thought of my lumpy pile of scraps. My body feels as limp as a deboned pheasant and I intend to fall through the door and sleep for days, but something crunches beneath my boots as I trudge up the steps. I squint through the shadows at what appear to be tiny bits of cracked white paint. Mirabelle is reaching for the door when I realize where the paint came from. I fling my arm out to stop her.

"Don't!"

"I swear on my father's grave if you try to—"

I put a finger to my lips and point up at the glaring brown hole in the center of the lintel, then down at the flecks of paint littering the steps like snow. "Someone's inside." I am barely short enough to pass through the door without disturbing the decaying paint, which means whoever entered is taller than I and still within, else their boots would have scattered the paint chips to the cobbles.

The color drains from Mirabelle's face, and we retreat down the steps to consider the shop. It looks exactly as it did when we left—windows blackened, shutters drawn, and the door shut tight—but those tiny flecks of paint scream, *Go no farther.* "Wait over there." I point to the alleyway between the millinery and a gambling den.

Mirabelle crosses her arms. "I don't need you to defend me."

"I never said you did. But I followed your lead on the rue du Temple and at the Hôtel-Dieu. Now it's your turn to follow mine."

Mirabelle scowls but complies.

Once she's safely tucked away, I draw the dagger from my boot and edge toward the door. Most likely it's a vagrant who took shelter in this seemingly abandoned shop. Nothing to fret over. Or it could be a Shadow Society patrol. Or what if it's La Voisin herself? Or Lesage?

A thrill courses through me. Terror, yes, but also a vicious, ravening hunger. A burning hope that it *is* one of them. My bones scream for vengeance—for Rixenda, who took a knife for me. For my sisters, who deserve a life in the sun. For Mirabelle, who was rejected and forsworn to the enemy. And for my father—

as much as it pains me to admit—who will never have the chance to see me as anything more than a bastard.

I roll my shoulders back and jam my boot into the door.

I'm so intent on finding La Voisin, shrouded in her double-headed eagle cape, I almost fail to recognize who stands before me.

"Desgrez?" A pulse of panic knocks me off-balance and my dagger clatters to the floor.

"You knew I would find you eventually." His voice spreads like ice beneath my skin, and I step back. He stands in the center of the room, stance wide and arms crossed over another disguise—this time a tattered brown priest's cassock.

"Desgrez," I say again, cursing the bedamned tremor in my voice. "I can explain."

"What is there to explain? You're a liar and a traitor. You *attacked* me and ran off with the poisoner. You abandoned your sisters."

"I haven't abandoned anyone. And I didn't betray you without reason. You're my best friend—"

He laughs—a quick, mirthless rush of breath. "You're no friend of mine." He means to lash me with his words, but a hint of emotion creeps into his voice, and he coughs to chase it away.

"I'm telling you, everything I've done is for good reason. We have a plan to take back Paris."

"Would you listen to what you're saying? Referring to yourself and the poisoner as *we!* Yes, I'm sure she'll *help* you hand the city right over to her mother. And your sisters along with it. Where is she?"

"Mirabelle wants nothing to do with her mother or the Shadow Society." I drag my fingers through my hair. "If you would just listen—"

"And you're foolish enough to believe her?"

"Has she ever given us reason to doubt? She guided us to safety during the procession, she healed the girls, she healed *you*. Or have you conveniently forgotten?"

Desgrez grunts. "I would have recovered on my own."

"You were a dead man."

"Better dead than a traitor."

"For the millionth time, I'm not a traitor!"

"If you're not a traitor, what, pray tell, is all of *this*?" He flings his hand at the counter cluttered with phials and forceps and herb packets. "It looks like a damned poison laboratory."

"That's part of our plan. If you would care to *listen* instead of snarling like the chimera atop the towers of Notre-Dame, I'd be happy to explain."

Desgrez folds his arms and glowers—the closest I'm going to get to an invitation.

"We're brewing curatives—*not poison*," I say pointedly, "which we've been distributing to the common people in the name of the royal family—to earn their favor and support. In addition to medication, we're offering the people a say in the government once Louis is restored to the throne—elected officials who will bring their concerns before the king. And we are devising an antipoison to administer to the remaining nobles whom La Voisin plans to target, so they will be indebted to us too. It will be a union of the common man and noble man—something neither Father nor La Voisin could accomplish. We'll be able to overthrow the Shadow Society with the strength of a unified city behind us."

I look triumphantly at Desgrez. I'm getting rather good at making these speeches.

He's silent for an endless moment, then he tips his head back and laughs. It feels like thousands of needles jabbing into my ears. "You poor witless fool! Please tell me the poisoner has tainted your water or sprinkled you with her devilish powders and that you don't honestly believe this ludicrous plan will work."

"It will work!" I bite back. "It's a good plan!"

"Perhaps it would be if you could believe a word out of her wicked, lying mouth."

"She's innocent. She was used and betrayed by her mother— just like us." Desgrez makes a show of wiping beneath his eyes and shaking his head, and my fingers curl into fists. "Stop laughing," I say, my voice a growl.

"I'll stop laughing as soon as you start using your head. I don't care what she told you or what she claims. She's lying. She's still one of them. She will always be one of them."

My heart bashes against my ribs like a caged bird, and my vision darkens around the edges, narrowing on Desgrez's infuriating face.

"You're impossible!" I shout. Then I do something very stupid—I lunge forward and ram my shoulder into Desgrez's chest, which I know will end badly, since he's the one who taught me to fight. He topples backwards and slams into the counter but somehow still manages to hook his foot around my ankle as he falls. Before I know what's happening, the back of my head cracks against the dusty floor.

Desgrez scrambles on top of me. I kick out and my boot sinks into his stomach. He doubles over, wheezing, and I try to roll away, but there's nowhere to go and I smash into the counter. A gallipot clangs to the floor, reverberating like a bell, followed by the crash of at least a dozen glass phials.

"What the devil is going on in here?" Mirabelle bangs into the shop. She looks first at her shattered equipment and then at Desgrez. *"You."*

Desgrez props himself up onto his elbows, his blue eyes dancing with amusement. "How precious, Josse. Your poisoner has come to rescue you."

"Tell him," I say to Mirabelle as I rub my throbbing head. "Tell him he can trust you. That you haven't hurt anyone, and you had nothing to do with the attack on Versailles."

She blinks as if I'm speaking in tongues. "What?"

"Tell him what you told me."

Slowly, she steps back and steadies herself against the door. Her eyes are wide and haunted, her cheeks the same chalk-white as the moon. "I don't understand. I can't. . . ." She grips her forehead. Droplets of sweat bead along her hairline. Her lips open and close, but she can't seem to find her voice.

A prickle of dread traces up my spine. "Mirabelle?"

She clasps her hands and looks heavenward.

"Mirabelle!"

I can feel Desgrez watching us. His eyes flit back and forth as if this is the most enthralling tennis match he's ever witnessed.

I clamber to my feet, heart battering inside my chest. "What, exactly, are you trying to say?"

"I'm sorry." A shudder grips her shoulders. "So sorry."

"*Why* are you sorry?" She's silent so long, I want to launch across the room and shake her. "Answer me!"

Finally, she looks down. Her gaze is as vacant and as faraway as it was at the Duc de Luxembourg's château.

"It's all my fault," she says softly.

"I don't understand," I say again.

A sob burbles up her throat and her voice breaks. "My mother delivered the poisoned petition into the Sun King's hands, but *I* made the poison. I am ultimately responsible for his death."

A burst of bone-chilling cold spreads through my chest and curls its icy fingers around my throat. I shake my head vehemently. "No. That's impossible. You said you had nothing to do with the attack on Versailles."

Mirabelle speaks to the floor, her voice flat and matter-of-fact. "I said I knew nothing about Mother's plans, which I didn't. But that hardly makes me innocent. I knew she would administer the poison to someone. And beyond that, I created the blood draught to make Lesage's magic tactile—his lightning, the smoke beasts, none of it would exist without me. I am the reason the Shadow Society was able to seize the city."

The ringing in my ears drowns out the end of her confession. *She* is the reason my sisters nearly died. *She* killed my father. And Rixenda . . .

I gape at Mirabelle, hunched in the doorway, trying to reconcile the girl I watched lovingly administer curatives with the monster she's describing. And I can't. It's impossible.

"Forgive me," Mirabelle chokes out.

"You see!" Desgrez jumps to his feet and points. "She admits it herself! She murdered the king—your *father*. Which is a capital offense in itself. But then she also claimed responsibility for the deaths of half of the nobility and the Paris Police. *This* is who you've chosen to align with"—he sneers at me—"but I'll not make the same mistake." He extracts a rapier from the folds of his brown robe and stalks to where Mirabelle stands. "On your knees."

The door is open. She could attempt to flee. But she gazes up at Desgrez with watery black eyes and complies. Her lips tremble and her breath comes short and fast. She doesn't beg for mercy. Doesn't look away.

Desgrez lifts his blade to her throat and twists the tip so it digs into the flesh below her ear. A ribbon of crimson snakes down her neck. I watch it trickle lower. Every heartbeat slams against my temples. My dagger lies on the floor within reach, but I'm unable to move. Unsure if I want to.

Mirabelle swallows against the pressure of Desgrez's blade

and lifts her chin higher. "Do it," she breathes. But at the same moment, a grating *scrape, scrape, scrape* comes from outside on the street. Like a sword dragging across the cobbles. It draws closer, louder, and a terrible stench fills my nose—like rotting eggs and gunpowder. Billows of oily blue smoke pour into the millinery and curl around our ankles.

Desgrez reels back, shouting oaths. Mirabelle collapses to the floor and clutches her neck. I quickly gain my feet. And we all stare out the door at an enormous indigo smoke beast that ambles into sight. It has long leathery wings, claws the length of my forearm, and a spiked tail that looks unnervingly like a mace. It *scrape, scrape, scrape*s from side to side as it lumbers down the rue de Navarine.

The creature stops directly in front of the millinery and turns its golden eyes on us, the pupils slitted like a snake's. It cocks its head and lifts its blunted snout into the air. Hot, rancid breath curls from its nostrils.

Mirabelle gasps. "He set them loose."

Desgrez shoves her aside, slams the door, and casts around for something to use as a barricade. I spring to assist him, wedging a chair beneath the handle. Which is laughable. The smoke beast could burst through with the flick of a single claw. Or burn the entire shop to cinders.

We retreat to the far corner of the millinery—me, Desgrez, and Mirabelle crouched behind the counter. Gasping. Trembling. Waiting for fire to engulf the shop or for the beast's massive weight to buckle the stairs leading to the door. The seconds pass. Droplets of blood leak from Mirabelle's neck and speckle the dusty ground. Eventually the scraping resumes—moving distinctly *away*.

We rush to the window as the beast's spiked tail vanishes around the corner of the rue de Navarine. Desgrez releases a breath and crumples against the wall. I grip the windowsill for support. But Mirabelle races to the door and knocks the chair aside.

"No, no, no," she mutters.

"You can't run from me," Desgrez says. "I'll easily overtake you."

"*You* are the least of my concerns," she says. Then she bangs out the door and flies down the street. Chasing after a beast made of smoke and flame and nightmare. Running, most assuredly, to her death.

17

MIRABELLE

There's only one reason the smoke beast would retreat. Only one reason it wouldn't destroy the millinery, and the entire city, if Lesage has set them free.

Mother wants to capture us alive—so she can make a bloody, public display of the royals' execution and my punishment—and Lesage's creatures are her hunting hounds, sent to sniff us out.

I grip an iron garden fence, propel myself around the corner, and tear down the winding street. The creature moves like an azure wave. Its spiked tail bobs and flashes like lanterns in the moonlight, and its slitlike ears swivel, listening to my footsteps. But it never turns to blast me with its fiery breath. Confirming my suspicion.

I fist my petticoats and will my feet to move faster. Each breath cuts through my lungs like a scythe, and icy waves of fear crash through my limbs, but the pain is nothing, *nothing*, compared to the look on Josse's face when I confessed. How his eyes widened with horror. How he recoiled in absolute disgust. As if I'm a monster.

Maybe I am.

I did terrible, unforgivable things. Things I can't change. But I *can* stop the smoke beast from reaching the Louvre and revealing our location to Lesage.

I *will* stop it.

We tear around another corner. Window coverings flutter and candles flicker to life as we fly past, but not a soul ventures into the street to help. They saw what the creatures are capable of during the procession, and I'm glad they stay away. Fewer innocent lives on my conscience.

I lengthen my stride and summon a final burst of speed, but the beast is faster still. It pulls ahead, snorting as the Louvre comes into view along the riverbank.

If I don't stop it now, I never will.

Desperate, I heft a pitchfork from a hay cart on the roadside, aim the tines at the smoke beast, and heave with all my might, sending a silent prayer with my makeshift spear. The tool is heavier than I'd thought and my aim is far from perfect, but the steel teeth manage to nick the creature's hind leg. It whirls around and blasts the cobbles with fire. I slam to a halt a hair's breadth from the scorched stones and roll to the side, narrowly avoiding a second strike.

The beast dives toward me, shaking the ground beneath my boots, shaking every quivering bone in my body. Its golden eyes lock on my frame and a scream burbles up my throat. I cast around for a weapon, an idea. *Anything.*

Think, Mira!

The river's to my left. I could lure it to the water. Beasts that spit fire shouldn't take kindly to water. Or I could run right, toward one of the armories. If the beast's flames ignite the gunpowder, the explosion might kill it.

And half a block of innocent souls!

The creature hisses and stretches up to its full height. Its noxious breath pours over me like scalding water. I veer to the left. Not fast enough. Fire claws at my dress, and I curse myself yet again for not rendering Lesage's blood draught so *I* could control the monsters as well. Pain burns up my leg, but a second later it's gone. Arms wrap around my chest and drag me to the street. We roll into the gutter, my skirts sizzling as the dreck douses the flames.

"Are you insane?" Josse shouts.

"You followed me." I blink up at him, not certain he's real.

"A little help!" Desgrez bellows. He's dodging in and out of doorways across the street, stabbing wildly at the beast between bursts of fire.

Without looking at me, Josse pushes to his feet and comes at the beast from behind. He removes a dagger from his boot and manages to sink it into the smoke beast's left hind leg. The creature screams and spins around. Its mace-like tail splinters through a wooden pillar, nearly beheading Desgrez.

"On second thought, maybe you shouldn't help." Desgrez ducks behind a crate, and Josse streaks across the road to join him.

Panting, I push up to my knees and gather rocks into my skirt.

Then I hunker behind a vegetable cart and toss the stones at the smoke beast. When it turns to snarl at me, Josse and Desgrez leap from their hiding places and slash at its legs and neck. They manage a few decent blows, their faces and tunics covered in a spray of thick black blood, but the creature catches on. The next time I hurl my rocks, it swivels the other way and knocks Desgrez's blade from his hand. The rapier spins into the road, and when Josse tries to grab it, the smoke beast nearly sets his hand aflame.

Exhausted and unarmed, Josse and Desgrez hunker behind the wooden pillars that hold the half-timbered houses aloft. The beast rears back and draws a snarling breath. It's going to incinerate them—and the house too. I dart forward, pebbles falling from my skirt, and run at the creature, screaming.

Fire flares overhead. I gasp, assuming the beast breathed on the thatching. But instead of flaring upward, the fire rains down atop the monster—little balls of flame made of bundled twigs. The smoke beast screeches and lurches to the opposite side of the road, but a barrage of fire descends from that rooftop as well.

Down the block, two small figures dash from an alleyway waving their arms. The smoke beast rounds on them, but before it can lunge, someone whistles and a weighty bundle unfurls from the rooftops. It appears to be a net of some sort that drapes across the beast's back and tangles in its lashing wings. While the creature struggles, more shadowed figures burst from the alleys and climb down gutters. Half of them run toward the beast's head with daggers and fire pokers that they stab into its legs and underbelly, and the other half scurry around its stumbling feet like ants, reaching to secure the rope.

The smoke beast roars and swings its head, but before it can breathe its deadly fire, more figures emerge carrying pots of water, which they splash into the beast's face. Scalding billows of steam churn into the sky, and the lethal tang of sulfur and brimstone is so overwhelming that I gag. As the creature struggles, the net tightens. The beast attempts to turn but stumbles over the rope and crashes to its knees.

I watch, stunned, as the group pins it to the ground and a boy—a gawky, pole-armed *boy*—raises an ax and cleaves the smoke beast's head from its neck.

He laughs as slick blood sprays his face.

"What in Heaven's name . . ." Desgrez's voice trails off as the boy struts toward us, wiping his ax clean on his stained tunic. His straw-colored hair is matted in clumps and his eyes are feral and hungry. He couldn't be more than fourteen, but he carries himself with an air of authority—shoulders square, brows set in his serious, crinkled forehead. He whistles and the shadowy figures that had been holding the net hustle to join him. They continue to pour from the crevasses and spindle down from the balconies like spiders. Every one of them is rail-thin with scraggly hair, and they're armed to the teeth with daggers and pokers and clubs.

Shivers flash down my arms, and I take a stumbling step back.

A street gang. Paris is crawling with them—children who run

from the orphanages, preferring to eke out an existence picking pockets in the gutter. It's a cruel and merciless life, according to Gris, who took up with one of these gangs before Mother found him. He says the children are as hardened as any proper criminal. That they would have happily mugged Louis XIV himself had they spotted his carriage rumbling down the street.

They surround us like a pack of wolves, and I shrink closer to Josse and Desgrez—though I'm not entirely sure they'll protect me again. Neither has so much as looked in my direction.

The boy slings the ax over his shoulder and says, "You'd be dead if it weren't for us, and our protection doesn't come free." Desgrez edges toward his rapier at the side of the road, but the straw-haired boy swings his ax into the cobbles. Jagged bits of rock fly into the air, and he laughs when Desgrez jumps back. Which seems to be an invitation for the rest of the band to laugh. "I wouldn't do that, monsieur."

"Let us pass," Desgrez says.

"Gladly. *If* you pay." The boy cocks his head and grins, poking his tongue through a hole where one of his front teeth should be.

"We haven't got any money." Josse pats his filthy tunic and breeches.

"Surely you've got something worth taking?"

"We didn't ask for your assistance," Desgrez says. "You cannot hold us hostage."

"Can't we?" The boy swings his ax again. Josse and Desgrez narrowly dodge the bit, but I'm far enough away to notice how the boy's voice cracks when he laughs. The way he winces when he returns the ax to his shoulder.

I look at him more closely. His eyes are sallow, his neck swollen, and his skin is slick and wan. Behind his cocky grin, his breath is shallow and rattling.

Scrofula fever.

And his bandmates are no better off, sweating and coughing, their skin riddled with scabs.

"You will let us pass," Desgrez hollers. "Or—"

I rush forward and place a hand on Josse's arm. He recoils with a hiss, as if burned by my touch. "What do you want?" he says without meeting my gaze.

I remove my hand and swallow hard. "T-they're ill," I whisper. "And I can help them."

Josse says nothing, but the accusation in his eyes hurtles through the silence: *The same way you* helped *my father? Why should I believe a word out of your deceitful mouth?*

"If we help them, we might be able to recruit them to our cause. . . ."

Josse bristles, and I'm certain he's about to inform me there is no cause, but at last he gives me a curt nod, snags the back of Desgrez's brown robe, and hauls him away from the boy before their argument can come to blows.

Taking a deep breath, I skirt around Josse and Desgrez and approach the children as I would injured animals, holding out my hands for all to see. "When did you start coughing?"

The boy's eyes narrow and the children behind him regard me with suspicion.

I press on. "How many days ago did the pustules appear? It's important you remember exactly."

Still the boy says nothing, but several of his bandmates glance down and tug their tunics.

"I can help you, but I need to know how far the sickness has progressed."

Two children grunt and poke the boy in the back. The straw-haired boy glares at me, stone-faced. "The first of us noticed the sores last week."

"There's still time, then. I haven't a curative with me, but—"

"You know the remedy?"

"I do. I can distill it and bring it to you later tonight."

The boy shakes his head. "You'll do it now. Under our watch." He gestures down the road with his ax, like a gaoler marching prisoners to the stocks. I suppress a smile. This boy is unflinching. Exactly the sort of ally we need.

"I've one condition," I begin, but Josse clears his throat and steps in front of me.

He points at the hulking shell of the smoke beast. "That was an impressive feat."

The boy shrugs, but a satisfied smile teases his lips. "That's the third one we've killed this week. We used to rob carriages and carts coming to and from Les Halles, but after the beasties burned the riverbank, people are willing to pay dearly for protection."

"Very clever," Josse says.

"Aye." The boy pulls back his bony shoulders. "We behead the monsters and harry the masked patrols. And before the king's death, the Paris Police trembled at the mere mention of us."

Josse studies the boy as if they are long-lost brothers. "What's your name?"

"Gavril."

"What would you say to a partnership of sorts, Gavril?"

"Depends what you're offering."

"Why would we offer them anything?" Desgrez cuts in. "They're a group of feral brats."

Gavril spits into the road and bunches back his shirtsleeves.

"With a very useful skill set," Josse says in a rush, placing himself between Desgrez and Gavril. "What if I told you, in exchange for continuing to hunt the smoke beasts and badgering the Shadow Society patrols, I could offer you not only medication for your illness but all the food you can eat? And a proper roof over your heads. No more stalking the streets—unless you wish to, of course."

The children whisper in excitement, but Gavril holds up a hand. "Who are you to offer such things? And to what end?"

"I'm Josse de Bourbon, bastard son of the late king. My brother, Louis, is alive and plans to make a stand against the Shadow Society and reclaim the throne. But he needs the help of the commoners to do so. We need *your* help."

"We've no need for a king!" one of the children yells, and several others agree. "What did he ever do for us?"

"The dauphin will be a different sort of king," Josse says. "He will listen to the voice of the people. You will have representatives at court and proper food and shelter. As well as medication, as I said before."

The children sneer and roll their eyes. I don't blame them. Every time we make these proclamations, a small measure of doubt simmers in my own belly. I want to believe our plan will work, but we're making an awful lot of promises on behalf of a person who detests me. Who wants to kill me. Who has probably never even considered these orphans' existence. I can't imagine Louis will be eager to work with them—or any of our recruits.

Gavril chews the inside of his cheek and his eyes take on a mischievous gleam. "What if I said our price was the Palais Royal? Would you let us live there?"

He knows it's a monumental demand.

So does Josse. He tugs his collar and swallows several times before saying, "Consider it done."

Desgrez coughs so hard, I'm shocked his eyes don't burst from his head. "Josse, be reasonable! That's the residence of the Duc d'Orléans, second only to the Louvre in grandeur! The duc and nobility will never stand for it."

"*If* he's alive, the duc will be forced to accept it. In this new era, we all must make accommodations. The Palais Royal is a small price to pay for such an advantageous alliance."

A delighted smile illuminates Gavril's dirty face, and he looks up at the bastard princeling as if he were the king himself.

How does Josse do that? Make a person feel needed and confident, no matter their status. He makes you *want* to help him because he genuinely wishes to help in return. I think of how he spirited me from the sewer and snuck me into the Louvre, how passionately he argued to convince me to join him on this crazy venture to unite the people, and warmth rises within me like heat in a forge.

My eyes flit to his face, but he stiffens and clenches his jaw, refusing to turn.

Gavril spits into his palm and offers it to Josse, who returns the handshake with gusto. Something a true royal would never do. "A pleasure doing business with you, Master Gavril," Josse says with a bow. The children burst into applause, whistling and clapping.

"Now, about that curative . . ." Gavril says.

"That, you'll have to take up with her." Josse gestures over his shoulder at me, and after a deliberate pause, he finally meets my gaze and grinds out, "Mademoiselle La Vie."

A lump of emotion gathers in my throat. For a moment, I can't speak. It's far from absolution, but if he's still willing to call me that, it gives me hope that someday I might be able to crawl out from beneath the weight of my crimes. It gives me the strength to stand a little taller and hold my chin a little higher and make a somewhat unorthodox request.

"Of course," I say, bobbing a curtsy at Gavril. "I just have one small favor to ask. If we're all headed in the same direction, would you mind helping me carry the body?" I point to the hulking smoke beast, and the gaiety dies out. The children stare as if I've lost my mind.

Desgrez, who hasn't stopped grumbling since Josse began negotiating with Gavril, slaps a palm to his forehead and groans. "What could you possibly want with the creature's body?"

"What any good alchemist would want," I say fiercely. "To experiment."

18

JOSSE

The millinery feels oppressively quiet after Gavril and his gang depart with their tincture. Every crackle of the fire makes me jump; the steady drip of the smoke beast's blood on the floor bores a hole into my brain.

I would have left with them, but the majority of the orphans made it clear they're not comfortable rubbing elbows with a royal just yet. And I couldn't return to the sewer with Desgrez to check on my sisters, despite how desperate I am to see them. Apparently Louis isn't ready to see my "traitorous, double-crossing face." I'm not ready to see his haughty, piggish face either. Which means I'm trapped here, inside these four shrinking walls, with Mirabelle.

We both retreat to our separate corners and fall asleep immediately—a welcome reprieve. But as soon as she wakes, I can feel her looking at me. She's pretending not to, hunched over the grotesque body of the creature on the counter. It looks like a gutted fish on the wharf—or a whale, more like. She had to cut it into pieces to fit it through the door. Most are still piled in the alleyway behind the millinery. A portion of its belly is splayed across the board, and despite being elbow-deep in its foul black innards, she glances my way every few seconds. Hoping to catch my gaze as she did on the street.

Stare all you'd like, I want to snap. *It's not going to help.* But that would require speaking to her, which I'm also unwilling to do. With an overloud sigh, I turn to face the wall and tip my tricorne hat over my face. It's the easy way out, but I don't know what she expects me to say. I can't pretend I'm not bothered by the fact she murdered my father—and Rixenda, too, in a way—then conveniently omitted those details when I asked her about Versailles.

So, I settle in and pretend to be exhausted. Which doesn't require much acting at all. My limbs still feel like curdled pudding, and I'm covered in cuts and bruises from the bedamned smoke beast.

The creature continues to assault me, even in death. Its drying scales reek of rotting eggs and it makes horrid squelching noises as Mirabelle drags a knife down the center of its gut and peels back the pulpy skin.

My stomach flips and I gag. This is, without a doubt, the most disgusting thing I've ever witnessed. Even worse than helping Rixenda disembowel lambs. I stuff my nose down my shirt and close my eyes, but after three more nauseating incisions, I can't take it anymore.

"Haven't you cut it into enough pieces?" I wave at the hunks of mutilated flesh lying across the table.

Mirabelle's eyes flit to mine, but she must not like my expression—which I admit feels rather hostile—because she hurriedly wipes her sweaty forehead on her sleeve and returns her attention to the beast. "Not until I discover its inner workings. The beasts are half mine, so I should be able to control them the way Lesage does." She blows a curl away from her eyes, slices off another hunk of meat, and tosses it into the nearest pot.

"And how do you plan to do that?"

"By boiling it down to a broth, which I will then drink—*if* I can swallow it," she adds when she sees my horrified expression, "with the hopes that it will join my composition with the beasts'."

I shudder and avert my gaze. "I still don't understand why we can't allow Gavril and the orphans to take care of them. They're good at it, and they seem to *enjoy* it."

"It's not enough. No matter how many they kill, Lesage can always conjure more. In order to defeat the Shadow Society, we will need command of the monsters."

"And if your putrid stew doesn't work?"

She looks down at the pot with a wary yet determined expression. "Then I'll try making its skin into an amulet or grinding its bones into powder."

"So much to look forward to," I groan.

"You can leave if you need to," she says, and I spring to my feet faster than a jackrabbit. But before I reach the door she adds, "Or you can help."

"I think I'll pass."

"Not help with the beast, obviously."

"What, then?" I turn and let my arms slap against my sides. "I'm not permitted to do anything other than chop herbs, and as much as I enjoyed that . . ."

Mirabelle purses her lips and pushes her father's red grimoire across the table toward me. "Help me brew another antidote to Viper's Venom."

My laughter is sharp and cynical. "I thought I'm not to be trusted with your father's recipes." Which I've decided is fine by me. I don't trust myself with them either. Not after seeing Mirabelle, a trained alchemist, fail to create the proper antidote. "I know nothing about alchemy."

"Lucky for you, I'm an excellent teacher. I'll walk you through each step. I haven't enough hands to dissect the smoke beast and distill the antipoison at the same time. I need you, Josse. *Please*." The way she says *please*—so soft and beseeching—it sounds more like an apology than a request. But I'm even more dumbfounded by what she called me—my name, rather than "princeling." I can hardly bear to look at her, yet my traitorous ears revel in the sound of my name on her lips.

"Fine," I grumble, and skulk back to the counter. "But if this goes horribly—"

"You will be held blameless," she promises. "Now take up a gallipot and set it on the fire, then pour two measures of hyssop into the mortar bowl and grind the leaves to a fine pulp. I think that's what the previous antidote was missing."

"Two measures of what?" I stare down at the cluster of herbs and instruments, most of which I can't begin to describe, let alone operate. I wipe my palms down my breeches, but they're as cold and clammy as a herring.

"Father's notes should answer all of your questions." Her lips are pinched and her hand hesitates, but Mirabelle eventually opens the grimoire and sets it on the tiny corner of the counter not overtaken by her beast.

I stare at the lines and lines of messy, cramped writing and puff out my cheeks, once again feeling like the incompetent little boy listening in on Louis's lessons. Mirabelle is making a grand gesture including me like this, so I'm not about to ask her to read it to me, but I feel even more uncomfortable and out of place than I did among the courtiers at Versailles.

Take it one word at a time. Pretend you're in the kitchens with Rixenda and her recipes. How hard could it be? But the thought of Rixenda makes my stomach twist with rage and grief. She's dead because of Mirabelle.

The pain is still sharp, like the tip of a poker burning my flesh, but when I start to stagger back, I'm overwhelmed by the memory of Rixenda's craggy face. The scent of her lavender soap tickles my nose, and her rasp of a voice fills the smoky shop.

Be strong, Josse.

Holding a grudge will help nothing. It's not what she would have wanted.

I roll up my sleeves and lift the pestle and mortar bowl.

Despite my struggles reading, in an hour's time I've made decent headway on the anti-venom. Turns out alchemy *is* quite similar to working in the kitchens, and I'm more proficient than I could have hoped. I know this because Mirabelle keeps checking my progress and humming with surprise. Or lifting her brows in shock.

We work like this for several hours. Neither of us say much, but the silence isn't uncomfortable like before. And I no longer stand at an arm's length as if she has the pox. I even ask her to pass me a stirring spoon and neither of us recoils when our fingers accidentally brush on the handle.

When the sun falls behind the buildings, melting like a pat of butter into the river, Mirabelle lights the tapers situated throughout the room. She pauses after lighting the final one beside me and whispers, "Thank you."

"Don't thank me yet. There's a good chance I've fouled this up completely."

"It couldn't be worse than my first attempt." She flashes a strained smile. "That's not what I was thanking you for, anyway— at least not only that. Thank you for coming when I ran after the smoke beast. I would have died had you and Desgrez not followed."

She waits for me to say something, but I didn't make a conscious decision to follow her. My feet just carried me down the steps as if an invisible cord was tied around her waist and the other end was wrapped around mine. I'm not about to tell her that, though, so I mumble unintelligibly and return to spooning the antipoison into phials.

"Why did you come after me?" she presses, looking at me with those big black eyes. "You could have let me die and had your vengeance."

I pound the phial down harder than necessary, partially to fend her off and partially to harden my focus. "You may be a liar, but aligning with you is still my sisters' best shot at freedom. And our only chance of reclaiming the city from the Shadow Society."

Mirabelle gives a tight nod and bustles behind the counter, biting her lips to conceal their slight trembling. I want to ignore it, I *command* myself to ignore it, but it's so pitiable and heartbreaking, words spew from my lips. "And I suppose a small part of me might understand why you withheld the truth."

Her knife clatters to the table, and she peers at me from beneath her messy curls, the brown turned to gold in the candlelight. "You do?"

I sigh and scrub my hand over my face. It would've been so easy for the common people to blame me for my father's negligence, but they were willing to hear me out and judge me by my own merit. Doesn't Mirabelle deserve the same?

"We were both blind," I say slowly. "You may have brewed the poison, but you had no way of knowing how your mother planned to use it. You were doing what you thought was right. If I condemned you for that, I'd have to condemn myself too. I *knew* I was acting like a wretched miscreant. I *tried* to cause as much mayhem as possible. If I'd spent a little less time raising hell and a little more time educating myself on important matters, trying to be the prince the people needed, perhaps I would have seen how terribly my father was failing them. Perhaps none of this would have happened."

"This situation is bigger than any one person," Mirabelle says. "And you're no wretched miscreant. A hoodlum, certainly. And a scoundrel, definitely. But not wholly wretched." She gently knocks my shoulder, and our sides press together. To my astonishment, I don't lean away. Neither does she. We shiver there beside each other for a breath of a moment before the millinery door slams open.

Mirabelle yelps and stiffens. I turn, the spoon still in my fist, expecting to see Gavril returning with additional demands, but it's Mirabelle's assistant from the Louvre.

The one who doesn't know I exist.

"Gris!" Mirabelle's voice is an entire octave higher than normal. "What a pleasant surprise. I thought I'd have to wait another two nights to see your smiling face."

Which is the wrong thing to say, since the expression on his face is hardly a smile. His lips are curled back so far that he resembles a growling dog. And his brows crumple as his gaze darts between Mirabelle and me, as if he can see tiny, invisible threads connecting us from every place we've touched. He tightens his grip on his leather satchel, and his knuckles shine like bone.

"Who's this?" Gris says, looking me up and down. "I didn't realize you'd recruited additional help." The way he growls the word *help* makes it perfectly clear the sort of *help* he thinks I'm providing.

I set the spoon on the counter, don my most innocent smile, and wipe my hands on my tunic before offering one to Gris. "Pleasure to finally meet you. Mirabelle speaks of you constantly. I'm Jo—"

"Just a blacksmith's apprentice," Mirabelle interrupts. She brushes past me, links her arm through Gris's, and pulls him into the shop—decidedly away from me. "One of the pots cracked, and he came to repair it."

"What's he still doing here?" Gris asks. "He doesn't seem to be fixing anything. He didn't even bring tools."

"Oh, he fixed the pot days ago. Turns out he knows a thing or two about alchemy and offered to help me," Mirabelle says with a forced laugh, compulsively tucking the same wayward curl behind her ear.

Gris glowers down at her. "You're lying. You're doing that thing with your hair. The question is, *why* are you lying?" He glances to me.

"Don't blame her," I say. "It's a common problem. Most people are embarrassed to be seen with me. I'm Josse de Bourbon."

"*Bastard* son of the king," Mirabelle cuts in, emphasizing my title—or lack thereof.

"I know who he is," Gris mutters. "But I still don't understand what he's doing here. I'm happy to help *you*, Mira, but this . . . I was under the impression he was dead. And what's all *that?*" The color drains from his face as he finally looks beyond Mirabelle at the carcass of the smoke beast splayed across the table. "Is that one of Lesage's creatures?" He stumbles back, shaking his head.

"What are you really up to?" He shoots another look at me. As if I somehow forced her into all of this.

"I'm only healing, as I told you," Mirabelle says quickly. "And Josse is assisting me."

"Why would a royal do that?"

Mirabelle shoots me a look that says she'll toss me into one of her pots and boil the skin off my bones if I speak. "The princeling sought me out after I escaped because he wishes to be a different sort of royal than his father. One who actually cares for the people. He's more like us than any of the nobility. His mother was a scullery maid. The king was ashamed of him and banished him to the kitchens. The courtiers rejected and reviled him."

"I love when you extol all of my finest accomplishments," I say, pretending to be stung. Which isn't difficult because I do feel *a little* stung. I told her those things in confidence, not so she could disparage me to strangers. I part my lips, but Mirabelle shoots me another dangerous look.

"Josse sought me out because he wishes to heal the people. Who am I to refuse help? You know how having such a purpose can change a person." She stares up at him until he grudgingly sighs.

"And the other royal children?" he asks. "Do they live as well? I've been hearing rumors about the dauphin and some ill-conceived rebellion." Again, he glowers over at me, as if my brother and I are one and the same.

Mirabelle's eyes briefly catch mine, radiating both fear and elation. News of our rebellion is spreading, just as we hoped. But neither of us had considered what might happen if the rumors got back to the Shadow Society.

I hold up both hands. "If the dauphin is alive and leading a rebellion, I'm the last person he would recruit. He loathes me."

The lie is true enough. If the rebellion were Louis's idea, I wouldn't be included. Just as he isn't included in our plans—not yet.

"When I escaped, all of the royals were ailing in a dilapidated hovel," Mirabelle adds. "It would've taken a miracle for them to survive."

Another clever half-truth. And deliciously ironic since *she* was our miracle.

"I've heard nothing about the royals or a rebellion," she continues, "but the smoke beasts are rather worrisome." She artfully steers the conversation to the carcass on the board. "I found this one dead in the road and decided to study it to see how I might help the innocent people caught in the crossfire of their attacks, since they are evidently roaming the city."

"I didn't know Lesage had set them loose." Gris studies the beast with a concerned expression.

There are a lot of things you don't know, I'm tempted to say. But since I'm certain Mirabelle would kill me for admitting this, I keep my lips tightly stitched.

"Thank you for bringing more supplies," Mirabelle says, reaching for Gris's satchel, but he steps back and holds it out of reach.

"I want to help you, Mira, but you're putting me in a difficult position."

"I know," she says quietly. "I would never ask you to go behind Mother's back unless I was certain it was the right thing to do. And I'm certain. This is best for the people—I've already healed scores of men and women on the rue du Temple as well as the infirm at the Hôtel-Dieu—just as the Society used to. I'm asking you to trust me over her this once. To choose me this once."

Gris looks down at Mirabelle, who clasps her hands before her chest and makes a pleading face. With a final glance at the smoke beast, then me, he relinquishes the satchel with a sigh. "Very well. But only because I'm slightly afeared for the people—that's the reason I came tonight. I overheard Fernand and Marguerite whispering earlier today of a mass execution of the fishmongers on the Quai de la Grève. I'm certain La Voisin is only trying to appease the masses, but—"

"How would executing innocent men and women ever be the best way to go about anything?" I accidentally blurt.

Gris shoots me a hateful look and Mirabelle stomps her heel down hard on my toes before turning back to Gris. "Why would Mother attack the fishmongers? That doesn't sound like something the Society would condone."

"Apparently she demanded they donate two-thirds of their daily catch to distribute to the starving people, but they refused to comply."

"Refused or simply cannot?" I interject. Gris scowls, but I press on. "It's a valid question. Two-thirds is a staggering amount. They'll starve to death and fall to ruin themselves, giving away so much."

Gris says nothing, just frowns at the floor.

"How does she plan to kill them?" Mirabelle asks, pacing back and forth in front of the counter. "When?"

"Viper's Venom, of course. And it's already done. I distilled the poison yesterday with the understanding it would be used on traitorous nobles, but Marguerite collected it from the laboratory while I ate my midday meal. She tainted their nets and baskets not an hour ago while they supped. The fishermen will be poisoned when they return to set their nets and traps for the night."

"Only an hour . . ." Mirabelle fumbles with the half-filled phials on the counter.

"Can we finish the antidote in time?" I ask.

"If we work quickly . . . all of us together." She adds the last part with an imploring look at Gris.

He starts to nod but then bites his lip. "You realize she'll blame me? I want to help, truly I do, but if the fishmongers survive, La Voisin will presume I made faulty poison."

"She'll test your work, to be sure," Mirabelle agrees, "but since we're administering an antidote and not altering the poison, she'll find nothing amiss. Just make certain *you* are not the tester."

Gris moans and drags his fingers down his face.

"We haven't time for your dithering," I bark out. "Either help us or go."

Gris whips around to face me. He's a good hand taller and nearly twice as broad. He could easily haul me up by the back of my tunic and toss me out the door—which is precisely what it looks like he means to do. "Don't act as if you'll be of any help—"

Mirabelle bangs her fist on the counter. "Every second could mean a man's life. We need every pair of capable hands."

Gris gives a reluctant nod. "Very well."

Mirabelle straps on her goggles and calls orders at us both, and half an hour later we stuff the still-warm bottles of finished antipoison into sacks and start for the door.

"I wish I could accompany you," Gris says as we step out into the chilly, rain-soaked evening. "But it will look suspicious if I'm missing from dinner. Especially after word gets back to your mother about the fishmongers' miraculous recovery. Do you think you can manage on your own?"

On her own?

He's worse than Father's bedamned ministers, looking through me, pretending I don't exist. I give an exaggerated wave, but Mirabelle steps between us and throws her arms around Gris.

"We'll manage fine. Thank you for coming—for telling me about the fishmongers. I'll find a way to send word of how they fare."

"And I'll return if I hear of any more worrisome developments."

Mirabelle leans on her toes and kisses his scruffy cheek. For some reason it makes me stiffen. "Thank you, my friend. Be safe."

Gris squeezes her hand, pulls up his hood, and jogs off into the driving rain, but not before throwing one last glare in my direction.

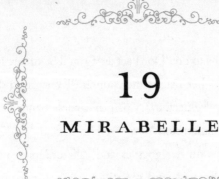

19

MIRABELLE

"We need to make a quick stop," Josse says as we race toward the Quai de la Grève. The rain falls in lashing torrents, making it difficult to see, and my boots are heavy with the fetid gutter water that's streaming down the streets.

"Where?" I demand. "There isn't time."

"It's on the way. We need to collect Desgrez from the Méchant Meriée."

"Why in the world would we do that? He made it very clear he doesn't wish to work with me. He stalked off before we even moved the smoke beast to the millinery."

Josse wipes his face on the back of his sleeve. "This healing could turn him fully to our cause."

"We don't need him committed to our cause!"

"Trust me. I know you two don't get along exactly, but think of Desgrez like Lesage's smoke beasts—hotheaded and difficult, but undeniably useful."

"You have twenty seconds," I say when we reach the tavern. I begin to count aloud as Josse bangs through the door. To my surprise, he returns with three seconds to spare, and Desgrez doesn't even scowl too deeply at the sight of me. He presses a gray wool cloak and tricorne hat into my arms.

"You're welcome. I won them straight off the back of my opponent."

"What's this for?"

"For wearing—what else? You're too conspicuous in that palace maid's uniform. If I'm joining you on this senseless endeavor, I'd rather not be caught. And the leader of a rebellion should have a bit more . . . panache."

"How can you be worried about *panache* at a time like this?" I say, but I pull the cloak around my shoulders and tug the hat over my drenched curls, thankful for the extra layers.

The bottles of antipoison rattle and clink in our sacks as we run down the rue Saint-Denis, and my nerves rattle with them. My lips move in silent prayer when the riverside comes into view.

Please let them live, I beseech God and all his heavenly angels.

Please let it work, I beg Father for alchemical blessings from beyond the grave.

When we reach the waterfront, we duck beneath the shadowed awning of a boathouse and inch closer to the docks, straining to see and hear over the drum of the rain. The long, wood-planked wharf is packed, as it always is each evening. But instead of fishermen gutting the day's catch, and merchants haggling at the fishwives' stalls while mud-caked children race past on bare feet, everyone lies writhing and flapping on the moss-slicked boards.

The wind batters us with rain and river water, and the scent is so foul, it drops me to my knees. The wharf is never pleasant-smelling, but now it's unbearable: blood and vomit, mingled with damp wood and rotting fish innards. And the sounds are even worse. Wailing and moaning and retching like I've never heard.

I clench the bottles of antipoison tighter, wanting to charge down the quai and help, but a few Society soldiers linger at the water's edge, watching and laughing.

I sink my teeth into my trembling lip to keep from screaming. This is not the Shadow Society I knew. How could Mother allow this?

"It sounds like a massacre," Desgrez says, his voice hoarse. "Worse than the dungeons of the Châtelet."

"It *is* worse," I say. "Prison would be a mercy compared to poison. Never have you felt such pain, like claws sinking into your gut and twisting your innards."

Josse stiffens beside me, and his mouth pinches into a line. "You speak as if you know from experience."

"It happened fairly often when I was young. Father claimed poisoning was essential to my training—to know how the body reacts to different toxins in order to determine which herbs would counteract the damage. He also wanted to be certain I could perform under pressure, in case of accidental—or not so accidental—poisonings. An alchemist must always be ready."

Both men gape at me, blinking through the rain streaming down their faces.

"It wasn't so bad," I say. "Father's methods may have been unorthodox, but he wouldn't have let me die."

Josse's frown deepens and he scoots closer. As if protecting me from events that took place half a lifetime ago. A prickle of warmth stirs in my belly, like coals being prodded by a poker, but another moan from the wharf douses the ember. I ball my fists and glance up and down the riverbank. The Society soldiers are finally gone. "Let's go."

"I'll start at the far end, near the Pont Marie," Josse says, gripping his bottle of antipoison and casting me a look that is equal parts reassurance and fear. Desgrez heads to the nearest shacks to see if anyone is still inside, and I pick up my skirts and wade straight into the center of the carnage.

I come first to a man lying prostrate on the slippery boards. He's twice my size, with deep brown skin and thick black hair. It takes all my strength to turn him over, and the sight of his bloated face is so horrific, I gag. Froth seeps from his lips, and his breath rumbles like boiling water.

I close my eyes and dig my knuckles into my thighs, but still the faces of the dead rise like phantoms from the mist: the Sun King, Madame de Montespan, and now the Duc de Luxembourg. A whimper escapes my lips and tremors start in my smallest toe and overtake me to the crown.

The man's eyes flutter open, and he thrashes beneath me. The phial slips in my sweaty hand. I can't bear to fail again. I won't survive it. I want to scramble back. I want to return to the dark safety of the millinery. But Father's hands shove me forward. His voice hums in my ear. I bring the bottle to the man's lips, but they're cold and stiff and his head flops to the side.

No, no, no. I can feel the scream welling up inside of me. My hand shakes so hard, the antipoison splashes across his lips and dribbles down his chin. I climb atop his chest and force the neck of the bottle between his lips.

Then I wait.

Each second lasts a lifetime.

I'm about to slide down to the slimy boards and never rise again when a door slams open and a squalling woman with the same dark skin and long black hair storms across the quai, Desgrez on her heels.

"Étienne!" she shrieks at the motionless man beneath me. "I forbid you to be dead!" She elbows me aside and slaps the man across the face. "Wake up this instant!"

Just as I'm about to tell her it's useless, she slaps her husband again and his eyes fly open. He clutches his chest and is immediately gripped by a fit of coughing.

My eyes burn with tears and I bury my face in my hands, crying and laughing so hard that I can't catch my breath.

He lives.

It worked.

"Don't sit there blubbering!" the woman shouts at me. "The rest, girl. Tend the rest."

Desgrez helps me to my feet and we continue our work down

the river, doling out antipoison and whispering my new name, La Vie, until it's on every tongue. Floating down the riverside. Once again shaking the bearings of my soul.

"We knew you'd come," a girl says as she pushes up to her elbows. "Rumors have been swirling down the dock and tangling through Les Halles. They say you're an angel, sent from God himself."

I'm no angel, that's for certain, but I feel something powerful, something transcendent, stir deep within me as I watch the dead return to life. Women and children rush from the shabby riverside shacks and collide with the men in great, weeping hugs. A small dark-eyed girl throws herself atop the first man I healed and clutches his face, kissing his scruffy cheeks.

My eyes sting and my lips quiver. Father's voice drifts past me on the wind. *You will be a great alchemist one day....*

This is what he meant. This feeling gave him the courage to stand up to Mother, to prize alchemy above all else.

"Miraculous," Desgrez whispers.

My eyes widen. "Is that a compliment, Captain?"

Desgrez scoffs and assaults me with the full force of his most intimidating scowl. "If you're trying to get an admission out of me, poisoner, it will never happen."

"I think the tears glistening in your eyes are admission enough."

"Raindrops. Obviously." He wipes his sleeve across his face.

A few minutes later, Josse comes tearing down the dock, whooping and wide-eyed. "It worked! Our antipoison worked!"

He catches me up in his arms and we spin across the rain-slicked boards.

For a second, I can't breathe—it's so reminiscent of the day I healed Anne and Françoise. And yet, everything has changed. Instead of pushing him away, my arms tighten around his neck. My fingers hungrily clutch his tunic. And instead of freezing with horror, I bury my face in his chest.

He sets me down, takes my chin in his hands, and presses his forehead to mine. He's laughing and misty-eyed, and his lips are so close I can practically taste them. The tiny space between us bubbles and pops. His warm breath spills across my frozen cheeks. His hands slide down my neck and tangle in my hair. It would be so easy to lift my chin a fraction.

Josse glances down, and his lip catches between his teeth.

I close my eyes and lean up on my toes.

"Focus!" Desgrez yanks Josse back by the shoulders. "This isn't the time to be . . ." He waves a hand between Josse and me and makes a disgusted face. "We've work yet to do." He nods to the scores of people still gathered on the wharf. "Make your speech so we can be off before a Shadow Society patrol spots us."

I never dreamed I'd say this, but Desgrez is right. We've a city to retake. No time for distraction.

"Do you want to do the honors?" Josse asks me.

"And deny you the pleasure of touting your royal heritage?" He clutches his chest, as if wounded, and I grin. "You're the link to Louis. And you've got a knack for making these speeches."

A slow smile tugs his cheeks. He straightens his cloak with a flourish and climbs onto an overturned crate. "My good people! I am Josse de Bourbon and this is Mademoiselle La Vie. We bring you these healing tonics from His Royal Highness, the dauphin! He is alive and plotting to reclaim the throne from La Voisin and the Shadow Society, even as we speak. But he needs your aid and loyalty to do so. If you will join us in this battle, we will continue to provide curatives and protection. Once order is restored, you will also be given a voice in the new government. Representatives will bring your complaints before the dauphin and the Parlément de Paris."

"Sure they will!" calls the fishwife who slapped her husband, Étienne, back to life.

"Ameline, hush," the man orders, but she elbows past him to the front of the group and stands before us with her arms crossed. "I'm just as likely to have a say in the government as I am to dip my fingers in the mucky Seine and have them come out plated gold."

A few fishermen snicker, and the rest stare—awaiting our reply.

"I assure you—" Josse begins, but Ameline cuts him off.

"Save your assurances! We want proof!"

Josse looks down at me, and I shrug helplessly. We have no proof to give them. We haven't needed it. The poor and sick have been so grateful for aid, they willingly put their trust in us. I had assumed the fishmongers would be the same, especially with all their happy tears and thankful cries. But Ameline tilts her head back and laughs bitterly, pointing a finger at us.

"Just as I suspected. If the dauphin is so eager to join with us, where is he? Where is any of the royal family? Shouldn't they be the ones distributing the curatives?" She looks all around for royals who are distinctly absent and more and more of the dockworkers begin to murmur and shout.

Josse waves a hand overhead. "I am the bastard son of the late king and here on behalf of the royal family—"

"Not to disparage your status, as I'm certainly in no position to do so"—Ameline tugs on her ragged skirts coated in mud and fish guts—"but sending the royal bastard and runaway daughter of La Voisin to do their bidding hardly inspires confidence."

"His Royal Highness wishes to walk among you, of course," Josse grinds out, "but you must understand how dangerous—"

"Exactly!" another man cries. "How do we know the dauphin lives at all? These could be cruel, empty promises. We were betrayed by another *champion* this very night. Seems foolish to put our trust in someone we can't even see, who could be hiding in a lavish castle, swathed in velvet and silk, while we are poisoned and left to perish."

"Louis and my sisters are living in conditions no better—"

"Prove it!" someone yells. And then all of the Quai de la Grève is shouting it.

Josse steps down from the crate with a heavy thunk and rakes his fingers through his soaking hair. "I give up. There's nothing I can say to please them."

"We appreciate what you've done for us," Ameline calls above the tumult, "but if we're to believe your promises, if you want commoners to rally behind royals who have always reviled us, we need to see them with our own eyes. And if it be as you say it is, then we'll cast our lot with yours."

A hundred *Aye*s rise up in agreement, followed by a hundred more.

Josse gives a curt nod and stalks off. Desgrez follows. I linger slightly longer, forcing a smile and calling out assurances. Then I rush to catch up to Josse and Desgrez.

"The healing was impressive, I'll give you that," Desgrez says. "But the response wasn't quite as enthusiastic as promised." He casts goading smiles at Josse and me in turn.

"Save it," Josse says.

"That went *differently* than expected," I agree, "but we knew we would have to include Louis sooner or later."

"I was hoping for *much* later," Josse growls.

"Not looking forward to your glorious family reunion?" Desgrez continues. "But Louis has missed you so!" He tries to sling his arm around Josse's shoulders, but Josse buries his elbow in Desgrez's side. After a long, drawn-out wheeze, Desgrez chuckles. "Not to worry—I'll protect you."

I accidentally laugh, and Josse shoots me a glare. "We'll *both* protect you," I say. Then slowly, so as not to draw Desgrez's attention, I slide my fingers between Josse's and give his hand a faint squeeze.

20

JOSSE

A foul taste lingers in my mouth from the Quai de la Grève, and it has nothing to do with the fish.

Once again, I am not enough.

Once again, I'm cast aside in favor of my brother, who hasn't lifted a bedamned finger.

Granted, we haven't asked for his help, but Louis wouldn't have offered it even if we had. Not willingly, anyway. He couldn't care less about fishmongers. Or the poor and sick.

Yet still they cry for him.

Still I am forced to grovel at his feet and beg for his support—then give him credit for everything *I've* accomplished.

I suppose I knew it would come to this—I proposed returning him to the throne. I just didn't expect to feel this bitterness churning in my belly. These sharp claws of jealousy dragging through my skin.

Desgrez keeps snickering as we walk, as if this is all a hysterical joke. I want to punch him in the throat, but hold back because he's finally warming to our plan.

Mirabelle squeezes my hand, trying to get me to slow down

and look at her, but I charge ahead, my fingers rigid against hers. I haven't a clue why she wants anything to do with me—I clearly have nothing to offer.

I turn to start up the rue Saint-Denis toward the millinery, but Mirabelle and Desgrez stop and look the other way—down the rue Saint-Honoré toward the pâtisserie.

"*Now?*" I groan.

"There's no reason to delay," Mirabelle says. "The sooner we enlist your siblings, the sooner we can recruit more allies."

"But it's so late. . . ."

Desgrez rolls his eyes. "The sun has barely set. And you know time means nothing down below."

I groan again, louder.

"I know you're anxious to see Anne and Françoise," Mirabelle persuades.

Their names stop me short. Anxious is an understatement. Two tiny holes have been drilling into my chest since the day I left the sewer. I'd do anything to see them, to protect them. Even face Louis. "Fine." I let Mirabelle pull me toward Madame Bissette's, but I drag my feet as if I'm marching to the gallows.

"Quit being so dramatic," Desgrez says. "This was your idea, was it not? Uniting the nobility and the peasants?"

"Yes, but I never considered *who* would do the actual uniting."

"Who better than the noble commoner?" Desgrez opens the pâtisserie door and waves me in with a gallant sweep of his hand. "After you, my lord."

I bite my thumb at him and slip inside. By some miracle, Madame Bissette is in her apartment abovestairs, so I lift the hatch and descend into the tunnels without her pecking and pestering.

As soon as my boots sink into the muck, I cough at the vile stench. After a few weeks aboveground, I had forgotten how the vaporous fingers reach down your throat. I step forward to make room for the others and walk directly into a cobweb. While I bat the sticky strings from my face, a rat the size of Rixenda's rolling pin scampers along the side of my boot.

I can't do this. Especially knowing the foulest creature of all waits for me at the tunnel's end. There must be another way to appease the people. Something, *anything,* else we can try.

I pivot, ready to bound back up the stairs and run far away from this hellhole, when two high-pitched voices trill down the tunnel like birdsong.

My heart stutters at the sound.

My girls.

Their laughter pulls me into the dark and dreck. I place my hands against the dripping walls and push into the blackness. Desgrez and Mirabelle follow.

Anne's and Françoise's voices grow steadily louder; my heart beats steadily faster. When we round the final bend and torchlight from their chamber illuminates the pits and holes in the ground, I break into a run. Needing to see them. Needing to hold them.

"Anne! Franny!" I shout.

There's a beat of silence, followed by delighted screams and claps as I burst into the chamber.

"Josse!" Anne fists her filthy skirt and runs for me. "You're back!"

I kneel down and catch her in my arms. Françoise crashes into my side a moment later and we three topple over sideways and splash into a puddle, laughing too hard to care about the cold and wet. I rain kisses on their cheeks and smooth my hands over their hair, inspecting every inch of them. "Are you well? Have you regained your strength?" I can't stop babbling and my eyes sting with tears, which is slightly mortifying, but it's so good to see them alive and well and warm and solid and—

"Stop!" Françoise giggles and bats my hand away. "We're fine. Where have you been? We were beginning to worry you'd never return."

"Some of us were beginning to celebrate," Louis calls from his corner.

Marie shoots him a disapproving look as she crosses the chamber to where I sit with the girls. "This is a happy moment, Louis. No need to sully it with old quarrels. We're glad to see you're safe," she says to me.

"I'd hardly call them old quarrels!" Louis's voice rises as Desgrez and Mirabelle duck into the chamber. "He brought the poisoner back! Captain Desgrez, how could you allow—"

"Mirabelle!" the girls shriek over Louis. They scramble up and attack her with only slightly less gusto than they did me. They jostle for position in her lap and laugh like they haven't since the attack on Versailles. Something squeezes in my chest, seeing the three of them together. Desgrez shakes his head at the smile creeping across my lips.

"You look different," Anne says, studying Mirabelle's close-cropped curls.

"I had to disguise myself," she explains, "and your brother thought this would be the best way."

"But your curls were so big and bouncing and lovely!" Françoise laments, swirling her arms around her head just as I did outside the Louvre.

Mirabelle chuckles and cuts me a glance. "I don't think anyone has ever called my hair *lovely,* but thank you. How are you both feeling? I've been longing to check on you. Have the spots faded? Have your coughs ceased?"

Anne holds out her arms for inspection, and Françoise bobs her head, insisting she's never felt better.

"So what have you been up to, now that you're well?" I say, plopping down beside them.

"We've been hunting rats," Anne pronounces.

"Rats!" Mirabelle glances at me, trying not to look disgusted.

Françoise nods eagerly. "They like to chew our skirts, so I ripped off bits of material and put them in the corner, and when the rats came, I trapped one all by myself. I hit it with my shoe and cooked it on a stick and ate it for supper."

"You ate it?" I laugh. Foul as it sounds, I'm brimming with

pride. Spoiled, pampered princesses would never stoop so low. My girls are strong. Resilient. A new breed of nobility.

"We gobbled it up, even the tail. Just like our kitten who lives at the palace," Anne tells Mirabelle. "When we return, I am going to help her hunt. I would make a good kitten, don't you think?"

"You would be a wonderful kitten," Mirabelle agrees.

"Enough of this blessed reunion." Louis stamps to where we sit. "I demand to know why you're here. And why you would allow it, Captain." He glowers at Desgrez. "Josse betrayed me. And assaulted you. He can't come parading back after weeks of carousing with our enemy and expect to be received with open arms."

I regain my feet and draw a deep breath. Heaven help me, it will take every morsel of patience I possess to survive what comes next. "So lovely to see you, brother," I say. "Before you run me out, you might be interested to hear we've devised a new plan to see you out of the sewer and reinstalled on the throne, but we need your cooperation to carry it out."

Marie lets out an uncharacteristic squeal and claps her hands to her chest. "Thank goodness. I was beginning to fear—"

Louis silences her with a look and turns back to me, his face crumpled with distaste. "Not another one of your ill-conceived plans. We've been through this before."

"You were the reason my previous plan fell through. And you haven't even heard our proposition," I say, trying and failing to keep my voice from rising.

"I don't need to. I have no faith in anything devised by the two of you. You have no experience in political matters, and it's no secret you abhor me. Why would I believe, for a moment, that you'd wish to return me to the throne?"

"For the sake of my sisters, and the people of Paris, and because sometimes doing the right thing involves making compromises," I shout.

Desgrez places a hand on my shoulder and tugs me back. "Which is what we've come to discuss with you, Your Royal Highness."

"I cannot fathom why you'd cast your lot with theirs, Captain." Louis sniffs. "I thought you to be of a sounder mind. Josse is a heinous rebel. You told me he was dead as far as you were concerned."

"And I meant every word. I had every intention of punishing him for his crimes, but then I saw their plan in action. I urge you to at least listen to our proposition." Desgrez's voice is indulgent and he sketches a ridiculous bow that makes me want to kick him. Louis doesn't deserve a scrap of our respect. He's impossible. Unbearable. I don't know why I ever thought this could work.

"Fine," Louis says. "I'll listen—to *you*, Captain. But I promise nothing. And I shan't withhold my feelings."

"I would never expect you to do so," Desgrez says, and I roll my eyes so hard it's a wonder they don't get stuck backwards.

"Josse, I need your help with the girls," Mirabelle says, even though they look completely content sitting beside her. She thumps her palm against the ground and casts me a look that says, *Before you ruin everything.*

Sighing, I join her as Desgrez launches into an explanation of how we healed the fishermen and how we intend to save the targeted nobles and unite the common man and nobleman in order to overthrow the Shadow Society. "The nobility, of course, will welcome your rule," he says, "but in order to keep the people on your side once you've obtained the throne, we must prove you're going to be a *different* sort of ruler than your father."

Louis frowns. "Different how? My father was the Sun King. There has never been a more glorious and celebrated monarch in the history of France. His military successes were unparalleled. He was an enthusiastic patron of the arts. He encouraged industry and fostered trade and commerce. Shall I go on?"

He was so vain and drunk on flattery, he ignored his subjects entirely, I want to say.

Thankfully Desgrez has a bit more tact. "Louis XIV was without comparison, it's true," he carefully agrees. "However, he was not the most *mindful* of his lesser citizens. And in the end, they killed him for it."

"So what are you suggesting?"

Desgrez takes a deep breath. "In exchange for helping you rise against La Voisin, the commoners will be given a voice in the new government—representatives who will ensure you are aware of their needs."

"That seems reasonable," Marie says, looking to Louis with hope. But his lips pinch and his face grows steadily redder until he resembles an overripe tomato. The seed pearls on his frockcoat tremble.

"Are you proposing I work *with* the rabble?" he demands.

"Brace yourselves," I whisper to the girls. "He's about to scream louder than when his breakfast tray arrives late to his levée."

Mirabelle lowers her eyebrows at me, but Françoise and Anne toss their heads back and giggle.

"This is no laughing matter," Louis rejoins. "I am king! Which means the common people work *for* me. I am the single brightest star in the sky. The sun around which they rotate. I shine down upon *them*."

"Pardon my insolence, Your Highness," Desgrez says, "but you are none of those things yet. You could be," he adds swiftly when Louis's eyes flare, "but I fear you will never have the opportunity unless you agree to this proposal. Your father was extraordinary, but he was not well loved by the people. This is the only way to be both."

Louis gnaws on his pinky finger, spitting out bits of nail and skin.

"It's a small concession," Marie says, though I suspect she'd crown a fishwife to get out of these tunnels.

Louis looks at Desgrez, then Marie and the girls, his gaze falling last upon me and Mirabelle. He closes his eyes and pinches the bridge of his long nose. "I don't like it. But since it seems to be our only option, I of course shall be the savior of my city. How do we proceed?"

Before Mirabelle can send word to Gris about our success with the fishmongers, the orphans deliver a note from him. Three short lines: *I'm fine. She's furious. Be prepared.*

Heeding his advice, we spend the next week alternating between brewing curatives and antipoison in the millinery and readying Marie and the girls to aid in the distribution—teaching them how to act and what to say to win the people's favor.

"All that groveling and pleading, insisting how badly you need me, and now you wish me to stay in these tunnels and do nothing?" Louis breathes down my back as I fasten a cloak around Françoise's shoulders.

"It's too dangerous for you to traipse around the city," Desgrez says for the millionth time. "If you're caught by the Shadow Society, we have no prayer of reclaiming the throne. You must stay hidden—for now."

"Forever would be preferable," I mumble under my breath.

"What was that?" Louis demands.

"Oh, nothing." I grin at his wounded expression.

Desgrez looks like he wants to strangle me, and Mirabelle frowns, but I'm not about to be reprimanded. Let Louis see how it feels to be useless and worthless and out of place for once in his life.

"You're welcome to join me in the millinery," Mirabelle offers. "I could use assistance brewing curatives."

Louis's face contorts and I edge closer to Mirabelle, ready to defend her from the horrible insults sure to fly from his lips like daggers. But to everyone's surprise, he mutters, "I'll bear that in mind."

The following evening, while Desgrez and Mirabelle take Anne and Françoise to the rue du Temple, Marie and I rendezvous with Gavril and a handful of orphans in the bramble beneath the Pont Neuf. In addition to killing smoke beasts, the little tricksters have been listening from rooftops and loitering near taverns, stealing snatches of Shadow Society conversation: plans and names and meeting locations. Tonight they claim the Duchesse de Bouillon is in danger, so Marie and I head to her household on the Quai Malaquais to equip her with Viper's Venom antipoison, should the Shadow Society attack.

Marie presses herself against the estate wall and I present myself at the gates. An armored guard appears on the other side, his hand on his sword.

"The duchesse isn't receiving visitors."

"I think she'll make an exception in this case," I say as Marie steps into the light and removes the hood of her cloak.

The guard's eyes widen and he drops to a knee. "Madame Royale!"

"This is no time to stand on ceremony!" I hiss. "Let us in, man!"

He fumbles with the lock and leads us through the forecourt

into the château. A tiny part of me is pleased to see these perilous times have affected even the highest born—the black and white marble tiles are smeared with muddy boot prints and the candles in the chandeliers are burnt to stubs. We find the Duchesse de Bouillon in the music room wearing a shabby muslin gown without a speck of powder on her face.

She glances up at the sound of our footsteps. "Did I not tell you, I do not wish to see . . ." Her voice trails off and a stifled cry burbles from her lips. "It cannot be!" She shoots to her feet and rushes across the room, slowing a few paces away to self-consciously touch her shabby gown before taking Marie's hand. "My dear girl. You're alive."

"It's nothing short of a miracle." Marie smiles, places her other hand atop the duchesse's, and guides her to a seat. I stand at a distance, melting into the wall like I always have—like a servant. The realization makes me jump forward as if the wainscoting bit me. I take a breath for courage and join them in the parlor, standing directly beside Marie. The duchesse frowns up at me, but my sister turns and smiles. "The dauphin lives as well, and it's in large part thanks to our brother, Josse."

The duchesse inspects me for another moment, as if I'm a fly that has landed in her tea, then returns her attention to Marie. "Praise be to God the rightful heir lives. I didn't dare to hope. That witch and her minions are threatening to exterminate anyone with a drop of noble blood."

I clear my throat, itching to point out that until recently *she* was a dedicated client of *that witch and her minions,* but Marie digs her elbow into my thigh and speaks over me. "Which is exactly why we've come." She removes the small phial of antipoison from her skirt and explains how we plan to save the nobility and unite the people.

"Yes, of course. I'll gladly pledge my support. Whatever you need. I also know the location of the Comtesse de Soissons and the Marquis de Cessac—they've gone into hiding but would be most grateful for this elixir. I'm certain they'll side with you as well."

And they do. Over the next few nights, Marie and I repeat the same routine, seeking out nobles of varying degree and title, sometimes in their grand châteaus, but more often hiding in dingy inns and hovels. As word of our visits spread, our hosts become increasingly more decent to me—clasping my shoulder and soggying my shirt with salty tears of thanks. And I'm horrified to discover that it plucks at my ribs and squeezes my heart, the same as when I healed the men and women on the rue du Temple.

These people mocked my heritage and spat at me at court. The laws of justice say I shouldn't care whether they live or die, but there's no denying the swell of emotion that thickens like cream inside my chest every time we deliver a dose of salvation. How it fills me up with a sweetness I've never known before.

The feeling only grows when I finally get to accompany Desgrez, Anne, and Françoise to the Quai de la Grève a week later to deliver coughing draughts and fever tonics and to seek the fishwives' help brewing antipoison. With the added capacity of so many kitchens, we would be able to distill more curatives than La Voisin could ever hope to counter with her Viper's Venom.

Anne knocks on the door of Ameline, the most outspoken fishwife. "Greetings, my good lady. I am Louise Marie Anne de Bourbon, Mademoiselle de Tours." She lowers into an impeccable curtsy that would have made Madame Lemaire coo with delight.

"And I am Louise Françoise de Bourbon, Mademoiselle de Nantes," Françoise says, bobbing a curtsy of her own. "We are here to deliver medications and beseech your help in reclaiming our city. We hear you and your colleagues are most proficient in the kitchen, and we were hoping you might assist us in brewing antipoison."

"Well, I'll be damned!" Ameline crows, wiping tears from her laughing eyes. "Your cock-and-bull story was true," she says to me and Desgrez.

"We're not supposed to say *damn!*" Anne looks at me with worried eyes. Ameline laughs harder, her black hair shaking like a waterfall.

"Let them in already." Ameline's husband, Étienne, appears behind her in the doorway. "It isn't proper to keep the king's daughters waiting in the cold."

The only dark spot to our otherwise extraordinary progress is that I'm forced to spend far more time with my *beloved* brother than I'd prefer. Which isn't surprising, since the amount of time I'd prefer to spend with him is none.

He passes his days either skulking around the sewer complaining about being left behind, or hovering over Mirabelle's shoulder in the millinery, pretending to take an interest in alchemy. A poorly veiled ruse to nettle me. I wish Mirabelle hadn't suggested he assist her. The millinery was our safe haven. Where this rebellion began. Where *we* began. And now Louis is there every waking moment. Driving me within an inch of my sanity.

"It turns out I've a natural proficiency for healing," he tells me late one afternoon when I come to collect the curatives to be delivered to Les Halles that night. He's working a pestle and mortar, and a sheen of sweat coats his face, making his golden hair stick to his forehead. His *real* hair. The wig has been tossed to the corner like a wet rag. And he seems oblivious to the smears on his doublet.

I scowl at his insipid act. He may fool the others, but not me. "The only thing you've a natural proficiency for is irritating everyone around you."

"You're *both* irritating me." Mirabelle slams her father's grimoire down on the counter. "Would it kill you to be civil to each other?"

Louis and I both respond with a zealous *"Yes."* The first time in our lives we've agreed.

When I return hours later, I'm eager to tell Mirabelle of the rumors swirling through Les Halles: tales of the angel,

La Vie, whose phials of antipoison are said to raise the dead; how La Voisin can be heard howling with rage from the Louvre each night; and—most shocking of all—that Shadow Society heralds have been crying from the crowded square of the Palais de Justice, condemning anyone found brewing, distributing, or using antipoison.

Our plan is working. The Shadow Society is losing control.

But before I can utter a word of this good news, Louis launches into an interrogation: "Describe the exact expression on the peasants' faces when you said my name . . . Did they seem inspired? Uplifted?"

"If they were *inspired* and *uplifted* it was due to the curatives, not you," I say.

"Yes, but they must have some opinion of me. If only I could go before them—"

"Absolutely not. Even if it wasn't too dangerous, you would sway them from the cause entirely."

Louis sets his pestle down and says in a pathetic, warbling voice, "Am I that unbearable?"

"You are worse than unbearable."

Mirabelle pins us both with an imperious look. "Will the two of you please stop? Or take your quarrels elsewhere. I'm trying to concentrate."

"I'll stop squabbling as soon as he stops being . . ." I can't even think of the proper word to describe how annoying Louis is so I settle for, ". . . *himself!*"

He's quiet for so long, I silently congratulate myself for winning this bout, but then he speaks, his voice low and hard. "For all you complain about me being insufferable and difficult, you're just as impossible. I was a selfish, mule-brained puttock when I was blind to the needs of the people. Now, when I am actively trying to help, I'm bothersome and unnecessary. No matter what I do, it's never good enough for you."

A punch of disbelieving laughter bursts from my mouth, and the more Louis insists it isn't funny, the harder I laugh. "Do you expect me to feel sorry for you? I've felt that way every minute of my life! *You* made certain I felt that way! So excuse me if I don't take pity on you after a few paltry weeks of dithering."

"When are you going to open your eyes and realize it wasn't I who ostracized you? Nor Father nor his ministers nor even the courtiers. We didn't need to. You sabotaged yourself! You made certain no one would ever see you as anything more than a worthless bastard."

"That's all I was permitted to be! Father despised me. I had no opportunity—"

"Wrong!" Louis shouts with more vehemence than I've ever heard. "In the beginning, he preferred you."

"No one believes your lies."

"It's true. You were more like him in every way—confident and full of swagger, loud and brash and physically capable. Everything I'm not. I overheard him once, when we were twelve years old, complaining to the Grand Condé that he wished you'd been born legitimate, as you'd have made a better king—notwithstanding your rakish ways and boorish behavior."

I slap both hands down on the table. "Stop! Lying!"

"Stop blaming me, and everyone else, for not living up to your potential. You've no one to blame but yourself!"

A high-pitched ringing fills my ears. Dark spots bloom across my vision, devouring the counter and phials and herbs until all I see is black. Until I'm certain I'll rip the millinery down board by board and bury Louis in the wreckage if I don't leave this instant.

"Josse—" Mirabelle takes a cautious step toward me.

I stumble back, growling a slew of profanities, and slam out into the night. I gulp back the chilly air and run down one street and up another without a care for where I'm going. Faster, faster. Farther, farther. But I can't outrun those bedamned words:

He preferred you.

You sabotaged yourself.

Lies. They have to be. But the sobs in my throat are so thick now, I have to stop to catch my breath. I reach out to steady myself on a tree, but my shaking hand misses its mark and I crash to the mucky ground, melting into a pathetic puddle of tears. Every interaction I ever had with my father flashes through my mind, colored by this horrifying new revelation. What if his pinched expression wasn't born of disgust, but dismay? What if he sent me to work in the kitchen not to hide me away or punish me, but to reform me?

He wanted me to be something more. He waited patiently,

giving me chance after chance to prove myself, and I was so indignant and impatient that I squandered every opportunity.

I gave him no choice but to push me away.

I lie beneath the tree like a boneless, vacant-eyed drunkard, thankful for the deepening sky that hides my tear-streaked face. Finally, when I haven't a tear left in my eyes nor a heart in my chest, I stagger to my feet and continue down the road. Not hearing, not seeing, just floating along like a ghost.

I stumble into scores of people, but one of them is so tall and solid, it feels like I've dashed my head against the city wall.

"Princeling!" Gris shouts, gripping my shoulders and shaking me. "I know you heard me. I've called your name a dozen times."

"Leave me be," I grumble. I try to push away, but Gris tightens his grip until I yelp and look up—into eyes that are as bloodshot and bewildered as mine. He's gasping for breath as if he ran all the way from the Louvre.

"What's wrong with you?" I ask.

He releases me and folds in half, bracing himself on his knees. "I came . . . to warn you . . ." he pants. "La Voisin is planning something terrible. We haven't much time."

21

MIRABELLE

A familiar prickle of pain grips my chest as I watch Josse tear down the rue de Navarine. He vanishes into the violet-stained twilight, and the tether between us pulls taut. My mind screams to go after him. I know precisely how he feels. His entire world—everything he thought he knew—came crashing down around him. But I also know there's nothing I can say to ease his pain. Not yet.

"Is it true? What you said about your father?" I ask Louis after we've spent a full minute staring at the door in silence.

He wipes his hands on his smudged doublet and turns to the counter. "What reason would I have to lie?"

"You saw Josse storm out of here. It destroyed him."

"I assure you, if I was lying, the story would have painted me in a better light." He picks up a pestle and mortar bowl and resumes crushing fennel seeds with frightening intensity.

"That must have been a difficult conversation to overhear."

"It wasn't difficult in the least," Louis snaps, making it clear it most certainly was difficult. "That's where I and my bastard brother differ. Father thought I was ill-suited, so I did everything in my power to prove him wrong. Josse assumed he was ill-suited and proved himself right."

"And I'm sure you did nothing to reinforce his beliefs?" I shoot the dauphin an accusatory glare. "I have an older sister. I know how it goes."

Before Louis can respond, the door flies open and a handful of orphans parade into the shop bearing a scaled smoke beast atop their shoulders. "Special delivery for Madamoiselle La Vie," Gavril sings.

This smoke beast has a long serpentine body covered in blood-red scales. The orphans coil what they can atop the board, leaving a good ten lengths trailing across the floor.

"Dead, I see." I try not to sound disappointed as I circle the table inspecting the creature. I lift one of its short, clawed forearms and let it fall with a thump. This is the third beast they've brought me. I feel horrible asking for more, but I've had no luck controlling the creatures, no matter how I mince or boil or combine the dead with my blood.

To find the secret link to my alchemy, I need a live specimen. I don't know how else to proceed. I'm no closer to understanding how the beasts function, and with our rebellion gaining traction, the day looms ever nearer when our success or failure will hinge upon whether or not I can stand against Lesage and the unnatural power I gave him.

"We tried to capture it live, honest we did," Gavril says, "but the battle got rather *heated.*" He points his thumb at a boy whose pants are singed at the knee and a girl whose thigh-skimming braids are now blunt, uneven locks.

"Don't apologize, this is fine," I say. "I'll make it work."

Somehow.

I roll up my sleeves, seize a knife, and bury it in the silver underbelly of the smoke beast. The orphans scream and scatter to the far side of the room to avoid the midnight spray of blood and I presume the dauphin will do the same, but he steps closer, leaning over to inspect its innards.

"Fascinating. May I try?" He holds out his hand for my knife, and I laugh with surprise. He is pompous and tedious, without question, but he's also gritty and determined and unflinching. Josse has been unfair to him. But Louis hasn't exactly been fair to Josse either.

"You and your brother are more alike than you think," I say.

"Since you're fond of the bastard for some unknown reason, I shall take that as a compliment. But in truth, I'm horribly offended."

He takes up the knife and I show him where to make the incision, but before the blade breaks skin, the door opens once again and Josse trips across the threshold. He's still panting and wild-eyed, but now, instead of looking like a raspberry, his face is completely drained of color.

I dart out from behind the counter and place myself between the brothers. "If you've returned to fight. . . ." I warn Josse, but my voice falls away because Gris barges in on Josse's heels. His golden curls are plastered to his sweaty forehead and he's gasping so hard, he has to steady himself against the wall. Both boys look near about to faint.

"What happened? Are you hurt?" I rush to Gris and begin inspecting his arms and chest for wounds. "Did Mother do this to you?"

He shakes his head and puffs out, "It isn't me . . . you need . . . to worry about."

"Who, then?" I spin to Josse. "You?"

"Tell them what you told me," Josse says.

Gris draws a deep breath and straightens, but his eyes widen at the absolute pandemonium of the overcrowded millinery, and he lurches back.

"No need to worry," I tell him. "These are people I've healed. They're trustworthy."

He nods, but continues to back away. "The princeling will tell you. I can't stay."

"But you ran all this way, surely another minute—"

"They'll notice I'm gone." He shakes his head and takes off down the street, even though he's hardly caught his breath.

"What was that about?" I turn to Josse.

"La Voisin is growing desperate," he says. "She plans to raze the fields in the Faubourg Saint-Germain once Gris has brewed more of Lesage's blood draught. Gris says the longest he can pretend to struggle and dither is three days."

I feel as if I've plunged into the icy Seine. Why the devil would she do such a thing? If the barley and rye are lost, the people will starve before the year's half through. "Mother cares for the common people. She would never . . ." Gavril and the children fall eerily quiet, making my voice sound high and shrill. "How does she plan to win back the people's support if they're starving?"

"She no longer plans to *win* their support," Josse says. "She plans to *take* it. By decreasing the food supply and controlling what remains, she can choose whom she distributes rations to. The rebels will have no choice but to come crawling back and fall at her feet."

"No." I whisper at first, but my anger is a live and coiled thing, slithering up my throat. I pound my fist against the counter. "NO! Thousands will perish. Our uprising will crumble."

"Can we head them off on their way to set the blaze?" Louis asks. "Engage the Shadow Society in battle?"

"Only if we wish to lose." Josse says it as if Louis's suggestion is the daftest thing he's ever heard.

"But their ranks are composed of inexperienced soldiers just like ours," Louis says.

"Hey!" Gavril puffs out his chest and gestures to the smoke beast on the table. "I'd hardly call us inexperienced."

"You're definitely experienced," I agree, "but they have magic. Not even you could contend with a dozen beasts at once." The thought makes guilt rise up my throat like a sickness, and I wrap my arms around my stomach. Perhaps the orphans *would* be able to contend with that many beasts if I could decipher how to seize control of them, even partway.

"So we trap the poisoners in their palace somehow," Louis suggests. "As they did to us at Versailles. Or we poison them, the way they've been poisoning half the city."

I rub my arms and begin pacing back and forth behind the counter. "I'll not stoop to their level. There must be another way." My heartbeat quickens with my steps. The air is hot and thick and it is hard to breathe. I cast around the millinery for something, anything, and like always, my eyes are drawn to Father's grimoire, half buried beneath a sack of feverfew.

You will be a great alchemist one day.

Of course.

I grapple for the book and flip furiously through the pages, a tiny ember of hope reigniting in my chest. When I find the recipe I'm looking for, I squeal and tap my finger excitedly on the page. "Gavril, do you think you can collect Ameline and Ètienne, as well as one or two representatives from the rue du Temple and Les Halles? And Josse, go drag Desgrez from whatever gambling den he's hiding in, and fetch the Marquis de Cessac. We'll reconvene here in an hour. I have an idea."

I have never seen a more unlikely grouping. Duchesses stand beside beggars. Fishwives rub elbows with royalty. No one looks particularly comfortable, and they all attempt to keep to their own, but they're here. Together. And the dinginess of the cramped shop has given them something to commiserate about. They frown at the explosion of herbs on the counter and bemoan the smears of black smoke-beast blood coating the floor and sticking to their boots. I stand off to the side, clutching Father's book and collecting my thoughts. Convincing the nobility and commoners to work together in theory is one thing, but saving the crops will require everyone's cooperation. And I haven't an alternate plan if they refuse.

"You get the most adorable little wrinkle between your eyebrows when you're anxious," Josse says, nudging my shoulder with his.

I swat him with the book. "Focus, princeling! The wrinkle between my eyes is the last thing you should be thinking about."

"Second to last. Because I also like the way you twirl your finger through that curl above your ear."

I immediately drop my hand. His goading smile is so devilishly handsome, I either want to kiss him or punch him—I'm unsure which. "You're impossible," I hiss.

"Or am I a genius? For a moment, you forgot to be nervous."

I blink up at him. I suppose I did.

"Whatever you're planning, I'm sure it's brilliant. And even if it's not, I'll fight anyone who disagrees." He puts up his fists, and a smile steals across my lips. "Come on."

After taking a deep breath, I stride to the front of the group and call them to attention. "Thank you for coming. We've recently learned of the Shadow Society's plans to raze the fields in the

Faubourg Saint-Germain. By greatly diminishing the rye and barley, the people will be forced to turn to my mother and the royal stores for support. Our rebellion will die—and thousands of starving souls along with it—*unless* we save the crops and reveal the Shadow Society's plan. Then we shall be the saviors of the city, and hopefully those who have remained loyal to my mother will be turned to our cause instead. With the entire city behind us, we may have the strength to stand against them."

Questions and suggestions fly at me—mostly the same worries we discussed at the outset—so Josse and Louis help me answer queries and make assurances. It's most of our allies' first time meeting Louis, and for all Josse worried about him "ruining everything," the dauphin is doing splendidly. Everyone seems to hang on his words. They grin at his tattered doublet and seem to stand taller when he acknowledges their opinions.

"If we cannot fight the poisoners or prevent them from leaving the palace, how do we proceed?" Desgrez asks.

I hold up Father's grimoire, the worn red leather catching the torchlight. "Through an alchemical process called fixation. My father studied it in depth and developed a powder resistant to flames. All we have to do is produce the powder and spread it over the crops *before* the Shadow Society sets them ablaze."

"And when do they plan to do that?" the Marquis de Cessac calls.

"How long will it take to make the powder?" Étienne asks.

"My informant can hold off for three days, which gives us two and a half days to produce and distribute the powder," I say.

Ameline fixes me with a steely expression. "Can it be done?"

"Yes, but only if everyone contributes. Do you think you can convince the other fishwives to help? We'll need a good many kettles."

"Aye, aye. I'll rally them straight away. Even those without a heart for rebellion won't refuse if the alternative is starvation."

"Excellent." I rip an empty page from the back of Father's grimoire, copy the recipe, and hand it off. "Étienne . . ." I turn to her husband. "Can you recruit your fellow fishermen to help us distribute the powder? And you"—I look to the haberdasher and milk maid, representing the merchants from Les Halles—"can you assemble carts to carry the powder? They need to look like those that come and go from the market."

They nod and set off, and the pressure on my chest—which felt as crushing as an iron cauldron—lifts considerably. I steal a glance at Josse, and his enthusiastic smile makes my stomach dip. I quickly look away before my cheeks grow any hotter.

"We'll begin spreading the word," Gavril says, "so a crowd will be present to witness La Voisin's treachery and our miraculous powder."

"And I'll scrounge up tunics and hats and such, to ensure we look like a proper vendor train," Desgrez offers.

"And myself and the Marquis de Cessac shall lead the expedition," Louis adds excitedly.

"Perfect," I say.

But as soon as our allies are out the door, Josse turns to Louis and says, "Absolutely not. *You* cannot lead us anywhere."

His words echo around the shop, sharp as nails. Thankfully most of our allies are already down the street, but Ameline and Ètienne stop and turn on the bottom step. All eyes lock on Josse, and Louis doesn't just stare—he shoots daggers of fire. The air is so thick with tension, I can scarcely breathe.

Devil's horns, not again. "This is no time to—"

Louis cuts me off, his voice a low growl. "Why not, *brother?*"

"It's too great a risk, of course." Josse gives a flippant wave of his hand. "You must stay hidden."

"We both know you're not concerned for my well-being. Which makes me think the risk is to *you* and *your pride.* You're worried the people will forget you the moment they see me."

"I'm worried you'll foul up our carefully laid plans and ruin everything. I could lead the mission just as easily and far more effectively."

"I disagree. In order for the greater plan to succeed, the people need to see me and nobles like Cessac defending them, fighting with them."

Josse buries his hands in his hair and looks to me, begging me to jump to his defense, but I bite my lower lip and glance at Louis. It's a risk to let him leave the safety of our hideouts, but we'll be there to assist and protect him, and I do think it would be good for the people to see him engaged in their struggles. I don my most pleading expression. "Perhaps we should allow the dauphin this chance. I've been working closely with him this past week, and I think you'll find he's far more competent—"

"He doesn't truly wish to help," Josse interjects. "You don't know him like I do."

"I do wish to help," Louis insists. "I've had time to think, to consider—"

"Yes, I know. I was trapped with you for weeks. I heard plenty of your *thoughts* on our accommodations and the fare and the company, and none of it was helpful in the least."

Louis lowers his chin and draws a ragged breath. "I haven't complained in weeks. I'm trying to change. I want to be a better king. Help me do this, Josse." He looks up at Josse with the most open and earnest expression. The closest a king could ever come to pleading.

I hold my breath, willing Josse to agree. Marie looks fit to burst with pride from where she sits with the girls off to the side. But Josse pulls his tricorne hat lower and turns his back to Louis. "I'm afraid that's beyond me."

Louis makes a pitiful sputtering noise. I press my lips tight and look up at the ceiling. What I really want to do is slap Josse hard across the face. All he had to do was give the tiniest fraction—Louis was willing to bridge the rest—but he couldn't do it. He *wouldn't* do it.

Damn the princeling and his pride.

The Marquis de Cessac glares at Josse, then places a hand on Louis's shoulder. "Thankfully, we all have a say in this, and I say you lead."

Josse whirls on the nobleman. "I saved your life!"

"Technically, she saved my life." He nods to me. "And it sounds as if His Royal Highness assisted in making the antipoison. And Madame Royale delivered it. . . ."

"I took part in all of those things! And you're still outnumbered at any rate."

Ameline whisper-shouts from the bottom of the stairs. "I think the dauphin should lead."

"As do I," Marie calls from the corner. Anne and Françoise clap their agreement.

"And I." Desgrez shrugs guiltily when Josse glares at him. "Sorry, mate. It's for the best."

Josse turns last to me. "Are you against me as well?"

I look down and finger the cover of Father's grimoire. "I'm not against you so much as I'm *for* allowing Louis to do this."

"Fine." Josse rips off his hat and wrings it through his fists. "Fine. But when this ends poorly, don't say I didn't warn you."

His cryptic words spindle down my neck like spiders, but I brush them off and find a smile for the eager faces around me.

Our ranks are swelling. We have a plan, with a clear end in sight.

There's no reason to believe this will end poorly.

22

JOSSE

They've all rejected me: Desgrez, my sisters, even Mirabelle. I don't know why I ever thought I could lead this bedamned rebellion.

Perhaps try a different way of leading, my father whispers. Not in the short, clipped tone I came to expect from him, but in a gentle, coaxing manner that makes everything worse.

Because I'm doing it again—lashing out and pushing everyone away and refusing to acknowledge my fault in any of it. The worst part is I *know* I'm doing it now, but I still can't stop. I'm like a hedgehog, raising my spines and curling in to protect myself from the truth.

I lean against the counter, close my eyes, and pull several deep breaths through my nose. I can be gracious. I don't have to let this get to me. But when I look up and see Mirabelle fussing over Louis, sending him off with the Marquis de Cessac to ready for the expedition, my irritation flares again, burning like a pan straight from the oven.

"You need to be seen aiding the rebels, but not necessarily looking like one," Mirabelle tells Louis. "The people still need to view you as king, so after the crops are saved, remove your disguise to prove you're alive and well. Let the people see you fighting for them."

Louis beams, and I can't stomach another bedamned second of it. I storm out of the shop, not knowing where I'm going. I just have to get away.

I don't get far.

Mirabelle's quick footsteps chase me down the street. "Josse, wait."

"Why? So you can twist your knife deeper? Sell me for thirty pieces of silver?"

She grabs my shirttail and pulls me into an alleyway. "Don't you think you're being slightly overdramatic?"

Yes. I know I am. But I growl adamantly, "No."

"You honestly can't see the benefit of allowing the people to see Louis defending them?"

"Yes, but—"

"Can't you see he's trying? Would it kill you to give him a chance?"

"Why should I when the same courtesy was never extended to me?"

"Wasn't it?" she says quietly. "Or did you choose not to take it?"

It was bad enough having Louis hurl this accusation at me. Hearing Mirabelle repeat it feels like a punch to the gut. I can't catch my breath. Tiny stars explode across my vision and form a picture of my father's face. He looks at me, so warm and sympathetic, and I hear his voice again: *You don't have to sabotage these relationships, too.*

But I do. If I don't protect myself, no one will.

I draw my shoulders back, ready to tell Mirabelle to keep her nose out of my affairs, but she grips my shoulders and says, "You're enough, Josse. You always have been. You're the only one who can't see it."

Her declaration shatters the brittle walls around my heart. I gasp as the shards cut inward: stabbing and slicing and flaying me wide open. I sink slowly to the ground, my back scraping against the splintered wood of the building, and I plunk my forehead on my knees.

"You're right," I choke out. "Louis is right. You're all bloody right."

I feel Mirabelle ease down beside me. Her arm brushes mine, and the sage and smoke scent of her tickles my nose. She doesn't say anything, just sits there—a rope waiting to pull me to shore whenever I'm ready to grab on.

"I did care," I admit to myself as much as Mirabelle. The truth of it rattles through me, shaking the very foundation of my soul. My voice cracks, which is beyond mortifying, and when I try to cough it away, I end up making an even more pathetic sniffling sound. If Mirabelle didn't think me pitiful already, she certainly does now. Since I haven't a crumb of dignity left to lose, I let all of the words tangled up in my head—years and years of anger and heartache and frustration—tumble out like vomit.

"I've always cared. I wanted my father's approval so damned much it nearly killed me. He was so *big*. So bold and commanding. A veritable God on earth. And he was *my* father. It was almost too much for a motherless, sniveling nobody like me to fathom."

"Believe it or not, I know a little something about that." She knocks her knee against mine and leaves it there. The outsides of our thighs press together. "Keep going."

And I do. Now that I've started, I can't seem to stop. I'm desperate to purge these dark, festering feelings. "I didn't want much—just a scrap of acknowledgment. An occasional smile or a nod. But he swept past me in the halls without so much as a glance of recognition, as if I was nothing more than a statuary or a painting. Any nameless servant. So I *made* him see me—any way I could: I flirted mercilessly with the highest-ranking ladies at court, and I purposely mucked out the horses' stalls right before serving in the great hall, so the grime and stench would hang over his lavish feasts. I even tossed a wasps' nest through the window of his staterooms and laughed as he and his ministers ran down the stairs, shrieking.

"I didn't know *why* I was cutting up, of course. I told myself it was because I didn't care what he thought, that I didn't want his attention or approval. But I did. More than anything. And acting like a hellion was the only way to get it—or so I thought." I press the backs of my wrists into my eyes and let out a long, slow breath. "Apparently, he *did* see me, but I was too bullheaded to realize it. Or perhaps he was too proud to show it. Either way, I pushed and he retreated, and we grew farther and farther apart until there was no bridging the gap between us. I made him hate me. His final memories of me held nothing but exasperation and disappointment, and now I can't change that. He will never know me as anything more than a worthless bastard."

"I disagree," Mirabelle says. "After my father died, my mother tried to taint my memories of him. She insisted he never loved us, that he was consumed by his obsession, and for a time, I let myself be swayed. But now that I share his grit and conviction, I feel him grinning with approval every time I distill a batch of antipoison. I hear his voice in my head when I stand up to Mother. I *know* he's proud of me—that he forgives me for siding with her. And I have a feeling your father feels the same. How could he not? You're healing his people, reclaiming his city, and restoring your brother to the throne. I promise that the Sun King is smiling down from Heaven, urging you on."

A tingling sensation presses behind my eyes. I try to disagree, but I seem to be incapable of making any sound beyond a raspy wheeze. Mirabelle's words worm beneath my skin, burrowing deeper and deeper until they sink into the core of me. Like an arrow hitting its mark. All at once, a massive serving tray of doubt and inadequacy lifts from my shoulders, and the lightness is astounding. The relief is so complete. I tilt my head back and tears spill down my cheeks, purging the last of my bitterness.

When my eyes finally dry up, I wipe my nose on my sleeve with a self-conscious laugh. "Look at me, blubbering in an alley when there's so much to be done. You probably think me ridiculous."

"You're *completely* ridiculous," she agrees. But then she grabs my hand and squeezes until I look down at her. "But you're also brave and big-hearted and determined and bold and there's no one I'd rather stand against my mother with."

Her eyelashes bat softly against her cheek. The smattering of freckles across her nose shine like specks of gold. She glances at my lips, and the tiny gap between us is filled with so much sizzling energy, I can't think straight. *Do it, Josse. Lean in.* I suck in another breath, trying to muster up the courage. Mirabelle grips my collar with a laugh and pulls my mouth to hers.

The kiss isn't timid or questioning. It's a statement. A demand. Her lips move hungrily against mine, and her fingers dig into my shoulders. I slide my hands around her waist and pull her onto my lap, deepening the kiss. She sighs, and my entire body flares with heat. Ever since we first healed the homeless, I've wondered how this would be, what it would feel like.

Mirabelle's hands are everywhere; trailing down my chest and tangling in my hair, leaving a trail of fire. She rocks her hips, and I lean back with a groan. Only I lean too far and knock my head against the wall. We laugh against each other's lips and kiss slower. Deeper. Savoring and exploring. She tastes of mint and honey and magic. Smells of smoke and sage and night. I could kiss her forever and ever and . . .

"That's enough." She pulls back suddenly and taps the tip of my nose. "We can't spend all night kissing, princeling. There's work to be done."

"But—"

"Perhaps if we work quickly, there will be time for more of *this*"—she pecks me again, the barest brush of her lips—"later. But for now . . ." She claps and motions me up.

"You're killing me."

"No, my *mother* is trying to kill you—and everyone who disagrees with her." She winks and marches back to the millinery. I follow with a shake of my head.

We spend the better part of that night and the following morning strapped in goggles and masks, producing the flame-resistant powder. Instead of working in the millinery, we join Ameline and the fishwives in their homes on the Quai de la Grève so Mirabelle can trek from kitchen to kitchen to check the consistency and potency.

The powder is extraordinary—a shimmery silver substance composed of salts of ammonia and phosphate. I haven't a clue how it works, but when combined, they knit into a sparkling sheet of gossamer that's supposedly impervious to flame.

"This twinkly *powder* is going to protect the fields?" Gavril holds up a jar and inspects it with a frown.

"Do you doubt me?" Mirabelle's huff is only partly in jest.

"Not exactly . . ." he says, "but I think the lot of us would feel better if we tested it first."

"Very well." Mirabelle tugs a string from the ratty hem of Gavril's tunic, rolls it through the powder, then holds it directly over a candle. We gather round, leaning in to better see.

The string ripples and spins, glowing white and hot, but not a puff of smoke escapes into the air. And when Mirabelle removes it from the flame and tosses it at Gavril's face, his horrified cry quickly transforms into laughs. He waves the scrap overhead.

"It's not even warm! Does it work on larger things?" Before anyone can stop them, the orphans are sprinkling powder over everything—snippets of parchment, the window curtains, a dead mouse they find beneath the cupboards—and holding candles to them.

"Enough of that!" Ameline cuffs Gavril over the head. "You're making a mess."

By the morning of the third day, three separate kitchens are stacked floor to ceiling with bottles, and the stationers are loading them onto carts.

"This should hopefully be enough to cover the fields," Mirabelle says, stepping away from her cauldron to offer encouragement to the fishwives working near her. Once she's spoken to each of them, she joins Desgrez and Louis and the Marquis de Cessac to discuss our route through the city. But midway through her sentence, she peeks over at me, somehow sensing my gaze.

Her goggles are pushed high on her forehead, making her short curls stand in every direction. Her cheeks are smudged with streaks of silver. And the smile that steals across her lips sets my heart to racing. We haven't had another moment alone since the alley, but the memory teases and tempts me every time I close my eyes: the heat of her lips, the soft curve of her body, the heady scent of her corkscrew curls.

Maybe . . . if our plan is successful and Louis is restored to the throne . . . maybe there could be a future for us beyond all of this.

"You're not very discreet." Marie appears at my side, smirking.

I cough to mask my surprise. "I haven't a clue what you mean."

"It looks to me like you're in love with her."

"Josse is in love with Mirabelle?" Anne pops out from behind Marie and grins up at me. Françoise materializes on my other side, giggling hysterically.

"Josse is in love with Mirabelle!"

"Keep your voices down," I hiss. "Mirabelle and I are allies, nothing more."

Marie rolls her eyes. "Your words say one thing, but your actions say otherwise."

"You mustn't lie, Josse," Françoise says with a tut. "Madame Lemaire says lying is a mortal sin, and you'll surely burn in Hell for it. Though I think she'd also condemn you for loving one of *them*, so either way, you're doomed."

"I'm not in love with her!" I say again, nearly shouting.

"Not in love with whom?" Mirabelle strolls up behind us at

the worst moment possible, and she's grinning like she knows precisely whom. I want to crawl into one of the cauldrons and die.

"This isn't the time nor place for *love*." Desgrez shoots me and Mirabelle a ridiculous google-eyed look that sends Anne and Françoise into another bout of giggles. Then he calls the group to attention. "We have only until sundown to distribute the powder—the razing will take place after dark so there's no missing the blaze—which means we must focus and work quickly."

As promised, he passes out disguises. I don't know where he finds them, but today they're drab, faded farmers' rags, patched and pieced with crooked stitching. Mirabelle wears a brown scarf over her shorn hair and an oversized apron. My shirt has a yellow sweat stain around the collar that smells as if the previous wearer keeled over from exhaustion.

"If anyone should ask, we are farmers leaving Les Halles with our unsold wares," he announces.

When we pass Madame Bissette's, I kiss Anne and Françoise on the head and tell them to behave for Marie, and then we follow Louis and the Marquis de Cessac across the bridge and down the left bank, our haggard party bumping along like a convoy of swaybacked mules. For the most part, no one pays us any mind. We blend in to the dusty bustle of these outlying streets. The few people who do notice us either turn up their noses or yell at us to get out of the way. Swift carriages haven't the patience for a weary procession like ours.

The cluttering of townhouses with peeling shutters and slate roofs slowly gives way to a smattering of cottages followed by the occasional shack surrounded by fields and fields of green and brown and yellow. It's nearly summer and the waves of wheat sway like dancers in the wind. Wild and rippling, like Mirabelle's hair before she cut it. I gaze longingly at her back, five or six barrows ahead.

"Pull your head out of the clouds and start on that barley field down the way." Desgrez shoves my shoulder. He sounds annoyed, but he's grinning and shaking his head. "You might as well take the girl with you. I can't have you two mooning across the fields at each other."

"We wouldn't—we're not . . ." I stammer.

"Josse. I used to spend my days interrogating prisoners. Your lies are wasted on me. And it's unnecessary. She's agreeable enough . . . for a poisoner." He cuffs my shoulder and strides off, ordering the fishmongers and stationers to different fields, some within and some positioned around the exterior to achieve the fastest and most efficient coverage of the crops. Countrymen and field laborers wander over to ask what we're about and readily volunteer their help, nearly doubling our numbers. Louis remains with the carts so he'll be able to reveal himself when everyone returns with their empty jars.

Mirabelle trails her fingers gently across my back as she passes by to take her place down the fence line, and my entire body shivers. From beneath her scarf, her dark eyes sparkle with mischief and eagerness and *hope*. I feel it too—like a fountain bubbling to life inside my chest, rising higher and higher until it spills over the edges of my being. I tilt my head back and inhale the warmth and sunlight. For the first time in months, the sky is a vivid, watery blue, and the tiny white clouds look like dollops of cream floating toward the horizon. My jar of fire powder catches the light, throwing fractals of indigo and rose and saffron.

Desgrez climbs atop a stack of hay bales in the centermost field and waves his hands to call us to attention. He may lead with the authority of a police captain, but he doesn't resemble one in the slightest. Today he's wearing a frayed tunic and wool trousers that leave a wide swath of skin exposed above his boots. He's completed his ensemble with a limp straw hat, half eaten by moths.

I chuckle and remind myself to tell him the look suits him when we return to the millinery. I already know his response. He'll brush the dust from his shoulders, sweep the hair from his face, and say, *When you're this handsome, everything suits you.*

"On my mark," he shouts. "Let's be quick and efficient."

I uncork my jar. Desgrez raises his hands. But before I toss the first handful of powder, a flash of green explodes in my periphery.

I know only one thing that moves so quickly.

"Desgrez!" I scream, but it's swallowed by a crackling hiss. Lightning smashes into the bales of hay, and the fields burst to flame like a heap of dry kindling. A wall of scorching green rolls across the countryside, licking my cheeks and singeing my eyebrows. I hold up my arms, but the searing brightness blinds me.

Desgrez.

I throw myself toward the inferno to drag him out, but a second bolt strikes directly in front of me, so close that it sends me sprawling on my back. The impact of the ground punches the air from my lungs, and I'm coughing. Retching. But it doesn't register as pain. Not compared to the razor-sharp agony impaling my heart. The world goes dark, and waves of heat and dizziness batter me. I press my fists into my chest and command myself to breathe. *Breathe, Josse.* When at last I catch my breath, a splintering sound tears from my throat—like a howl or a scream but so much louder. So much wilder.

How did they know? The Shadow Society wasn't set to arrive for hours yet. We had plenty of time. It was supposed to be simple. It was supposed to be safe.

Biting my fist, I stare at the dark outline of Desgrez's body until it's consumed by the fire. Then my gaze flicks to the others who lie smoldering beside him—Ètienne and the other fishmongers and laborers who were stationed in the fields. It's too much. Gasping, I tilt my head back, but the sky offers little comfort. A piece of Desgrez's straw hat cartwheels through the smoke and lands on the grass beside my boot. I clutch it tight, even as it burns my fingers. It's all that remains of him. All that remains of any of them.

It could have been me.

Or Mirabelle.

A new wave of panic crashes through my body—cold and sharp

compared to the flames lashing my face. I can't see her. Can't hear her. I drag myself to my feet and stumble down the fence line, shrieking her name. But smoke fills my lungs and throat.

I am choking on the ashes of my friends. My boots slip through what can only be their blood. Cries pierce my ears, and I can't tell if it's their voices or the angry crackle of the fire.

I crash to my knees and vomit into the grass. The world flickers in and out, guttering like a candle. Until there's nothing. No one. Save for darkness and death.

23

MIRABELLE

My skin feels like it's been dipped in hot wax, and I think I'm bleeding; something warm and wet slides down the side of my face. I tell myself to get up. Get help. *Do something, Mira.* But my head is heavier than a mace and my legs are crumpled and boneless beneath me.

I can do nothing but stare into the blue-green inferno.

She knew.

How did Mother know?

I call for Josse but everything's lost in the roar of the blaze. I squeeze my eyes shut and pray he's alive and running to safety—and that he thinks to help Louis. The rebellion will be dead without him.

The rebellion is dead either way.

Our allies lie burning in these fields—my ears still ring with Ètienne's wails; he shouted Ameline's name until the flames leapt over his head. My eyes burn with the final image of Desgrez—his face contorted, his skin glowing the same ghostly green as the day we met. Only this time I couldn't bring him back.

I couldn't save any of them.

Guilt slashes through me like a cold knife, and tears spill down my face.

The fire burns hotter and higher, and shapes take form in the smoke: the flutter of a crimson cape, flashes of velvet masks. I push up to my elbows and try to crawl away, but I don't get far. Long, knobby fingers reach through the haze and grip me by the throat.

"There you are, La Petite Voisin," Fernand says in his slippery serpent voice. "Or should I call you La Vie? Though it looks to me like you bring more death than life."

He wrenches my arm so hard it feels like it's tearing from my body and drags me through the dirt to the road where Mother waits. Her lips are pressed into a determined slash, and triumph dances in her dark eyes as she looks out across the blaze—a victorious general surveying her battlefield. The mother I once knew would have wept and trembled to see so many people drowning in flames, but she no longer resembles the woman who cried beside Father's empty bed each night and lovingly traced the lines across my hands, teaching me and Marguerite to read palms. This monstrous version of Mother drinks in the bilious smoke and stands taller, the flames glinting through the folds of her black satin gown.

"Ah, my long-lost daughter, found at last. I've been sick with worry," Mother jeers. Fernand dumps me at her feet. "You look surprised to see me. Perhaps you weren't expecting me so soon?"

"How did you know?" I ask, but my tongue is as thick and

slow as a slug, and the words come out garbled.

Mother laughs. "Sometimes I forget how hopeless and naïve you are. Did you honestly believe you could outwit me? I have eyes and ears everywhere. Even among your *followers*." She accentuates the word *followers* as if it's ludicrous to think anyone would follow me.

"My people detest you. They would never take your side."

"That's your mistake—assuming they are *your* people. Some of them have always been mine—will always be mine." She claps and Marguerite parades forward, tugging a slack-eyed Gris behind her. "*He* came to *me*," Mother continues, "of his own volition. No threatening, no prodding."

No. An unbearable high-pitched buzzing fills my ears, and my vision swims as I gape up at Gris. He wouldn't. He promised to take my side. Mother is lying. I look into his light-brown eyes and wait for him to flash me a look of indignation. To fight and flail and loudly proclaim his innocence—that he had no part in this. He is my best friend. My brother. He would never betray me like this. He would never betray the people like this.

"Tell me it isn't true," I say, my voice a shaky whisper.

Gris bites his lip and refuses to meet my gaze.

Agony carves through me, and I moan as I curl into a ball. Suddenly my cuts and burns are nothing. *Nothing* compared to the storm raging within me. The scorched fields take on a blood-red hue, and I can't squeeze my fists tight enough, can't scream loud enough. I can't even tell if I'm breathing. It was excruciating to think someone else betrayed us, or that we weren't vigilant enough and the Shadow Society trailed us through the streets.

But *Gris*?

"How could you?" I shout. The sight of him standing there with his slumped shoulders and miserable expression makes me twitch with fury. I want to pluck his deceitful eyes from his skull. I want to strap him to the rack or hang him from the gallows.

Traitor. Traitor. Traitor. My heartbeat roars the word.

"They're dead! You killed them!" I spring to my feet and lash out with a scream, clawing for Gris's throat, but pain explodes across the side of my face. Bright bursts of white and twisting pillars of fire dance across my vision as I plummet back to the ash-covered ground. My breath whooshes out, and my pulse hammers at my temples. When my eyes clear, Fernand stands above me, shaking out his fist. Mother and Lesage join him, sneering down with disgust, followed by Marguerite and, last of all, Gris.

I knew the rest of them were lost, but I trusted him. Needed him. He promised to choose me this once.

"Why?" The word is mangled in my blood-filled mouth. I slide my tongue across my teeth and spit to the side. Gris's cheeks drain of color. "Answer me!" I shout. The exertion is too much, and I curl into the brittle grass.

"The dauphin was there, in the millinery," Gris says. "I'd heard the rumors, of course—La Vie is uniting the commoners and nobility—and I knew you were carousing with the bastard, but I said to myself, *Mira would never align with the dauphin. She swore to me she's only healing. The people are spreading false rumors.* But there he was. Assisting you!"

I think back to that night. How Gris froze in the doorway and left so abruptly. I'd assumed it was because he was hurt, because he was so distraught over Mother's plan to destroy the crops. And I was so distracted by the news, it hadn't even occurred to me that he would notice and recognize Louis, stripped of all his finery. But of course he did.

"So rather than give me a chance to explain, you thought dozens deserved to die?"

"It wasn't supposed to be like this," he stammers. Tears well in his eyes as he gazes across the burning fields. "You and the peasants weren't to be harmed. Only the royals."

"And you believed that?" I bark a bitter laugh. "Mother is full of lies on top of lies on top of lies."

"Silence!" She slaps me across the cut at my temple, and the world blurs and tilts—molten fire and charcoal smoke and their horrible, wicked faces.

Marguerite crouches beside me. "My apologies, little sister," she says, but her grin is anything but apologetic. She covers my face with a damp cloth, sickly sweet with ether, and my bones turn to puddles beneath my skin. I can't lift a hand, can't so much as scream, as she rifles through my bodice.

When she finds Father's grimoire, she clucks her tongue and tosses it into the fire. "Gone for good," she sings. Then she grips me beneath the arms and pitches me into a cart like a sack of grain.

I feel nothing.

Pain cannot reach me; disappointment cannot touch me. All I feel is emptiness—a cavernous, keening void where my heart once dwelt.

Gris betrayed me.

The cart lurches forward and we bump along the rutted Faubourg road. I fight to lift my head, but dark, curling shadows swallow the landscape. I'm shivering and sweating. Gasping and groaning. Sinking farther and farther into oblivion.

Marguerite leans over me and whispers in my ear, "Sweet dreams, La Petite Voisin."

I wake, not in the dungeon but in a featherbed. Which is worse. The silken sheets cling to me like tentacles, and I kick against them, ripping the bed curtains from their fastenings. Give me manacles or the rack, gladly. Anything but these plush pillows and luxurious linens that mean I belong here. That I am *one of them.*

My stomach flips and I vomit over the side of the bed, spattering the finely woven rug. After wiping the dreck on my sleeve, I cast around the room. The ebony armoire looms over me like a watchman. Two high-backed chairs stand sentinel on either side of the door like gates, ready to slam closed and lock me inside.

I scramble to the edge of the bed, my desperation booming fast and hard—like my heart: *Get out, get out, get out!*

I have to find Josse and the remaining rebels—if any of them survived. The contorted faces of my dead friends rise up around me, and for a horrible second, I imagine Josse among them, howling in agony, the whites of his eyes stained green by the flames.

My trembling arms give out and I gasp into the blankets, clutching my chest.

No. I didn't see him burn. He escaped. And he needs me.

I have to believe it.

The glowing window panes call to me, and I gather up my dressing gown. We may be four levels up, but I could leap from the ramparts if necessary. I swing my legs over the bedside, but as soon as my feet meet the floor it slides away like melted candlewax.

The blasted sedative still has hold.

I topple into the dressing table like a flapping hatchling, and a basin of water crashes over my skull. One of Mother's maidservants pokes her head into the room. "You're awake! I'll send for La Voisin at once."

Merde. I groan and wipe the steaming water from my eyes. Not Mother. Anyone but her. I press my burning face against marble and silently scream.

The maid bustles in. "Up, up. Your mother won't tolerate such wallowing." I don't move. I don't think I can. With a sigh, the maid grips me under the arms and drags me back to bed. I fight her every step—or try to—but my arms are slow and shaking. My legs drag through the carpet like plows. Marguerite must have administered enough sedative to fell a horse.

"How long have I been here?" I ask.

"Going on two days, miss."

Two days. Another punch of agony wallops me in the chest, and I wheeze out a stuttering sob. Two days might as well be a lifetime. Mother's soldiers could have easily captured Josse and Louis and the girls. Gavril and the orphans, too. What if I'm the only one left? I look out the window again, half expecting to see their bodies dangling from the battlements.

The maid is still wrestling me back to bed when the chamber door bangs open and Mother barges in. Her dark hair is pinned up with pearls and crimson rosettes, and her cream brocade gown trails behind her like a cloud. It's a mockery for anyone to be clad in such finery after the carnage on the fields.

"At last, you've awoken. We've much to discuss, my pet." She situates herself on the edge of the bed and reaches for my face. I lean back, pressing my shoulders into the upholstered headboard.

"I have nothing to say to you."

The light in her eyes gutters. "You had better *find* something to say, for I cannot execute the royal children unless I know where they are hidden, and I'm most eager to put this bothersome uprising to rest. Think of the people, Mirabelle—dying and suffering because you encouraged this revolt. Their deaths are on your head."

My head? I want to shout. But then the first half of her admission overshadows everything else. She doesn't know where the royals are hidden. That means they escaped. They're safe. Gris never knew about the sewer or the floor hatch in the pâtisserie. My head falls back against the headboard and I squeal with relieved laughter.

Mother grips my arm and yanks me forward. Up close, the heavy powder on her face cracks across her wrinkles. Her almond-scented breath makes me gag. "You will tell me where they are, Mirabelle."

I glare at her and shimmy lower. It's the first time I've defied her face to face. Red blotches bloom across her cheeks, making her garish rouge even more dreadful. She expects me to shrivel and shrink and break like before, but I'm no longer her blind, subservient daughter. I am La Vie. "I'll do no such thing."

Her nails bite into the flesh of my arm. "I think you will, given the proper motivation. Get up."

When I fail to comply, she snaps at the maid, who grunts and drags me from the bed. Two additional maids scurry in from the hall and bear me up. My legs wobble like a newborn calf's as they tug me from the royal apartments, through the salons, and belowground to my former laboratory.

Marguerite and Fernand are waiting outside the gray door at the end of the hall. My sister smiles at our approach, delighted, I'm sure, to see the icy waves of fury rolling off Mother. "Welcome home, La Petite Voisin." She brushes her lips against my cheek.

"So glad to see you're finally awake. My hand must have slipped with the sedative."

Fernand snickers and leads the way inside. Mother follows. The maids heave me forward, but I turn to face my sister. I have only seconds, so I must make them count. "Help me, Margot," I whisper in a rush. "This is madness. She destroyed the food supply and dozens of innocent people with it. You can't possibly support this."

Marguerite hesitates for half a second, then averts her gaze. "Don't try to claw your way back into Mother's good graces by dragging me out of them."

"I don't *want* to be in her good graces!"

Marguerite rolls her eyes and slams her palms into my shoulder. I tumble into the room.

Gris is here, of course. Mother's dutiful pet. He watches me from behind the counter, taking in my tangled hair and vomit-spattered dressing gown. His gaze feels like Mother's nails dragging through my flesh. I want to toss him into one of the great cauldrons and watch the skin boil off his bones.

Spineless, selfish, double-crossing coward!

Gris mouths my name, begging me to look at him, but I will never, never lay eyes on him again.

"While you were stirring up trouble," Mother begins, joining Gris behind the board. "We have been hard at work, altering the Viper's Venom formula. Not only is it more violent, but it's also impervious to your antipoison."

"I'll make another," I seethe.

"When do you plan to do that?" Her saccharine smile makes me want to scream. "Now tell me the location of the royal children or I will be forced to show you how effective our modifications are."

"And murder another innocent citizen? We are supposed to be the saviors of Paris, the voice of the people, yet you're killing them by the droves!" I don't realize how wildly I'm gesticulating or how loudly I'm shouting until Mother clutches my chin in her cold fingers and glares me into silence.

"You have no one to blame but yourself. The city would be at peace beneath the Shadow Society were it not for your machinations." She releases me with a shove and my stomach slams into the corner of the table. Gris tries to steady me, but I shrink away from his traitorous touch.

Mother pounds her fist against the worktable and snaps at Gris in warning. "A demonstration, alchemist, if you'd be so kind. Show Mirabelle precisely what she's brought upon her little band of rebels."

"My little band of rebels?" I know I should hold my tongue, but I can't bear to hear her speak so callously of Desgrez and Étienne and our allies who perished. "We were more than mice waiting to be exterminated. We were a revolution. We were poised to destroy you."

"Silence!" The back of Mother's hand strikes my cheek, and her rings leave long, stinging gashes. She turns to Gris. *Now.*

"H-how would you have me demonstrate?" he stutters. "I haven't anyone to . . . um . . ."

Mother's eyes flick across the room and settle on a guard near the door. He isn't much older than I, with blond hair and a hooked nose. He's done nothing wrong, nothing to differentiate himself. He simply was there, in her line of sight. "You'll do." Mother motions him forward.

All the color drains from his face. "Me, my lady? But I—"

"I see I've chosen correctly. I have no patience for dimwitted staff. Come now. Hurry, hurry."

The guard doesn't move. His eyes twitch from Mother to the poison. Then he throws himself at the laboratory door. Mother bellows, and the other guards scramble to respond. He's halfway out the door and I'm about to raise a cheer when Fernand streaks across the room like a diving falcon. He catches the guard by the arm, wrenches it mercilessly, and slams the guard's forehead against the wall. The guard howls and spits. Blood courses from a cut above his eyebrow as Fernand drags him back to Mother.

"P-please!" He fixes pleading eyes on her, as if that will change her mind.

"Drink," she commands, motioning to Gris, who brings the phial to the guard's mouth.

He squirms and bawls like a small child.

"Enough!" Fernand shouts. He rips the phial from Gris's hand and forces it between the guard's lips. The boy sputters and coughs. The poison dribbles down his chin and wets his tunic.

I heave toward him, but Marguerite tightens her hold on my elbow.

The effect is nearly instantaneous—like nothing I've ever seen. The guard's cheeks bulge, his hands fly to his gut, and he gurgles, as if choking on his own saliva. In less than thirty seconds, he drops to his knees, spitting phlegm and blood. By the time he hits the floor, his face is frozen in a grotesque mask of pain and his back is twisted at an unnatural angle.

A wave of nausea surges up my throat, and my hands fly to my mouth.

"Impressive, isn't it?" Mother pats Gris's stubbled cheek. He murmurs a quiet thanks, but his voice sounds choked. Only I would notice. His every breath, his every shrug, is so familiar to me—and I hate that. I hate that I know his fingers are rubbing the bottom of his tunic into frayed oblivion below the table.

He's a traitor. A murderer. Mother may be the head of the Shadow Society, but he is her hands—as I once was. Thankfully, I found a better way. I showed Gris a better way. Yet still he chose her.

How could he choose this?

Mother steps over the dead guard as if he's a mere puddle in the road and stands before me. "Now that you know what's at stake, I shall ask you again, Mirabelle. Where are the royal children hiding?"

I shutter my eyes and pretend I'm somewhere else—in a warm, peaceful fairytale world, complete with lush gardens and bubbling fountains. I'm happy and safe, brewing tinctures with Father, inhaling the sweet aroma of sage and honey tea. Far, far from Mother's reach.

She bangs her fist against the table. "You may not have a care for the lives of common men—despite your gallant claims—but I suspect you won't be so cavalier about *his* life." She turns to the door. "Lesage! Bring the prisoner."

The laboratory door slams open and unnatural emerald light cascades across the floor. Lesage struts into the room, his fair skin and red hair pulsating with the sickly glow of his magic, making him look demonic and wraithlike. Electric sparks crackle at his fingertips. He tugs a rope and Josse hobbles in behind him. He looks a few breaths from death; he's bare from the waist up, and his chest and arms are covered in gashes and burns as well as spatters of green *désintégrer* sickness. Lesage has clearly been busy for hours.

The walls of my fairytale world fracture, raining daggers of glass that slice through my heart. *Oh, Josse.* It was too much to hope all of the royal children escaped.

Lesage flashes a goading smile at me and runs his sparking fingertip down the side of Josse's face. A violent shudder drops Josse to his knees, and he grabs his cheek with a howl.

I lunge forward. I don't know how I'll protect Josse, but I must do something. Before I manage half a step, Mother's fingers sink into my hair. She yanks me back with such force, I fall back and my head strikes the ground. My scalp prickles and the walls of the laboratory spin. When I look up, a clump of hair dangles in her fist.

"You will not touch him," she says. "Answer the question if you wish to spare his life. Where are the royals hidden?"

Josse lifts his face. His eyes are wild and flashing—like a frightened horse's. He manages a brief shake of his head before Lesage slams a knee into his stomach.

Nothing. I am to tell them nothing.

Sweat gathers at my hairline and my breath comes quick. He cannot expect me to stand by and watch Lesage torture and kill him. But if I forsake his siblings, he will never forgive me. I will never forgive myself. Marie and the girls were the first to trust and accept me. And the rebellion will truly be dead without Louis. I dig my fingers into the dirty rushes, grasping for anything I can cling to, any way to stop this. But there's nowhere to go. The dream of a better future—for Paris, and for *us*—comes crashing down around me. I wish the palace would collapse with it and bury us all. It would be easier than this.

I take a shuddering breath and nod to Josse. A promise.

"Where are the royal children?" Lesage demands.

"I don't know." My voice wavers only slightly.

"You've always been a deplorable liar." Lesage places his palm against Josse's chest, and cerulean flames crawl across his skin. He writhes and screams, his back arching completely off the ground and his mouth open in a soundless scream. It's so grotesque, even Marguerite and Fernand gape in horror. From somewhere far off in the corner, it sounds like Gris is crying.

"Stop," I beg. "Please, stop!"

When Lesage finally relents, Josse collapses with a thud, a jade scorch mark branded in the center of his chest. His skin pulsates with sickening light, and blood trickles from his nose, his lips, his ears.

I clutch my chest, as if my own insides are liquefying.

"I shall ask you again, Mirabelle." Mother speaks this time. "Where are the others hidden? If you do not tell me, I will move on to more lethal means." She points to the phials of altered Viper's Venom on the table.

Josse's head lolls to the side, and his gooseberry green eyes paralyze me. "Don't," he gasps.

Tears stream down my cheeks and I bite my lips so hard, I taste blood.

"Very well." Mother takes up a phial of poison and stalks to Josse's side. "Once I've killed your bastard lover, we will be paying a visit to the rue du Temple and the Hôtel-Dieu. Perhaps the poor and sick will be more forthcoming with their knowledge."

I look up, cold with terror. Our allies saw Louis and the girls, of course, but we never revealed our hideout in the sewer for this very purpose. "They know nothing!"

"You'd better hope they know something. If they refuse to cooperate, I shall distribute a *special* hunger tonic we've created specifically for them." She rattles the phial of Viper's Venom.

"But they're innocent."

"They're hardly innocent," Mother says with a bitter laugh. "You made certain of that."

I bury my fingers in my curls and pull. "You can't poison half the city!"

"The choice is yours, Mirabelle. You can sacrifice hundreds of innocent lives to save a few worthless royals. Or you can tell me where they're hidden. Cooperate, and I promise to release him and leave the people be. This is the only way to bring peace."

My throat is on fire. A dozen boulders press upon my chest. I love Louis and the girls, but how can I condemn so many? Mother will never stop.

She brings the Viper's Venom to Josse's lips. My heart thunders faster—pounding, pounding, pounding until I'm certain it's going to burst from my chest. "They're hidden in a barn, just beyond the Port Saint-Antoine," I blurt out. But my voice is weak and I stumble over the lie. Mother hisses with disgust and tilts the phial. At the last moment I cry out, "The sewer! They're hidden in the sewer. The entrance is beneath the pâtisserie on the rue Saint-Honoré!"

The admission leaves me empty. Broken. Falling. I clatter to the floor, wishing I could dissolve straight through it. Josse's howl is a thousand times more painful than it had been during the jolts of désintégrer. He's thrashing and wailing and he won't look at me.

"I'm sorry," I cry as I curl into a ball.

"The *sewer*," Lesage marvels.

Mother considers it for a moment and laughs. "How appropriate. The royal children, living like rats and exterminated like them too. Go," she says to Fernand. "Quickly. Take as many guards as you need. Bring the dauphin and princesses back alive."

Then she turns to me, leering with delight. "My poor, foolish girl. The heart makes one weak. It clouds your judgment. I was never going to poison the commoners. And I would never kill the bastard here, in the laboratory, when I could do it before all of Paris and make an example of him." She bends and gives my cheek a mocking pat. "Thank you. I could have never accomplished this without your help. But now I'm afraid you're no longer of use to me."

She motions to her guards and they fall upon me, their grasping fingers pulling my hair, their rough hands bruising my skin. They drag me from the laboratory and toss me into a dungeon cell.

Judging by his wild, animalistic screams, Josse isn't far behind.

24

JOSSE

Death would be better than this.

I am trapped in a godforsaken dungeon with *her* while Fernand and an army of Shadow Society soldiers storm the tunnels and capture my sisters. My eyes burn at the thought of Anne and Françoise and Marie stumbling and crying, screaming my name as they're dragged to their execution. Wondering where I am, why I haven't come to save them.

Lesage's magic still pounds through my skull like a sledgehammer. My limbs are so heavy, it feels as if my bones are made of iron. But I muster the strength to stand and dash myself against the bars.

The jagged protrusions pierce my palms but I grip harder—until blood runs down my wrists. I want to feel the pain. I deserve to suffer.

My sisters were my only priority. Not the city. Not Mirabelle. Nothing else. And I failed them.

I failed everyone.

The horrible image of Desgrez's hat fluttering through the

smoky sky is branded in my memory. I see the ravenous green flames devouring his face. I hear the stationers and farmers gasping and shrieking, burning alive. And I can *feel* Father's disappointment, hanging over me like the executioner's blade.

How many ghosts can haunt a single man?

I throw myself at the bars harder—howling and crying and shouting oaths. I know it's useless, but I have to do *something*. Have to keep fighting until I know my girls are gone. Then I'll die willingly.

"Stop! You're hurting yourself," Mirabelle pleads from the cell beside me. She's been sitting there, watching me with those wet black eyes. As if she gives a piss. As if she didn't just condemn my entire family to death.

"Do you think it matters?" I say with a growl. "Look at me. I've one foot in the grave already."

"I can help you. Most of your wounds are superficial. Some chamomile, tea tree, and yarrow will do wonders for your burns and bruises. And if we escape, I can distill the antidote to désintégrer."

I wave a dismissive hand at her. "We're not going to escape, and I don't want your bedamned antidote. I don't care what becomes of me if I cannot save my sisters."

"What if we *can* save them?"

"How?" I glower at her. Disgusted with myself for trusting her. For allowing myself to care for her.

She fidgets in the filthy rushes. "I don't know," she admits.

"But we'll think of something. And you'll be of little use to them if you turn yourself to mincemeat. I cannot bear to watch you—"

"Don't act as if you care."

"I *do* care!"

"You don't! If you cared for me at all, you would have kept them safe. If you *knew* me at all, you would have known I'd gladly die to protect them."

"It wasn't just about them." Mirabelle's voice trails off and she buries her face in her hands. "How was I to know Mother was bluffing? She's done such horrendous things. I was just trying to—"

"You sentenced my sisters to death." Saying it aloud gives it weight. Truth. I totter to the far side of my cell and crumple to the dirty straw. It smells of dung and vomit and I gag as I ease down on my side.

Mirabelle crawls closer, pressing her face between the bars. "*We* may not be able to save them, but who's to say Louis hasn't? He escaped the fire. Perhaps he had the foresight to hide them somewhere else."

My laughter is bitter and grating. "Perhaps your Mother will beg my forgiveness, release me from this cell, and crown me King of France."

Mirabelle lowers her brows. "I'm in earnest."

"So am I! In fact, I'd say my scenario is more likely."

"Why do you insist on underestimating Louis?"

"Because I know him."

"Do you?" she presses. "Or have you invented a convenient identity for him? So you always have a scapegoat?"

I shove up to my elbows. "He invented an identity for *me!*"

"Have you considered that perhaps you've been unfair to each other? How long are you going to cling to this senseless childhood grudge? If the two of you would just—"

"Stop!" I bang my fist against the bars and the impact rattles through me. The hair on my neck rises like hackles. "Is it not enough that you've sent my sisters to the chopping block? Do you have to side with Louis as well? Kick me while I'm down. Spit upon my rotting corpse."

"Josse, I—"

"No! Don't pepper me with your excuses and platitudes or pretend to understand my childhood grudges. You are oblivious. And careless. And disloyal. Rescuing you from the sewer was the worst decision I've ever made. If I'd let Desgrez finish you, he would be alive. My sisters would be alive."

Mirabelle shrinks back. She wraps her arms around her stomach and blinks at me through tear-filled eyes. "Do you honestly believe that?"

I ignore the tiny twinge in my chest, refusing to be deluded by her mournful frown and poisonous logic any longer. I regard her with my iciest expression. "I don't believe it—I know it."

She bites her lips together, but her shoulders shake. "Then I suppose there's nothing more to say."

"I suppose not."

I turn away and stare across the dungeon. It's a foul, low-ceilinged place. The wall opposite is fitted with chains, and an insidious black stain covers the stones. Mirabelle and I are far from the only prisoners. Each cell is occupied, and the poor souls are nothing but lumps of skin and bone and hollow eyes. The man on my other side scrapes at the bars in slow, eerie repetition, his fingertips raw and bloodied. And the old man across from me lies faceup on the ground, weeping the name *Jeanne*. And somewhere down the block, a woman cackles day and night like a bedamned jester.

But none of them is as irritating or as pitiful as Mirabelle. She cries quietly for what feels like an eternity, and the sound is worse than the squeal of pigs being slaughtered. Like nails hammering my eardrums. She has no right to cry like that. To act as if she'll die of heartache when she could have prevented this. All she had to do was hold her tongue and let me die. I clench my teeth and clamp my hands over my ears, but her whimpers still seep through the cracks. So I climb back to my feet and resume writhing and railing against the bars. Anything to drown her out.

Hours later, when we've both collapsed to the ground and sit in exhausted silence, she whispers, "I'm sorry, Josse. So very sorry."

I don't respond. Because *sorry* will never be enough.

I drift in and out of fitful sleep. My thin dressing gown clings to my skin, wet with sweat and tears and whatever ghastly horrors float in the puddles on the floor. My eyes are itchy and swollen, and my head pounds. I may not have been tortured like Josse, but I'm so heavy with grief, I haven't the strength to drag myself to the bowl of unidentifiable sludge that slides into my cell. Once I see the worms wriggling through the rotten fare, I haven't the appetite, either.

I shutter my eyes and rock forward and back, sobbing until there's not a drop of water left within me. Then I choke on silent tears as those horrible moments in the laboratory play again and again across the stage of my mind.

How could I have been so gullible?

I don't blame Josse for hating me.

I rather hate myself.

There's no way to tell how much time has passed. The single window, high up on the wall, is no wider than my hand, and the dim shaft of light that cuts through the gloom is a perpetual shade of gray. Every so often I allow myself to peek at Josse, and each time I immediately wish I hadn't. His speckled skin pulsates with the sickly glow of désintégrer, and he's so weak that he can hardly hold himself upright, yet he continues to throw himself against the bars. Blood weeps from the wounds on his face and arms and back, but the dull, vacant look in his eyes is most heartrending of all. It's as if he drank the Viper's Venom. As if by saving him, I delivered the final death blow.

I didn't want to betray your sisters, I silently shout. He must know that. I didn't have a choice! So many lives were at stake.

Or, I thought they were at stake.

After what could be hours, or possibly days, a guard ambles over and upends a bucket of water over Josse's sleeping form. Josse bolts upright, gasping and coughing, and the guard laughs. "Wakey, wakey, *Highness.* Can't have you smelling like a hog for your execution." Then he turns to me and pours a second freezing deluge over my head.

He unlocks our cells and Mother's maidservants file in bearing cakes of bergamot soap and piles of finely tailored clothing. Josse slaps at their hands and shouts, "Why bother? Do you think the executioner will care how I look?"

But I know why. It's the same reason we wanted Louis to look presentable while saving the crops. Mother wants the people to recognize us. She wants them to know not even her daughter or the son of the king can defy the Shadow Society.

The maids scrub my face until it's as raw as my splintered heart and apply my makeup to match Mother's—making my eyes into sunken pits. Then they squeeze me into a revealing gown of lavender satin, which I suspect will match Marguerite's. When they finish, I look ghastlier than I ever did in the sewer.

La Vie is gone. Mirabelle is dead. Only La Petite Voisin remains.

The guard who "bathed" us returns with several masked comrades and they clamp shackles around our wrists and ankles. The cold metal gnaws at my skin as they lead us from the dungeon—Josse first and me trailing behind. I try to catch his eye, but he refuses to look up from his ridiculous heeled slippers. They're pristine white with blue ribbons—something fit for Louis, not a bastard kitchen boy. Josse's entire outfit is as gaudy and degrading as mine: a sumptuous brocade doublet cut in Bourbon blue with red braiding and miniature fleur-de-lis buttons at the cuffs. The royal crest is embroidered in gold across the whole of his back.

There will be no mistaking his identity.

I wonder, for a second, if it bothers him to be publically acknowledged more in death than he ever was in life.

When we emerge into the courtyard, the sunlight stabs my eyes. I squint, but it's like staring into the heart of a fire. I'm almost relieved when they stuff us into the musty dark of the waiting prison wagon. It, too, is dressed for the occasion—festooned with emerald and plum drapes and Mother's double-headed eagle banner—to ensure we attract as much attention as possible as we make our way through the city.

The guards shove me onto a bench along one wall and Josse

falls onto the bench opposite. Still not looking at me, even though our knees are practically touching. I force a cough, but he continues to ignore me.

Do you really want to go to our deaths like this? Without a word?

The fine black carriages carrying Mother and Lesage and Marguerite depart to the sound of trumpets and fanfare, and our wagon rumbles after them. It's eerily reminiscent of the ride to Versailles at the birth of this madness: Here I am, bouncing over the ruts and peering out the window, fretting over where we're headed. My stomach tangles into knots as the horses clop over the Pont Neuf and carry us to the far end of the Île de la Cité, where the twin spires of Notre-Dame disappear into the clouds like ladders to heaven. The cathedral frowns at our approach—the delicate flying buttresses lower like eyebrows; the rose window purses like lips. As if it senses the horrors to come.

We enter the courtyard through the western gate, and our wagon slows to a crawl as we weave through the thronging crowd. Shadow Society miscreants teem around us like dogs fighting over a scrap of meat. Everywhere I look are velvet masks and vibrant capes. They cheer and shout and bang upon the sides of the wagon. Calling for our execution.

I clutch the bench and let out a slow breath, but the wagon walls press closer. The shouts grow louder. I cannot lift my hands to cover my ears, so I fold in half and bury my face in my skirts. When we rumble to a stop, I make the mistake of looking up. Beneath the cathedral's archivolt is a hastily constructed scaffold bearing a cauldron of the altered Viper's Venom. My hands begin to tremble. I can't look away from the insidious curls of sapphire smoke rising into the air.

At least it will be quick, I tell myself. But that's little comfort when I imagine Josse and Anne and Françoise shrieking and twisting like the guard in the dungeon. A sickness rises up my throat and I vomit onto the wagon floor, narrowly missing Josse's boots. He curses and scoots away.

He should be disgusted.

I am to blame for everything. I told Mother where the royals are hidden. I invented the antidote to Viper's Venom, prompting this devilish new mixture. It was my idea to dust the crops with fire powder. I am the reason Lesage can wield désintégrer and conjure smoke beasts, and I'm so daft, I never did find a way to control the magic myself.

I tilt my head back and stare up at the ceiling, silently screaming at Father for promising I would be a great alchemist when my talents have brought far more pain and suffering than relief.

The wagon's doors swing open, but instead of Shadow Society guards, it's my sister who's come to collect us. For a brief instant, my heart drums with hope. She has heeded my words when we were outside the laboratory. She's going to help me.

But then her lips twist into a sneer as she takes in my gown. As suspected, it matches hers exactly. She grabs our chains with a disgruntled huff. "Once again, you've ruined everything. I must bear the disgrace of wearing the same gown as a traitor.

I must haul you around like a nursemaid rather than standing at Mother's side, where I belong." She yanks the chain and I nearly tumble from the cart face-first. "Keep up."

"Wait, Margot. Please." I grab her arm, but she breaks free and spits on my dress.

"Don't touch me."

"*Please,*" I beg, my voice small and broken. "Think of all the nights we spent crouched inside the cupboard, holding hands—"

"Not another word!" She turns her back on me and drags us up the scaffold steps.

I can feel Josse watching our exchange, and for a brief second, I see a flicker of empathy cross his face. But when I glance over, he irons out his expression and looks away.

Once we're positioned beside the cauldron, Mother alights from her carriage, waving to her raucous followers and flashing her most honeyed grin. Lesage escorts her through the crowd, which has grown so thick that it spills from the courtyard into the surrounding streets. There are Shadow Society supporters and rabble alike. Everyone has come to see the commotion. I squint into the sea of faces, hoping to spot Ameline's defiant scowl or Gavril's gap-toothed grin, but La Trianon and Abbe Guibourg are the only familiar faces near the platform. Beyond them, the people blend together like herbs in a cauldron. Even if our old allies are present, they've no reason to help us again. Not when they've lost so much.

"Are we ready to proceed with the *festivities?*" Mother asks

Lesage through a tight-lipped smile as they take their places beside us.

"Fernand should arrive with the royals any moment," he assures her.

Mother's eyes simmer with annoyance. "How hard could it be to apprehend a few little girls and the inept dauphin?"

Lesage places a steadying hand on her shoulder. "The bastard and your daughter are at the ready. Shall we begin with them?"

"Very well." Mother cuts a withering glance at me and Josse, then turns to address the crowd, her face oozing with sudden warmth and affection. "My good people!" she bellows in her most enthralling voice. "Since the inception of the Shadow Society, we have dedicated ourselves to serving you, the citizens of Paris! It is our greatest desire to ensure that you are well-fed and finely clothed and prospering—unlike the lecherous, self-serving kings who came before. But our great purpose has been thwarted by these grievous rebels"—she motions back at us—"who have robbed us of peace and fractured our city by attempting to pit us against one another. Royals who wish for things to return to the way they were before. Who want to keep you low and see you suffer."

From all across the square, people raise their fists and shout in agreement. But I'm pleased to find just as many come to our defense.

"La Vie kept us from starving with her hunger tonic," calls a girl near the front.

"We were on the brink of death when she administered a fever draught" comes a deep voice from the center of the throng.

More and more voices cry out, like the patter of rain as storm clouds descend.

Mother waves her hands to quiet them. "The Shadow Society will provide those services. We *would* be doing all of that and more, were we not constantly harried by rebellion. Once *they* are disposed of and we, as a city, are united in purpose, all of our time and resources shall be dedicated to the care of the common man. You have no need of this *La Vie*"—she spits my new name—"or her pathetic uprising."

A good half of our defenders fall quiet. The rest whisper to their neighbors. Cold fingers of panic trace along my spine. With a few clever lies, Mother is going to undo weeks' worth of progress. Everything we've fought for—a future Desgrez and Ètienne and so many others died for. I look helplessly to Josse, but of course he isn't looking at me. His shoulders are hunched and his hair hangs in his downcast eyes. His skin has that awful greenish hue, and his face shines with sweat. He looks finished, defeated. If I were in the audience, I would abandon our cause too.

A numb, tingling dread slowly claims my limbs. If I don't act quickly, the same despair will consume me and drag me down to the scaffold. I ball my fists and lunge forward against my chains. "Lies!" I shout. "Don't believe her lies! The moment the Shadow Society rose to power, they abandoned you! They will never keep these pretty promises because the rebellions will never cease. Even if we perish, others will rise. *We* are your true advocates, and we have a plan to—"

"Silence!" Mother shouts. Her guards haul on my chains and I crash to the platform. My face smashes into the boards and blood pours from my nose, filling my mouth with the taste of salt and rust. But my outburst did the trick. The people agitate and churn once more, like a boiling kettle.

"These hopeless rebels are not your allies," Mother says with perfect calmness. "Who do you suppose is responsible for destroying the crops? We caught them sprinkling a poisonous powder across the fields, tainting your food so they could then 'save' you and gain your support. We razed the fields to protect you. And the Shadow Society will distribute the royal stores of grain to accommodate for the shortages caused by this heinous act."

The crowd shifts yet again, like the changing of the wind. A thousand voices shout. Louder and faster and angrier until, like the snapping of a bowstring, they hurtle forward and slam against the scaffold. The hastily constructed boards judder beneath my boots, and I stare at Mother slack-jawed as I fight to keep my balance.

She smooths her hands down the front of her immaculate golden eagle cloak and shoots me a gloating smile. She got everything she wanted. She destroyed the crops and found a way to spin it in her favor. "Anything more you'd like to add, daughter?" she taunts.

Because she knows there's nothing to be done.

She has thought of everything.

The roar of the mob grows to a fever pitch—clanging and

clashing louder than the cathedral's great bells. Which can only mean one thing.

"At last." Lesage points across the square to where Fernand appears, cloaked and masked, tugging four plodding forms behind him. Josse moans and my heart wrings in my chest like a washrag. Fernand plunges into the crowd, and I shudder when Gris appears behind the royals, prodding them along. He already made it clear where he stands, so this shouldn't come as a surprise. But watching him lead Josse's sisters to the scaffold shatters the final fragment of my heart.

I heave forward against my chains. I howl and shake and scream. Fighting to the last. Until there's nothing left inside of me. Then I collapse to the boards and stare at the cauldron of Viper's Venom, wishing I had the strength to break free and cast myself into its depths.

26

JOSSE

I force myself to look up.

Watching the girls march to their death is the last thing I want to witness, but I can hold my chin high, muster a smile, and pretend to have a plan if it will make them even a little less afraid. If it will make their last few moments slightly more bearable.

Fernand and Gris push through the mob like tunneling ants, vanishing and reappearing in the turbulent sea of masks and cloaks. Each step feels like a league, each second a lifetime. I can't recall the last time I breathed. It isn't until they're halfway across the square and La Voisin gasps that I realize the prisoners are a wearing dirty tunics and breeches rather than skirts. Instead of Marie and Louis's blond and Anne and Françoise's rich mahogany, one has hair as black as charcoal and another is white blond. The foremost prisoner has hair like straw and flashes a wide, toothy grin at me when they reach the base of the platform.

"You look surprised to see us," Gavril says. "Though not as surprised as her." He laughs at La Voisin, and Fernand yanks the rope, sending Gavril crashing to the scaffold steps.

I blink and my mouth falls open. A thousand questions rattle around my head, but my tongue has forgotten how to form words.

"The royals never returned to the sewer," Gavril says with an innocent shrug. "Haven't a clue where they could be."

I don't mean to be callous—I would never wish to see our little allies shackled here beside me—but I'm so relieved the girls are safe, I fall to my knees.

I'll die knowing they're alive—that they still have a chance.

I immediately look to Mirabelle. I don't mean to, but my eyes are drawn to hers. She tilts her head back and lets out an exultant whoop.

I clutch my stomach, half laughing, half crying.

"Stop that!" Marguerite shouts at us.

"Get up!" One of the guards slams his boot into my thigh. But the pain doesn't register. I am out of my body with joy.

Mirabelle and I continue celebrating while La Voisin and Lesage stitch strained smiles across their lips and try to act as if this development was expected. But sparks jump between Lesage's clenched fingers, and La Voisin is practically vibrating with fury. She fists Fernand's cloak and drags him into what may resemble an embrace to the people down below. A very forceful embrace.

"Where are they?" she demands.

Fernand mumbles something unintelligible.

"Where. Are. They?" La Voisin's voice is a deadly whisper.

Gris elbows Fernand aside with an exaggerated swing of his arm and smiles at the crowd, as if jostling for his share of favor.

While they cheer, he lowers his head and mutters, "If we knew their location, they would be here. We were ambushed by these little miscreants."

"The dauphin said the sewer was sure to be filled with Society roaches," Gavril pipes in, "so he placed us in the tunnels to exterminate them. Which, I'd say, we did rather well." He smiles wickedly at Gris and Fernand, and that's when I notice the blood smeared down the length of Gris's face and the gruesome spray across his cloak. Fernand is equally covered in gore, but it's difficult to see beneath his mask and raven-black ensemble.

"It took those two plus half a dozen less fortunate guards to apprehend just the four of us," the black-haired orphan boasts.

My brows rise so high and quick, they practically leap off my face. Not because the orphans slayed so many guards—I've seen them take down far worse—but because *Louis* organized the ambush. He spirited our sisters away and arranged to have the orphans waiting in their place.

Mirabelle shoots me a goading look, and I can't even pretend to be annoyed. I would willingly throw myself at my brother's slippered feet and kiss his ringed fingers and even powder his bedamned wig.

He saved my girls.

"Unbelievable!" La Voisin's voice rises.

Lesage rushes forward and places a firm hand on her shoulder. "There are many watching eyes, my love," he says through his teeth. "The royals can't get far, but I suggest we take care of the rebels already in our possession or we're like to have a riot on our hands."

As if on cue, someone tosses a turnip at the stage. The shouts redouble. The people came for blood, and unlike La Voisin, they don't care whose is spilled, so long as someone pays for the decimated crops.

"Act as if everything has gone to plan; the people will have no reason to think otherwise," Lesage continues. Gris and Fernand drag Gavril and his three comrades into position beside us. The orphans balk and bray like stubborn donkeys until Lesage holds up a crackling hand in warning. All four of them flinch and one accidentally whimpers—reminding me how young they are. My heart squirms inside my chest; they shouldn't have to make such a sacrifice. I may be prepared to die for my siblings, but I would never ask them to do the same.

Once we're all lined up before the cauldron of Viper's Venom, La Voisin takes a deep breath and returns to the front of the platform to address the crowd. "Do you wish to see them punished?" she bellows.

The roar of approval is thunderous. I wonder if Anne and Françoise can hear from wherever they hide.

Don't worry about me, I want to tell them. *Just live. Live and be well.*

I tilt my head back to gaze up at the unbearably cheery sky— the clouds white and airy, like spun sugar; the warm breeze dances through my hair. I release a breath I've been holding for a lifetime, and with it I expel every morsel of resentment and frustration and inadequacy until I'm cleansed—but not empty. I let the best moments and sweetest memories fill the newly purified spaces: Rixenda's crinkled grin and the feel of her old, withered hands clasping my cheeks; the echo of my sisters' giddy laughter and their small arms draped around my neck; Desgrez's sly smile concealed beneath an outlandish disguise; and finally, Mirabelle's intoxicating scent of sage and smoke and the feel of her callused fingers sliding between mine.

I long to reach for those fingers now, but cold shackles cut into my wrists.

A look will have to do.

I turn to Mirabelle and find she's already looking at me, her dark eyes burning with fearless determination. She says something, but it's swept away in the deafening clamor.

Words are needless anyway.

I smile and shift a hair closer, holding her gaze. And she knows.

That I'm sorry.

That I forgive her.

That there's no one I'd rather stand by—in life or death.

Six guards file onto the platform, collect phials of Viper's Venom, and stand before Mirabelle, myself, and the orphans. They hold the sparking blue liquid aloft for the crowd to see.

Gavril and his comrades shout at the guards and pull faces. We're a sip away from death, but they haven't a speck of remorse or fear.

I roll my shoulders back and look out across the writhing mob, hoping I look half as brave and defiant. But when La Voisin raises her hands to quiet the crowd, I have to clasp mine tightly to hide their shaking. "Let this be a warning to any other rebels who attempt to destroy the peace and endanger the good people of this city," she cries. "This shall be your end."

Her hand drops in a swift arc, like an ax, and the guards lower the poison to our lips. I draw a final shaky breath as warm curls of steam tickle my nose. Then I tense every muscle. Waiting for the poison to wet my lips. Waiting for it to twist and claw my innards.

A hair-raising cry rings out down the platform.

I presume it's either Mirabelle or one of the orphans—that their guard had a swifter hand, and I lean into my own phial, not wanting to be the last. Not wanting to watch them suffer. But the cry comes again and a blue-green flash streaks through the corner of my vision. Lightning crashes into the center of the crowd, and suddenly the entire mob is screaming. Shoving. Running.

My guard whirls around and the phial of Viper's Venom shatters on the scaffold with a hiss.

I look to my right, down the line of prisoners, and we're all standing. All staring at Lesage, who collapses to his knees and releases another errant bolt of désintégrer. It smashes into the carvings of Saint Anne along the front of Notre-Dame, and as the smoke dissipates, I watch in stunned confusion as Fernand pulls a bloodied dagger from the sorcerer's back.

Marguerite's shriek is so loud and shrill, it feels like shards of glass stabbing my ears.

Lesage falls forward and coughs a spray of blood. He raises a quivering hand and streams of colored smoke explode overhead, forming into teeth and scales and claws.

With a furious howl, La Voisin rushes toward Lesage. Gris watches her approach, his eyes wild and feverish. Right before she reaches the sorcerer, he lunges. His shoulder slams into La Voisin's stomach and they crash to the platform, tumbling end over end.

The guards abandon us and sprint to La Voisin and Lesage. Gavril and the orphans whoop like little devils and give chase. As if they expected this. They pull their ropes taut between them, which they use to trip and entangle the guards.

Go! Move! my mind screams, but unlike the orphans, I'm bound wrist and ankle by shackles and I still don't understand what I'm seeing. I look over at Mirabelle and she's gaping with equal shock.

From around the corner of the Hôtel-Dieu, a surge of stationers and ducs, fishmongers and viscounts, charge into the square led by Ameline and the Marquis de Cessac. They stampede through the riotous crowd and cut their way toward the scaffold, looking for all intents like angels, for they seem to be glowing.

No, *sparkling.*

With the last of his flagging strength, Lesage fires a cascade of désintégrer at them, but still they advance. Untouched. Unburned. "Impossible!" he gasps.

I laugh because it most certainly *is* possible. They are covered in the fire powder we brewed for the crops, and they are tossing it into the air as they batter through the throng, covering as many as they can.

Back on the platform, La Voisin howls as Gris wrenches something from her hand and tosses it to Fernand. Then Gris rolls off the front of the platform seconds before a gargantuan black smoke beast breathes a stream of fire precisely where he stood. Fernand vaults over Lesage and sprints toward us. Marguerite tries to intercept him, but he bludgeons her over the head with the butt of his dagger, then throws it into the chest of an advancing guard. Without slowing, he brandishes his sword and spins to fend off the blow of another assailant.

The hairs prickle down my neck, and my mouth falls open. There's something strangely familiar about his thrust and parry. The way he lunges and ducks, as if carried by wings. I know only one person who fights with such grace. One person who is small enough and slender enough to pass for the mercenary. When the guard's sword glances off Fernand's mask, shredding it from his face, I'm not surprised to see it isn't Fernand at all.

Louis drives his sword through the guard's stomach, kicks him to the ground, and skids to a stop before us. He releases Mirabelle first then moves to me, glancing up as he fits the key into my manacles. "Do you have something to say to me, brother?"

I stammer incoherently, still not believing he's here. Rescuing me. It's so absurd, I laugh as the iron cuffs fall away.

"I fail to see anything funny about this," he snaps.

"Where are the girls?" I finally manage.

"With Marie, safe at the Marquis de Cessac's château."

"Good."

Louis arches a blond eyebrow. "Anything *else* you'd like to say?"

"Honestly? You want me to grovel *now?*" I wave a hand at the grisly pandemonium.

Louis crosses his arms.

"Fine. Thank you." I can be gracious. I can admit I needed him—this once. "What do we do now?"

"Get down!" Mirabelle screams. We flatten against the boards, narrowly avoiding the claws and flame of a pearl-pink smoke beast. The back of my tunic sizzles and I roll to snuff the sparks.

Louis drags his sleeve across his sweating face, and says, panting, "I suggest you deal with the beasts. Or *that.*" He points across the platform to the cerise and emerald capes falling into formation around La Voisin. She rises slowly from Lesage's lifeless body, shouting and pointing in our direction. "I'll help Ameline and the rebels reach the platform. Hold La Voisin and her guards off until then." He removes a dagger from his boot, tosses it to me, and shuffles to the edge of the boards.

The crowd below heaves like a great, surging whirlpool. And above the courtyard, the beasts circle and swoop, breathing swaths of fire and roaring with fury when it fails to catch.

Louis takes a steadying breath. Before he leaps, I stumble forward and clasp his shoulder. "Be safe," I say.

He stills, looks down at my hand, and slowly returns the gesture. Neither of us recoils. I stare at his sweaty, blood-streaked face, and a burning sensation swells inside my chest. A feeling akin to pride. Or respect.

"Thank you, brother," I say with a squeeze.

"This is no time to grovel, Josse." A tiny smile quirks his lips, and before I can think of a retort, he bellows a war cry and dives into the chaos.

Mirabelle and I watch him vanish into the sparking haze. Then I take her hand and together we turn to face her mother.

27

MIRABELLE

The smoke from the beasts is so thick, it shrouds the cathedral, blocking all but the tops of the twin towers. My eyes water and my lungs burn, but once again Mother seems to revel in the flames and heat. She charges through the fog, shouting my name. At least ten Society guards surround her, as solid and imposing as the city wall, and another ten are flying up the scaffold steps. Instinctively, I fall back, but my heels leave the edge of the platform.

Merde.

Josse's fingers tighten around mine. "You don't happen to have a sword hidden in your skirts, do you?"

I force a laugh. It's supposed to sound incredulous, but it comes out high and quivering.

"Pity. You're always so prepared with antidotes and curatives and Heaven knows what else you keep buried under there." He waves his fingers at my gaudy purple dress and flashes a smile. I could kiss him for that smile, for attempting to sever the tension with his black humor. "No matter. We'll think of something."

Unfortunately, the time for thinking has passed.

Mother's guards streak toward us with all the ferocity of Lesage's smoke beasts: their masks curling away from their faces like horns, their teeth gnashing. Josse's eyes meet mine and we turn to jump from the platform, but another slew of guards waits below. The tips of their swords jut through the smoke like seedlings from the gray winter ground.

We have nowhere to go. Nothing to defend ourselves with but a single dagger.

Fear clamps around my chest as we wheel back around. The guards barrel closer. Josse pushes me behind him, and my heart swells with tenderness and then breaks into a million jagged pieces. He's so weak from Lesage's torture, his breath comes in ragged gasps and he can hardly keep his feet, yet still he darts forward and slashes his tiny blade. "Stay back!"

The guards lunge with a sinister laugh. One knocks the dagger from Josse's hand and another takes out his legs. As soon as he hits the platform, the rest of the guards descend like a pack of jackals, mauling and tearing and ravenous.

They're going to kill him.

Rage ignites me. Terror propels me. I launch myself at the horde of guards, but someone else reaches them first. From the other side of the platform, Gavril and his small band of orphans hurl daggers and brandish swords they must have stolen from the dead. I crow with triumph, but before I can join them, vicious fingers dig into my sides and haul me back. I scream and kick as

I'm dragged across the platform and dumped at Mother's feet.

"Go deal with that," she says to her guards, motioning to Josse and the orphans. "I wish to have a word alone with my daughter." A shudder works through me because I'm fairly certain her *words* will end with me lifeless on these boards. "Are you happy?" she spits at me. "Lesage is dead, the city is burning, and the people we swore to serve are suffering."

I push up to my elbows and look into her cold, dark eyes. "I'm happy everyone can finally see what a monster you are."

"*I* am not the monster. This is *your* doing, Mirabelle!"

"I'm not the one who assassinated the royal court at Versailles and obliterated the Paris Police. I'm not the one who poisoned my former allies along with any noble who dared to stand against the Shadow Society. I did not attempt to exterminate the fishmongers or raze the fields to coerce the people's obedience and loyalty."

Mother steps closer. "I wouldn't have needed to take such measures if you hadn't turned the people against me. Order was nearly restored."

I tilt my head back and laugh. "The riots were never going to cease. You cannot forsake half the kingdom in favor of the rest. That was the Sun King's folly, and it was yours as well. For all you despised him, you made the exact same mistake."

Mother slaps me across the face. Her handprint throbs against my cheek, but I revel in the pain. I drink it in, laughing and laughing until Mother looks ready to burst. "Enough!"

"The only way to truly restore the balance is by *uniting* the people."

Now it's Mother's turn to laugh. "The aristocracy will never unite with the commoners."

"Won't they?" I point to the front of the crowd, where Louis, Ameline, the Marquis de Cessac, and a host of nobles, fishmongers, and stationers cut through her Shadow Society guards, drawing ever nearer to the scaffold. "Because they look rather united to me."

With a growl of fury, Mother reaches into her golden eagle cloak and extracts a dagger the length of her forearm. The steel glints as she adjusts her grip, reflecting the fires in the crowd. The fire in her eyes. Quicker than I've ever seen her move, she slashes at my face. The blade whistles as it hurtles toward me. I dodge to the left, but searing pain flares across my cheek. When I bring my fingers to my ear, they come away hot and wet.

"You're destroying everything I've worked for," she sneers as I scramble out of reach. "All the good the Shadow Society has done. You're just like your father. Meddling and discontented. Reckless and deceitful."

"That's the finest compliment you've ever given me," I pant.

With a vicious scream, she hurls the dagger at my chest. It spins end over end, quicker than Lesage's lightning. I ball my fists. Close my eyes. Ready for the spike of pain. But rough hands slam into my shoulder, and the world spins sideways. My head cracks against the ground, and a high-pitched ringing fills my ears. But still I hear it—the wet thunk of metal piercing flesh. The sharp intake of breath.

I bolt upright as Gris staggers to his knees, one hand stretched across my skirt and the other raised toward Mother. The dagger meant for me protrudes from his chest. He looks down at it and his eyes flick to mine, wide and petrified.

"Gris!" I cry as he collapses with a shudder. Blood courses from the wound, drenching his tunic and wetting my petticoats. I take his hand in a vise grip, as if I can squeeze my strength into him. "You're going to be fine," I say fiercely. But already the color is leaching from his cheeks.

No, no, no.

Despite what he did, he's still my brother. My best friend. He saved us in the end.

With frantic hands, I attempt to stanch the blood flow with my skirt, struggle to scrape it back inside his chest. He cannot die. Not like this. When my last words to him were so ugly. I press my hands around the dagger in his chest, but the crimson stain flows faster, thicker. Nearly black.

"Stop," he wheezes. "There's naught to be done."

"Don't say that. I'll get you back to the laboratory and—"

He gives my fingers a faint squeeze. "I'm sorry, Mira." His face is chalky now—a sharp contrast to the red stain sliding from his lips. His cinnamon eyes wander, searching me out through the pain. "So very sorry."

"Hush." I brush the hair from his eyes. Tears fall from my chin and spatter his face, but he doesn't seem to notice. He reaches up and his fingers skim my cheek. So cold already. I place my hand over his and lean in to his palm—big and strong, etched with so many familiar calluses.

"You were right not to tell me." He coughs blood between each word. "I should have chosen you sooner."

"Shhhh." I kiss the inside of his palm, crying so hard that I can barely form words. "Your timing was perfect. You saved me. Twice now."

A wisp of a smile lights his face. A final glimpse of his crooked grin. He takes my hand and presses my fingers against his trembling lips. "Dagger."

I shake my head. I'm not strong enough to free it. Gris grunts, and with the last of his strength, he guides my hand to his hip. To *his* dagger. And mouths a single word:

Poisoned.

My lips drop open, and his eyes fill with relief. He lets out a long breath, and then stills forever. Limp and heavy and gone. My chest splinters down the center and my shredded heart tumbles out, leaving me gaping and gasping and empty. I fold in half and lay my head against Gris's stomach, my cheek drenched with blood and tears.

"Another death on your conscience," Mother mutters. I'd forgotten she was there, watching. "Perhaps it's for the best. Perhaps *his* death will teach you the consequences of defying me, since annihilating half the city hasn't."

"How can you be so heartless?" I shout, hugging Gris close. "He was our family. All he ever wanted was your approval."

"He certainly didn't deserve it."

"No. You never deserved him." Rage carves out my insides until there's no bottom to the well of my fury. Then hatred fills me back up, pumping its greasy blackness through my veins. In one fluid motion, I free Gris's dagger from its sheath and pounce toward Mother. She jumps back, tripping over her ceremonial cape and gaping as if I'm a rabid beast. Maybe I am—the low growls pouring from my lips are more animal than human.

I slam into her and we roll across the boards. She claws at my face and bucks beneath me, but I'm far stronger from years of hefting cauldrons. I bear down on her shoulders and raise the dagger to her throat. At the last moment, she heaves to the side and the blade barely nicks her arm, just below the shoulder.

Thanks to Gris—brilliant, loyal Gris, who thought of everything—a nick is all it takes.

I fall back, panting. Mother rises to her hands and knees, a smirk on her lips. Thinking I missed. She prowls closer, and I let her come. Her elbow wobbles after a few lengths. Before she reaches the edge of my skirt, her arms give out entirely.

She sucks in a breath and looks down at the tiny line of blood on her gown with horror. "What have you done?"

Before I can answer, a violent, shuddering cough sends her sprawling. Thick white foam burbles from her lips, and her eyes roll back. She's taken in a fit, shaking and thrashing wildly, and

I can't tell if I'm laughing or weeping. I wanted to be better than Mother. I wanted to beat her by giving life, not taking it, but she made it clear she would never stop. She would kill the beggars and fishmongers and orphans. Everyone I've come to love. Everything good.

"How could you?"

I look up into my sister's horrified face. Marguerite clutches her head with one hand, her eye already swelling where Louis bludgeoned her, and the other hand rises to her quivering lips. "How could you?" she repeats—so soft that it's lost in the roar of the smoke beasts and clashing swords. With a wail, she crumples to her knees and crawls to Mother's side. She gently prods her shoulder. She traces her fingers down Mother's face— whispering, crying, begging her to rise. Mourning over her as I just mourned Gris.

I have never felt so alone. So apart.

Shout at me, I silently beg as I watch. *Attack me. Rail and fume and fight!* That would be easier than watching her cling to Mother's cold, limp arms.

My eyes burn, and an uncomfortable thickness fills my throat. I have to look away.

"Congratulations, you've won," Marguerite says. "Kill me and be done with it."

"I don't want to kill you, Margot."

"You might as well. I have nothing left. You killed our mother. And Lesage. And where's Fernand?" A sob bursts from her throat.

"End my misery. Or leave me here and let the beasts devour me."
She lays down beside Mother, face up to the sky.

A roar rattles the platform, and the long snake-like beast flies
across the stage as if summoned by Margot's defeat. Without
thinking, I fling myself on top of my sister, clutch her to my
chest, and roll away from the wall of fire eating up the boards.

"Let me go!" She slaps at my face. "It doesn't matter. We're all
going to die."

"We're not. Look!" I point to Louis and the rebels as they
bound up the scaffold steps. The smoke beast circles back around
and swoops low to breathe its fire, but the rebels duck their
heads and thrust through the inferno. They emerge completely
unscathed, their skin shimmering like diamonds. "I distilled one
of Father's compounds. It's impervious to—"

My explanation is drowned out by the rose serpent's furious
snarls. It howls across the square, and the midnight-black creature
growls in response. Together they dive at the rebels, their razor
claws extended. Louis and Ameline drop to their stomachs, but
not everyone is quick enough. The Marquis de Cessac and an
unlucky fishmonger are crushed by the beasts' talons, lifted high
above the courtyard, and shredded to bits.

I scream into the back of my hand as blood and flesh fall from
the smoky sky.

"Your precious powder can't protect us from *that*." Marguerite's
voice is flat and listless.

I shudder as the truth of her words seeps through me.

Lesage is dead. But still the beasts live. Because of me. Because I cannot control my portion of his magic.

I press my cheek against the ground and scream with frustration.

The impossible has happened. Mother and Lesage are gone. Louis rose from the sewer and the rebels rallied behind him. They even thought to distill additional fire powder. But it still isn't enough.

Lesage's beasts will be the death of us. Just as I feared.

28

JOSSE

I had no grand illusions of besting a dozen Society guards with a single dagger, but I had hoped to at least put up a decent fight in front of Mirabelle—to die with a scrap of honor and buy her a few extra minutes. But my arms are slow and shaking. My legs tremble and drag. Lesage's désintégrer has ravaged my body so completely, the guards disarm me with a single blow. Louis's dagger spins away across the platform. Knuckles smash into my jaw and someone tackles my legs before I can even think to get my hands up to protect myself.

As I crash to the boards, I can hear Desgrez groaning with mortification from beyond the grave.

Punches rain down on my face and ribs. The edge of a knife grazes my side. Clumsily, I kick out, but the guards strike faster and harder. The best I can do is curl into a ball and pray it ends quickly.

It does. And, shockingly, not because I'm dead.

At first I think someone has set loose a pack of wild dogs, with the high-pitched yips and growls and the way the guards are screaming. But when I open my eyes, Gavril's filthy face hovers over mine. "Not your best fight, Highness," he says with a cheeky wink. He pulls a dagger from his waistband and hands it to me. "Try not to lose this one too." Then spins and buries a sword in the chest of an advancing guard.

I fist the dagger and scramble to join them, but an earsplitting cry stops us all where we stand. Needles flash down my spine, and I slowly turn.

The first thing I see is blood. Everywhere. A deep crimson stain oozes across the boards. It's impossible to tell where it's coming from. Both Mirabelle and La Voisin are sprawled across the platform along with a third hulking body that I realize—with a pulse of shock—is Gris.

The smoke beasts roar overhead, blades crash, and shouts rise from the square below, but on the scaffold, there's a single second of absolute silence.

Then La Voisin begins to shake. She tosses and twists, her arms flying and her back arching. It goes on and on and on, and we watch in stunned horror until she falls still. Even then, none of us move. The remaining handful of Shadow Society guards glance nervously at each other, then us, unsure whether to leap back into the fray with both of their leaders dead.

My eyes keep darting back to Mirabelle. Her face is blank and haunted as she looks at her mother's body. Marguerite barrels across the platform and drapes herself across La Voisin, which causes Mirabelle to retreat even farther.

The unnatural pause finally shatters when a smoke beast the color of sunrise—pink and gold and dusty gray—careens across the scaffold and nearly burns us all to cinders. I hit the ground so fast, my breath rushes out in a sharp punch. Once the creature's wingbeats recede, I allow myself to look up. Which is a horrendous mistake. The beast and its oily-black brother circle back and dive at Louis and the other rebels who have finally reached the platform. They pluck up fishmongers and stationers like birds pecking worms and devour them in messy, shredding bites.

I press my fist to my forehead and scream. No matter how much we accomplish, there's always another disaster.

"Hurry, Josse!" Gavril shouts in my ear. Instead of running *away* from the beasts with the remaining Shadow Society guards, Gavril and his gang sprint toward the danger. "The nets! Ready the nets!" they yell at the orphans in Louis's company.

By the time we reach the group, the lengths of rope are unfurled and Gavril barks orders at everyone, including Louis, telling us where to stand and how to position the nets. Mirabelle hurries to join us, dragging her squalling sister behind her, and Ameline douses us all with fire powder.

Then we wait, eyes fixed skyward.

The black beast dives first. It ripples through the smoke like a shadow and we hurl the net into the air, but without the height of the rooftops and the narrow streets to hem it in, the creature has plenty of room to rear back. The net slides from its wings and crashes to the platform, nearly crushing several of our allies.

As we scramble to regroup, the rose-gold smoke beast attacks. It catches the net in its claws and hurls it across the stage—along with everyone still clutching the rope. I make a sound like a screaming teakettle as I watch Mirabelle tumble across the platform. She lands like a rag doll near Lesage's body and doesn't rise.

No. I sprint toward her, my vision darkening around the edges until she is all I see. My body howls with each step. Lesage's handprint pulses against my chest, burning hot and tight. But the sight of Mirabelle lying motionless on the boards relegates my pain to a dull ache.

It's not until I'm halfway across the scaffold that I realize her eyes are open and she's staring down at her blood-soaked palms, opening and closing her fingers. All at once, she pushes up to her knees and glances over her shoulder. I think she's looking at me, and I call her name, but before I drop down beside her, she knocks past me and crawls to Lesage's body.

"What are you doing?" I ask.

"His blood," she sputters frantically. "That's what I've been missing. When I rolled across the stage . . ." Her voice trails off, and with shaking hands, she removes the dagger from Lesage's baldric, draws it across her palm, and presses her hand into the gaping stab wound in his back. She twists deeper and deeper until she's up to her wrist in gore. I wince at the horrid squelching noises—like boots sticking in mud—but Mirabelle grits her teeth and tightens her fingers.

The black smoke beast screeches above us, bending as if

Mirabelle's fingers are clamped around its neck rather than Lesage's innards. She changes her grip and it plummets to the platform. The boards crack beneath the creature's weight and splinters spray into the air, some as long and jagged as spears. The pearl-pink dragon roars with fury and dives to protect its companion, but Mirabelle wrings her hand again, sending the second beast rolling sideways across the sky. It crashes into the façade of Notre-Dame, and every panel of stained glass shatters. The beast hits the ground with a shudder so violent, I bump into Mirabelle.

Across the platform, the black beast moans and flaps. Louis advances from one side, Gavril charges from the other, and together they bury a sword and dagger into the creature's long neck.

"The other one!" Mirabelle yells at me, sweat streaking down her face. "Finish this."

With the last of my strength, I heft a fallen Society guard's sword off the ground and drag myself to where the creature lies. It hisses at my approach, its ears pinned back and its yellow eyes wild. One shimmering wing is shredded, and its front leg is twisted—the scales torn away to reveal pale, pitted flesh. I edge closer and it rears back, like a snake coiled to strike, but when it attempts to lunge forward, it shrieks in pain. Its head wrenches to the side, and I take the opening Mirabelle made for me.

I thrust the sword deep into the creature's side. A geyser of hot black blood sprays my face, and I reel back. Just out of reach of the smoke beast's claws.

It keens and groans. Or maybe that's me. My entire body is screaming with pain. The world flickers in and out, growing darker and darker until I can't see the beast or the cathedral or even the smoke. I am alone, floating through the blackness. Cradled by the glorious sound of silence.

I don't know if this is the end. Or if it's the beginning. But either way, it feels like victory.

When I wake, I'm in a bed. An enormous bed with fresh ticking and a silk coverlet. Since I've never in my life slept in a bed so fine, I figure I must still be dreaming, and I close my eyes to bask in the slippery warmth a while longer. But then my limbs begin to prickle and the horrific scenes from Notre-Dame replace the hazy gray nothingness: the blood, the beasts, the bodies strewn across the courtyard.

How did it end?

I push up to my elbows, but pain explodes across my chest, forcing me back to the mattress. Carefully, I reach up to touch the outline of Lesage's awful handprint on my chest, but I find a knife wound instead, along with a thick crusting of herbs.

Mirabelle's remedy. The one she used to heal Desgrez and my sisters. The curative that started everything—and ended it as well, it seems.

"Mirabelle?" I slit my eyes to peer around the room. The walls are covered in deep burgundy brocade. A velvet fauteuil rests in the corner, and the side tables are made of polished rosewood. The river Seine meanders lazily past the window, throwing fractals of fading red sunlight across the ceiling. We are in the Louvre. Which can mean only one thing: the Shadow Society is truly vanquished.

"Mirabelle?" I call again, and a thick, low voice coughs in response from the door.

"It's about time you awoke," says the piggish steward. He wears a white wig and a condescending frown. "His Royal Highness has been waiting all day. I am to escort you to him at once."

Before, I would have bristled at such a summons. Heaven forbid I keep Louis waiting even a minute after we all nearly perished. Doesn't he need to eat and bathe and sleep? But I allow the steward to help me out of bed and escort me down the hall because I'm eager to know what happened after I collapsed.

And I'm even more eager to see my sisters.

The steward leads me through the clock pavilion, clucking at my limping step, and into the Grande Galerie, where a massive armchair is arranged before the fireplace. Louis sits rigidly atop the cushion, clad in white from head to toe—white kidskin breeches and a white doublet with golden studs. He looks so pristine compared to the grime and wreckage from Notre-Dame. As if he's forgotten the battle already. Attendants rush around him, stoking the fire and bearing trays of thinly sliced meats and soft cheese. Several nobles I recognize from the battle are clustered behind him, returned to their satin doublets and powdered wigs. But there's no sign of my sisters anywhere.

Louis sees me and gestures to the ground before him. "Come forward."

"Isn't this a tad excessive?" I say with a laugh.

Louis's face pinches as if he ate an unripe berry. "Is that any way to greet your king?"

"You've been king less than a day. And I thought—"

"I've been king all my life. Chosen of God from the moment I was born."

I slap my hand to my forehead and drag it through my hair. For some reason I presumed things would be different now. We will never love each other, but after the time we shared in battle and the change I saw in him . . .

"Where are Anne and Françoise?" I ask. "And Mirabelle?"

"You cannot just barge in here, making demands. I shall dictate this conversation."

"First, I didn't barge in anywhere. *You* summoned me. And if you want to dictate, get on with it already."

He sniffs and glares expectantly.

Sighing, I drop into the world's most overwrought and condescending bow. "Get on with it already, *Your Majesty.*"

A smile flutters at the corner of his lips. "As you may recall, I saved your life several times at Notre-Dame. . . ."

Several times is generous, but I grit my teeth and nod. "And I thanked you."

"Such a life debt deserves more than a mere thanks."

I glance miserably at the door. All I want is my girls. And Mirabelle. And to leave behind my brother and the battle and all of *this*. "Why don't you tell me what you want so we can be done with it?"

"It's most inconvenient for a new king to have a bastard brother milling about. You are uncouth and unpredictable. Some of my new ministers have advised that I banish you from court. . . ."

My mouth falls open and I gape at the noblemen standing behind Louis. We fought side by side only yesterday. And, before that, I spared their lives with antidotes. A surge of old, familiar pain bubbles inside my belly, but instead of lunging at them as I would have done before, I ball my fists and stand my ground. Let them whisper and jeer. I have nothing to prove. I am enough. "Thankless, scheming sots," I mutter.

Louis laughs. Even though nothing about this is funny. He fans his face with a gloved hand. "While my ministers think I would be better off without you, I am of a different opinion. I made a promise to my people, and it would reflect poorly on me if I ousted their champion straight away. So I've another proposal for you. It seems I'm in need of a new police captain, and I believe you are the man for the job. An old friend claimed it would suit you."

"*What?*" All the anger drains out of me, puddling in my boots. My eyes sting. "You want me to take Desgrez's place?"

"I need someone I trust patrolling the streets, and it would please me greatly if that man was you."

I shake my head slowly. I could never fill Desgrez's shoes. And I don't want to fill them. Not if it means moving on. Forgetting him. I have other responsibilities, besides.

"I can't. The girls . . ."

"Have been placed in excellent care."

"What do you mean, they've been 'placed in excellent care'? Where? With whom?" I look all around the room, as if somehow Anne and Françoise will appear.

"Madame de Montespan's elder sister, the Marchioness de Thianges, volunteered to oversee their upbringing, and I thought it a splendid idea."

"How could you think that? They need to be here. With me."

Louis steeples his hands and waits for me to stop shouting. "Be reasonable, Josse. It isn't fitting for little girls to be raised by us. They will be happy with their aunt. And it's not as if they've been sent across the sea. They're on the other side of the city. You can visit as you please."

"Doesn't the marchioness prefer to be at court?"

"She thinks they will benefit from living somewhere quieter for a time, to recover. But they've a place here whenever they wish to return."

The thundering in my chest slows, and I grudgingly nod. "You could have at least waited until I awoke. So I could see them off."

"You would have never let them go. You're allowed to be both a brother *and* an officer, you know. And the girls aren't your only sibling in need of assistance."

Behind him, Louis's ministers whisper at this admission. He stiffens in his armchair. "I expect an answer in the morning, Josse. Now run along." He lifts a gloved hand and waves me away. "I've important matters to attend to that are far above your station. I'm sure you'll find the company in the millinery more suited to your tastes."

This makes his ministers chuckle, but a ghost of a smile floats across Louis's lips and his blue eyes twinkle with mischief.

I manage a bewildered bow and drift out of the palace and up the streets. Toward Mirabelle and the millinery. Marveling at how everything has changed. And how everything in the world feels oddly right.

29

MIRABELLE

The millinery is dark and I am alone—basking in the stillness, luxuriating in the comforting darkness that seeps around me like steam. It's so warm and quiet. So opposite the fray at Notre-Dame.

I sit beneath the window, legs tucked against my chest and chin atop my knees, and stare at the moonlight passing through the papered windows. It paints the floor with brushstrokes of pewter and indigo, and I twirl my fingers idly in the light.

Mother and Lesage are dead. Marguerite and the members of the Shadow Society who surrendered are locked in the Châtelet, awaiting trial. Gavril and the orphans have already taken up residence in the Palais Royal. Ameline and the fishwives returned victorious to the wharf. And Louis and I carried Josse to the Louvre, though I left directly after administering the cure for désintégrer.

That palace makes my skin crawl. I saw Mother's face in every stone and tapestry. Her voice echoed down the halls and hovered in the silence of Josse's sickroom. So I started walking, hoping to outrun the horrifying images of her writing on the scaffold at Notre-Dame. But the memories followed me clear to the millinery—I suspect they will follow me always.

And not just the ones of Mother.

Gris's warm brown eyes haunt me from the goggles resting on the table. His crooked smile shines in the glass of every phial. I hear his laugh in the belly of each cauldron. A tear slides down my cheek, and when I wipe it away, I recoil at the metallic scent of blood.

His blood.

Agony flays me open like the smoke beasts' claws. He took a dagger for me. And he gave me the means to kill Mother. Even though I tricked him, and condemned him, and said so many awful things.

"I'm sorry," I whisper. "Forgive me."

After Gris comes my sister. Marguerite didn't attempt to fight when she was apprehended and marched to the Châtelet. She didn't even look up to say goodbye. The last I'll ever see of her is the glass-eyed expression she wore when she sagged over Mother's corpse.

We may have retaken the city, but a small part of me can't help but feel defeated.

My entire family is gone.

Father's voice comes swiftly, right at my ear. I can almost *feel* the whisper of his breath. *I'm with you always. And I've never been so proud.*

The door snicks open, and Josse's beautiful, moonlit face appears through the dust and dark. Despite the shadows, I can tell his skin is glowing and golden rather than stained with Lesage's sickness, and he stands, tall and strong, like the statues in the Tuileries. He squints across the shop, and when his gooseberry-green eyes fall on me, warmth and light and hope tingle through my body.

He's alive. He came for me.

"I thought I might find you here," he says as he pads across the millinery. "Don't you know it's impolite to heal someone and vanish? How am I supposed to offer my thanks?" He collapses beside me, and the shadows highlight the sharp planes of his cheeks. His hair hangs in his eyes, painted black by the darkness. He catches me staring and shoots me a mischievous grin that makes my toes curl inside my boots. "I intend to thank you for a very, very long time."

I try to laugh, but it catches in my throat and sounds more like a sniffle. The grin quickly slides from Josse's face, and his brows pull together. "Mira, are you *crying?*"

"No." I wipe my tattered sleeve quickly across my eyes.

"What's wrong? Are you injured?" He cups my chin and sweeps his fingers below my lashes. Then he pulls me against his chest and his hands rove up and down my sides, inspecting every inch of me.

I slip my arms around his waist and clutch his tunic. As if I am a listing ship and he is my mooring. "I'm fine."

"What, then?"

"Gris." I try to say more, but the name alone slashes through me, reopening my wounds. After several shuddering breaths, I quietly add, "My mother. Marguerite. All of it. I know it needed to end this way, but they were still my family. It was still the only life I knew."

Josse's hold tightens and his lips brush feather-soft against my temple. "We'll make a new life, you and I."

A few short weeks ago, I would have laughed at the impossibility of his suggestion—a princeling and a poisoner. But now it seems like the only constant point on the horizon. The brightest guiding star. "And what will that life look like?" I ask.

Josse presses another kiss to my temple and then at my ear, trailing slowly and maddeningly down my neck. "I shall wake you every morning like this."

"That would be acceptable," I say with a shiver.

"Then I will obviously do the cooking, since we ought to take advantage of my kitchen skills." I laugh and he continues, "After which you will spend the rest of the day ordering me about your laboratory, and I won't once complain, because you're brilliant and beautiful, and watching you work is like watching a master painter at the easel."

"I might even let you help," I say. "And of course I'll teach Françoise and Anne."

Josse stiffens and falls silent.

"What happened? Are they injured? Or unwell?"

"Louis sent them to live with their aunt, the Marchioness de Thianges."

"Why would he do that?"

"He says we're in no position to raise little girls. He's given me *other* duties."

I cock a brow.

"He asked me to captain the police."

"Josse, that's wonderful! Aren't you happy?" I shake his shoulders to knock the somber expression from his face.

"I think I will be once I recover from the shock. I would have liked to see my sisters before they left. To ensure they're well. So they know I didn't choose to send them away."

I lean up on my knees and press my forehead to his. Pressing my strength into him, as he just did for me. "They know you adore them. And we'll visit them soon. Imagine how they'll coo over your officer's uniform. They'll be so proud."

He nods and summons a small smile.

I grip the standing collar of his doublet, crawl onto his lap, and kiss his scruffy cheeks. He traces his finger over my lips, and goose bumps ripple through my skin. Then he repeats the motion with his lips. I return his kiss with a ferocity that thrills me, exploring his jaw line, his neck, the tender area beneath his ear.

Josse groans and lifts me up onto the counter, hitching my petticoats above my knees so my legs encircle him. My elbow knocks against a gallipot and we laugh against each other's lips as it clatters to the ground. Camphor floats into the air, dusting us like pollen, but we don't pull away, not even to breathe. His hands glide up my thigh, trail down my neck, and gently graze my breasts as they heave against the stays of my bodice.

"Mira?" he breathes. His fingers hover over the laces.

I answer with a kiss, nibbling his lower lip and dragging my hands down his chest.

He climbs onto the counter and hovers over me. Presses into me, whispering things that make my cheeks burn. He kisses my neck and eyelids, then my shoulder as he pushes my gown aside.

When we break apart, minutes or hours later, I lay my cheek against his chest and let out a long breath. Grief and uncertainty battle to reclaim me, but I hold tighter to the boy beside me until my resolve hardens and my skin thickens, forming a barrier so strong, not even Mother's memory can penetrate it.

At the end of June there is a bonfire at the Place de Grève, as is tradition for the Fête de la Saint-Jean. But I do not attend. I have no desire to dance around the roaring flames—not when I know they are fueled by my sister, as well as La Trianon and the other devineresses. Twenty-six members of the Shadow Society met their end this morning, and their ashes paint the sky a sinister shade of ochre and brown.

We'll all burn at the Place de Grève. La Trianon's words echo through my thoughts as I work my pestle, grinding leaves of heather and sprigs of holly.

Not all of us, La Trianon. Not me.

It's no coincidence Louis chose this day for their execution—the day of the solar Sabbat, a day celebrated by witches and sorcerers. It's a warning and a promise, though I alone am left to hear it.

The millinery looks nothing like it did a few short weeks ago. I stripped and scraped and scoured every corner of it, and when I hung the sign on the door—*LE APOTHICAIRE LA VIE*—I'd never felt more proud. My own place. Where I belong. With my grimoires and ewers and phials.

With Father and Gris.

Sometimes, if I am very quiet, I can hear Father quizzing me in the bubbling of the cauldrons. When I lean forward to stir a gallipot, Gris brushes the hair from my face with a gentle breeze. And always—*always*—I keep Gris's goggles on a nail beside the hearth, the worn leather and dirty lenses watching over and guiding me.

Just after midday, when I'm half finished with a gout tonic ordered by one of the fishmongers, a sharp rap sounds at the door. Josse strides across the shop and leans against the counter. His lips curve into a wry smile as he plucks at the strap of my goggles. "Don't you look fetching."

"I'm *working*." I swat him with a spoon, but he still manages to peck my cheek. He looks so striking in his officer's uniform—a black doublet with golden epaulets, the buttons shining and his rapier hilt a-twinkle at his side. His dark hair is tied back and his hat is cocked at an angle on his forehead. He would have rivaled

Desgrez for the handsomest police captain in Paris.

He tugs at my goggles again and pouts when I shoot him an exasperated look. "Can't you take a break? Come with me to the Place de Grève."

"I told you, I have no interest in seeing that funeral pyre."

"And you shan't. The blaze is long dead."

"Then why go?"

"For the maypole."

I snort. "If you plan to dance about with ribbons, perhaps I do need to bear witness."

"Not me," Josse says, taking my hand and tugging me across the shop. "Them."

The bustling square is festooned with white and yellow banners that flutter like butterflies in the summer breeze. The tables are heavy-laden with hamhocks and relish, as well as fruit tarts and buttered bread and sizzling turkey legs, for the community feast. Madame Bissette waves from behind the table, still preening over her promotion, careful to keep her royal purple uniform free from a single speck of flour. Josse and I weave through the crowd hand in hand, dodging jesters with colorful balls and flaming batons and revelers with casks of ale. Marie joins us, and we make for the maypole at the center of the courtyard, each step more eager than the last.

Thick silk streamers of purple and blue and gold weave around the pole, guided by many hands below. I watch them parade past, a blur of laughter and color, until I spot two auburn-haired tornados. Then everything stills. Anne spins in a circle, her arms tangling in her golden streamer. Françoise tips her head back and laughs as she tugs Anne forward. Wreaths of baby's breath crown their heads and their pink cheeks look ripe as summer berries. We've visited them several times at the Marchioness de Thianges's estate—as often as Josse's position permits—but it's never enough.

When the ribbons are bound and the lutes and fiddles cease, Josse cups his hands to his mouth and shouts their names.

In a whirl of lace and satin, Françoise and Anne turn. We raise our hands, and I know the instant they spot us. It's like the moment herbs coalesce inside a cauldron—coming together to form something greater, something stronger, something whole. Their eyes spark with recognition, and their squeals of delight are more healing than any antipoison, more fortifying than any elixir or draught. As they rush toward us, crashing into our open arms, I know I have discovered the greatest compound of all. A formula Father would be proud to have in his grimoire. A force that lifts us higher and makes us braver and sheds light into even the darkest of corners:

The recipe for happiness.

Author's Note

From the moment I first read about the infamous devineresse Catherine Monvoisin and the Affair of the Poisons, I felt a spark: this was a story I wanted to tell. While I decided to take a fantastical, alternate-history approach, I would like to take a moment to separate fact from fiction and introduce you to the true La Voisin and her involvement in one of the most notorious episodes in French history.

Known as a Duchess Among Witches, La Voisin held an incredible amount of power and influence for a woman of her day. Taught by her mother at the age of nine to read faces and palms, La Voisin turned to fortune-telling to support her family when her husband, the jeweler Antoine Monvoisin, was ruined. At first she offered only tips and suggestions to make her clients' wishes come to pass, but as she began to notice similarities in their requests—that someone would fall in love with them, that someone would die so that they might inherit, or that their spouses would die so they might marry someone else—she decided to supplement her suggestions with potions and deadly "inheritance powders." La Voisin was not alone in this dubious business; by the end of the seventeenth century, there was a vast network of fortune-tellers, alchemists, and magicians providing similar services throughout all of France.

As La Voisin's reputation grew, she began to attract the noblewomen of Paris, including high-profile clients such as Madame de Montespan. It's difficult to determine the extent of Montespan's involvement with La Voisin, as all evidence implicating the noblewoman was sealed in a coffer and burned by Louis XIV himself. It is generally agreed that La Voisin provided Montespan with aphrodisiacs and black masses, which she believed were responsible for helping her win and retain the king's favor. When the king eventually dismissed Montespan in favor of Angélique de Fontanges in 1679, it's rumored that she hired La Voisin and her associates to poison the Sun King and his new mistress. According to multiple testimonies, La Voisin did create a poisoned petition to be delivered into the king's hands, but due to the overwhelming crowds that flocked to court with petitions, it was extremely difficult to gain access to the king. La Voisin attempted to deliver her petition three times to no avail. Before she and her accomplices could regroup, they were arrested, having been incriminated by a rival poisoner, La Bosse. La Voisin and 33 of her associates were executed between 1679 and 1682, and another 218 were arrested and imprisoned. The scandal ended when Louis XIV closed the investigation in order to protect members of his inner circle, and, most important, his reputation.

While these events are scandalous and gripping in their own right, I found myself wondering what could have happened if this plot to kill Louis XIV had been successful. I was also fascinated by La Voisin—this woman of little means or consequence, who became a successful businesswoman and leader of a network of witches and alchemists, obtaining fame, fortune, and influence beyond her wildest dreams. (She truly wore a crimson cloak studded with 205 golden eagles that cost as much as garments owned by the queen!) It seemed to me that someone with such drive and ambition might have had higher political aspirations. Since I was already changing history, I decided to give La Voisin her own motivation for killing the Sun King and imagined how things might have played out had her secret society taken hold of Paris.

Most of the characters in this book (excluding Josse and Mirabelle) are historical figures who played a part in the Affair of the Poisons. I endeavored to represent them as accurately as possible; however, I did take some liberties with personalities and timelines to suit my alternate version of history.

La Voison's husband, Antoine Monvoisin, was alive and well—much to La Voisin's dismay. She despised the man, whom she complained was financially inept and a vicious drunk. Lesage encouraged La Voisin to murder Antoine on several occasions, but she never followed through with it. It actually became something of a joke among her friends and colleagues; the proper way to greet La Voisin was to ask if her husband had dropped dead yet.

When La Voisin was arrested on March 12, 1679, her eldest daughter, Marie-Marguerite, was treated as a key witness rather than an accomplice in her mother's criminal network. Marie-Marguerite's testimony was paramount in incriminating La Voisin and other important players in the Affair of the Poisons. However, it would be hasty to assume she was wholly innocent. Having grown up in such a dangerous and volatile environment, Marie-Marguerite was a very conflicted individual who sometimes assisted her mother and other times did not. I wanted to play with this idea of guilt versus loyalty to one's family, which is why I chose to make one daughter fiercely loyal to La Voisin and the other rebellious and wary. Guilty or not, Marie-Marguerite was arrested on January 26, 1680, and imprisoned for life by lettre de cachet—a direct order from the king, which could not be appealed—due to her damning knowledge regarding Madame de Montespan and other prominent members of court. The Abbé Guibourg, Lesage, and everyone who was a witness to Montespan's involvement were similarly imprisoned. I would also like to note that La Voisin attempted to arrange a marriage between Marie-Marguerite and one of her associates, a man named Romani, whose name I changed to Fernand to avoid any confusion or association with the Romani people.

Louis XIV was actually residing at the palace of Saint-Germain when La Voisin and her associates attempted to deliver the poisoned petition into his hands. But since the palace at

Versailles is so widely known and associated with the Sun King, I decided to set my coup d'état at this more dazzling location. Historically, it could have been possible. While the courtiers and other officials did not take up residence at Versailles until 1682, Louis XIV began staying there as early as 1674.

I also decided to give Josse's siblings happier endings than they experienced in life. Louis, the Grand Dauphin, was never king, as he died before his father in 1711. Marie Thérèse, Madame Royale, died at the age of five of tuberculosis; however, I thought this story needed a fierce princess—someone to be caught between Josse and Louis's quarrels. Louise Marie Anne de Bourbon (Anne) died at the age of six in 1681, which devastated her older sister, Louise Françoise de Bourbon (Françoise), as the girls were exceptionally close.

"Captain" Luc Desgrez was actually Lieutenant François Desgrez, right-hand man to La Reynie, the lieutenant general of the Paris Police and principal investigator in the Affair of the Poisons. Desgrez made several important arrests, including that of La Voisin. For the sake of my story, I aged him down to make him a contemporary with Josse. I like to think of my Desgrez as the younger brother to the actual policeman.

Additional Reading

For additional reading, I highly recommend the following:

- *The Affair of the Poisons: Murder, Infanticide and Satanism at the Court of Louis XIV* by Anne Somerset

- *The Affair of the Poisons: Louis XIV, Madame De Montespan, and One of History's Great Unsolved Mysteries* by Frances Mossiker

- *Princes and Poisoners: Studies of the Court of Louis XIV* by Frantz Funck-Brentano

- *Archives De La Bastille* by Francois Ravaisson

- *City of Light, City of Poison: Murder, Magic, and the First Police Chief of Paris* by Holly Tucker

- *The Oracle Glass* by Judith Merkle Riley

Acknowledgments

My road to publication was long and winding, but the good thing about taking the "scenic route" is the ample time I had to surround myself with an amazing group of people who made this journey an absolute joy.

Endless thanks to my fabulous agent, Katelyn Detweiler, for being my champion, for your lightning fast emails and insightful notes (you seriously have an eagle eye!), and for your guidance and enthusiasm. I'm so grateful to be on this crazy publishing adventure with you.

A million thanks to my brilliant, talented editor, Ashley Hearn, who helped me shape this manuscript into something far better than I could have dreamed. Thank you for loving Josse and Mira as much as I do, for helping me find the heart of this story, and for pushing me to make it truly shine. #BestEditorEver #HashtagQueen #TeamPoisons!

Thanks to the entire team at Page Street Publishing, including Will Kiester, Lauren Knowles, Marissa Giambelluca, Hayley Gundlach, Lauren Cepero, and Chelsea Hensley. Extra special thanks to Kylie Alexander for designing such a beautiful cover and interior, to Allison Kerr Miller for catching all of my mistakes and making each sentence shine, to Lauren Wohl and Deb Shapiro, my amazing publicists, and to the fabulous Macmillan sales team.

So many wonderful critique partners helped me on my journey to publication. Thanks especially to J.C. Davis for answering thousands of frantic texts and phone calls, for shredding this manuscript with your Red Pen of Death more times than I can count, and for being the best, most amazing friend; to Kristin Hale for being my first and biggest fan: thank you for reading every word I've ever written and for gushing over my stories (even in the beginning, when they were TERRIBLE!); to Laura Irrgang for your helpful notes and inspiring creativity; to Jen Brailsford for your excitement over an early draft; to my Princeton writing crew (even though we're not all at Princeton anymore *sob*). Jessi Cole Jackson and Hannah Karena Jones: Thanks for good times at bookish events and for listening to me whine. I owe you both Gingered Peach for life. Thanks to Erin Cashman, my big sister at Page Street, for taking me under your wing and showing me the ropes; and to Nicole Lesperance and Maria Hebert-Leiter for being fabulous CPs and friends.

Thanks to Pooja Menon for being the first person to believe in this book, and to Kathleen Rushall for your determination and hard work on my behalf. It was a delight to work with you both!

I'm so grateful for the incredibly kind and gracious authors who took the time to read and promote this book, including Lyndsey Ely. Your support means the world to me. I can't thank you enough.

I am blessed to have the very best family in the world. Thanks to the Hair and Thorley clans for cheering me on and encouraging me to pursue this "writing thing." A special shout-out to my dad, who allowed me to write my first two novels on his dime when I was supposed to be answering his office phones and scheduling appointments. Eternal gratitude to my husband, Sam, for believing in me when I didn't believe in myself and for knowing how to motivate me when the going got tough (I am never going back to Texas Roadhouse!). Thank you for being so patient and supportive and for putting up with me. I love you so much! Thanks to Kato, my plot hole–smashing pup—all of my best breakthroughs happen on our long walks. And to Kaia, my girl, thank you for showing me what truly matters and for bringing so much joy into my life.

All my thanks and gratitude to my Father in Heaven for blessing me with this wonderful opportunity.

And thanks to you, my marvelous readers. (I still can't believe I get to say that!) Thank you for coming on this journey with me and Josse and Mirabelle. This is an absolute dream come true, and I wouldn't be here without you.

About the Author

Addie Thorley spent her childhood playing soccer, riding horses, and scribbling stories. After graduating from the University of Utah with a degree in journalism, she decided "hard news" didn't contain nearly enough magic and kissing, so she flung herself into the land of fiction and never looked back. She now lives in Princeton, New Jersey, with her husband, daughter, and wolf dog, and when she's not writing she can be found gallivanting in the woods or galloping around the barn where she works as a horse trainer and exercise rider. *An Affair of Poisons* is her debut novel. You can find her online at www.addiethorley.com or on Twitter @addiethorley.

COMING SOON FROM
ADDIE THORLEY...

The first in a fantasy duology, transforming the
Hunchback of Notre Dame into a tundra-inspired epic.

KEEP READING
FOR AN EXCERPT...

CHAPTER ONE

Darkness waits like a devil outside my window—curling its shadowy fingertips beneath the shutters, drawing its inky claws across the latch, raising every hair on my body as temptation trickles down my spine.

Enebish, it whispers. Not with words that anyone else can hear; the ghostly plea lives inside my mind, inside my entire being, coursing through my veins like blood and filling my lungs with breath.

I grit my teeth and nestle deeper into my bedroll, one hand clenched around my prayer doll, the other fingering the small circular stone embedded at the base of my throat. The harder I press, the quicker its calming tingles flow into my bloodstream, filling me with warmth and steadiness and light.

The perfect antidote to darkness.

Tonight, I will not listen. Tonight, *I* am in control.

The night slams against my window in protest, lashing the glass like rain.

Enebishhhhh, it cries.

It feels like thousands of tiny fire ants are burrowing beneath my skin. I toss and turn and sweat for as long as I can stand it. Then I bolt upright and turn to the window.

Just a peek. One tiny glimpse and I'll be satisfied. There's no danger in simply *looking* at the darkness. . . .

Lies! my conscience screams. *A glimpse is never enough. Remember what you did. Remember why you're imprisoned.*

I squeeze my eyes shut and try to picture the rolling fields of Nariin drenched in vicious orange flames. I press my fists to my stomach, trying to evoke the shredding pain I felt when the monster inside me ripped through my bones and seized control of my Kalima power. But thanks to the glorious, gleaming moonstone in the center of my collarbone, there's nothing. No monster. No memories. Just a swirling, amorphous darkness and a crushing weight upon my chest. Making the incident feel less real, less horrific.

Hardly dangerous, the night coaxes.

With a pathetic squeal, I kick out of my blankets like a fly escaping a spider's web, and limp across my chamber to the window.

Even though I know what I'll find, I gasp when I fling the shutters wide. Millions of ebony tendrils crash against the glass. To anyone else, the midnight sky would look empty and quiet. Peaceful, even. But to me, it looks like a tangled mass of coal-black snakes: frenzied and teeming and *alive*.

Each ribbon of darkness is roughly the length of my forearm, and together they form the undulating tapestry of night.

I lift a finger to the frosted pane and trace a slow, looping spiral. The whorls mimic me, so close that I can feel their heat through the glass. Begging me to flatten my hand. To press my entire body against the window. Needing more, *More, MORE.*

I stagger back and stab my nails into my palms.

There. You've seen them. Now close the shutters, bury your head beneath your pillow, and pray to the skies for forgiveness.

But the night won't let me go so easily. Not when it's lured me this far.

Come, it beckons.

My throat tingles.

I won't give in.

Sweat beads along my hairline.

I *can't*. The moonstone severs my ability to wield the darkness.

Precisely, it hums. *There's no risk, no reason to resist. . . .*

My resolve snaps like a bowstring, and I snatch my crumpled cloak off the floor and steal into the dormitory hall.

The narrow corridor is twice as long as the throne room at the Sky Palace, and I limp past door after door with careful, measured strides. Unfortunately, no matter how softly I tread, the *thump-slide* of my injured leg echoes off the unforgiving tiles and high, frescoed ceiling. I tighten every muscle and will my body to cooperate. One wrong step will bring every monk at Ikh Zuree running. They all watch me like hungry, circling hawks. Eager to earn their salvation, and more important, the king's favor and a seat on his Council of Elders, by "saving" sinners like me. Which isn't done through selfless service and finding harmony with one's family, one's enemies, and one's self, as the First Gods taught. No, followers of the New Order attain exaltation by reporting the mistakes of others. The more grievous the infraction, the closer they come to rapture. And I, the most notorious criminal in the empire, am imprisoned in the heart of their den. Constantly bombarded by hundreds of predatory eyes and salivating mouths.

Thankfully, the rushes I laid this morning help to muffle my uneven gait. The rushes aren't technically my duty, but the old ones always smell of rat piss, so I've taken to changing them out of the goodness of my heart. Not because I *plan* on sneaking out.

At the end of the hall, I crack the door and slip like smoke into the moonlit courtyard. The night chitters in welcome, flocking to me like bees to budding globeflowers, delighted to have won our battle of wills *again*.

Now that I've submitted, the tendrils no longer growl like hungry panthers, but rub against my hands like sweet, purring kittens. I sigh and tilt my face skyward. The sensation is euphoric. More freeing than galloping across the grasslands with the wind in my hair. More satisfying than the whistle of an arrow flying straight and true toward the center of a target. Even better than the memory of Ghoa's proud smile.

The thought of my sister makes my stomach lurch.

Ghoa wouldn't be smiling if she could see me now. She risked her reputation and position as commander of the Kalima warriors to secure my sanctuary here. These midnight jaunts could jeopardize everything she's worked for—and possibly her life. If I'm caught meddling with the darkness, the king could easily execute us both. And while I came to terms with my own execution long ago, I would rather die a thousand deaths than watch Ghoa swing beside me.

The horrifying image nearly sends me scuttling back to my room, but the night kisses my cheeks and buzzes in my ears, singing my worries away. In order to punish me, the king would have to visit Ikh Zuree to witness my disobedience, and since neither he nor Ghoa have set foot inside the monastery compound since my banishment, they never need to know I've allowed myself this tiny taste of freedom.

The chilly autumn breeze whispers through my cloak, and I draw the hood around my face as I hobble down the pebbled pathways. The monastery at Ikh Zuree is massive, with hundreds of bone-white prayer temples and dormitories encircling a towering jade assembly hall that stands in the center like an ever-watchful eye.

Tonight, the moon hangs heavy and full overhead, bathing the snow-dusted pathways in brushstrokes of light. Beautiful, yes, but it makes sneaking around far more difficult. My fingers twitch out of habit. Before my imprisonment, I could have gripped the threads of darkness spooling down my arms and swathed myself in shadow. I could have flounced across the complex as I pleased, invisible as a ghost. The only one able to see through the oppressive blackness. But now I'm forced to dart from temple to temple like a petty marketplace thief, my Kalima power nothing more than a fuzzy memory that passes swifter than the glacial breeze.

When at last I reach the mews at the northern edge of the compound, my convocation of eagles screeches in welcome. They flap their wings and blink down at me from their perches. Feathers litter the floor like gold-spun carpet, and the familiar sounds of nesting and preening make the tightness in my chest and shoulders vanish. At least the birds are always glad to see me.

The king keeps his hunting eagles at Ikh Zuree, and it's my duty to feed and train them. In the kingdom of Ashkar, even prisoners must make themselves useful. Most dig trenches or haul heavy artillery to the war front, so I'm grateful to have a position I like so well. With the birds that never cower in my presence or call me ugly names that make me cry in my chamber late at night.

They are my only friends. Other than Serik.

I flit around, patting and scratching a few, until Orbai shrieks with impatience and scuttles back and forth on her perch. "You're even more demanding than the night," I mock-scold her. She always encourages my midnight rebellions because it means she gets a few extra hours of freedom—and she has developed a taste for bats. I offer her my arm. "Just because you're my favorite, doesn't mean you get to boss me around."

Except it does. And she knows it.

We return to the waiting darkness, and Orbai shoots into the blackness like a comet. Her feathers glint like liquid amber and her massive wings send the ribbons of night swirling. I smile at the chaos. Wanting to follow. Needing to be up there too.

While she stalks the skies, I duck behind the smallest

400

prayer temple and run my fingers along the mosaic wall until I find the bloodred eye of a serpent, which I *accidentally* wiggled loose when I scrubbed the temple last month. I jam my boot into the hole, hold my breath against the pain, and heave myself up. Between my ruined arm and wounded leg, it's difficult to get a firm hold on the ledge, and while I hang there, grunting and wriggling like a marmot, Orbai dives past me. The tips of her feathers tickle my cheek.

What's taking so long? she seems to say.

"Impatient eagle." I shake my head at her. "Not all of us have wings."

Eventually I swing my leg over the edge and roll onto the roof. The ceramic tiles are cold and wet through my cloak, but I hardly notice the chill. I'm too consumed by the towering ebony swells crashing over my body like waves.

The sky doesn't care that I am wicked and ugly. The clouds never rain down judgment for my crimes, and the moon shines without flinching on my injured limbs and scarred face. The majority of Ashkar may despise me, but the heavens will always embrace me in arms of frost and wrap me in a blanket of starlight. In the eyes of the Lady of the Sky and Father Guzan, I am accepted.

Wanted.

The king can decree all he likes about the First Gods being dead, but I refuse to believe it. I *cannot* believe it. Not when I feel the Lady and Father thrumming in every wisp of blackness.

The hours fly like minutes, and too soon the first rays of pink kiss the horizon, cutting like a saber through the gray. *Stay. Just a little while longer*, I beg. But as the treacherous sun creeps higher, the spools of night slip through my fingers like tadpoles. Abandoning me, yet again. My lungs heave against my too-tight rib cage as I watch the darkness race frantically toward the east. Toward the shadow of the Ondor Mountains in the distance. The last place the light will touch.

I would give anything to leave the monastery so easily.

It has been two long years since the king banished me to this holy prison. "A sanctuary," he said. "Be grateful," he said. "It is more than you deserve."

But what does a criminal like me truly deserve?

Sighing, I slump down hard on the tiles and stare out at the hazy landscape. I can see everything from up here: the outer wall of the monastery compound, white with twisting iron spires; the endless frost-tipped plains I used to gallop across in full armor, the grass rolling beneath me like a great green sea; and far, far in the distance, the capital city, Sagaan, where Serik and I dueled in the streets with sabers made of sticks, and lay beneath the larch trees, imagining what our Kalima powers might be, telling stories of how we'd ride into battle side by side.

That part, at least, came true. We're together.

I don't know if that makes it better or worse.

I sit there, fingers pressed against my eyelids, wishing I could turn back time, until the shuffle of slippered feet rips me from my desolation. In perfect harmony with the rising sun, the monks emerge from the dormitories in lines of two. Their crimson robes look like a gash against the silver-white snow, and they spread like a slow-moving stain toward the prayer temples.

Toward me.

Blazing skies! I always return to my chamber long before they can spot me up here, committing treason. If I'm caught, I'm certain my punishment will be worse than the twenty lashes and fifty serenity prayers I'm assigned each time I skip midday supplication.

They could alert Ghoa.

Or the king.

I scramble to my feet and duck behind one of the snarling stone gargoyles perched on the corner of the rooftop. The statues are meant to ward off evil spirits—that's why they look so fearsome—and with the three jagged scars marring the left side of my face, marking me as an imperial traitor, I fit right in.

The king made the cuts himself, slashing his keris dagger alongside my nose, through my eyelid, and over my cheekbone. The wounds bled and festered for weeks—healers weren't permitted to clean or dress the cuts—so I suppose I should be grateful I didn't die of infection or lose my eye. Many criminals do.

I hold my breath as the abba shuffles into the prayer temple. A brass censer swings from his sunspotted fingers and he chants the Song of the Sky King in his dissonant voice. The other senior brethren follow him without a glance in my direction. As the highest-ranking monks at Ikh Zuree, with secured seats on the Council of Elders, they have no need to meticulously scan for infractions. The younger acolytes at the rear of the convoy, however, spot me immediately.

"You aren't permitted to leave your chamber until after morning supplication, when it's fully light!" One of them points up at me.

"Or desecrate our holy temples with your bloodstained hands!" another calls.

"Are you plotting to murder us as well, Enebish the Destroyer?"

That terrible name makes me flinch. I blow out a breath and scan the line of crimson robes for Serik's freckled nose and devious smile. He'll shut them up.

But he's late for morning supplication. Like always.

"Of course she's plotting our murder!" the first acolyte jeers. "And the Sky King will immediately promote me to Abba when he learns I stopped her rampage."

"Only if you reach her first!"

A dozen of them rush toward the temple, leaping over one another like snarling jackals as they scale the mosaicked wall.

I stumble back with a yelp. Which is mortifying. The old Enebish—Enebish the Warrior—could have silenced these sniveling fools in seconds. But now my bad leg snarls in my cloak and I thump down hard on the tiles.

I whistle and Orbai dives at the monks with her talons bared. A few stragglers wail and lose their grip, but the majority surge across the roof like a swarm of frenzied bees. I barely have time to curl into a ball before their bruising hands paw my sides. Before their grasping fingers tangle in my hair.

"Stop!" I cry.

But that only makes them more zealous, more ravenous. "What are you going to do, Enebish the Destroyer?"

The monster inside me rears its head and flicks its pronged tail, exhaling a fiery breath up my throat. I squeeze the tiles so hard, one cracks beneath my fingertips, splintering like my feeble control. Before I realize what I'm doing, I fist a shard in my good hand and lash out blindly. I may not be able to wield the night, but that doesn't mean I'm helpless.

My makeshift knife collides with something warm and soft, and a second later there's a wail. The acolytes fall back. I barely nicked the blubbering monk's forearm, but the way the others are hollering, you'd think I stabbed him through the heart. They attack as one: a ten-headed, twenty-armed beast. I swing the shard wildly and dodge to the left—dangerously close to the upturned ledge. But they anticipate my move.

What they don't anticipate is the combined force of so many people lunging at once. Instead of pinning me to the rooftop, we plummet over the edge.

My arms pinwheel and the wind steals my scream. I close my eyes and brace for impact—thankfully, the temple is barely taller than two men—but before I hit the ground, someone calls my name. My eyes fly open just in time to see Serik leap forward. My stomach slams into his bony shoulder and while I wheeze, he curses. Words a monk shouldn't even know, let alone shout.

"Have you lost your mind?" he groans as we collapse into the frosty grass. "Why would you attack them? You know they're going to run straight to the abba."

"I didn't attack them. *They* attacked *me*. They're *still* attacking me." I point to the other acolytes, thumping down around us like the world's largest, and loudest, hailstones.

"You'll pay for this with your life!" the one I cut bellows.

Serik struggles to his feet and steps in front of me.

"Leave her be."

"Why would we listen to *you*?" The other acolytes sneer at the hundreds of thin white scars climbing Serik's forearms. After six years at Ikh Zuree, there's hardly an inch of him that hasn't felt the sting of the abba's whip. He's nearly as scarred as I am.

"*I said* leave her be," Serik snarls.

"Or what?"

I expect Serik to bunch back his crimson sleeves and start throwing punches like he does every time they corner me, but he squares his shoulders and says in a strange, official tone, "Or you'll have to answer to Commander Ghoa. She just arrived from the war front and has requested I bring the prisoner."

The acolytes halt and their eyes widen. This is not what they expected.

This is not what *I* expected.

A warbling sound halfway between a sob and a laugh bursts from my lips, and a spark of pure joy flares through me before fingertips of dread slowly close around my throat.

Ghoa has no reason to come now, after all this time.

Unless the abba somehow alerted her to my treason . . .

Unless she knows I've been meddling with the darkness . . .

My heartbeat throbs at my temples. Serik's bluffing; it's just a clever lie. I would have seen Ghoa arrive. I was on the rooftop all night.

And you were so consumed by the darkness that you wouldn't have seen your own hand waving in front of your face.

I gape up at Serik, praying he'll flash me a quick smile or wink. But he continues glaring at the other acolytes until they finally retreat toward the assembly hall, their lips curled into gloating sneers.

Then it's just Serik and me, gulping back the chilly morning air. He exhales and scrubs his palm over his head, tugging at phantom locks of floppy brown hair. His hair was shaved to the scalp when he joined the brotherhood, like every acolyte at Ikh Zuree, and I'm still not used to it. Neither, apparently, is he. Though it does make his chin look stronger, the angles of his face sharper. Less like the boy I grew up with and more like a man.

"Thank you," I say, panting. "That was a brilliant lie. Though they'll find out soon enough and make you pay for it."

There's a long beat of silence before Serik looks down at me. His lips are pressed into a thin line and his cheeks are so pale, his light brown freckles look like peppercorns. "It wasn't a lie."

I scrabble to my feet and spin around, as if Ghoa might materialize behind us in the courtyard. "When did she arrive? And *why*?" I add in an anxious whisper.

"Just this morning. And I don't know why. Do *you*?" He shoots me a meaningful look, then glances up at the temple rooftop. "What were you doing up there, En?"

"I just needed some air." The thought of having to admit, even to Serik, how desperate I feel and how reckless I've become makes my cheeks burn. He's no lover of rules, but even he would scold me. Or pity me. Or worse, think me a thankless wretch.

Serik crosses his arms and narrows his hazel eyes. They're the same color as the grass poking through the frost, which is convenient, as I'd rather stare at the ground than answer his questions. He clears his throat loudly, but I keep my eyes fixed on the dirt. Finally he lets out a dramatic sigh and pats the cherry-sized lump on his forehead. "Do you think the abba will believe it's from spending so much time with my head to the floor in prayer?"

I bark out a laugh. "Not a chance. You are the worst monk at Ikh Zuree."

"That's the finest compliment you've ever given me."

"It wasn't a compliment."

"Exactly." Serik grins—a rare, true smile he once shared with every gardener and chambermaid when we were carefree wards running wild on Ghoa's parents' estate. A smile I've only seen a handful of times at Ikh Zuree.

"She's really here?" I knot my hands and look toward the assembly hall. Part of me wants to sprint across the compound and fling myself into her arms. I've dreamed of this moment every day for two years. Missed her every day for two years. But the other part of me is sweating and trembling and compulsively licking my lips. Blood thunders in my ears, beating a frantic refrain: *She knows, she knows, she knows.*

"She's really here," Serik affirms.

"And she summoned me?"

He nods once.

It feels like the ground is rolling beneath my feet. I reach out and steady myself on Serik's shoulder. "Come with me?" I beg.

"I think I'd rather attend morning services."

"You would not."

"You're right." He tilts his head back with a groan. "Both prospects are equally horrendous."

I consider swatting him but decide I've injured him enough for one day. "*I'm* the one who should be dreading this. You have no reason to—"

"Oh, I have plenty of reasons," he interjects. "Ghoa's going to be as fake and infuriating as always, pretending to be a doting mother hen so she can bend us to her will."

I roll my eyes. "Ghoa has only ever tried to help us. And she's your cousin. Practically your sister."

Serik mumbles something about *family* and *obligation* and *already having a skull-splitting headache*, but he dusts off the black cloak with the golden sunbursts he always wears over his robes and then waves me toward the assembly hall. "Fine. But I won't pretend to be happy to see her."